This Bloody Shore
Book 3 of the Manxman series

By

Lynn Bryant

Copyright © 2022 Lynn Bryant
All rights reserved.
No part of this publication may be reproduced or transmitted in any form or by any means without the prior written consent of the author.

Front cover artwork
Copyright © 2022 Richard Dawson
All rights reserved.
No part of this cover image may be reproduced or transmitted in any form or by any means without the prior written consent of the illustrator.

To my good friend Suzy Holland
(Who never expected to enjoy my books)

About the Author

Lynn Bryant was born and raised in London's East End. She studied History at University and had dreams of being a writer from a young age. Since this was clearly not something a working-class-girl-made-good could aspire to, she had a variety of careers including a librarian, NHS administrator, relationship counsellor, manager of an art gallery and running an Irish dance school before she realised that most of these were just as unlikely as being a writer and took the step of publishing her first book.

She now lives in the Isle of Man and is married to a man who understands technology, which saves her a job, and has two grown-up children and two Labradors. History is still a passion, with a particular enthusiasm for the Napoleonic era and the sixteenth century. When not writing she waits on her Labradors, reads anything that's put in front of her and makes periodic and unsuccessful attempts to keep a tidy house.

She is the author of the popular *Peninsular War Saga* and the *Manxman series*. The first two books in the *Manxman* series, **An Unwilling Alliance** and **This Blighted Expedition** were both shortlisted for the Society for Army Historical Research fiction prize in 2019 and 2020.

Acknowledgements

Once again there are many people who have helped in the writing of this book. Research is a huge part of the writing I do, and I'd like to thank various historians and writers who have helped me with the maddest questions; especially Jacqueline Reiter, Rob Griffith, Rory Muir, Andrew Bamford, Charles Esdaile, Zack White, Gareth Glover and many others on social media and in person. There will be some I've missed out and I'm sorry, but thank you all.

As always, I'd like to thank Mel Logue, Jacqueline Reiter, and Kristine Hughes Patrone for reading sections of the work and making helpful suggestions.

I'd also like to thank my fellow admins from the Historical Writers Forum who have been so supportive of me as I struggled through the past difficult couple of years. Paula Lofting, Sharon Bennett Connolly, Stephanie Churchill Ling, Samantha Wilcoxson and Kim Barton have made me laugh and pulled me round on some of the worst days.

Thanks to Richard Dawson, my husband, for his amazing cover, for technical help and for endless support and patience during the writing of this book.

Thanks to my son, Jon and his girlfriend Rachael for cooking for the family on the days I forget to leave my desk. Thanks to my daughter Anya, for sharing my study and for being the best motivational cheerleader in the world.

For four years I struggled to find the right editor and then I discovered she'd been there all along. I don't know why I didn't approach her sooner. Thank you, Heather Paisley, my editor, proof-reader, and partner-in-crime for more than thirty years.

Finally, thanks to Oscar and Alfie, the stars of *Writing with Labradors* for sharing my study and bringing me joy.

And in loving memory of Toby and Joey, the original inspiration behind *Writing with Labradors* who will always be with me in spirit.

Chapter One

The *Maid of Castletown*, a square-rigged Manx schooner, trading wool and linen into Liverpool, sailed with a cargo of wine, brandy and luxury goods into Derbyhaven, bringing four passengers with their accompanying servants. The Captain, a young man new to his command, was a little overawed by his company and Captain Hugh Kelly RN thought he was slightly relieved when the ship docked into a warm, mellow late afternoon and his passengers disembarked. Hugh, who had been young and unsure himself once, took time to speak to Captain Faragher to compliment him on his running of the ship and was rewarded by an approving smile from his wife as they stood watching the unloading of their luggage.

"That was very kind of you, Hugh. Did he manage to stammer out his thanks?"

"I think so," Hugh said, considering. "He definitely said something, and he looked happy, but Mr Durrell interrupted me before I was able to make sense of it."

"I apologise if my interruption was ill-timed, Captain, but it seemed to me that if the young man was unable to complete a sentence fairly soon, you were likely to lose your patience," Lieutenant Durrell said. "I recognised the expression, having been so often on the receiving end of it."

"In your case, fella, it's not because you've a stammer, it's because once you've embarked on a sentence, it could run to three volumes and a second edition before you're done with it."

Durrell grinned. "You would miss it if I stopped, sir."

"I know I would. Come on, it looks as though they've sent the carriage, and a cart for the bags."

It took some time for Hugh's coachman to organise the transfer and Alfie, Hugh's three year old son, was restless and bored, having slept on his mother's lap for the past few hours. Hugh collected the boy, swinging him up onto his shoulders, and walked with Roseen and his First Lieutenant along the quay and down a flight of stone steps onto a narrow stony beach. Hugh set Alfie down and watched him run joyously down to the sea, bending to pick up a stone to throw.

"He's going to get soaked," Durrell commented, watching as Alfred raced through the shallows.

"He'll dry," Roseen said placidly, and Hugh shot her an amused glance. Alfred's clothing was new and most women would have been fussing at him to keep it clean, but Roseen took a relaxed attitude to motherhood. A boy of Alfred's age would generally have remained in petticoats for at least another year, but just before their departure from Chatham, Roseen had regarded the nursery maid's pile of mending and the condition of most of Alfred's clothes and had announced that it was enough.

"He's too active to be dressed up in skirts, Hugh, look at him. I don't intend to waste any more of Beth's time and energy repairing these things. I'm putting him into breeches."

Hugh raised no objection. Not having been raised amongst the gentry, the celebration of breeching when a boy grew old enough to leave his baby skirts behind meant nothing to him. The boys he had grown up with were bundled into their brothers' hand-me-downs as soon as they might be expected to fit and Hugh found he rather liked his son's newly mature appearance in trousered skeleton suits which Roseen insisted were made in dark material so as not to show the stains. Alfred was ecstatic with his new clothing, both as a sign of growing up and for the freedom it gave him.

A shout from above informed Hugh that the carriage was ready to leave. He watched as his First Lieutenant ran down the beach to his Godson, roaring like an enraged tiger. Alfie shrieked with laughter and fled, splashing through the waves until Durrell caught up, swept him up in his arms, planted a kiss on his face, then carried him back up to the steps, both of them laughing. Hugh felt a twist of emotion. Only a few months ago he had thought he would never see Durrell laugh again. The younger man was still not back to full health after almost dying from Walcheren fever, but he was well on the way and Hugh found himself thankful for every small sign of recovery.

It was a short carriage ride to the Kellys' home at Ballabrendon, and Hugh sat back, listening to his son's chatter. Alfie had still been a baby when he was last here and everything was new and exciting to him. Durrell held him on his lap, oblivious to the fact that his uniform was now covered in wet sand and gave serious attention as Alfie pointed out every cow, sheep, and goat on the way.

They were greeted on arrival by Isaac and Voirrey Moore, childhood friends of Hugh, who were employed to run the estate and the house in his absence. Hugh had only managed one brief visit in the last few years, although Roseen had spent eight months there before joining him in London. It was good to be back and Hugh recognised a sense of belonging that he felt nowhere else. A long, distinguished and very profitable career in the navy had taken him all over the world, but here, in the green fields and dramatic landscape of Mann, he felt at home.

Dinner had been held back for them and, with no guests other than Durrell, Hugh insisted that Voirrey and Isaac dine with them instead of retreating to their own cosy apartments in the East Wing. Hugh wondered, as they settled around the table, what Durrell would make of the arrangement. His First Lieutenant came from a more genteel background than Hugh and there was a lot of difference between social customs in London and Mann. When Hugh had first met Durrell, he had thought him inclined to be toplofty, but longer acquaintance taught him that Durrell's reserve had more to do with shyness than any sense of superiority and watching Durrell talking to Voirrey reassured Hugh. Here in this family environment, Durrell looked relaxed and happy and very much at home and did not seem to care that he was dining with Hugh's housekeeper.

Hugh's decision to invite his First Lieutenant to join his family party on their visit home was made on impulse. Durrell had worked alongside Hugh through the past weeks, supervising repairs to the *Iris* and the recruiting of a new crew. Hugh had been given advance notice that he would be joining the Mediterranean fleet when the *Iris* was ready to sail; but while she was still in dock, he had been granted leave to take his wife home.

Durrell was officially still on sick leave and Hugh had deliberately extended it. The disastrous campaign in the Scheldt and the ensuing inquiry had left Durrell physically frail and emotionally bruised. It had also left him temporarily unpopular at the Admiralty. It was felt that his testimony at the inquiry and his defence of Lord Chatham, the disgraced army commander, bordered on disloyalty to his service. Hugh had come under considerable pressure to take on a new first lieutenant, leaving Durrell to languish on half-pay while he was recovering. Hugh had refused as politely as he could and made it very clear that Durrell would return to duty as soon as the doctor declared him fit.

Hugh had suggested several times that Durrell take some leave and visit his family, but he had refused. Hugh was not surprised. The rift between Durrell and his brother which had developed during the Walcheren campaign meant that Durrell had seen little of his family since his return. Henry Durrell had recently married, and Durrell had made a formal call to pay his respects to his sister-in-law and had received visits, when he was in London, from both his mother and his younger sister. When Hugh suggested he might wish to spend a few weeks in London while they were in Mann, Durrell shook his head decidedly.

"No thank you, sir, I will remain with the *Iris*."

"Nonsense. The *Iris* doesn't need you and you've spent the past weeks of what was supposed to be your convalescence working bloody hard. Is it because of your brother?"

Durrell nodded. "Yes, sir. For the sake of my mother and my sister, I will try to remain civil to him, but I can only achieve that by remaining at a distance. I've no wish to stay in the new house he has purchased with his wife's money or hear tales of political success which was achieved over the ruin of another man's career."

Hugh smiled faintly. "Your brother didn't bring down the Earl of Chatham, Mr Durrell. Walcheren did that."

"I agree, sir. But we both know that Henry helped. Besides, even without that, I will never forgive him for what he did to Miss Collingwood."

Hugh regarded him sympathetically. "Have you heard anything of her?"

Durrell shook his head. "No, sir. I asked Mrs Kelly if she could think of any way to make enquiries and she did the best she could, making an excuse of her brief acquaintance with Miss Collingwood in Walcheren. All we could find is that she has been sent away to Norfolk in disgrace while my brother struts about London like a Bond Street dandy. I'll remain with my ship."

"No, you won't. You need a break. Come to Mann with us. You've never been, and I realise I've a strong wish to show you my island home. Join us for a week or two and make your Godson very happy."

Durrell assented so gratefully that Hugh realised he had not been looking forward to spending his final weeks on shore alone. Durrell had few close friends and had spent previous periods of leave in London with his family. Hugh knew that his friends, Ben and Maria Thurlow had invited him to stay but Hugh suspected Durrell was reluctant to go into society after the brief scandal of his supposed flirtation with his brother's disgraced fiancée. Hugh thought the matter a five days wonder which would have been quickly forgotten if Collingwood had not over-reacted so dramatically and he did not think it would do Durrell any lasting harm.

Durrell's reputation at the Admiralty was another matter. Durrell was the best first officer Hugh had ever had and had also become a close and valued friend. Durrell was still junior enough for his reputation to recover, but he needed to be at sea, both for his career and his peace of mind. An out-of-favour officer could languish on half-pay for a long time and Hugh was not prepared to allow it to happen to Alfred Durrell. Knowing his junior's tendency to speak his mind when he would do better to keep his mouth shut, Hugh thought it was probably a good idea to keep Durrell a long way from London society where he might be tempted to express his opinion on the late campaign.

It was good to be home and even better to watch Roseen's sheer joy at being back on the island she loved. She was awake at dawn, racing out into the garden with her hair down and dew on the hem of her skirts, to watch the sun come up over the hills. Hugh joined her and they stood for a long time without speaking while the grey half-light turned pink, staining the hilltops with a rosy hue.

"It's going to be a glorious day," Roseen said eventually. Hugh was standing behind her, his arms wrapped around her to keep her warm. He dropped a kiss on the top of her head.

"It is. What do you want to do first?"

"We should go over to the Top House to see my father and I imagine he'll want us to stay for dinner. It will be good for Alfie to meet his cousins, he's too young to remember them from last time he was here."

"We'll do that today then. Tomorrow I'd like some time with Ise and the books, and we'll take Mr Durrell on a tour of the estate. Do you think your father might have a horse he can borrow? The only spare I have is the grey mare and he's too tall for her."

"He can borrow Teddy, my brother's gelding."

"As long as your brother doesn't want to accompany him."

Roseen gave a splutter of laughter. "Hugh, behave yourself. Ffinlo can't help being a little stolid."

"Roseen, I will be unfailingly polite to your entire family, but I think your brother must be a changeling. You, your father – even your aunt - can manage an entertaining conversation. Your brother just talks farming and glares disapprovingly at you. It's hard work."

"Poor Ffinlo. He's never got over the scandal of his younger sister getting taken up by a press gang while she was dressed as a boy. And he's never really come to terms with the fact that I not only survived, but also made a very good marriage and am extremely happy. He'd be more comfortable if I'd been permanently disgraced and penitent."

"Penitent? Ha! He can't know you very well, love."

"Nobody knows me the way you do, Hugh. Let's go in, I'm getting cold."

They took the carriage down to Malew. Dinner was a lengthy affair and Hugh sat beside his father-in-law, who was also his business partner, and talked of trade and politics and the progress of the long war with France. He shot sympathetic glances at Roseen who had been drawn into an excruciatingly dull conversation about children with her sister-in-law, Mary. Hugh could see his wife planning her excuses for an early departure.

Durrell was in an even more unenviable position, seated between Mary and Ffinlo, Roseen's elder brother. Hugh caught snatches of what appeared to be a lengthy monologue on cattle prices and he thought with some amusement that it would do Durrell good to be on the receiving end for once. Durrell had excellent company manners and seemed to be handling it well, nodding politely and applying himself to the food, which was very good. Hugh relaxed into his conversation with Josiah Crellin and was fully engaged in a discussion of the difficulties experienced by the officers of the West Africa squadron when he realised that Ffinlo had moved to a new topic, less palatable than agriculture.

"My sister tells me you've made a good recovery from the fever, Lieutenant."

"I have, sir. I am looking forward to returning to duty."

"Aye, so I should think. Back at sea where you belong eh? And a long way from the army."

Durrell reached for his wine glass with a faint smile. "I prefer to be at sea, sir, but I made one or two good friends in the army during the recent campaign."

Ffinlo Crellin snorted. "That's as may be, sir, but the ones I've encountered are wastrels in red coats. All too happy to waste public money in a quest for glory. It's the navy will win this war and defend Britain from Bonaparte, mark my words."

Hugh saw Josiah Crellin cringe. He gave his father-in-law a reassuring grin and turned his attention to Ffinlo, whom he suspected had drunk more wine than he should have.

"As navy men, we're flattered that you have so much faith in us, Ffinlo, but I think the army is doing its part as well."

"If that's what you can call it. A small fortune wasted, good men dead of the fever and nothing achieved but a toothless Parliamentary inquiry. Though at least it got rid of..."

"I have high hopes of Lord Wellington achieving something in Portugal and Spain," Roseen said, cutting her brother off ruthlessly. "He has always seemed to me to be a very determined gentleman."

"If he don't go the way of Moore," Ffinlo said. He seemed determined to take a negative view of the army. Hugh wondered if he had recently lost a large sum at cards to a member of the Castletown garrison at the *Glue Pot.*

"I don't think he will," Hugh said mildly. "I've met him once or twice and I've a friend serving in Portugal with him who describes him as an excellent general. Roseen..."

"I didn't realise you were so friendly with the army, Captain Kelly," Ffinlo said, more loudly than was necessary. Hugh decided he was definitely drunk. "And what of you, Lieutenant Durrell? I'll wager you've formed an opinion of the boys in red based on what you saw in Walcheren, eh? Friends or no friends, you can't deny they were a pack of incompetents led by an idle fool not fit to command."

Josiah Crellin made a sound in his throat that sounded suspiciously like a growl. Roseen caught her breath and shot Hugh an agonised glance. Hugh watched Durrell's face. The younger man had been frowning down at his plate, but at Ffinlo Crellin's words he raised his eyes. They were an unusual colour, a mixture of blue and green. Roseen had once compared them to a smooth summer sea, but there was a stormy light in them now. Durrell had known the Earl of Chatham since boyhood and had recently and very publicly demonstrated his willingness to put loyalty to that languid gentleman ahead of personal interest.

Hugh was still frantically considering the best method of intervening without embarrassing his host further when Durrell looked over at him and caught his eye. Hugh held his gaze, giving a tiny shake of the head. Durrell did nothing for a moment, then to Hugh's surprise he gave a broad smile and turned his gaze back to Roseen's brother.

"I am delighted you have asked about the recent campaign, Mr Crellin. I am always pleased to share my knowledge, as well as my opinions, with a man such as yourself who has no military training or experience" he said earnestly. "As it happens I spent a good deal of my time on shore so I am in an excellent position to explain the progress of the campaign from both the army and the navy's perspective. Before I go into any detail about such matters, however, or indeed before I even describe the planning and logistics that went into the expedition to the Scheldt, I feel you would benefit from a brief history of the region to explain why it appeared to be such a valuable target. Wait, I have my note tablets in my pocket. I will draw you a map."

Hugh watched in awe for a while, before turning back to his host and their interrupted discussion about the exploits of the anti-slavery squadron. Roseen had taken the opportunity to move her conversation away from babies and was answering her aunt's enquiries about her recent visit to

Mrs Maria Thurlow in London. Mary Crellin joined in with a question about the Thurlows' London home and around the table, the tense atmosphere relaxed again.

In the background, Durrell's voice went on. Ffinlo Crellin had made several attempts to interrupt the steady stream of information, but Hugh knew very well that once Durrell was in full flow only a surprise bombardment by the French navy could stop him. His First Lieutenant had moved on from an extremely informative history of Walcheren and its environs to a lecture about the problems of supplies, with some useful facts about the shortage of ready coin which had temporarily halted Lord Chatham's progress. He was now drawing a sketch map of the siege works of Flushing, pointing out where the dyke had been cut and sharing a detailed description of the town's water and drainage system that he must have picked up from one of the local engineers.

Ffinlo was slumped over his empty plate staring into his wine glass with a glazed expression. Hugh decided he would allow it to go on for a while longer before calling his junior to order, collecting his son and going home. Tomorrow, if the weather was fine, he thought they might go sailing. Durrell would enjoy taking charge of Hugh's beautifully restored Manx-built yacht and Hugh considered he had earned a treat.

"Hugh, are you almost ready to leave?" his wife whispered softly. Hugh took her hand and raised it to his lips lovingly.

"In a while. Why don't you go and find Alfie and take him out into the garden to play? I want your father to try the port I brought over and I think Mr Durrell will be happy to take a glass and sit a little longer, don't you? I'm not sure about your brother. He may have drunk enough wine for today."

Roseen suppressed a giggle and rose, collecting her aunt and her sister-in-law with a suggestion that they take the children for a walk down to the stream. Hugh watched her go then sent a servant for the port. He poured four glasses and passed one to his father-in-law, one to Ffinlo and one to his First Lieutenant. Ffinlo took it and gulped half of it down in one go. Durrell thanked Hugh absently and his glass sat untouched as he began to describe the contrary winds and difficult channels which had made the naval aspect of the campaign so frustrating and unpredictable.

"He's an interesting fella, your first officer," Mr Crellin said, sipping the port. "I don't think I've ever seen my Ffinlo sit that quietly for that long. It's like he's in a trance or something."

Hugh surveyed Durrell. He decided that his First Lieutenant was finally fully recovered from his illness. "It gets you like that after a while," he said. "I find it quite soothing. So what do you make of this port, sir?"

***

It was raining on the beach, the wind whipping the dull grey waves into white foam and Faith Collingwood was wet through. There was no sign of her maid. She was not permitted to walk out without her maid, but she had found that Rigby, whom she cordially disliked, would not follow her out of the house or the carriage if the weather was bad. She had scolded irritably when Faith put on her walking shoes and announced her intention of going to the shore. A year ago, Faith would have taken notice and reluctantly curtailed her walk, but she no longer cared for the opinions of either Rigby or Mrs Irwin, the tight-lipped woman hired as her chaperone. Since she was already disgraced and banished from society, Faith had decided to do as she pleased. She reasoned that neither woman would have the audacity to physically restrain her, and she had been proven right. Possibly they wrote angry letters to her father in London, but Faith did not care about that.

Being wet was uncomfortable, but curiously liberating. Faith had been raised to consider the cost of her clothing and shoes and the thought of potentially ruining both on a soaked, sandy beach would once have terrified her. Almost a year into her exile, she found that she did not care, and she splashed through the shallows, soaking her hem and her kid boots with some enjoyment.

A year ago she had walked on a beach in Walcheren with a young naval officer. The sun was shining, and Lieutenant Durrell's awkward admiration had made Faith very happy, despite the fact that she knew very well that her father intended her to marry Durrell's older brother. She had done her best to accede to his wishes and had allowed herself to be betrothed to Henry Durrell, trying hard to push her misgivings and actual distaste to one side.

When Henry Durrell had broken their engagement, publicly shaming Faith with a spurious accusation of improper behaviour with his younger brother, Faith was shocked, bewildered, and for a time felt wholly adrift. Her entire life had been spent trying to do the right thing, walking on eggshells through her father's angry outbursts and vicious personal criticisms. He had beaten her when the scandal broke, ignoring her passionate assertion that she had done nothing wrong and then sent her away. Wickham House was a damp, gloomy house on the Norfolk coast which Mr Collingwood had received in payment of a debt. He had never visited it and had not bothered to check its condition before banishing his disgraced daughter in the company of a spiteful maid and a disapproving paid chaperone. The house was freezing, the roof leaked and the windows were ill-fitting and let in the wind from the sea.

Faith sometimes wondered if the inhospitable nature of both the house and the countryside had been good for her. Coddled in luxury, she had never had cause to search for inner resources; but Wickham House, with its miserable conditions and uncooperative servants showed her a new side to herself. Many miles from her demanding, bullying father, she learned how to manage the staff and when that proved impossible, to manage herself, so that she could light her own fires and make her own tea at need. She realised that the overbearing manner of Mrs Irwin meant nothing without the support of her employer, and that Rigby's spiteful tale-bearing could not work without a master to listen to her stories. Faith wept, then when she was tired of crying, she got up and went outside and learned how to walk in the rain.

She walked today until she became too cold, then turned back. Norfolk beaches were wide and flat, reminding her a little of the beaches in Walcheren. When she had first come here, Faith had thought the countryside boring, but she had come to love it. The endless miles of sand, sometimes fringed with low dunes, proved to be a palette of constantly changing colours, with the sky reflecting a glorious flat light off the sea or the marshland. A wide variety of sea birds inhabited the dunes and swooped lazily over the water. Faith loved to watch them, envying their freedom. Away from the beach there were broad grassy meadows, home to shy deer which became accustomed to her silent presence and came ever closer. The boggy marshlands were rich with wading birds, stalking elegantly through the water snapping at insects; whilst in the background, the incessant calling of the natterjack toads disturbed the peace.

Raised mainly in her father's London home, Faith knew nothing about birds or wildlife, but several weeks into her stay, she made the acquaintance of Abel Turner. Faith had seen him about the gardens, a tall thin man of around forty, who seemed to fulfil the role of gardener and general handyman. Faith found most of the servants uninterested and somewhat resentful at having to cater for the daughter of their absentee master, and after a few weeks she gave up trying to win them over. She had not spoken to Turner until he found her shivering in the summer house one afternoon, working on a watercolour of the overgrown gardens. He stood watching her work for a moment.

"Not bad, that. You had lessons, then?"

Faith looked up in surprise at his tone. She was not sure if he was being disrespectful, but he sounded simply curious, so she replied:

"Yes. I didn't enjoy the lessons at all, but I wanted something to do here and I find that I'm enjoying the challenge. So many colours."

"You should try the beach or the marshes for that."

"I'd love to, but it's so cold and windy at present. And I don't have an easel. I've not been used to painting for pleasure, it's surprising I brought my paints at all."

"Use the master's. He won't mind, been dead these six years."

"The master?"

"Mr Copperfield. He was a rare one for his paintings. Got some of them framed, they're in the hallway, and up the stairs."

"Those were his?" Faith said in dawning delight. "I've been studying them, wondering how he caught those birds so perfectly."

"He used to spend hours at it. Had a hide built overlooking the estuary; I did it myself. Good place for the sea birds."

Faith studied him. Turner had the weathered look of a man who spent his working hours out of doors, but there was something different about his manner which suggested that he was not simply another member of the staff. Awkwardly, she said:

"I'm afraid I seem ignorant but I'm not sure who you are. Do you work here?"

"Aye, some of the time. They pay me to cut the shrubs back and cut the grass, do a few odd repairs. I'd do more if I were asked, but yon new owner's a miserly begger, won't do more than he has to. He'll come all to grief when the place falls down and isn't worth the debt he took it for."

Faith wondered if Turner knew he was speaking of her father. "Was Mr Copperfield living here then? Was it his debt?"

"Nay, miss, weren't him. He died and left it to his nephew, his sister's boy. Not worth a tinker's cuss, that one. Owed money through half the county and up in London too. Lost this place over a year ago, and we've heard nowt since apart from to keep it aired and ready for buyers. None been by, mind, but they won't be, the state of it. He's none too quick on paying the wage bill either, so I'm told, but that don't affect me. I've my own cottage and my own land over by Fenton Wick. Just a smallholding, but it's mine by right, and I get by."

Faith took a deep breath. "He's my father."

"Lord love you, miss, think I don't know that? Place was shut down apart from a monthly clean and me checking on the doors and windows and doing the garden, but he got Mr Forbes, the local agent, to bring back some of the staff when you was coming. Gave 'em a chance for a good mardle trying to guess what you'd done to get yourself sent away."

Faith blushed deeply. "I suppose so," she said. "Perhaps that's why I can't even get them to lay a fire when I want one, they don't pay the least heed to me."

"Well you could write to your Pa telling him so, miss."

"I don't think he'd care, Mr Turner."

The long, lined face studied her for a moment then split into a broad grin. "Happen that's right, m'dear. I'll have a word with Mrs Blake, tell her to buck up a bit. Or I could show you how to light your own fire."

The remark was outrageous, but for some reason it made Faith laugh. The thought was unexpectedly appealing. "Would you?" she asked.

Turner grinned. "Aye, why not? Can show you around a bit if you like. Tell you something about those bird paintings you're admiring. But for now, come with me, I'll take you up to master's room."

Faith followed a little nervously. She had not really explored the house, being content with the rooms she had been allocated. She had been faintly curious about the stubby tower on the eastern corner of the house, but Mrs Blake, the housekeeper, had shaken her head when asked.

"You don't want to go up there, ma'am. Floorboards are rotten."

The stairs creaked ominously but felt perfectly safe as Faith followed her guide up the stairs. At the top she stopped with a little gasp at the unexpected vista from the windows on three sides of the room, overlooking the shoreline and the marshes. The room was laid out as a studio, with an easel set up before the window with a faded, half-finished canvas on it. Faith stepped into the room, looking around her with dawning delight.

"This is astonishing."

"Aye, master spent most of his time up here. Used to ask me up for a glass or two sometimes, to talk about his painting. Weren't much for the social rules, the master."

Faith turned to him, her face alight. "May I use this room? I mean, there is such a beautiful view. And so much here...brushes and pencils and...probably the paints are no use after all this time, but even so. Would he mind, do you think?"

"I think he'd be glad, miss. There's a good fire there as well, keep you warm in the cold afternoons. Tomorrow I'll bring up some wood and show you how to get it going."

It was the beginning of an odd, but very rewarding friendship. Under Turner's guidance, Faith explored the surrounding area with new eyes. He showed her the birds and the wildlife and the best places to watch them. He taught her to light a fire and to make her own tea in a bracket over the hearth in the tower room, and on one wet afternoon he drove her into Yarmouth in an old, battered gig, to a dim stationer's shop which sold paints and canvasses and paper, regaling her with local history and legends to pass the time on the journey. Faith was well aware of the frozen disapproval of her maid and endured several lengthy scoldings from her hired companion; to each she turned a deaf ear. When Mrs Irwin seemed inclined to take the matter further, Faith fixed her with a cool, uninterested stare.

"If you think my father would be interested in my enthusiasm for painting, Mrs Irwin, and the help of Mr Turner to find the best locations, feel free to write to him. If he disapproves, he can come and tell me himself."

Mrs Irwin lapsed into indignant silence and Faith, who had come to understand that the woman would never trouble her employer lest he blame her for his daughter's poor judgement and dismiss her, continued to walk on the beach in the rain.

Returning to the house that afternoon, she was surprised to see a carriage on the driveway. In the time she had lived at Wickham House, the only vehicles to visit the house were local deliveries to the kitchen or Abel's tatty gig, but this was a gentleman's carriage. Jackson, the only groom employed at the house, was struggling with the horses with Finley, the manservant giving ineffectual assistance. Faith felt a twist of fear, wondering if her father was here, but she dismissed the idea immediately. Mr Collingwood would not have arrived without notice. He had a great sense of his own consequence and would have sent servants ahead to prepare the house for him.

Faith walked up the shallow steps and went into the hallway, leaving a trail of water from her shoes and hem. She untied the ribbons of her bonnet, looking around her curiously. The door to the parlour opened and Mrs Irwin stepped into the hallway, followed by a portly middle-aged gentleman dressed very neatly in dark clothing with a navy blue coat. His eyes widened at the sight of Faith. Faith stood looking at him, thoroughly enjoying the expression of horror on the face of her father's man of business at the sight of her soaked clothing and dripping hair. She smiled, swinging the bonnet a little to widen the pool of water she was making on the boards.

"Mr Glinde, what an unexpected surprise. You should have written to tell me of your visit, I'm afraid you will find the house very unprepared."

"Miss Collingwood. You are...you are so wet!"

Faith looked down at herself and then up at Glinde, affecting astonishment. "So I am. How very vexing, I did not notice. I have been walking on the beach, you know."

"In this weather, Miss Collingwood?"

"Well I suppose it must have been, since this is the only weather we have at present. I collect you have a message from my father, but I think I should probably change first. The carpet in the parlour is sadly worn, but I do not think it will be improved if I stand there dripping over it. Will you excuse me? I will be down presently. Mrs Irwin, perhaps you can see if the kitchen can manage some refreshment for Mr Glinde. I haven't the least idea what we have in the house, but they can usually manage a pot of tea if they are in a good mood."

Faith took her time changing her clothing. Rigby kept up an unceasing stream of complaints as she rubbed Faith's hair with a towel, brushed it out and dressed it in a neat chignon.

"There's no time to curl it, it's still too wet, miss."

"It hardly signifies, Rigby, it is only Mr Glinde. No, not that gown. I'll wear the blue, it's warmer and I'm chilled."

"Hardly surprising, gallivanting about in this weather. It's surprising you don't catch your death."

"It has ceased to surprise me, Rigby. Now that I come to think of it, I have never yet heard of anybody dying of a cold that they caught in the rain. I suspect it is a tale they invented to keep us locked up indoors on a wet day. Do I have a pair of stockings without a hole in?"

"There are these that I've darned."

"They'll do. Thank you."

Rigby eyed her. "You need new stockings, miss. And new shoes."

"Well, I don't have the money for them."

"You spent all your allowance on paints and such rubbish."

"They are more useful than stockings just now. There, that will do."

Faith found Glinde seated in the parlour before a fire. There was a bottle and glasses on a small table, something that Faith had never seen at Wickham House before. Glinde rose as she entered and bowed. There was no sign of Mrs Irwin, which surprised Faith. Her chaperone liked to keep up with whatever was going on and Faith was sure that if she was not in the room it was because Glinde had told her to leave.

"Miss Collingwood. Are you feeling warmer? Here, come closer to the fire."

Faith did so, looking at him warily. She had known Glinde all her life and did not like him, but that was simply because she associated him with her father. At the time of her exile, he had made the travel arrangements and it had been he who had informed her of her destination, of the limited allowance she would be given and the strict terms of her imprisonment. He had not shown any sympathy for her tearful bewilderment and Faith felt no need to pretend to be pleased to see him.

"I don't wish to sit too close, Mr Glinde. None of the chimneys here have been swept properly for years and we are likely to be overwhelmed by a belch of black smoke at any moment; it has happened to me several times. Have you a message from my father, or did he merely wish to check that I was still alive? He could have written to Mrs Irwin for that; I am sure she would have been delighted to send a full report on my iniquities."

"Miss Collingwood, please sit down. I have some bad news for you, and I fear it will come as a shock."

For the first time, Faith realised that he was nervous. She froze, staring at him. "Bad news? My father? Has something happened to my father?"

"I am afraid so."

"He is not dead?"

"No. No, he still lives. But I have to tell you that his doctors are unable to say for how long. It was a stroke, they believe. A massive stroke. He collapsed at a board meeting and was taken home. His own doctor was called and after that, a specialist was brought in, but there is nothing they can do. He lies unconscious: he cannot move or speak, and we are not sure how much he understands."

"Oh. Oh, dear God."

Glinde came forward, took Faith gently by the arm and steered her into a chair. "Sit down, my dear, and have some sherry. It is perfectly good, I brought it with me. This must be a shock for you."

"It is," Faith said. She accepted the sherry and sipped it, feeling it warm her chilled body. "Forgive me, I did not expect this."

"None of us did, ma'am. There was no sign of it. I dined with him the previous day and he was as hale and hearty as ever. I'm sorry to be the bearer of such dreadful news."

Faith said nothing. She remembered her father as she had last seen him. His face had been scarlet with fury as he had screamed at her, calling her names that she had not even understood although she could guess their meaning. Faith had tried hard to explain to him, to tell him that she had done nothing wrong, and that Henry Durrell's accusations of impropriety with his younger brother were completely untrue; but it was impossible to make herself heard, and she knew that her father did not want to listen. His contempt and disappointment with her had nothing to do with the ending of her betrothal. He had despised her and bullied her all her life, as he had bullied her mother before her simply because she was a girl and not the son he wanted.

Faith had tried, over the years, to find ways to mitigate the offence and to please her father. She had studied hard, obeyed every petty rule and restriction, and had never complained about his bullying, his scathing remarks, and the times he had beaten her. She had even tried to make the best of the match he had made for her, although she could not like Henry Durrell and rather dreaded the idea of being married to him. But when she was sent into exile, to the cold damp house on the Norfolk coast in the care of a disapproving hired chaperone and a maid who was paid to spy on her, something had changed for Faith. She had sat in the coach, shivering with cold and shock and still aching from the worst beating she had ever received, and promised herself that she would never again try to please her father. Whatever he did to her in the future, she would not bend her head and apologise for being a woman. Her meekness had not made him love her and Faith had lost all capacity to love him. She was willing, at their next meeting, to tell him so.

It had never occurred to her that she would not have the opportunity to do so.

The sherry glass was half empty. Faith set it down on the table and Glinde immediately refilled it, along with his own. "Give yourself a few moments," he said gently.

Faith looked up and caught his expression. She had never seen him look at her so kindly, and for a moment she could think of nothing to say. Finally she found her voice.

"What do you think I should do, Mr Glinde?"

"I believe you should return to London, Miss Collingwood. I do not think your father will know you are there, but..."

"That is probably just as well, Mr Glinde, as at our last meeting he expressed the hope that he should never set eyes on me again."

"I am sorry, ma'am. Your father could be a harsh man at times, I know. I have felt for your difficult situation, although it was not my place to say so. But as his daughter - and his only child - you should be with him. For the sake of appearances if nothing else."

Faith did not reply immediately. She thought about his words and realised suddenly that she was being very stupid while Mr Glinde was being very clear. She picked up the sherry and sipped it again, raising her eyes to his face.

"I am extremely ignorant about my father's business affairs, Mr Glinde, and I have no idea what happens next."

"Your father is still alive, ma'am. As his man of business, I have full authority to continue to manage his interests if he is unable to do so himself. I have no idea how long that is likely to be."

"Nor have I. But I suppose that means that in his unavoidable absence, you are also my guardian, as I am not yet twenty-one."

"Not in legal terms, Miss Collingwood. Were you younger, I believe I would need to apply to Chancery to be appointed as your legal guardian. However, if I have correctly remembered, your twenty-first birthday is less than five months away."

Faith was sure he had checked. "That is so," she said sedately.

"It would probably take that long for the court to hear the case, and by then it would be irrelevant. I know how your father has left his money and property, Miss Collingwood. Often, when the only heir is a young woman, her father will leave the money in trust, to be managed until she is either married or rather older and more capable of running her own affairs. In your father's case however, he has never made any secret of intending you to be married young. And he was, as far as we knew, a fit and healthy man. It probably seems wrong to be considering the provisions of his will when he is not yet dead, ma'am, but since it is just we two..."

Faith waited, watching as Glinde chose his words carefully. Eventually, he said:

"There are a number of provisions relating to your future husband and children. But should you be of legal age and unmarried at his death, his estate will go to you with no ties or restrictions. If your father's doctors are correct, Miss Collingwood, you are about to become a very wealthy young woman. That is why I believe your place is in London and not out here in this dreadful house in the middle of nowhere."

Faith looked around her at the walls. There were signs of damp and the wallpaper was peeling in one corner. "I have become quite fond of it," she said. "Really, if it was properly taken care of, it might be a very lovely house."

Mr Glinde said nothing. Faith allowed the silence to go on. She realised that it was going to take some time for the reality of her situation to sink in. She sipped the sherry and, for a while, thought of nothing but the rich taste. She was aware of her companion's discomfort and she thought that she understood it, but she felt no desire to reassure him at this moment. They sat on either side of the fire, which for once was not smoking too badly.

The warmth and the wine began to make Faith feel drowsy. She stirred a little. "Are you staying in the house tonight?"

"I have booked a room at the *Stag*, ma'am. I was not sure..."

"I think you were wise. The sheets would undoubtedly be damp. I have become quite used to it, but I would not wish you to be ill."

Glinde blushed scarlet. It was very satisfying. "Miss Collingwood. Please do not think that I have not felt sympathy for your situation out here. A young girl alone, and under such difficult circumstances, you must have felt...I tried to talk to your father, to tell him..."

"Oh let us not," Faith said sharply. "If we are to go over the circumstances of the past year of my life and your part in them, I will say things that will make it difficult for us to work together in the future. I do not know you as a person, Mr Glinde, merely as an instrument of my father, and in that capacity you have given me no cause to like you or trust you. But I know that you were the man he trusted more than any other, which means you must be very good at what you do, as he was not a trusting man. And if I am to step into his shoes, I will need a man I can trust. I am prepared to give you a chance. You are right, I need to go to London and play the devoted daughter while my father still lives. You, I imagine, would like to continue in your position. Let us see, shall we, how we manage the next few months? But let us be honest between us, if nowhere else. My father has never given me the love or care that most men give their daughter, and although I spent many years trying to pretend otherwise, I will not do so any more. He despised me. And now I despise him. He is a cruel, vindictive, and unprincipled man and he will be no loss to this world. When he dies, I will mourn the father I longed for, not the one I had."

Glinde did not speak for a while. Faith finished the sherry and set the glass down. "I would ask you to dine, Mr Glinde, but with so little notice, the food will be terrible."

Glinde got up. Suddenly there was a sense of energy about him. "Miss Collingwood, I would like to invite you to dine with me at the *Stag* today. We will need to invite Mrs Irwin as well."

"I accept, sir," Faith said calmly. "However, I need to tell you that I am not at all happy with Mrs Irwin as my companion, she behaves as if she is my gaoler. At some point I also wish to employ a new maid, since Rigby was my father's creature, and I will never be able to forgive her for that. But for now, let us proceed as we may. Please make the travel arrangements, and I will pack. I hope it will be possible for my journey home to be rather more comfortable than my journey here."

"It will, ma'am. I will see to it."

"Very good. Thank you for your frankness. If you would send your carriage for us later, I would be very much obliged since I do not have one here. In the meantime, I think I need some time alone. I have a lot to think about."

Chapter Two

Hugh's stay in Mann was extended by the news that the repairs to the *Iris* had encountered unexpected problems. The ship had been hit several times during the campaign on the Scheldt, but the worst damage occurred during the voyage home. They had sailed in December, and several troop transports were lost in the storms which chased them back to England. The *Iris* had weathered the squalls very well, but her masts and rigging had suffered and the temporary repairs done in Walcheren would need attention. Hugh had supervised the initial work before leaving for Mann and hoped to be ready to sign on crew within six weeks, but he was disappointed. Chatham dockyard was frantically busy with winter repairs and there was a shortage of expert craftsmen, wood and other supplies. The repairs would happen, but it would take time.

Hugh decided to contain his impatience and enjoy his extended time at home. The weather was good and it was wonderful to be able to spend time with Roseen and his son. They went for long rides through the countryside with Durrell, skimmed stones on the beach with Alfie and went sailing. Alfie quickly made friends, not only with his older cousin but with several of the servants' children as well.

Local society was keen to entertain Josiah Crellin's daughter and her husband. The scandal surrounding their marriage four years earlier was not exactly forgotten, but was very easy to ignore. Captain Hugh Kelly had returned to the island a wealthy man. The purchase of an extensive estate and considerable investment in local trade made it clear that he had every intention of settling on the island when his navy days were done, which made him a man to be cultivated. Manx society was less rigid than its English counterpart and Hugh's money, rank and distinguished navy career made it easy to forget his relatively humble origins. The Kellys and their guest were invited everywhere.

Durrell was obviously enjoying his unexpected holiday. He looked relaxed and happy and Hugh was relieved. For a long time after their return from Walcheren, Durrell had worn an expression of taut misery and London had not helped at all. The tranquil beauty of Hugh's island home seemed to be having a very soothing effect on Durrell and the informality of local society, coupled with the relief of being a long way from Durrell's obnoxious brother and his new wife, was exactly what he needed to complete his healing.

Nevertheless, Hugh was not surprised that Durrell became impatient about the extended delay long before he did. Hugh received regular letters from his master and his new bosun as well as from Lieutenant Paisley who was currently Hugh's deputy aboard ship. Durrell awaited each report with ill-concealed anxiety and Hugh took to reading them quickly then handing them on to his junior to reassure him.

"I cannot believe it is taking them so long," Durrell said, after finishing the latest lengthy report from the bosun. "What is your opinion of this new man, Captain? I must own he gives very detailed reports and he sounds as though he knows his work, but I would feel happier if Mr Keig were still in charge. Or even if we had been able to appoint a new bosun from our own crew."

Hugh grinned. He and Durrell had disagreed on his decision to take on a new bosun on their return from Walcheren and although Durrell had reluctantly accepted his decision, he could not resist reminding Hugh of his doubts. Hugh understood, but his own uncertainty about his choice was rapidly receding with every report from Bosun Geordie Armstrong.

Nial Keig, Hugh's long-term bosun had been Manx, appointed in 1805 when Hugh was first given command of the *Iris*, a French-built 74-gun third-rater taken as a prize after Trafalgar. Keig had been one of the victims of the winter storms on their return from the Scheldt, hit by a falling mast only hours from the safety of Portsmouth. His leg had been so badly broken that it had to be amputated and there was no possibility of him sailing with Hugh again. Hugh had grieved the loss and engaged in a brief and spirited fight with the Admiralty over Keig's pension, which he won. He was then left to survey his current selection of bosun's mates and other petty officers for a replacement.

Hugh was not sure that any of them were ready to replace Keig. A ship's boatswain, more commonly known as bosun, was a warrant officer, employed by the Navy Board and was one of the standing officers who remained with the ship as a ship-keeper even when it was in dry dock. This was intended to provide continuity and specialist knowledge of a ship's rigging and equipment. Many bosuns remained with one ship for most of their career and their experience was invaluable to a captain taking over a new command. While Hugh dithered over his decision, the matter was taken out of his hands by a letter from the Admiralty, informing him that the former bosun of *HMS Hera* was currently unemployed and in search of a new warrant.

Hugh might well have registered a formal protest at having a stranger foisted upon him, but mention of the *Hera* gave him pause. The ship, a 74-gun third rate of a much older design than the *Iris*, had been lost off the coast of Spain during a storm in the winter of 1810. Hugh had heard the full story from one of the *Hera's* former officers at a dinner in Chatham. Lieutenant Powlett was a good storyteller and held the other officers around the table spellbound with his description of the shipwreck.

The *Hera* was badly hit by the storm and found herself with damaged steering, drifting dangerously close to the rocky shore, with her crew scrambling for the boats. That section of the coastline was in the hands of the French and Powlett was resigning himself to being taken as a prisoner of war, when the ship's bosun had taken charge.

"Rigged up a temporary steering mechanism from the gun deck. They did something similar on the *Victory* at Trafalgar, you know. Apparently he'd read about it and had been experimenting to see if it could work on the *Hera*. And it did. Got us to within sight of the fleet, but she was taking on water too badly and we had to let her go. Still, we were all picked up from the boats and no prison camp for us. Clever man, Armstrong."

Hugh had decided that as the *Iris* was due some time in dock after the Walcheren campaign, he would postpone any objection until he had met Geordie Armstrong and seen what he could do. He was surprised and a little impressed that a man of Armstrong's age was so determined to find a new ship and return to sea, and he was also sure that somebody with influence had intervened on the man's behalf, which was interesting.

What Hugh had seen so far was impressive. Armstrong, a stocky weather-beaten borderer in his fifties, took possession of the bosun's cabin and stores with calm authority and spent long hours inspecting and testing every area of Hugh's ship. The bosun was responsible to the captain and the master for the rigging, sails, blocks, anchors, cables, ships' boats and all other aspects of seamanship and it was clear to Hugh that by the time the *Iris* sailed, Geordie Armstrong intended to know every inch of her.

With Armstrong came his wife Janet, a comely woman ten years younger than him. Hugh had no objection to his bosun bringing a wife to sea even though it was not strictly allowed. His current master, James Manby not only brought his wife, but a young daughter with him and Hugh found the women helpful in nursing the sick and dealing with domestic matters aboard ship. Sometimes he wished Roseen could sail with him, but he knew he would worry about her too much and neither of them were prepared to risk their son aboard.

Armstrong's detailed reports of the progress of the repair confirmed in Hugh's mind that he had made the right choice and he was looking forward to getting to know his new bosun better. He suspected that Armstrong was using the refit to make changes to the set-up of the rigging and, given his long experience, Hugh was happy to give him his head, though when he returned to the ship he intended to spend some time learning how the changes would affect the way the *Iris* sailed. Hugh had reached his present rank the hard way and as a captain, he insisted on knowing every detail of his ship and being involved in every aspect of its design and practical application. It made him a hard taskmaster but he had a feeling that might be something he shared with his new bosun. It was certainly something he shared with his First Lieutenant and watching the younger man poring over Armstrong's reports to make sure he understood the fine detail of the work, Hugh felt thoroughly pleased with himself.

The most difficult aspect of putting to sea was not likely to be the condition of the ship, but finding enough men to crew it. The navy worked very differently from the army, where a new recruit signed up for life until the army decided it was time to discharge him. With the exception of a few ship-keepers, a ship was paid off when it returned home and it was the responsibility of the captain to recruit a new crew. Recruitment was challenging, with the competition for experienced seamen being fierce. Most men preferred to sign up with merchant ships where the pay was significantly better, and a navy captain had to rely on a good reputation, luck and the press gang. Many ships were undermanned when they set sail.

Hugh usually did well with recruitment. He had the reputation of being a lucky captain with respect to prize money and a fair one with respect to discipline. He had a core of experienced sailors who returned to him for every voyage. The challenge was to make sure that these men were not scooped up by the press gang for service aboard another ship. Hugh had issued shore passes to each of them confirming that they were signed up to the *Iris* and promised a bonus to each that chose to do so, but he would need more men. Lieutenant Paisley and his other officers were working hard to make up the numbers but Hugh thought that he and Durrell would probably be needed back in Chatham soon.

The post had been delayed for a week due to summer storms in the Irish Sea, but when it arrived there were several letters for Hugh. Durrell was out riding. He had struck up a friendship with a former navy officer who had resigned his commission and married into a wealthy local family. Thomas Young had been badly wounded at Trafalgar leaving his face a scarred horror, but he had clearly settled happily into his new home after a difficult few years. Roseen knew his young wife from girlhood and had renewed their friendship during this visit. On this occasion Hugh was glad Durrell was out as he wanted to speak to Roseen first. He found her in her favourite room, the large saloon in the tower, with enormous windows looking out towards the sea. She was reading a local newspaper while Alfie and his cousin Freddie played with a collection of wooden toy soldiers and Beth, Alfie's nurse, sat sewing in the corner.

Beth rose as Hugh entered. "Are you wanting to speak to the mistress, Captain? I'll take the children down to the kitchen for their milk and bonnag."

"Thank you, Beth."

Hugh waited until the door closed behind them then turned to his wife. Roseen's dark eyes were studying the letters in his hand.

"Orders?"

"Yes. At least it isn't my formal orders, they'll be sent to the house in Chatham, but I'll need to get myself back there. I'm sorry, Roseen."

Roseen rose and came to kiss him. "Don't be daft, fella, we've done far better than we could have expected this summer. It's been wonderful having you for so long, and it's been good for Alfred as well, he's looking so much better. But if this went on much longer, I'd have been worried they would be putting you on to half-pay."

Hugh grinned. "I'm not ready to be put out to grass just yet. Though spending this time here makes me look forward to the time I am. Roseen...I've something to ask you."

Roseen met his gaze and he saw the sparkle of amusement in her eyes. "Have you, Hugh? You're an observant man, it must be all those hours paying attention to your ship."

Hugh's smile widened. "You're sure?"

"Yes. I've not spoken to the doctor yet, but I'm fairly sure. The only thing that's stopped me mentioning it is that I've not been sick this time, though my appetite has been a bit off. But Mary tells me she was never ill with Freddie but as sick as a dog with Erin, so that probably doesn't mean anything. Have you only just guessed?"

"I've suspected for a couple of weeks but I was waiting for you to tell me. Does anybody else know?"

"Only Mary. I wanted advice." Roseen hesitated then gave a slightly embarrassed smile. "I've been rude about Mary over the years and I remember when Ffinlo married her I thought she was dreadfully tedious. But this visit I've found her a comfort. There's something very reassuring about being around family at a time like this. And it's very different here. In London, even in Chatham, I'd be surrounded by doctors and nurses and very expensive accoucheurs."

"I seem to remember we managed very well last time without those, out in Gibraltar."

"Exactly. I'd like to again. I wish you could be here with me this time as well, Hugh, but I know you can't."

"But your family can. You should stay here, Roseen. No point in making that long journey to the ship with me, when for all I know we'll only get a few days together at the end of it. Look what happened to poor Jane early this year when she took the children all the way to Plymouth to be with Ned, only to find he'd had to set sail before she got there. I'd rather you stayed here and let them spoil you."

"Thank you, I knew you'd say that. Once the baby is born and I'm fit to travel I'll go back to Chatham and wait for you there."

"You don't have to."

"I want to. I'm already missing Maria and Ben, and I've made other friends there now. It's as much my home as this is."

"Not quite, Mrs Kelly. But I'm both amazed and impressed at how well you've adapted."

Roseen laughed and kissed him again. "Not so bad for a little Manx tomboy."

Hugh held her close for a long time. "You are, and will always be, my lady, my love and my best friend. I'll miss you all the more for this time we've had together, but I'll rest easier knowing you're safe and being bullied by Voirrey into eating properly and drinking plenty of fresh Manx milk. And Alfie will love staying here. I'm going to get Ise to teach him to swim."

"Good. I'm also in search of a pony and a puppy for him. He should have both, even if the dog runs wild with him and he can only go round the paddock on a leading rein for a while. Harder to do all of that in Chatham. Who are your letters from?"

Hugh led her to a sofa and brought a footstool for her, insisting that she use it mainly because he knew it would make her laugh. There would be some tears before his departure, for both of them, but by now he was used to Roseen's practical hardiness and he knew she would make the best of it.

"This one is from the Admiralty, with news of my posting. It's as I thought, I'm bound for the Mediterranean. Initially I'm to report to Sir Richard Keats who is stationed off Cadiz. I've a letter from him too."

"Oh how is he? I like Sir Richard. Isn't Cadiz still under siege by the French?"

"Yes, for now. There's been a battle at a place called Barossa as part of an attempt to raise the siege. The French were beaten, but the Spanish were unable to provide support, so nothing came of it. I believe Sir Thomas Graham is being packed off to join Wellington to prevent a major diplomatic incident with the Spanish; he was furious according to Keats. The siege goes on, but there's a lot of French activity on that Eastern coast. They're going to detach a squadron under Ned Codrington, to include a few English ships and some Spanish gunboats. Keats wants me to join them."

Roseen regarded him with interest. "Serving under Ned? Is that the first time you've done so, Hugh?"

"It is. Commodore Codrington, no less. I hope it doesn't go to his head or I'll be obliged to kick him overboard." Hugh scanned the letter again then grinned. "You can read Keats' letter for yourself, love. He's sending me to keep an eye on Ned, in case he goes off on some mad crusade without authorisation."

"Heavens, is he likely to?"

"You never know with Ned. He's an excellent commander, no question, but he occasionally lacks respect for the chain of command."

"So do you."

"That's fair enough, but I'm more likely to keep my mouth shut and work around it, whereas Ned is likely to go in bellowing. Keats likes Ned, so it's my job to keep him out of trouble."

"Rather like the navy version of Major van Daan," Roseen said, and Hugh gave a smile.

"You're not up to date with the news, my love. That's my other letter."

"Paul van Daan? It's been a while since we heard. How is he, Hugh?"

"You can read that one for yourself as well, since it's addressed to both of us. It's rather more serious than usual."

Roseen studied him. "Is he all right?"

"Very much so, it seems, he's been promoted to colonel. But his wife died, giving birth to a daughter." Hugh paused, suddenly wishing he had not told Roseen that, given her own pregnancy.

"Oh no, the poor man."

"Yes. Although it seems he has remarried again rather quickly. A young widow he's known for a while."

Roseen did not speak for a moment. Finally she said:

"Known for a while?"

"I know no more than you do, *my chree*. I always gained the impression he was genuinely attached to his wife, and we don't know the circumstances."

Roseen gave a little smile. "Nor should we try to guess. God knows I've spent enough time with the gossips making free with my personal life, I'm hardly likely to pass judgement on another. I was just trying to work out how to write a letter of condolence. Or congratulation. How typical of that man to present me with a social problem. Never mind, it will give me something to do. Let me read the various letters and you can ride out to meet Mr Durrell and give him the good news."

"Yes. I'll need to think again about my recruitment problem, we're still a few short. Perhaps I can try recruiting locally before I leave."

"Manx seamen are the best, Hugh."

"Don't I know it," Hugh said. He kissed her and left her in charge of his correspondence.

***

The manner of Faith's return to London was very different from her departure. She made the journey in a hired post chaise, spent the night in a very comfortable coaching inn which catered to the gentry and was accompanied by her new maid, Dalton, who had been hired in London by Mr Glinde's wife and who had been sent to join Faith in Norfolk to assist her with her packing and on the journey. Faith had requested the dismissal of both her maid and her hired companion. She asked Glinde to pay them for the rest of the year which was more than generous, but she refused to see either of them for a farewell interview. Both had been employed by her father with specific instructions to report back to him and neither had showed any kindness or understanding. Faith would not see them starve but she refused to listen to excuses or explanations from two women she cordially disliked.

Mr Collingwood's London house was in Russell Square; an impressive Georgian mansion which he had bought many years earlier from the widow of an East India merchant who no longer had need of a London home. Faith had been raised in the spacious, lonely nursery under the care of a series of nurses and governesses. She had learned not to become too attached to any one of them, since Mr Collingwood was a demanding and capricious employer and staff tended not to remain with him for very long.

The house was very quiet, making Faith feel as though she should tiptoe. Hudson, her father's very correct butler greeted her formally and gave instructions for the disposal of her luggage and the accommodation of her maid. Faith asked for a message to be sent to Glinde and requested that the housekeeper attend her in the small drawing room, then went up to change her clothes.

Mrs Bell arrived with the tea tray and poured for Faith, making enquiries about her journey, the weather in Norfolk and whether Miss Dalton, the new abigail, was proving satisfactory. Faith answered politely but cut the conversation short when Mrs Bell began to tell her about the shortcomings of the new laundry maid.

"I am sorry to interrupt, Mrs Bell, for it is very good to see you again, but I am keen to have news of my father. I will visit him presently but before I do so, I would like to know all that you can tell me about his care. Who nurses him?"

"Well, miss, Dr Mercer arranges all that. There are two nurses living in, with a third who comes once a week to give them some time off, or to stay through the night if the doctor thinks they're too tired. They share the room opposite the master's, but we've set up a truckle bed in Mr Collingwood's dressing room for the night shift. Mr Hudson has sent a boy to ask Dr Mercer to call as soon as possible. It's all taken care of, so no need to think you'll be having to nurse him yourself, it would be very unsuitable."

"Given my complete inexperience in matters of nursing, you would be right, Mrs Bell. I would like to speak to the doctor, but I think I will visit my father now."

"As you wish, miss. Should I accompany you?"

"No, thank you. Later on, once I have seen Mr Glinde and Dr Mercer, I will talk to you about how I wish things to be done now that I am home, but we have time for that."

Mrs Bell looked taken aback. "How things...well, miss, I suppose I thought that with your father in the house, we would continue to do things..."

"When my father recovers enough to give orders, Mrs Bell, I've no doubt he'll give them. Until then, I am afraid you will have to put up with me."

The housekeeper bobbed an uncertain curtsy. "Miss...ma'am, what about your companion. Mrs Irwin? I was expecting..."

"Mrs Irwin is no longer in my service, Mrs Bell. I have dismissed her, along with Rigby, which is why I was in need of a new abigail. I shall ask Mr Glinde for assistance in finding a new hired companion, one who is rather more attuned to my requirements. In the meantime, since this is all very new to me, I am hoping I can rely on all the staff to help me."

Mrs Bell's mouth was hanging open. She appeared to realise it and closed it quickly. "Yes. Yes, ma'am, of course. I hadn't thought...but of course you won't be wanting things to remain the same. Nor should they. Nor should they indeed. I'll be off then, to let you rest until Mr Glinde arrives. Unless...are you hungry, ma'am? I've some cake just out of the oven, I could send Sarah up with a slice for you."

Faith opened her mouth to refuse and then changed her mind. Such luxuries as cake had not been on offer at Wickham House. Besides, she sensed a sudden change of attitude in Mrs Bell that she was keen to encourage. "I would love some cake, Mrs Bell, I cannot remember the last time I had such a thing. The cook at Wickham House was...well, barely a cook at all."

Mrs Bell gave an expressive snort. "And I could have guessed that just by looking at you, there's nothing of you. That Mrs Irwin, giving herself airs and looking down her long nose at those of us in service, but not able to see that her young lady is being half-starved. Or not caring, more like. Well she's gone now, and good riddance in my opinion. Don't think of it again, ma'am, that young woman you've employed as abigail seems very well indeed, and I'll speak to the rest of the staff and make sure they know what I expect of them. We'll look after you properly while the poor gentleman is so ill, and if it should be that the good Lord doesn't see fit to return him to health, I'm sure Mr Glinde will do all that you need. I'll send that cake up right now, and then you should have a lie down."

She bustled away and Faith watched her go and found herself smiling. She knew very little about her father's servants, as he had allowed her no responsibility about the house, but she had a strong sense that her situation had been much discussed in the servants hall, possibly not to her father's advantage. She poured more tea and ate the cake, when it arrived, with very good appetite.

Faith did not go for a lie down. Instead, she walked up the stairs and along the corridor to her father's bedroom. She had almost never entered the room and she opened the door with a flutter of anxiety which she knew to be nonsense.

John Collingwood lay in the big bed. He was very still, apart from the rise and fall of his chest. Faith was surprised to see that his head was swathed in bandages. He looked oddly smaller than she remembered. A middle aged woman in a dark gown sat beside the bed. She rose at the sight of Faith and dropped a curtsy.

"How do you do?" Faith said. "I am Miss Faith Collingwood, I have come to see my father. You must be...?"

"Mrs Smith, ma'am, the nurse. Doctor told us you'd be home soon. Staying in the country, weren't you? This must be a terrible shock for you. They say he was a healthy man, no warning, like."

"Yes, I was very shocked. I am not sure I have really come to terms with it. Why are there bandages?"

"The surgeon operated, ma'am. He thought he might be able to relieve the pressure on the brain. He's tried bleeding him as well, every day. And leeches."

Faith tried to repress a shudder. "Is it helping at all?"

"No, ma'am, and it won't," Mrs Smith said bluntly. "I expect the doctor will be here any minute, now that you're back, they'll have sent for him. He might ask if you want him to try more surgery. That's what they do, these doctors. The more they do, the more they charge, especially with a wealthy gentleman like I'm told he is. You tell him no. I've seen a dozen or more cases like this. It's different if there's some sign they might recover. Sometimes they lose movement or speech, or their face is all twisted up. I've seen some good come of it then. But with a gentleman lying like one dead, like he's been for days, it's going to go one way. I calls it cruel, pulling him about and cutting him open. Bleeding is all right. Certainly won't do him any harm, though I doubt it will do him any good either."

Faith moved close to the bed, looking down at her father's face. There was something wrong with it, as though he had been pulling a face and been somehow frozen in the act. It made him look angry, as he had the last time she had seen him.

"Does he regain consciousness at all?" she asked.

"No, ma'am."

"What of food and drink?"

"We spend a lot of time getting water and wine into him. Been trying with gruel, but it chokes him. He'll keep going as long as he's drinking. But it's not much."

"Do you think he knows I am here?"

"Probably not, ma'am, but you can try talking to him. Hold his hand. I'll step outside for a bit. Call me if you need me."

When she had gone, Faith stepped closer to the bed and reached for her father's hand. It felt dry and rather cold.

"Papa. It is I, Faith. I've come home to see you. Can you hear me?"

There was no response. Faith stood studying him. She felt foolish, as though she had been caught talking to a statue. She could not ever remember holding her father's hand before. It felt alien and almost wrong.

"Father, can you hear me? Can you squeeze my hand a little?"

There was no movement, not even a light pressure. He was not there and for the first time, Faith thought that the nurse might well be right and that nothing would bring her father back.

"Miss Collingwood. My dear Miss Collingwood. I understand your desire to see your father, but you should have waited, indeed you should. It is not fit that you should do this alone, with nobody to support you."

Faith turned in surprise. The gentleman in the doorway was probably around forty, prosperous and portly with thinning hair and a waistcoat which looked perilously stretched. Behind him, Mr Glinde met Faith's eyes.

"Miss Collingwood, it is good to see you. This is Doctor Mercer, who has been treating Mr Collingwood. I am sure that you have many questions for him. Perhaps Miss Collingwood and I should return to the drawing room, Doctor, and you can join us there when you have seen your patient."

In the drawing room, Faith rang the bell. She was surprised when Hudson appeared with a drinks tray, but she supposed he knew the preferences of her guest. She allowed Hudson to pour her a small glass of sherry. When the door closed behind him, Glinde said:

"How was your journey?"

"It was very comfortable. Thank you for making the arrangements. I was shocked at my father's condition. I know you told me, but seeing him like that..."

"I'm sorry, ma'am. It must be very distressing."

"I've spoken to the nurse. She said that there was some kind of operation?"

"Dr Mercer hoped that he might be able to release some of the pressure on the brain, but it has made no difference. He has spoken of trying again. It will be your decision, ma'am, but I do not think..."

"No. Dear God, no, look at him. My father is a man I dislike very much, but I could not put him through that. I have no idea what he can feel or what he knows, but I will not allow it."

"I agree. With your agreement, ma'am, we will wait until you have had the opportunity to speak to Dr Mercer, and then I think we should talk about your situation."

Dr Mercer appeared shortly and accepted sherry. "Miss Collingwood, how are you? I am so sorry for this dreadful shock, you must be wholly overcome."

"I will try not to be so, Doctor. I would like you to tell me, if you would, what treatment my father is receiving. The nurse spoke of an operation."

"I called upon Dr Fleetwood, ma'am, who is an expert in matters of the brain. He was of the opinion that your father might benefit from an attempt to relieve the pressure within his skull. I believe Dr Fleetwood to have had some very good results from the procedure, but in your father's case, it did not answer. Since then, I have been bleeding him daily and have applied leeches. So far, we have had no success."

"The nurse said it is difficult to get him to take nourishment."

"It's impossible," Glinde said bluntly.

"My dear Miss Collingwood, we should not take such a pessimistic view. For the time being, it is true that although my nurses are able to get him to drink a little, he is not eating. However, if we can but..."

"Doctor, please." Faith could feel herself becoming uncharacteristically angry. "I realise that is must be difficult for you, having to deal with a young female instead of an older relative, but in this case, I am the only option. I have come home to find out the true case of my father's health. You will not help me with meaningless platitudes."

Both men were visibly shocked, which Faith found very satisfying. She was a little shocked at herself. Throughout her girlhood she had never stood up to her father although his contempt had reduced her to tears many times. It had never occurred to Faith that she was also angry. Since being beaten and sent away for a crime she had not committed, she had been constantly furious, and she was amazed at how much she was enjoying it.

"My apologies, ma'am," Mercer said huffily. "I merely wished to spare one of such tender years and delicate sensibilities..."

"Let us pretend that I am older and have no sensibilities at all. What is the likely outcome for my father?"

"He is going to die, ma'am. We could try another operation, but I do not think it can succeed. I am very sorry."

"How long do you think he will live?"

"I cannot say. As you correctly suggest, getting sustenance into him is crucial, but he will take very little. I have instructed the nurses to concentrate on getting him to drink, since that is vital, but without food he will eventually weaken and die. That could take many weeks, possibly months. Or, he may have another stroke which will kill him. I am very sorry."

"Thank you. It is better to know the truth."

Faith sat thinking for a moment and neither man spoke. She supposed that Dr Mercer, without knowing the facts, thought her upset. Glinde probably knew better, but he was unsure at present. His previous interest in Faith, as his employer's despised female heir, had probably been entirely based around the best way to get her married to a man of influence. It had not been easy, since John Collingwood's huge fortune was not enough to offset his humble beginnings and his blunt and often vulgar manners. Some men made the transition from trade to gentry very easily and a marriage into society or political circles could smooth the path. Collingwood had not been successful, and Faith had always known that her extremely expensive education had been intended to attract a son-in-law who would make it possible. Faith had dreaded her father's choice and the prospect of being able to make her own decision made her feel slightly dizzy.

"You are upset," Glinde said finally. "May I suggest that you allow Dr Mercer to continue with the current treatment, Miss Collingwood? He is very experienced, and unless you intend to allow further surgery, I see no need..."

Faith looked up. "Yes. Yes, of course you are right. Thank you so much for all you've done, Doctor. How often do you visit?"

"I have reduced my visits to alternate days, ma'am, but if there is any change, I will come immediately."

"Do as you think best. I have no medical experience and will be guided by you and your excellent nurses."

When Mercer had gone, Faith sat opposite Glinde and watched him refill the sherry glasses. He was looking at her with an expression that she found difficult to read.

"How are you really, Miss Collingwood?"

Faith thought about it. "I don't know," she said honestly. "This has all happened so fast. Last week I was in Norfolk, shivering in a room with cracks in the windows and lighting my own fires because the servants saw no reason to obey me. And now I am back here, and people are fussing over me as if I am some fragile creature in need of protection and care."

"That is how you should be treated, ma'am."

Faith stood up and walked to the fire. She picked up the tongs and took several pieces of coal from the scuttle, arranging them carefully, then applied the poker until the fire blazed brightly again. Straightening, she turned and looked at Glinde.

"Well it is a little late for that, sir. When I needed your care and protection, you were nowhere to be seen. Now I find I do not need it at all."

Glinde flushed a little. "I cannot put that right, ma'am, all I can do is continue to apologise. And to offer what help I can."

"Very well. I have some practical questions. We spoke before about a legal guardian, and you said that we should wait until we had further news of my father. What is your opinion now?"

"It remains the same. For form's sake, I will write a letter enquiring about it. They will probably take a month to reply. Every week that passes brings us closer to your twenty-first birthday. I think it very unlikely that your father will survive until that day, but we need take no action, I think."

"What happens when he dies?"

"You are his undisputed heir, Miss Collingwood, but you will need a man to manage the business. I have been effectively your father's deputy for many years. I would be honoured to serve you in that capacity, but I should advise you that you should appoint somebody else as well, to oversee my activities. A matter of good faith, you understand."

"A matter of keeping you honest, Mr Glinde?"

"I am honest, ma'am. But it is important that you know that I have no opportunity to be otherwise. Normally this would have been managed by a Trust until you marry, when your husband can take over the management of your affairs. As your father did not appoint Trustees, I would suggest that you meet with his solicitor. He may be willing to act, or he may have a suggestion as to whom he could appoint. One of your father's City friends might be willing to act..."

"I don't want any friend of my father's."

Glinde gave a flicker of a smile. "I meant a business associate, ma'am. Remember they will simply be supervising how I run the business, not arranging your personal life."

Faith was surprised at how accurately he had read her thoughts. After a moment, she nodded grudgingly. Glinde sipped his sherry.

"There are other matters which we should consider, ma'am. I did suggest when we were in Norfolk, that you might wish to discuss some of these with my wife, but I understand you would prefer not."

"I mean no disrespect to your wife, Mr Glinde, but I cannot see how she can be helpful in this matter. You are speaking of my living arrangements, I collect."

"I am, ma'am. Your situation is difficult. I am delighted that you agreed to return to Town, and I understand and fully support your decision to dismiss Mrs Irwin as your companion. Nevertheless, this leaves you in a somewhat ambiguous position. You are a young, unmarried girl, and even if you were of age, it would be expected that you would have some lady to live with you. In addition, you left London under a cloud of scandal. Oh - I accept your word unreservedly that you were not to blame and that you did not deserve the opprobrium, but Society will remember."

"I am sure it will."

"Naturally, you will not be going into Society at present, given the circumstances of your father's health, and also given the fact that you have not yet made your formal debut. Did your father ever discuss his intentions in that direction?"

"Mr Glinde you must know him well enough to know that he is likely to have talked to anybody other than me about what he meant to do. He treated me as if I were an idiot child for my entire life."

"I am beginning to think that was his mistake, ma'am," Glinde said surprisingly. "It is my understanding that Mr Collingwood hoped that a formal debut would not be necessary. He intended to find you a husband so that your first appearance at Court would be as a married lady."

"Yes, he made that clear when he ordered me to accept Mr Henry Durrell's offer."

"The situation now is quite different. You are unattached, you are about to become very wealthy, and your fortune is unencumbered. In addition, and I am speaking candidly here, your social position will be very much enhanced by the absence of your father. He is not generally liked, and his manners were not always those of a gentleman, which made it difficult for him to rise to the position he hoped to attain. To be frank, I think that many gentlemen would have hesitated to contract a marriage with the prospect of him as father-in-law. You, on the other hand, would be accepted anywhere."

Faith felt unsuitable laughter bubbling up. She tried hard to suppress it then changed her mind and laughed aloud. "Really? That is very funny, Mr Glinde, when I think of all the things he said to me. Are you trying to warn me against fortune hunters?"

"I am trying to tell you, Miss Collingwood, that even without a formal debut, you are likely to become very popular once your situation is known. One or two of the highest sticklers may hold up their noses at your father's origins or even at the unfortunate scandal last year, but I rather suspect that most gentlemen will find it very easy to forget both."

"My goodness, how that would annoy my father."

Glinde permitted himself a faint smile. "Very much, I imagine. Miss Collingwood...is there any gentleman that you...?"

He broke off delicately and Faith felt herself blush and wished she had not, because she knew it would give him entirely the wrong impression. She looked at him and said as calmly as possible:

"I collect you are referring to Lieutenant Alfred Durrell, sir? Do I need to repeat, yet again, that the story told by his brother was a lie from start to finish? Mr Henry Durrell became engaged to me because he wanted my father's money. After we returned from Walcheren, he found a better prospect in Miss Cornell, who could offer not only money but also political influence. Our betrothal had been announced and he knew that there was no way that he could withdraw with honour, so he chose the dishonourable path instead. He told my father, and anybody else who was willing to listen to him, that he was repudiating our betrothal because he had discovered that I had been intriguing with his younger brother when we were in Middelburg and I am very sure he paid my maid to corroborate the story. Another man would have defended the honour of his daughter. My father took a riding whip to me and beat me until I bled."

Glinde's face blanched. "My dear Miss Collingwood, pray..."

"Pray what? Do not speak of it? Let us not do so indeed, I would not wish to offend your delicate sensibilities, sir. You will not offend mine, since after how that man treated me, I have none left. I discovered I have no use for them."

Glinde did not speak. Faith allowed the silence to lengthen. Eventually, she said:

"In answer to your question, no, I have no ongoing attachment to Lieutenant Durrell or any other gentleman, although I liked him very much. He was very kind to me, which is more than I can say for his brother. But I believe we were speaking of my future. For the time being, I think I should remain here. Until my father is dead, and my proper period of mourning is over, I will live quietly, although I suppose I do not need to shut myself up wholly?"

"No, indeed, ma'am. Not at all. I am afraid you must resign yourself to employing a lady to live with you. The world will expect it. For the time being, I have a suggestion. My wife has a sister who lives with us, and acts as her companion. I am aware that you are determined to select your own companion this time, so will you take Miss Caddick on a temporary basis? She will not wish to leave my wife long-term and we could not spare her, but for a month or two, she is very willing."

Faith was rather taken aback. She wondered if Mrs Glinde had made the suggestion, but whoever it had come from, she was a little touched and felt ashamed of her outburst.

"Thank you, sir, that is a very good idea."

"I will bring her over tomorrow so that you may meet her and, if you agree, she can move in immediately. Once you are known to be properly chaperoned, you will not find yourself short of callers, I imagine, and you may receive some invitations. I suggest you ask Miss Caddick for advice about what it may or may not be advisable to do."

"Thank you," Faith said. "I was rude earlier. I am sorry."

"Please don't be, Miss Collingwood. I think you have a right to be angry, you were treated appallingly. I will leave you now to settle in. If there is anything you need, please do not hesitate to apply to me. I will escort Miss Caddick over tomorrow."

He bowed and Faith gave him her hand. "You're being very good, Mr Glinde, and I don't think I am being very grateful."

The older man smiled, and Faith decided that it improved him considerably. "Ma'am, I think in the coming months, and even years, if we can develop a good working relationship it will benefit both of us. I hope I have made my position very clear. I have been employed by your father for twenty years and I have been very well paid for my service. I am still employed by him while he lives, but within these walls I answer to you, as his undisputed heiress."

Faith returned his smile. "I am very glad you said that because it has just occurred to me that I have no money. I had a very small allowance and I spent most of it on new art materials. I am afraid the state of my clothing is woeful, and I haven't a feather to fly with."

Glinde bowed again. "I should have thought of it myself. I will make arrangements to rectify that immediately, ma'am, and as for dressmakers and the like, you will set up whatever accounts you need. Good afternoon to you."

When he had gone, Faith went over to the fireplace, studying herself in the huge mirror above the mantle. The lace collar of her gown was frayed in places and she was aware of a darn in her stocking and a small stain on the hem of the gown which her maid had not managed to remove. The thought of ordering new clothing, of replacing her battered straw bonnet and of a pair of shoes which were not patched, filled her with happiness. Then another thought occurred to her.

The door opened and Mrs Bell entered. "Has Mr Glinde gone, ma'am? I was wondering when you'd like your dinner, and where we should serve it, when you're on your own? The master used to eat in his study often as not, but you won't want to do that."

Faith turned. "Oh no. No, not at all. But I wonder - could we move a small table into the back parlour? The one that opens up onto the garden."

"Of course, ma'am. I'll speak to Hudson."

"Thank you, Mrs Bell. Oh, and while you are speaking to Hudson, do you think he could discover the best shop for art materials?"

"Paints and suchlike? Oh that will be Ackermann's on the Strand, for sure. I didn't know you enjoyed painting, ma'am. Will that be all?"

"Yes, thank you," Faith said absently. As the housekeeper left, she went in search of her note tablets and sat down to the enjoyable task of making several shopping lists.

Chapter Three

Hugh was writing letters regarding his journey back to Chatham when his wife suggested a riding expedition. Hugh managed just in time not to ask if she should be riding in her condition and was rewarded by an approving smile from Roseen.

Durrell was mounted on a tall, skittish, black gelding borrowed from Roseen's brother. They rode through Castletown, along the quay and out towards Derbyhaven to the peaceful beauty of St Michael's Isle with its tiny fortress and ruined eleventh century chapel.

With the curiosity common to isolated communities, the people of Mann peered out of cottages and houses and several of them emerged at the sight of Roseen who was well known and very popular among the fisher-folk. Roseen reined in to speak to each of them. She knew them all by name and made enquiries about children and extended families, held a proudly offered new-born and exchanged banter with a toothless elder smoking a pipe. Hugh glanced at Durrell and saw that he too was watching her and was smiling broadly.

"Mrs Kelly is very well liked here."

"Mrs Kelly is one of them," Hugh said with a grin. "When I first met Mrs Kelly she was running wild with the lads from the fishing fleet and giving her father sleepless nights over it. An unconscionable young hoyden."

"I heard that," Roseen said, turning her horse. "Do not pretend that you didn't make the most of it, Captain Kelly. Do you mind if we make one more stop? I'd like to call on Mrs Kissack."

"Of course, lass. Take all the time you need."

Outside a neat white cottage at the end of the row, a middle aged woman with iron grey hair and a weathered face was operating a wooden butter churn with great concentration. She looked up at the sound of the horses and her face softened into a smile as Roseen dismounted and came forward.

"Mrs Kelly, it's good to see you. Your pardon, ma'am, I can't stop..."

"No, of course you can't, and there's no need. I just wanted to see how you are doing."

"Very well, ma'am, as you see. We took on an extra patch of land when Jemmy Corrin died early last year and we're growing barley as well now. You know my Jonny married last year?"

"I've already seen him. And the baby. She's very pretty."

"They couldn't have wed so soon if Mr Moore hadn't taken him on as a farm hand, with the cottage as well. I was that grateful, ma'am. Your family has been a good friend to us these past years."

"Your eldest son saved my life, Mrs Kissack, and he was my friend. There's no debt between any of us. How is..."

"Roseen Crellin." The man who had emerged around the back of the cottage was a stocky Manxman in his twenties. He was halfway across the small front garden when he realised what he had said and remembered his place. He stopped dead, flushing scarlet, but before he had time to stammer his apologies, Roseen reached him and put her arms about him.

"Davy Kissack don't be so daft, you've known me since I was a scrubby brat. How are you? How is Mary and your boy? He must be a giant by now, where is he?"

Kissack gave her a quick hug and released her, shooting an apologetic grin at Hugh. "You never change, Roseen. He's with Mary over at her mother's. I'm sorry you've missed them. I've been hoping to run into you, but we've been that busy."

"There's no rush, Davy. Captain Kelly has to return to his ship, but I'll be staying on a while. I want to bring Alfie down to meet Illiam, he's in need of playmates."

"How old is he now?"

"He's three and so active he's a danger to his surroundings."

Kissack laughed. "If you like, I'll take him out on the boat."

"Only if I can come too," Roseen said. "I've missed fishing with the Kissack boys."

"Oh no," Hugh said firmly. "You're very welcome to take them out, Kissack, but not without me. I've no reason to assume that the impress service is in these waters, but if they are, the sight of a post-captain and his first lieutenant will get rid of them."

"I wouldn't mind seeing that Captain."

"I'll just bet you wouldn't," Hugh said with a grin. "Roseen, we'll need to get home, we're supposed to be dining with the Quayles later. You'll have plenty of time to come back. I know very well where you'd rather spend your time and it's not doing the pretty with the Lieutenant-Governor."

"You're no better, Captain," Roseen said serenely. She bent to kiss Mrs Kissack's cheek. "Goodbye, ma'am. I'm looking forward to meeting little Illiam soon."

The older woman looked up at her, still wielding the butter paddle rhythmically, and gave her sweet smile again. "You've no reason to be calling me 'ma'am', Mrs Kelly."

"It's what I called you when you gave me slices of buttered bonnag when I was just a little girl and I've no reason to change it."

Kissack came to help Roseen onto her horse. He straightened and gave a little bow to Hugh, who acknowledged it with a salute. "She'll be back, Kissack. In the meantime, I've a favour to ask. Since I'm going back to the *Iris*, I'm on the lookout for a few more crew members. We're in need of another thirty or so and I'll welcome any Manxman who wants to volunteer. Would you put the word out?"

"Aye, I'll do that, sir. Might be a few, times have been hard for many and they've not all been as lucky as us."

"You should ask around in the ale houses up Ramsey way," Mrs Kissack said. "I heard Orry Gelling has laid off a lot of men since he's realised he can't get around these slave trading laws. He was boasting about how they wouldn't stop his ships, but he seems to have changed his mind a bit."

"He'll have changed it since Parliament made it a felony to engage in illegal slave trading," Hugh said grimly. He was aware of an angry tightening in his gut which was only partly because of Gelling's slaving history. During a painful separation from Roseen during her early love affair with Hugh, Gelling had shown an interest in marrying Josiah Crellin's lively daughter and when Roseen refused, had made a serious attempt to force the issue. The assault had ended badly for Gelling. Hugh hoped it had taught him not to try conclusions with a girl who had grown up wild and knew exactly where to kick a man to disable him. Hugh had not encountered Gelling since. He studied Mrs Kissack with sudden interest.

"Do you happen to know if Gelling is still running any merchant ships, ma'am?"

"Lord yes, sir. He'll ship anything if the price is right, he's still got the *Ramsey Maid* trading to Liverpool and Glasgow and the *Josephine* and *Clara May* shipping luxury goods from the West Indies. But he's stood down his other two ships, and I'm told some of the men are finding it hard; catching a passage when they can or doing casual work loading and unloading at the quayside, or during harvest. It's no way to support a family as we well know. Happen the men with families won't care to sign up but there are plenty of young men idle and there's not the work for them."

"Thank you, ma'am, that's useful information," Hugh said seriously.

They were halfway back to Ballabrendon, when Roseen said:

"Hugh, what are you up to?"

"Up to?" Hugh turned innocent grey eyes towards her. "Nothing, love. I'm just turning over what Mrs Kissack said about recruiting locally. We're still short-handed and you know how I love to take on Manxmen, especially if they're experienced seamen and volunteers."

Roseen nodded, seeming satisfied, and Hugh made himself join in the conversation for the rest of the ride home. His wife was sharp-eyed and knew him very well and he had no wish to arouse her suspicions. Hugh spent an hour playing with Alfie in the garden and then went to wash and change for dinner. He left Roseen in the hands of her maid, knowing that her toilette would take some time, and sped downstairs. As he had expected, he found Durrell in the drawing room, already dressed, and reading a copy of the Manks Advertiser with a stunned expression on his well-bred face. Hugh enjoyed the view for a moment.

"Seen anything you like, Mr Durrell?"

"There is to be a sale of the goods and chattels of Mr Thomas Roberts of Santon. Items include a goat, three Loaghtan ewes and sundry broken fence posts. Do you think they have listed the most appealing of the lot?"

Hugh considered. "Well they can keep the fencing, but I might get Isaac to have a look at those ewes, Mr Durrell, thank you." He saw his junior's expression and laughed aloud. "Don't look so shocked, fella, you're on my home ground now and there's more to me than the captain of the *Iris*."

"I've always known it, sir, but it's been a revelation seeing it first-hand. And your wife..." Durrell waved a hand in the air, apparently lost for words, something which seldom happened. Hugh shook his head and removed the newspaper from Durrell's hands, tossing it onto a table.

"My wife is in her element. Just watching her here makes me feel guilty that I've kept her away for so long. I'm glad she's decided to stay on. But listen, I want to talk to you before she gets down. How many crew are we short?"

Durrell blinked in surprise. "Approximately forty, sir, according to Paisley. We have enough to sail, but if we do not manage to recruit more, we might be somewhat exposed in a battle or in some other difficult conditions. I was thinking that I may travel back a little ahead of you to see if our press gang can..."

Hugh shook his head decidedly. "I don't want landsmen if I can avoid it, Lieutenant."

"None of us do, sir, but it may be necessary."

"It won't be necessary, as I have come up with a brilliant idea. Mrs Kissack suggested it."

"The former crew of this slaver? I agree that we may pick up a few, sir, but not enough to bring us up to full strength."

"Oh, you've misunderstood, Mr Durrell. I wasn't intending to trail around the taverns and ale houses of Ramsey searching for unemployed sailors. We'll put up some posters though; I'll ride in to Jefferson's in Douglas tomorrow to arrange for them to be printed up and Isaac can send a couple of the men around to the most likely places. We'll pick up a few that way."

"And the rest?"

Hugh smiled broadly. "Mr Orry Gelling, leading light of Ramsey Town and former slave trader, currently has two ships in port, waiting to be loaded up with finished cotton and woollen goods from the mills of Manchester and Lancashire which he ships to markets all over the world. I've been talking to Ise, who tells me Gelling keeps a small crew of experienced men aboard and then takes on the rest of the crew two weeks before he sails, so he doesn't have to pay them for time ashore, the miserly bugger."

"Sir, that's common practice."

"I know. However, I'm delighted to find that the weekly newspapers are as reliable as ever with the local shipping news. I can tell you to within a day or two when that bastard will have his ship ready to sail with a full complement of very experienced Manx seamen."

Durrell stared at him, his mouth hanging open. Hugh considered suggesting that he close it but found that he was enjoying having reduced his talkative First Lieutenant to speechlessness.

"Sir, you cannot."

"Oh yes I can."

"But sir, have you thought this through? While I understand your enthusiasm for an easy way to press so many men at once, surely it is going to cause problems on the island for you? The press gang is hated here. It's hated everywhere."

"I don't care. Once they're pressed, I'll call for volunteers. If they're signing up to Gelling's ship they're definitely up for going to sea and I have immense faith in my First Lieutenant to work out which ones we want to keep. I'm going to write some letters to go off with the packet in the morning, I've some favours I can call in so I'm hoping we can borrow an impress brig to transport them to the *Iris*. I'm sure I can find a way to ensure that the captain gets his bonus, I just need to know where the nearest one is."

"It's illegal," Durrell said flatly. "The Royal Navy is entitled to do whatever it likes with merchant seamen returning to shore, but if this Gelling knows the law, he'll know you can't board a ship that's about to sail from port."

"I can do what the hell I like before they board."

"Not if they're already signed up."

"He'll advertise the signing on day. Generally there's a nice queue that forms while the shipping clerk is setting up, and all we have to do is watch and wait. If I can get an impress crew down there in plenty of time, it'll be like falling off a log, Mr Durrell."

Durrell looked appalled. "Are you serious about this, Captain? Do you not think that this will have a detrimental effect on your relationship with some of your countrymen?"

"If it does, they'll get over it. I doubt they'll care, I'm Manx and these lads are already seamen. But don't mention it to my wife just yet, it's a sensitive subject with her."

"I can see why, sir."

"Mr Durrell."

"I will not say anything, sir, since I would have no idea what to say. But if you will forgive me for mentioning it, I find it impossible to believe that this notion you have taken into your head is simply about finding crew members for the *Iris*. I have known you for several years now and during that time I have found you to be generally a rational man, often in circumstances where other men would allow their emotions to get the better of them. It seems to me that from the moment that woman mentioned Mr Orry Gelling, you have behaved in an uncharacteristically irrational manner which seems to suggest that you have some grudge against Mr Gelling, which might possibly be related to his prior involvement in the slave trade. I know that you are a supporter of the abolitionist movement. I am myself, as was my father. But if you are allowing your sentiments about this to cloud your good judgement, I would urge you..."

Hugh stepped forward and very gently placed his hand on Durrell's mouth. "Alfred, you know that thing that you do?"

"Yes, sir." Durrell's voice was muffled. Hugh removed his hand.

"You're doing it now, and I think my wife is coming down. Stop worrying about it, I've not gone mad, and it will work. And if Orry Gelling wants to speak to me about it, he's more than welcome to call."

Durrell was frowning a little. "That is why I am worrying, sir. Because I think that is what you are hoping he will do."

***

During the following week, Durrell tried to put the matter of Gelling's crewmen from his mind. Durrell had thoroughly enjoyed his introduction to island life, although he was also looking forward to getting back to sea.

A good deal of his enjoyment was due to Roseen, whose happiness at being home was infectious. On dry days, they had explored the small island on horseback; picnicking in rocky coves, walking on broad sandy beaches and exploring the winding streets of Peel Town, Castletown, and Douglas. To his amusement, Durrell was introduced to both the local gentry and the farming and fishing population, since both Roseen and Hugh seemed equally comfortable in both settings. Durrell knew that Hugh had not been born into the gentry, being the son of a tenant farmer who drank himself to death after the loss of his wife, leaving Hugh the choice of taking employment as a farmhand or a fisherman or joining the navy. Durrell had wondered at first why the orphaned boy had not simply chosen to sign up to the crew of a merchant ship, but over the past years he had got to know Hugh better and he recognised that under Hugh Kelly's relaxed facade burned an ambition as fierce as his own. Hugh had used the navy and his own intelligence and courage to lift himself out of the sphere into which he was born, and Durrell respected him for it. He also respected how comfortable Hugh was with both parts of his life. He was as much at home with the farm labourers and fishermen as he was with Josiah Crellin and the Manx gentry, or some of his wealthy and aristocratic fellow officers.

Durrell's Godson was immediately at home at Ballabrendon. He had two cousins through Roseen's brother, Ffinlo, but on a daily basis he played with the estate children, taking part in the rough and tumble in a way that Durrell found frankly terrifying. Beth, his Manx nursemaid, had two young nephews who were a year or two older than Alfie, and the three of them were quickly inseparable under Beth's competent supervision. On dry days they roamed the gardens and fields of the estate, returning home filthy and starving. On wet days, they played in the nursery, building towers and defences from wooden building blocks to the disapproval of Ffinlo Crellin.

"You'll have those two thinking they belong in the big house at this rate, Roseen."

"Good. Perhaps they'll join the navy, make their fortunes, and buy the Top House when you've gambled away your sons' inheritance," Roseen said serenely.

"Gambled away...?" Ffinlo broke off as he saw his sister's expression and made a sound like a growl. "You don't improve at all, Roseen."

"Isn't it fortunate then, dear brother, that my husband likes me the way I am. Stop being so top-lofty, you played with all the farm boys and fisher lads when you were young, and it didn't do you any harm."

"You did as well, as I recall, but we cannot say it did you no harm since it led to you being taken for a boy and impressed by the Royal Navy," Ffinlo said waspishly.

"Think of how well that turned out for me, though, Ffinlo." Roseen spread her hands to indicate the comfort of the house around her. Durrell turned away, trying hard to conceal his amusement. He thought that he was not entirely successful as Ffinlo gave a muttered excuse and left. Durrell opened his mouth to apologise then realised that Roseen was openly laughing.

"I'm sorry, ma'am."

"Don't be, Mr Durrell, this has nothing to do with you. My brother and I were very close when we were young, but when he reached the age of twenty-one he appeared to turn into a different person. I did not. I have no idea how he manages to be so stuffy, he must bore himself I should think. He is constantly furious that I was on the verge of total disgrace and have somehow managed to emerge from it very happily. You would think he would be pleased. I shall put him from my mind since he irritates me. I was wondering if you would be my escort into Castletown. I have several errands, and Captain Kelly is closeted in his study writing letters again. It is clearly time he was back at sea although I shall miss him dreadfully."

"Gladly, ma'am," Durrell said offering her his arm. He wondered when Hugh was intending to tell Roseen his plans for acquiring the remaining crew for the *Iris* and hoped, with shameless cowardice, that he would be a long way away when she found out.

Durrell found himself wishing, during the following week, that something would happen to scupper Hugh's plans. There were a number of things which could go wrong, but Hugh lived up to his reputation of one of the luckiest captains in the navy, and things fell neatly into place under Durrell's gloomy gaze. Letters arrived from Lieutenant Paisley aboard the *Iris* and from Lieutenant Leach of the impress frigate *Abilene*, which Durrell thought was a very pretty name for what turned out to be a very ugly ship. Leach anchored off the coast but had himself rowed ashore to meet with Hugh. Hugh and Durrell entertained him to a meal in the *Glue Pot* tavern in

Castletown to discuss arrangements. Hugh had obtained information that Gelling's agent was to begin signing on crew members for both ships the following Tuesday at his Ramsey warehouse. As Hugh had hoped, Gelling had given a specific time for willing crew to present themselves. This was common practice when there was no regularly manned ship's office. Depending on how many men came to sign up, it was likely to result in a large group of men milling about in the hope of getting a berth. Hugh's informants suggested that Mrs Kissack had been right when she said that times had been hard over the past year, and the posters Hugh had put up in taverns and ale houses around the island had brought a surprisingly good response.

"We've already signed twelve volunteers," Hugh said, pouring wine for Leach. I've asked them to present themselves at my father-in-law's sheds down in Derbyhaven on Wednesday morning."

"Paid them already?" Leach asked cynically.

"No. One or two might change their minds, but I've a feeling they'll show up. That will take us to only thirty or so short of a full crew. I've sailed with less, to be honest, but if I can pick up some from Mr Gelling, I'll be happier. Once they're all aboard, you can head straight to the *Iris*; she's left the dockyards and is down in Portsmouth. Once they're sworn in, you'll get your bonus, and if we can do this without fisticuffs and cracked heads, it'll be a bigger bonus. These are Manxmen, you don't treat them like some drunken landsman you pick up in an alley in Gosport, are we clear?"

"If you say so, sir." Leach grinned. "Do you know this Gelling, Captain?"

"I think we may have met in passing a few years back, when I first came home, but we've never had much of a conversation."

"Well I don't suppose he'll be inviting you to dinner now, sir."

"That suits me fine, Mr Leach, he's an unrepentant slaver and I wouldn't go."

Hugh and Durrell escorted Leach back to his boat and stood watching it leave, listening to the oars swishing through the quiet waters of early evening. After a while, Hugh said:

"I don't understand why you're so worried about this, Mr Durrell. I'm doing nothing illegal, and it's not as though you've ever been particularly squeamish about impressment. I'm telling you, once they're over their surprise, this lot are going to shrug their shoulders and sign up without a second thought, they won't give a damn whether it's a navy or a merchant ship as long as they get fed, people have starved over the winter on this island. For every Davy Kissack who has a few acres of his own and Jonny Kissack who has a good labouring job and a cottage to go with it, there are half a dozen lads with empty bellies hanging around the quays each morning in the hope that one of the fishing fleet is a crewman short. What is your problem with this?"

Durrell turned to look at him. "You are," he said bluntly. "I told you before, sir, there is something more to this for you, and that bothers me. But what worries me the most is that you don't want your wife to know about it.

The last time you kept a secret from her, I'm reliably informed she punched you in the jaw when she caught up with you."

Hugh gave a grin. "At least I know to duck this time."

"Why won't you tell her, sir?"

Hugh did not speak for a long time and Durrell decided that he was not going to find out. He sighed and turned away from the sea, where the boat was a dark speck on the horizon. They had stabled their horses at the *Red Lion*. Durrell took a few steps, waiting for his Captain to fall in beside him.

"He tried to rape her."

Durrell stopped in his tracks and turned round. Hugh had not moved. His tone had changed, and Durrell could hear raw anger such as he had almost never heard before in his level-headed Captain's voice. The light was beginning to fade, and behind them, up in the town, lamps were being lit: small beacons in the rapidly darkening streets of Castletown.

"I don't understand," Durrell said, and he could hear the pure shock in his own voice. "When? How?"

"Before she was picked up by that press gang and ended up half-dead with fever in my cabin in Copenhagen. I've never been sure exactly how much you know about what happened then, but we'd quarrelled."

"I rather suspected that, sir."

"I came home in '06 to take possession of my new house and lands, and to find myself a wife. A good sensible Manx woman who would take care of my home and give me children and wait patiently while I was off at sea. I had a list of requirements and romance was not one of them. Crellin wasn't stupid, he saw me coming, and he needed a husband for Roseen, since she'd been running wild since her mother died. I thought I'd consider her along with a number of other ladies." Hugh gave a self-conscious smile. "Looking back, I think I fell in love in a week."

"I think it was mutual, sir."

"It was. But I took my time coming to the point because I thought I had the time. I did have the time. But there was a misunderstanding over a young Englishman she'd had a liking for before we met. I thought I'd got it wrong, and I didn't wait to ask. I left the same day and went back to the *Iris* in the worst mood..."

"I remember that aspect of it very clearly, sir."

Hugh gave a shout of laughter. "I was so bloody hard on you," he said. Although you were also a royal pain in the arse. Anyway, she was here, with a brewing scandal which made her father even more determined to get her off his hands. Gelling had buried two wives and wanted a third. What made Crellin think he could get away with that I've no idea, he should have known her better. She was steadfast in her refusal, but Gelling was presumably used to pushing his women around. He caught her out on her own at some party and tried to force himself on her so that she couldn't say no."

Durrell felt sick. At the same time, he was genuinely curious. "What did she do to him?"

"How well you know my wife, Mr Durrell. I believe she gave him a kick in the balls that left him on the floor. When she told her father what had happened he was furious and told Gelling to stay away from her. My father-in-law is a good man, even when he can't see further than the end of his nose. And that was the end of it."

"But not for you, sir."

Hugh grinned, wiping away the unusually serious expression. "Well I don't think I'd have gone to the trouble of taking furlough and travelling a few hundred miles to challenge the fat bastard to a duel, Mr Durrell, I think she already gave him what he deserved. But when I find out I can solve my recruitment problem and bring a bit of pain to a trader in misery who also thinks it's acceptable to assault women, I am going to grasp it with both hands."

Durrell considered it for a moment and realised that he agreed. "I'm glad you told me, sir. I will render you all the assistance that is in my power to bring this to a successful conclusion. But..."

"There is always a 'but' with you, Mr Durrell."

"Tell your wife. You should not need me to say this to you. This will not be the first time that you have kept things from her in a misguided attempt to protect her, but in this matter more than anything else, she is personally concerned, and she should know."

Durrell forced himself to stop speaking, aware of how badly he wanted to continue. He could see his captain considering his words and knew that one of his lengthy speeches at this point would be unhelpful. Hugh did not speak for a long time, then finally he gave a slightly crooked smile.

"Who would have thought after those first weeks aboard the *Iris* with you, Alfred, that I'd be taking advice on my marriage from you?"

Durrell returned the smile. "Certainly not me, sir, I was unsure that I would make it as far as my first campaign with you."

"I'll speak to her. What I don't know, is what she'll say. Come on, let's get back. What do you make of Leach?'

Durrell fell into step beside him and began the walk back up towards the lights of the town. "I think he's looking forward to making a profit, sir, and he's probably puzzling over why you're willing to allow him to take the bonus when he's barely done any of the work."

"Does that matter?"

"Only if it leads him to believe that you're a man who can be easily duped."

Hugh shot him a sharp glance. "Do you think there's an outside chance I could arrive in Portsmouth to find he's taken a hefty bribe to offload some of my men to other ships in need of a crew, Mr Durrell?"

"I would say that is a possibility, sir. I have a solution, however. Should you manage to obtain the men you require, I suggest that I cut my visit short and take passage with Mr Leach aboard the *Abilene*. I can personally supervise the signing on of the recruits and do a final check of the *Iris* before we set sail."

Hugh studied him thoughtfully. "I can't decide if you're being your usual efficient self here, fella, or if you're fleeing before the enemy because you think my wife is going to launch a broadside at me over this and you don't want to get caught in the crossfire."

Durrell laughed. "I think you will talk her round, sir. I do want to make sure we don't lose our recruits, having gone to so much trouble to obtain them, and it will only be a week earlier. Also..." Durrell paused, thought about it, then decided to go on. "I know you are expecting orders the moment you report that the *Iris* is ready to sail, sir. I would like to visit my mother and sister before then."

"Have you heard from them?"

"I had a letter from my sister this week, sir. It appears that my mother has formed the intention of bringing her out this season."

Hugh raised his eyebrows. "How old is Abigail now?"

"She is sixteen, sir."

"Well I'm not all that conversant with the rules of polite society, Mr Durrell, as you know, but isn't that very young?"

"Yes, sir. In my opinion, it is too young. Abigail is very mature for her age, but most girls are at least seventeen or eighteen and it is not at all unusual to be older. There is no financial reason for her to be married very young. Since Henry's marriage to Miss Cornell he is very comfortably off and when I last spoke to my mother I know she had no intention of bringing Abigail out for at least another year and possibly two. And Abigail certainly did not wish it."

"So what's going on?" Hugh enquired. They had reached the main square of Castletown. It was well lit, with lamps hung outside most of the shops, houses, and inns. The looming bulk of Castle Rushen was dark against the lingering glow of daylight over the sea and there was a smell of woodsmoke from various chimneys as householders cooked their supper. The evening was very mild, with little wind, and as they approached the *Red Lion,* Durrell could hear a rhythmic clanging from the neighbouring blacksmith's where old Corlett was shoeing a horse by the light of several lamps and his glowing brazier. He looked up as they passed, recognised Hugh, and lifted a hand in greeting.

"I'm not sure what's going on, sir," Durrell said, as they walked into the stable yard. "I have no legitimate reason to intervene. Henry is my sister's legal guardian, and it is my mother's responsibility to organise her debut. Abigail said very little in her letter, but I have the sense that she is unhappy, and I would like to talk to her."

Hugh did not reply immediately. For a time, they concentrated on arranging for their horses to be saddled, paying the landlord and tipping the groom. It was not until they were walking their mounts through the town and onto the road towards Ballabrendon that Hugh said:

"Your bloody brother. You think he has an ulterior motive, don't you?"

"I have no idea, sir. What I fear is that he has his eye on a marriage for Abigail which will bring him some political advantage and he does not want to wait in case the gentleman makes other arrangements. If that is the case, then I will not allow it to happen. He can sell himself and his honour as cheaply as he likes in pursuit of his ambitions, but he shall not do the same with my sixteen year old sister."

It had come out more passionately than Durrell had intended but he found that he was not sorry. They rode in silence for a few minutes then Hugh said:

"Go. Get my ship ready for action, Mr Durrell and then post up to London and find out what the hell is going on. I'll be back myself the following week."

"Thank you, sir." Durrell shot him a grateful glance. "Mrs Kelly will miss the island."

"Mrs Kelly isn't leaving the island for a while," Hugh said. "She wants to go back to Chatham eventually, but for the next six months or so, she'll be better off here."

Durrell was puzzled and then suddenly understood. "Oh. Oh, you mean...?"

"Yes. We've suspected it for a few weeks, but it's confirmed."

"Congratulations, sir."

"Thank you. I'm glad it happened now, it pleases me to think my second child will be born at Ballabrendon and she'll have Voirrey and her sister-in-law and her aunt to help her."

"She'll have every woman on the estate wanting to help her, sir, she's well loved."

Hugh grinned. "We managed very well without any of them last time, of course. Come on, Mr Durrell, let's speed it up. That's rain I can feel and I've no wish for a soaking."

***

It was raining in Ramsey, a typically Manx fine drizzle. In the company of Hugh, Lieutenant Leach and eight armed sailors from the *Abilene*, Durrell waited inside a netting shed which they had found conveniently unlocked and which gave an excellent view of the substantial warehouse of Gelling Merchant Shipping. The company name was painted in huge white lettering on the side of the red brick building. There was no sign of life inside, but as a faint dawn light began to filter through the grey clouds, there was activity on the quay.

They came in ones and twos, quietly in the pale light, standing alone or in small groups. It was difficult to make out details in this light, but they were all men, shabbily dressed, wrapped up in the warmest clothing they had. Some carried small bags or bundles, and many walked with the rolling gait of men who had spent their lives at sea. Durrell found that reassuring. He would be even more reassured if he could be certain that Orry Gelling himself would not make an appearance at his warehouse this morning. Durrell knew it was unlikely that a wealthy merchant would trouble himself with the signing on of his ships' crew, but he also knew that the Manx did things differently to the English. Watching the men gathering before the building, Durrell was surprised at how many there were.

"A fair few of them, sir," Leach said.

"Yes, I'd guess he's signing on both ships at once," Hugh said. "How many can you take?"

"Thirty or forty at a push."

"Don't push. They're men, not cattle and I want them hale and hearty when they arrive on board."

Leach gave a little snort. "Thirty-five easily, sir."

"Plus one," Durrell said softly. Leach said nothing very eloquently. He had been rigid with indignation at the news that he was also providing transport for Hugh's First Lieutenant, which confirmed Durrell's suspicions that the man was up to no good.

"Sir." One of Leach's men who was close to the door pointed and Durrell heard the carriage. It approached through the misty rain from the direction of Milntown, clattering over the cobbled streets and into the yard before the warehouse. The men waiting on the street shifted and began to form themselves into a rough queue. The carriage came to a stop and two men alighted, both dressed in dark suits with hats pulled down against the rain. Durrell watched them as they hurried into the building, then looked over at Hugh and found him grinning.

"Not Mr Gelling, Lieutenant, so you can breathe. Mr Leach, are your men ready?"

"Aye, sir. Should we wait..."

"No, I want to catch them before they set foot in that building. Come along."

Outside the net shed, Leach's men fanned out, surrounding the group of men. Each one of them carried a stout cudgel and Leach himself was armed with a musket. Durrell drew his pistol although he had no intention of using it. He had no idea how these men would respond to being approached by the press gang, but if they decided to put up a determined fight, Hugh had given orders that Leach withdraw his men. It occasionally happened, and a mass brawl was only likely to end in death or injury on both sides.

The waiting men were looking around them, confused and apprehensive. One of them, a slight figure in an oilskin cape, stepped forward belligerently.

"What are you doing here, fellas? If you're signing on, the end of the line is over...oh bloody hell. Watch out boys, it's His Majesty's fucking navy."

Hugh moved out of the shadows, positioning himself between the men and the door. "You've got the right of it there, lad," he said, raising his voice so that it could be clearly heard. "Don't try to run, these men are armed, and you'll get hurt. I reckon most of you know how this works. Captain Hugh Kelly of HMS *Iris*, and I'm here to tell you that you're being pressed into service with the Royal Navy. Lieutenant Leach is in charge of the *Adeline* and his boats are ready. We'll march you down now and get you aboard, then Mr Durrell will get you signed up. You'll get the option of signing on as volunteers, in which case..."

"I want the bonus paid to my wife," one of the men said instantly. He had a deep voice, sounding Manx but with a hint of something other, as though he had travelled widely from these shores. Hugh regarded him then gave a faint smile.

"I know you, don't I? The *Newstead*. The name's gone, but you're a rigger and a bloody good one. Wait, it'll come to me..."

"Martin, sir."

"Martin, that's it. You got into a fight with Jones, the cook's assistant and the Bosun had to separate the two of you with a cooking skillet."

Martin was grinning broadly. "You've a good memory, Captain."

"I don't forget a face, though I'm bloody terrible with names. Are you coming to sea with me again, Mr Martin?"

"Gladly, sir, if you can make sure my wife..."

"Consider it done. Children?"

"Three, sir, and it was a hard winter."

"My wife is expecting our second and staying home for a while. I'll get her to go over, see how they're doing. They won't want for anything. Form a new line, Mr Martin, just over there and we'll see who else we've got."

Durrell let out a deep, silent breath of relief. The atmosphere had wholly changed, and he thanked God for Martin and for his Captain's admirable if erratic memory. The impressment had changed in an instant from an imminent threat to a new adventure. Hugh had been right, these men were ready and prepared to go to sea and it mattered little who they sailed for. Hugh's genial manner and Martin's positive response had shifted the balance, and men moved into line without even glancing at Leach's armed impress men. Durrell concealed a smile. Leach looked almost disappointed at not having had the opportunity to show what his men could do.

There were several stragglers, men who hung back. One of them was the man in the oilskin cape. Hugh approached him as the line began their march down to the dock. "What's your name?"

"Sam Cain."

"You'll call me sir, Cain, whether you join my crew or not. You're not a landsman, where have you served?"

"I'm Mr Gelling's man, Captain. Been to sea in his vessels since I was fifteen, I know the coast of Africa like..."

"You're a slaver," Hugh said flatly.

"I'm a seaman, Captain, I serve where the ship sails."

"And you'd rather serve Gelling than your country?"

"It's not my country."

"Fair enough." Hugh turned away. Two other men were hovering uncertainly. Hugh surveyed them thoughtfully. "I can call the impress men back and they'll give you a bit of help along the way."

The younger of the two hesitated then took off towards the retreating line at a run. The other, a solid Manxman in his twenties, stood his ground. "I'd rather sign up with Mr Gelling, begging your pardon, Captain."

"You don't get a choice when the Navy calls, fella, but I'm curious. What's your objection?"

"Press gang took my brother. He died at sea of fever. He'd no wish to join the navy, he got no choice."

"What's your name?"

"Kinvig, sir."

Hugh looked thoughtful then shook his head. "I'm sorry about your brother, Kinvig, but I'm taking you anyway. That one over there, I don't want him. He can wait here and sign up with Gelling and I don't give a damn. But you? I think you're a bloody good sailor and you'll do well aboard my ship. I don't want to have to get those bastards up here to drag you aboard. You're a valuable man. Give me a chance."

Kinvig hesitated for a long moment, then shrugged. "Don't look as though I've got any more choice than my brother, does it?"

"Not really. But fever's just as likely to strike on a merchant ship as a navy frigate and you've a better chance of prize money, I'm known to be a lucky captain."

"I know who you are," Kinvig said. "I knew your wife when she was younger."

Durrell looked quickly at Hugh, who was staring at Kinvig, an arrested expression on his face. "Was your brother aboard the *Flight*?"

"Aye, sir."

Durrell knew what was coming. Hugh held up his hands. "I'm sorry. Go or stay with Gelling, it's up to you. I know what those lads did for my wife aboard that impress brig. You're released if you want to go."

It was Kinvig's turn to look startled. "You mean you won't press me?"

"No, I owe your family a debt that I can't repay. I'd still like you to sign up with me, but the choice is yours."

"What about me?" Cain said. He sounded almost aggrieved.

"I don't want you," Hugh said dismissively. "I can smell a troublemaker from ten feet away, you'll spend more time in irons than doing your job and Mr Durrell here has better things to do."

There was a sudden commotion and the door to the warehouse burst open. A stout, bald-headed man erupted through it.

"What is going on?" he demanded furiously. "Where have those men gone? Get them back here immediately, they are Mr Gelling's crewmen."

Durrell turned to look at him. "Are you Mr Gelling, sir?"

"I am not, sir. I am Benjamin Caldicott, chief clerk to Mr Gelling, and I am here to sign on his crewmen, which is what I intend to do."

Durrell bowed. "My apologies, Mr Caldicott, but I am afraid the men waiting on this quayside have now been pressed into service by the Royal Navy, with the exception of these two. I fear you will have to advertise for more crewmen. I regret the inconvenience."

"Inconvenience? Inconvenience?" Caldicott's voice rose to an indignant squeak. "How dare you do this, sir? You have exceeded your authority. You have no right to impress men from an outbound merchant ship. I am fully aware of the regulations and there will be consequences to your actions unless you release our crew immediately. Many of them have served aboard Mr Gelling's ships for many years. They are experienced seamen. They are our seamen, sir, and you shall not take them." Caldicott's face was scarlet with rage. He paused to take a deep breath. Durrell held up a hand to stop him.

"Allow me to introduce myself, Mr Caldicott. I am First Lieutenant Alfred Durrell of the *Iris* and I assure you that my understanding of the law with regard to impressment is at least equal and probably far superior to yours, given that it is part of my duties to manage the recruitment of crew for my ship. The law states that the captain of a Royal Navy ship may press into service any seagoing men within the prescribed age limits and with one or two very specific exceptions. I can assure you that I intend to examine each man personally to discover if he is exempt under these rules, and men who are will be released immediately as I do not hold with the unscrupulous although unfortunately not uncommon practice of some captains who will put to sea before making these enquiries thereby making it difficult or impossible for these men to avoid at least a period of navy service before the vessel is in a position to enter a port convenient to put them ashore to allow them to return home."

Durrell paused to take a breath. Caldicott looked stunned. Durrell did not have to look at Hugh to know that he was enjoying himself.

"Furthermore," Durrell continued, just as Caldicott looked as though he had recovered himself enough to make a protest, "I am sure that you are aware that the impress service is fully entitled to take any man from the crew of a merchant ship returning to port or any former crew member of the said merchant ship who happens to be on land. The fact that these men have served aboard Mr Gelling's ships before does not provide any exemption at all from their legitimate obligation to serve their country when required to do so."

"That is where you are wrong," Caldicott blustered. "You have no right to take any crew member from an outgoing merchant ship, sir."

Durrell looked around him in mock surprise. "Can you show me the ship they are signed up to, sir?"

"Both ships are at anchor, but that does not mean the signing on has not occurred."

"You are perfectly right, sir. Bring your ledger immediately and I shall accompany you to the *Abilene* where we may ascertain which of these men is contracted to sail with you."

Caldicott hesitated and his expression made Durrell want to laugh. He did not dare to look at his captain. "Indeed. It is impossible for me to do so right now, I will have to ensure that I have all the records fully up to date..."

"If they're not up to date five minutes after you signed them up, fella, you're not that good at your job and Gelling should think about getting a new clerk," Hugh said pleasantly. "All that will happen is that you'll spend the next hour frantically forging signatures and putting crosses against the names of men who can read and write perfectly well. You've two men here willing to sign up and if there's any who turn out to be exempt from impressment and choose to come back, I'm sure they will. Otherwise, I'd pin up a few advertisements and see what you get."

"Landsmen and untried boys," Caldicott said bitterly. "You've got all our best men."

"And His Majesty's Navy is very grateful for them," Hugh said smoothly. "Now if you'll excuse us, Mr Caldicott, we've a good deal to do."

Hugh bowed politely and made his way down the road towards the quay. Durrell fell into step beside him. After a moment, he became aware of footsteps behind them. Hugh stopped and turned.

"Mr Kinvig. Have you decided to give the Royal Navy a chance after all?"

"Thought I might," Kinvig said casually. "Given I've got a choice, and all."

Hugh laughed aloud. "That is so bloody Manx, fella, it makes me proud. Come on then."

Chapter Four

It took Durrell several hours to arrange the signing on of Gelling's crewmen. With no particular reason for haste, and more men than he really needed, he took the time to examine them thoroughly and was pleased. All but three were experienced seamen who had sailed either with merchant ships or the Royal Navy for years. The three exceptions were all very young, but all had at least some experience of going out with the fishing fleet. Durrell offered them the option of returning to shore and one accepted with alacrity but the other two elected to remain. It had been Durrell's intention to remain aboard the impress frigate and send for his gear, but Hugh shook his head firmly.

"No need for that, Mr Durrell. Leach will have to wait for the tide anyway, no fear he'll slip anchor and sail off with our crewmen. We're attending the ball at Castle Rushen this evening and it promises to be a fine night. Come and dance with my wife; it'll be a while before you have the opportunity to do so again. You'll have plenty of time to get your boxes aboard in the morning before she sails."

Durrell was happy to agree. He had already visited the castle and, despite its run down appearance, Durrell had fallen in love with it. Privately, he thought it was like a traditional Norman castle but in miniature, but he did not say so as he suspected it might be taken the wrong way coming from an Englishman.

There were only a few companies of the Manx Fencibles stationed on the island and none were billeted in the castle due to the poor state of the accommodation. The castle was used as a prison, the island mint and as the local law courts. In addition the Governor's House stood within the walls, currently occupied by the Lieutenant-Governor, Colonel Smelt. Officers and men were billeted in houses and taverns in Castletown, but the castle was still used for balls and receptions and its tattered appearance was much improved by coloured lanterns hung around the courtyards.

There were several reception rooms, brilliantly lit with candles, and a small dais had been set up for the orchestra. Hugh's carriage dropped them in the town square where a carpet had been laid up to the narrow walkway of the castle. Hugh took his wife's arm and Durrell fell in behind them alongside Mr Crellin. Roseen looked very lovely in blue silk, with no sign yet of her pregnancy.

Durrell could remember his early debut into society in painful detail. Socially awkward and with no idea how to make small talk, it was an excruciating experience and no amount of tuition or family advice had helped. In desperation, he had concentrated on those aspects he could learn by rote and had achieved a level of skill in dancing which had carried him through a number of painful evenings.

On this occasion there was less pressure to achieve success and Durrell, although never wholly comfortable, was less anxious. He danced with Roseen, enjoying the sense of familiarity which overcame his nervousness and allowed him just to appreciate the music and the sense of movement. Buoyed by his success, he allowed himself to be introduced to several partners and managed some conversations about the weather, his imminent departure and his service aboard the *Iris,* which went better than he had expected.

Supper was served late, and Durrell shared a table with the Kellys and Thomas and Aalin Young. He had grown very friendly with the couple during his time on the island and had promised to write to them. Their company helped him to forget his awkwardness in his enjoyment of the evening. After supper there was more dancing, but Durrell was happy to sit back, until there were signs of the evening breaking up and people began to call for their carriages.

Hugh and Roseen joined Durrell at the table. "Don't get up, Mr Durrell, I think it will be a while, it's chaos out there. I've bribed Private Clague to come and find us when our carriage gets to the front of the queue so we may as well finish the champagne and wait in comfort."

Durrell sat down again. He did not particularly want more wine but accepted a glass to be social and watched Hugh flirt with his wife. The crowd was thinning out as more carriages arrived and Durrell wondered why theirs was taking so long, although he did not really mind. He was looking forward to going back to sea but it was good to have these few hours of frivolity before he sailed.

"There's Clague," Hugh said, getting to his feet. "About time too, I was beginning to wonder if he'd stopped off at the *Glue Pot* on the way and forgotten us. Roseen, you look tired. You're staying in bed late tomorrow, with no arguments."

Roseen took his arm with a weary smile. "I am tired," she admitted. "But it's nothing to worry about, it will pass fairly soon, I remember being like this last time. I hope you don't have to leave too early Mr Durrell."

"No, ma'am, we'll sail with the afternoon tide, I'll have plenty of time."

"Good. We will have a late and leisurely breakfast, and…"

"Kelly! Where the fuck is Hugh Kelly, I know he's in here!"

Durrell turned towards the door, along with every person left in the room. A man was pushing his way through a party that was leaving, causing a furious complaint from one of the gentlemen who had to catch his startled wife's arm before she fell. The newcomer did not even look round. He had seen his quarry and was stalking across the room towards him.

Durrell glanced at Hugh, then back at the stranger. He was a big man, probably approaching fifty and running to fat, with a florid complexion which was currently scarlet with rage. Durrell ran his eyes over him, checking for a weapon, but Orry Gelling did not appear to be armed.

"I've been looking for you, Kelly."

"And here I am," Hugh said genially. "It's a bit late for this conversation, though, Gelling, and I've a feeling your language is going to upset the remaining ladies. Why don't you come over to Ballabrendon in the morning if you want to yell at me?"

"Yell at you?" Gelling's voice was so loud that it seemed to echo off the stone walls. "Oh this is a matter for more than that, boy. Thirty-two of my best crewmen you've stolen, you thieving bastard. Thanks to you, my ships sit idle when they should be bound for the Indies on tomorrow's tide."

"I'm sorry for the inconvenience, Gelling, but you know the law of impressment as well as I do. And you'll find more. Now get yourself out of here and stop making a fool of yourself. I'm fairly sure Captain Corlett has just sent for some of his men to escort you out of the room. He probably thinks you're drunk." Hugh sniffed with what Durrell thought was deliberate provocation. "I think he'd be right."

"If any one of those scrawny soldier boys puts a hand on me, I'll break his fucking jaw," Gelling snarled. "I want my crew back. You'll put them ashore in the morning or you'll be sorry."

"Don't be more stupid than you can help, Gelling. They're legally signed up as volunteers to the crew of the *Iris* and there isn't a damned thing you can do about it. Go home and sober up."

Hugh turned to Roseen with a reassuring smile. Durrell glanced at her and could see from her bewildered expression that she had no idea what was going on, although knowing Roseen she was probably slotting the puzzle into place very quickly. Durrell felt a rush of exasperation at his Captain. Given that by the time it happened he would probably be at sea, he sincerely hoped that Roseen gave her husband the earful he richly deserved for keeping her in the dark.

"Come on, lass, let's get you home. I'm sorry about this, I…"

"That's what this is about, isn't it?" Gelling said suddenly. "This had nothing to do with needing crew. You went after my men because she told you to."

Hugh stepped neatly between Gelling and Roseen. "Mr Durrell, are you ready?"

"Perfectly, sir." Durrell moved to Roseen's other side. He did not think Gelling would start a brawl so publicly, but if he did, he wanted to be sure that Roseen was not at risk.

"Look at her," Gelling said. "Dressed up like a lady, though we all know she's not. I used to think, when I'd a mind to marry her, that she had the look of a good breeder but I'm glad it came to nothing as I'd never have known if the brats were mine or not. Still, I admit I envy you that enthusiasm in the bedroom. Wouldn't do for a gentleman in my position to wed a girl with the manners of a Liverpool doxy, but I don't suppose it matters so much to a man with your background, does it?"

Durrell felt rage flood his entire body. He took a step forward, then stopped, knowing that it was not his job. To his surprise, Hugh did not immediately move. Durrell knew that his Captain disapproved of duelling in any form, but he was sure that Hugh would not allow another man to insult his wife without answer.

Hugh turned very slowly to look at Gelling. The older man gave a short laugh, and moved, as if to turn away. Everybody else in the room seemed frozen with shock. Durrell saw the expression on his Captain's face and decided that he was going to have to intervene after all, or Hugh was going to kill the man. He took a step forward, but Roseen was quicker. To Durrell's complete astonishment, she took a long stride, lifted her knee, and drove it very hard into Gelling's groin.

Gelling cried out, a high-pitched yell of pain, and doubled over, clutching at his genitals. Roseen turned to her husband, ignoring Gelling.

"I'd really like to leave, Hugh."

"Of course. I'm sorry, love. I intended to tell you, but it didn't occur to me that he'd do anything this stupid."

"Well next time perhaps you'll have the wit to ask a woman with personal experience."

Hugh grinned and took her hand. As he led her towards the door, Durrell saw four red-coated soldiers entering along with an officer. Gelling straightened slowly and painfully, his eyes on Roseen. His expression was murderous, and Durrell wanted to be sure that the soldiers had a firm hold of the man. He was immediately reassured. Captain Tobin gave a brief order and Gelling was bundled through the doorway. Hugh drew Roseen to one side to allow them to pass.

Around the room people stirred as though woken from a trance and began to make their way to the door. One or two shot awkward glances towards Hugh and Roseen and Hugh bowed in response, his expression daring them to comment. As the last of them left, Colonel Smelt reappeared from the hall where he had been saying farewell to the guests.

"Mrs Kelly, are you all right? A shocking business, the man must be inebriated. He should never have been allowed to enter in such a state, I am very sorry."

"Think nothing of it, Colonel, I am not harmed, and I am very able to ignore a drunkard's words," Roseen said. Durrell thought appreciatively how well she was handling an unpleasant situation. He was not deceived, and he knew she was upset. Roseen's marriage to Hugh had taken place in unusual circumstances and there had been gossip about it, but after four years the tattlemongers had lost interest. This would undoubtedly revive the scandal, but Durrell thought that if Roseen continued to calmly pretend that nothing important had happened, it would be a five minute wonder.

"Thank you for having him removed, sir," Hugh said. "He'll have sobered up by tomorrow and realise he's made a fool of himself. I'm not surprised he's irritated given that the navy has purloined half his crew, but it won't take him long to find more and I'm afraid my need was urgent, I've orders coming."

They talked for a few minutes more, and the Lieutenant-Governor escorted them to the gate. It had rained while they had been inside, and the cobbles were slick and shining in the lantern light. Private Clague stepped forward and saluted Hugh.

"My apologies, Captain, we had to move your carriage on to make way for some of the others. It's drawn up over there by the quay. If you'll wait inside I'll run and…"

"No, please don't," Roseen said. "It's only a short walk and I would enjoy the fresh air; the rain has stopped now. Thank you for a lovely evening, Colonel Smelt. Good night."

The air was fresh with recent rain and a breeze had picked up. Hugh paused and inspected his wife, then drew up the hood of her evening cloak and fastened it properly as though she were a child. There was something very tender about his manner and Durrell looked back at the looming bulk of the castle, unwilling to intrude on their moment of intimacy.

"Come on, Mr Durrell, it's going to rain again in a minute, I want to get home," Hugh said briskly. They walked down towards the quayside, passing two noisy ale houses. Durrell could see the carriage drawn up outside the shuttered chandler's shop. As they approached, Hugh's groom jumped down to open the door and let down the steps.

"I wonder if Mr Gelling rode all the way from Ramsey in this weather to shout at you, Hugh, or if he's staying locally? It will be an unpleasant ride back if he did."

"Good. I hope he gets caught in a downpour and catches his death. Evening, Jed. Sorry we kept you so long."

Hugh handed his wife up into the carriage. His foot was on the step to climb in beside her when there was another yell from the darkness beside the shop.

"Kelly! We're not finished yet."

"Oh for God's sake," Hugh said irritably.

"Hugh, get into the carriage," Roseen said firmly. "He's drunk. He'll go away and sleep it off and in the morning he'll remember that he needs to at least pretend to have some manners if he ever wants to be invited anywhere on this island again."

"Is that bitch in there?" Gelling said, stepping into the lamplight. "She's half crippled me, the little…"

Hugh stepped back from the carriage. "If you don't shut your mouth and piss off, Gelling, I'm going to finish the job," he said shortly. "I've no wish to hit a man in your condition, but I will if I need to. Take yourself off to wherever you're staying and sober up. If you can't find the way, I'll ask Colonel Smelt to provide you with a military escort."

"Hiding behind the army, Kelly? Fucking coward."

"No, I'm just bored with you. Get lost. In you get, Mr Durrell, it's starting to rain."

"Your wife is a whore," Gelling screeched. "I wish you joy of her, Kelly. Perhaps you won't even care what she's doing with the boys from the fishing fleet while you're looting the French and kissing the Admiralty's arses in London. At least I married a respectable girl, not a…"

Durrell stepped back quickly, knowing that he was likely to get knocked over if he stood in the way. Hugh strode past him to where the older man stood waiting, clearly ready to fight. He did not wait for Hugh, but threw the first punch, catching Hugh a glancing blow on the edge of the jaw. It must have hurt, but Hugh seemed barely to notice it in his fury, and punched back, an enormous blow which sent Gelling staggering backwards. Hugh advanced towards him and Durrell glanced over his shoulder at Roseen.

"Stay in the carriage, ma'am. We might need to get him away from here in a hurry."

He turned back as Hugh hit the other man again. Gelling was the same height as Hugh, but some years older and a lot heavier. Gelling's nose was bleeding heavily, and Durrell thought that he had probably had enough, but it was clear that Hugh was not of the same mind. Gelling aimed another punch, but Hugh was ready this time, and dodged back with contemptuous ease, then swung his fist into Gelling's midriff. Gelling doubled over with a groan, then fell to his knees. Hugh stood looking down at him and Durrell breathed a silent sigh of relief. He was angry himself, but he was a little shocked at his Captain's single-minded ferocity.

"Sir, why don't you get in the carriage?" Durrell said quietly. "I'll go into the tavern and see if I can find one of Mr Gelling's friends to assist him, and then…"

"Mr Gelling doesn't have any friends, Lieutenant," Hugh said, and Durrell flinched at his tone. "Mr Gelling wore out his welcome years ago in most of the decent homes on the island, with his habit of forcing his attentions onto any young woman he could get his mucky hands on. Mr Gelling only has a collection of hangers-on and toad eaters who are out for what they can get, or who share his nasty habits."

"Sir…"

Gelling retched suddenly and was sick down the front of his tight-fitting green coat and onto the pavement. Hugh did not move, and Durrell decided there was no point in trying to make him. He stood poised, ready to intervene, but he was hoping that Hugh was done. After a long time, Gelling managed to look up, his heavy face a mess of blood and vomit.

"You arrogant bastard. You'll meet me for this."

"Don't be a bloody idiot, Gelling. I'd kill you in five minutes, you're overweight, out of condition and I'd be surprised if you could hit a barn door with a pistol. Be thankful that I'm a charitable man and get yourself out of here."

Hugh turned and walked towards the carriage. He had almost reached it when Gelling finally found his feet. Durrell looked around to make sure that the man was capable of staggering back to the inn. Gelling seemed steady enough, although he was swaying slightly. Hugh once again had his foot on the step, when Gelling's voice roared, hoarse with rage.

"Kelly. You're a low-bred son of a whore and you married another one. Your father died drunk in his own vomit on this same quayside, and that wayward bitch you're wed to will produce a string of ill-favoured bastards to whatever man she can talk into her bed…"

It had taken that long for Hugh to reach him. There was a brief scuffle and then a scream of terror, followed by an enormous splash. Durrell used an oath he would never generally have uttered in Roseen's presence, and ran to where his Captain stood, looking down into the inky dark water where the sounds of a man thrashing around were clearly audible.

The noise of the fight had finally drawn several men from the inn. One of them was carrying a lantern, and Durrell ran to take it from him and went to the edge of the quayside, spilling light onto the water below.

"Mother of God is that Gelling?" somebody said. "I knew he'd had a few, but I didn't know he was that bad."

"Can he swim?" another man asked.

Durrell listened, and decided that he could not. He swung the lantern around and located a wooden ladder leading down into the darkness, not far from where Gelling had gone in. Setting down the lantern, he began to take off his coat, but his Captain put a hand on his shoulder.

"I'll go. Grab me a boat hook, there's a couple by the shed over there."

"Sir…"

"Do it, Mr Durrell."

Durrell ran to get the hook then watched as Hugh, stripped to shirt sleeves, climbed carefully down the ladder to where the cold water lapped against the stone wall. Durrell passed him the boat hook and peered down anxiously, as Hugh reached out with the hook. It took several attempts, but Gelling had managed to keep himself afloat, and was able to grasp the hook and allow himself to be towed in. There was a brief scuffle at the foot of the ladder, then Hugh's voice said:

"Don't be stupid, Gelling, I'm only down here because my Lieutenant insisted. You give me any trouble at all, fella, and you're going right back in. Now hold on to that ladder and get yourself up."

Back on the quayside, the innkeeper offered blankets and a cup of brandy, and Gelling's acquaintances crowded around him. Hugh took his coat back from Durrell and waved away any further attentions.

Gelling was shivering violently, but Durrell thought that at least his impromptu swim had cleaned him up. Gelling turned to glare at Hugh and Hugh put a friendly arm about his shoulders and leaned in close, speaking softly.

"That's us done with, Orry. You've said your piece and you've got my answer. You say one more word either to or about any one of my family or friends, you'll regret it. And just so that you're aware, I know exactly what you tried to do to my girl when she was alone and vulnerable. If you give me any reason to come after you again, it'll be just you and me, and you won't be getting up. Now get yourself inside and warmed up, or you'll catch your death, fella. Goodnight."

The carriage door was closed as they approached. Hugh studied it with a thoughtful expression. "It's stopped raining," he said. "I was thinking I might do a spell on the box with Jed on the way home."

"I was thinking just the same thing, sir," Durrell said smoothly. "But you're rather wet, so you should travel inside. I expect Mrs Kelly would be glad of a chat with you."

Hugh gave him a look. "I will remember this piece of arrant cowardice, Lieutenant Durrell. The next time you go down with fever and can't remember your name, you're on your own."

Durrell saluted punctiliously. "Duly noted, Captain. Allow me to open the door for you."

***

Roseen dreaded her family's reaction to the scene with Orry Gelling, but nothing was said during Hugh's final week. Neither her father nor her brother had been present at the Governor's ball and Roseen was beginning to wonder if by some miracle the story had not yet reached them. She was not reassured. In the restricted society of Mann there was little to gossip about and she was sure the tale was being freely discussed at every dinner party where she was not present.

Roseen thought about it and discovered that she did not care. When she was younger and unmarried, she had loathed the tattlemongers and had felt at times as though her every move was under critical scrutiny. These days she was happy and secure, both in her marriage and her social position. She had travelled further than most of the ladies of Mann and had found her feet in navy circles. Thanks to her girlhood friend Maria Quayle's fortunate marriage to Mr Benjamin Thurlow MP, she was also very comfortable in London society. She no longer needed the approval of local society and if some of her father's friends chose to invite a known slaver rather than the young woman he had insulted, Roseen decided they were welcome to him.

None did. The invitations to dinner continued to arrive after Hugh's departure and when Roseen chose to attend she saw nothing of the objectionable Mr Gelling. She had reached the point where she hardly thought of him at all, when her father surprised her over tea at the Top House one afternoon by raising the subject.

"I'm guessing you heard nothing more from Gelling before he left, Roseen?"

Roseen put down her tea cup. Her aunt had excused herself with a headache and Roseen had rather looked forward to a comfortable hour alone with her father, but she realised now that she had been ambushed. She gave him a look.

"I didn't even know he was away, Father. Why would I? We're hardly on speaking terms."

"If I'd been your husband, I'd have insisted on a written apology."

"Hugh knows better. I'd only have thrown it in the fire, it would be a waste of paper and ink."

"All the same, it would have been good for him to have to write it. He's away to Liverpool, some tale of trying to recruit crew members there since your man took every useful seaman on the island. But to tell you the truth I think he went to let the gossip die down. He's not a man to weather that kind of humiliation easily."

Roseen reached for a slice of bonnag. "Good. The island is a more pleasant place without him. I'm surprised you haven't mentioned this before, Father, I was beginning to think you hadn't heard about it."

"Everybody has heard about it, Rose. We don't get that much excitement in these parts. In a way it was fortunate that Gelling chose to make a fool of himself so publicly, though it must have been unpleasant for you. It's distracted people nicely from your husband's antics with the press gang."

Roseen said nothing as eloquently as possible. She ate her bonnag and reached for the teapot. "More tea, Father?"

Josiah Crellin gave a grim smile and held out his cup. "Are we not talking about that, lass? It wasn't popular, you know."

"I don't suppose it was, but it's hardly unheard of on the island, as I know to my cost. As a matter of fact I thought it a rather clever solution to Hugh's recruitment problem. Every man he took was already willing to go to sea. And if it made life difficult for Orry Gelling, all the better."

"Was it your idea then?"

Roseen debated with herself for a moment, then shook her head. "No," she admitted. "I knew nothing about it until afterwards, though I knew he was recruiting. I was quite cross as a matter of fact, I thought he should have told me."

"Well a man's not obliged to tell his wife his business, Rose, but your man generally does. Happen he thought you'd object. Or at least ask him why."

Roseen put down her cup with a sigh. "Stop dancing around the subject, Father, you're as bad as he is. You're wondering if Hugh knew what Gelling tried to do to me four years ago and whether that had anything to do with what he did."

Crellin sipped his tea, watching her. "You're a grown woman, lass. You don't have to tell me anything you don't want to."

Roseen grinned. "It's a relief to talk about it," she admitted. "Yes, Hugh knew that Gelling attacked me back then. And no, I didn't know that he was about to enact such an imaginative retribution. I was furious that he didn't tell me to be honest. In fact, I spoke about it for quite some time, without taking a breath. It wasn't that he'd made use of the press gang, mind. After three years with the navy I've accepted that sometimes it's necessary, although I'll always hate it. But to go after Gelling as he did…"

Crellin smiled back at her. "So it was because of you."

"Partly, I think. Although he did need those crew members."

"I wasn't sure until now that he knew about Gelling."

"I told him even before we married," Roseen said. "When we wed…Hugh didn't hesitate, you know? He he must have known what people would be saying about me. That there would be a scandal. Another man would at least have taken time to think about it. Hugh didn't. He told me he loved me, that he should never have left me and he married me as soon as he could. I'll never forget that. I promised myself that in return, I'd tell him everything. I didn't ever want him to have reason to doubt me again. When I told him that Gelling had tried to rape me, he was furious but he's never really mentioned it again. I should have realised he wouldn't forget about it."

"Aye, he's that kind of man. And I'm not sorry Gelling got what was coming to him, Roseen. I've often thought I should have done more myself."

"You couldn't have without everybody knowing why and that would have reflected badly upon me. Hugh of course managed to goad Gelling into giving him an excellent excuse to punch him and throw him into the harbour. I don't think he expected Gelling to do it so publicly though, and he certainly didn't want me involved. He knew I'd tell him to leave it alone."

"Clever man, your husband."

Roseen gave a reluctant smile. "He is that. But it wasn't all about me, Father. Hugh needed the men, he'd have had to make use of the press gang at some point and he saw an excellent opportunity to make up his numbers with experienced Manx seamen. He also knows they'd be better off with him aboard the *Iris*. Gelling doesn't have a good reputation. Then there is the fact that Gelling is an unrepentant slaver."

Crellin lifted his eyebrows. "I knew Hugh wasn't fond of the trade," he said. "When we first talked of going into business together, he made very careful enquiries about where my money had come from. His advocate told me afterwards he'd stipulated that he'd have nothing to do with any venture connected to the Africa trade. But I didn't realise he felt that strongly."

"He won't even allow it to be called the Africa trade," Roseen said quietly. "When people do so, he'll correct them and call it slavery. He says it's a euphemism that people use to make themselves feel better and he'll have none of it."

"Not all the navy feel that way about it."

"Oh no. But I think that's rather the point with Hugh. When he was younger, he served on ships which escorted slaving vessels and he's seen what that was like. He also spent some time on a plantation after he was injured at sea. He's always said that once you've seen it, you can't close your eyes to it."

"I've never seen it, but I respect him for it. A relief that the trade is done with."

"It isn't done with," Roseen said. "As a matter of fact, while we were in London, Hugh became a little involved with a newly established society which is campaigning against the continued existence of plantation slavery in the West Indies. He was introduced to a young clergyman who is involved in it, by Sir Richard Keats. We attended a few meetings and Hugh made several speeches about his experiences. Maria and Ben Thurlow were there as well."

Crellin gave a splutter of laughter. "That's hard to imagine. If you'd told me a few years ago that Maria Quayle would bestir herself about the plight of the slaves, or indeed anything outside of the set of her gown and the arrangement of her hair, I'd have laughed in your face."

Roseen smiled. "She's grown up, Father. We all have."

"Aye. Well I'm glad you told me, lass. There's been some talk about your man's actions, bringing the press gang home with him. But now that I know he'd a good reason other than what happened to you, I'll be happy to tell them. It'll shut them up very nicely. There's a few folk on this island who go red in the face when you mention the Africa trade and with good reason. Won't hurt them to know we've a man of principle among us who's not afraid to stand up and be counted on the matter."

Roseen studied her father. There had been times during her growing years when their relationship had been difficult and she had felt the distance between them widening into what felt like an unbridgeable gulf. She thought now, that after all it had been nothing more than growing pains for both of them.

Setting down her cup again she got up, went over to his armchair, put her arms about him and kissed him. When she straightened, she saw that he had flushed a little, but he was also smiling.

"I love you very much, Da. I hope you know that. I don't say it that often."

Crellin laughed. "Aye, well that's not our way, is it lass? Doesn't mean we don't feel it. I've felt the loss of your mother keenly over the years, but when I look about me at you and at Ffinlo…she'd be proud of the things you've done and the people you are. As am I, Roseen. Never forget it."

***

Having dreaded a lengthy siege in winter, Captain Gabriel Bonnet of the second battalion of the 30th légère was surprised and relieved when the Spanish garrison of Tortosa surrendered in eighteen days. Bonnet was of the opinion that the governor of the town had yielded disgracefully easily, but it made life much easier for the men of General Suchet's army.

The approach to Tortosa had been a misery, over dreadful roads in appalling weather. An earlier French attempt had been called off and by the time Suchet received orders to proceed, he was faced with the task of moving his army and his siege train through boggy conditions. It was necessary to bring the fifty-two guns by river, on specially constructed rafts. Tortosa had solid-looking medieval walls and a garrison of more than seven thousand men and Bonnet foresaw months of digging trenches and building batteries in appalling conditions.

Tortosa's weakness, however, lay not in the state of its defences but in the character of its elderly governor, Major-General Lilli, Conde de Alacha. Lilli appeared to have been promoted beyond his abilities and the hardships of siege warfare proved too much for him. After repeatedly handing over to his second-in-command then reappearing to countermand the poor man's orders, he had apparently surrendered against the recommendation of his own council of war.

In the immediate aftermath of the surrender, Bonnet was kept busy dealing with a breakdown of discipline in the streets. The storming column, which included his men, began systematically to sack the southern part of the town in flagrant disregard of their officers' orders. Bonnet, who was out of wine, followed his men into a wine shop and collected several bottles along with a bottle of brandy, wedged them into his pack then drew his sword and chased the men out into the street clutching their loot before they noticed the wine merchant's extremely attractive wife who was cowering in the back room.

Bonnet briefly enjoyed the merchant's obvious confusion as he stammered thanks to the man who had just openly robbed him. He cut the man short, as he was in a hurry to catch up with his company. Bonnet had no expectation of being able to stop them stealing and getting drunk. However, he was armed not only with his sword and his pistol but also with a musket that he had prudently looted from a dead Spaniard on his way into the town, so he could probably stop them from raping or killing the townspeople. Standing in the broken doorway to the shop to prevent his men seeing past him he pointed to the frightened woman.

"Get her out of here and upstairs, and do it quickly," he said in fluent Spanish. "After that, if you've any sense you'll stand in this doorway handing out the rest of your stock to anyone who wants it and shouting 'Vive L'Empereur'. They'll be so drunk in a couple of hours they'll be no threat to anybody and then we'll get them out of here."

"Your men do not obey you?" the merchant said with a hint of contempt in his voice.

"They'll obey me fast enough over a wall and into the breach," Bonnet said shortly. "After that they want their reward. Better your wine than your woman."

Shouldering his heavy pack, Bonnet made his way through the narrow streets of the town. The looting appeared to be contained to one area and there were enough sober troops to guard the rest of the town and to bring the rampaging men under control fairly quickly. Bonnet decided that he would probably not be needed here, so he went in search of his commanding officer and further orders.

The 30th light infantry was commanded by Colonel Lacasse, a tall thin Breton who had taken command when the previous colonel was killed at Jena. Bonnet got on well enough with Lacasse, although he occasionally got bored with being treated as a regimental joke. Lacasse was a courageous, although not a brilliant officer who liked to place his juniors into neat categories that he could understand. Once labelled by Lacasse, there was no changing his opinion. He trotted out the same jokes again and again and expected the same responses from his officers. Change made him nervous.

There was only one battalion of the 30th with Suchet's army and after seven years of march and counter-march, Bonnet knew his fellow captains well and knew exactly what Lacasse thought of them. Faure was the serious one, Bergne the dandy and Foulon the rash and courageous one. Garreau was steady and reliable and Forget was good-looking and a womaniser. Lacasse had his jokes for all, steadfastly ignoring any behaviour that challenged his view of them.

Then there was Bonnet, the favourite butt of regimental jokes. Bonnet was the misfit, the battalion clown. He was a big man with a scarred face and a slight paunch which he cultivated in winter quarters and generally lost most of through the campaigning season. Bonnet could not be bothered to cultivate his moustache or trim his long dark hair or get his uniform brushed every day. He knew that he drank too much and swore too much and did not always show the proper respect for his senior officers. At the same time, he knew that he was a damned good soldier and he wished that somebody would mention that occasionally.

He eventually found Lacasse with the quartermaster discussing billets for his officers. He returned Bonnet's salute then looked around him as though something was missing.

"Where are your men, Captain?"

"Awaiting orders, sir, I left Sergeant-Major Belmas in command," Bonnet said. When he had last seen Belmas, he was seated astride a wine barrel, filling any cup or glass handed to him and singing an appallingly vulgar marching song, but Bonnet thought he had done it with a commanding manner as well as considerable panache, so it was not exactly a lie.

"Excellent. There are three inns along this square with rooms for our officers. Your men can billet in the church on the corner."

"I hope you've removed the church plate, sir."

"I imagine the priests have done so by now, I've given them time. Go down and inspect the place then march them up here. I think we'll have a few days here at least, while General Suchet makes his arrangements."

Even a night or two in an inn sounded good to Bonnet. He considered going in search of Pierre, his lazy servant, but decided that would be too much effort. Pierre would be down in the lower town, looting and pillaging with the best of them. He would come back when he sobered up and until then was no use to Bonnet anyway.

The rank of captain entitled Bonnet to a small room of his own when one was available, and he unloaded his kit and hid the wine and brandy before going back in search of his company. He found his two junior officers already there, arguing fruitlessly with half a dozen drunken soldiers who were attempting to break into a cellar. Bonnet assessed the situation and decided he would have to intervene. Two of the men, Pascal and Roche, were holding their bayonets with an air of menace and Lieutenant Allard and Sub-Lieutenant Duclos looked distinctly uncomfortable. Bonnet reminded himself to have a chat with his juniors about the best way to break up a drunken mob. He swung his looted musket from his shoulder, checked that it was properly loaded then walked forward and placed the barrel against the back of Pascal's bald head.

"How much of your head do you think will be left if I pull this trigger, Pascal?"

Pascal froze in sheer terror. "Captain Bonnet. Sir. Please. You will kill me."

"That's what I was just trying to tell you," Bonnet said in pleased tones. "You're not as drunk as I thought you were. Lieutenant Allard, where is your pistol?"

"I have it here, Captain."

"That's the wrong fucking place for it, it ought to be loaded and pointed at Roche's thick head. See to it, will you?"

Allard obeyed, fumbling nervously. Bonnet looked at Sub-Lieutenant Duclos and felt a flicker of sympathy. He looked genuinely terrified.

"Captain Bonnet," Pascal said again. "This musket is from the Spanish, no? What if it is damaged or defective. It could go off."

"It's quite likely, the trigger looks bent," Bonnet said happily. "Where's the Sergeant-Major?"

"In that house, sir. He has found a woman."

"Oh fuck. Allard, take this musket and give your pistol to Duclos. If any of this lot move, shoot them. I don't mean threaten to shoot them, I mean actually shoot them. Got it?"

"Yes, sir."

"I'll be back."

Bonnet found Belmas in a big kitchen. Several of his men sat around a scrubbed wooden table drinking and singing, but Belmas was dancing. Given how drunk he was it was astonishing he was still on his feet, but Bonnet realised he was being held up by a plump Spanish woman in a grey gown. Bonnet ran his eyes over her and decided that she was unharmed, though when Belmas finally passed out she was in danger of being crushed. Belmas paused in his lumbering movements and held his bottle to her lips and the woman obligingly drank.

"Sergeant-Major Belmas."

"Captain Bonnet!" Belmas sounded delighted. "You have come. No party is complete without my Captain. My Captain and my friend. Look, I have a woman. I saved her from those drunken beasts and now she loves me, and I love her. Have a drink, my love. You too, Captain. I love this woman. I will marry this woman and give her fine babies."

Bonnet met the gaze of the Spanish woman across the kitchen table and admired her composure. "Of course you will, Sergeant-Major, but not right now. I need you to march your men up to their billets and you need to do it soon because General Suchet is on his way and if he finds you like this, you'll all be sent to the colonies to die of yellow fever. Outside, all of you. The church is up the hill, you can see the spire from here. They're good billets but you need to be quick before the Italians get there first and you'll all be sleeping in the streets under the stars."

Belmas studied him thoughtfully for a moment then gave a wide smile. "Yes, Captain," he said enthusiastically. "I shall lead our brave lads to the church and if we find those bastard Italians there, we shall drive them out. Maria, my lovely Maria, I must leave you, but I will be back. Stay inside and take care of yourself and I will return when I can."

Belmas made his way to the door and crashed into the doorpost. He swore indignantly, made another attempt, and hit his other shoulder on the opposite doorpost. Bonnet caught him before he fell, steered him out into the street and pointed out the church. Belmas studied for a long moment and took a deep breath.

"I think I can do that."

"Excellent fellow." Bonnet clapped him on the shoulder. "Lead the men. I will make sure your woman is safe."

It took almost an hour to round up every member of Bonnet's company. One or two of them were less inebriated and given orders, were able to help in the search. Bonnet returned to his two rather shaken officers and nodded to the cellar door. "Is that a wine cellar?"

"No, Captain. It is where some of the women have hidden."

"Right. We'll need to set a guard on it for tonight – a sober guard if we can find one – and I'll direct any other stray females to come down and join them. Once they've sobered up, it'll be safe enough. Stay there until you're relieved and for God's sake, the next time a man points a bayonet at you, shoot him. It will save us the trouble of hanging him and burying you."

Bonnet returned to the kitchen where the Spanish woman was cleaning up the broken pottery and pools of wine. She regarded him warily over her broom, a plump woman in her thirties with huge brown eyes.

"Are you hurt, Maria?"

The woman shook her head. "No. He stopped them. The big man who dances like a bear. And I am not Maria, my name is Ava Sanchez."

Bonnet grinned. "To him, all Spanish women are called Maria. You should go over to your neighbour, some of the women are hiding in the cellar there. Soon the men will be sober, and you will be safe, but best not take the chance tonight."

She did not reply but disappeared into another room and reappeared clutching an embroidered quilt and a small bag which Bonnet guessed held her valuables. He held the door open for her and she preceded him into the street and over to the cellar door. Bonnet knocked and called out. As they stood waiting, the bag in the woman's arms wriggled and made a noise. Bonnet jumped.

"What in God's name…?"

The woman hoisted the bag and a head appeared from the top, a sandy coloured small dog with lopsided ears and big brown eyes. It regarded Bonnet with interest. Bonnet looked back. He reached out and scratched the dog's ear. It licked his hand. The door opened.

"Look after your mistress, she had a lucky escape tonight," Bonnet told the dog seriously. "Now in you go."

Ava Sanchez went through the door and turned. "Thank him for me, when he is not so drunk," she said. "The big man. He saved me. Tell him I said thank you."

The door closed. Bonnet was tired and hungry and wanted his supper, but first, he went in search of sober men who could guard the door. As he walked up to the inn to find food and his bed, he thought about Jacques Belmas and decided he had made a very good choice for his sergeant-major.

The officers dined together, waited on by a nervous innkeeper and his terrified daughter. Bonnet kept an eye on some of the younger men who were making the most of the wine and might be inclined to forget their manners with the young woman. It was not his responsibility to ensure good discipline in other companies but it had become a habit. The officers behaved and drifted away early to their beds.

Bonnet was the last to leave. He sat on alone for a while after Lieutenant Allard said goodnight, looking into the dying embers of the fire and wondered how many nights he had sat like this during his thirteen years with the army and how many of his companions from the early days were still alive. Bonnet had left them all behind when he had volunteered for the 30th légère and he was not even sure where his old regiment was fighting now.

The 30th was a new regiment when Bonnet joined it as a sub-lieutenant, or rather it was a new version of an old regiment which had been disbanded in 1802 and then revived two years later when the brief peace of Amiens fell apart and the Emperor needed more troops. Bonnet liked being part of the light infantry and promotion to command his own company had come quickly. There were four battalions plus a recruiting depot back in Calais and Bonnet served with the second, while the other three were scattered throughout Europe. Bonnet had friends in the other battalions, and he tried to keep up with their location, although he was a lazy correspondent which meant letters were only occasionally exchanged.

At thirty-eight, Bonnet knew that his ambition, which had burned brightly in his younger days, was now only an occasional flicker. He wondered sometimes about volunteering for a commissary or administrative post which would probably bring promotion, but the thought of sitting behind a desk at the depot or spending his days bartering with dishonest merchants for grain and flour depressed him. He had no family living, no wife or children who might be glad of his improved prospects. Sometimes, riding miserably through a wet dawn, he dreamed of an easier life, but Bonnet knew he would be unhappy away from combat. He resigned himself to the fact that he was unlikely to gain promotion within the battalion as he was hopeless at making friends with the right people.

He was also too experienced and too intelligent to attempt some spectacular feat of daring in battle which might bring him to the attention of a senior officer. He had been wounded several times during his career but the last had been the worst, a cavalry sabre at Jena which had almost killed him and left him badly scarred. The memory of that pain still had the power to chill Bonnet and he tried not to think of it.

Bonnet felt the scar, on his left cheek, long since healed. He had never been a man concerned with his appearance and he seldom looked in a mirror except to shave, but the scar made him stand out. It was the reason he had abandoned the customary moustache of the French light infantry because hair would not grow evenly on that side of his face. Bonnet had always found facial hair irritating and was glad of the excuse.

He had been cut down that day defending a fellow officer who lay wounded on the ground, and it had been instinct rather than an act of deliberate heroism. Bonnet had received much praise and a personal letter from the Emperor, but he was in too much pain lying in an army hospital to be properly grateful. These days the scar was a reminder that he was not invincible and that sometimes it was better to leave the heroics to others.

They remained for several days in Tortosa waiting for orders. With their men well fed and relatively sober, Bonnet and his fellow officers took the opportunity to explore the ancient town. Tortosa had been a Roman town and occupied an important defensive position for any invaders wishing to control Catalonia. Situated on the Ebro River, it was a town of glorious Renaissance architecture. Gothic churches rubbed shoulders with medieval fortifications, many of them partly ruined.

There was a variety of taverns and inns and few of the landlords chose to demand payment for food and drink. Bonnet paid anyway, providing the Spaniards were civil and the food was hot. He quite enjoyed their unconcealed surprise when he produced his purse. He also enjoyed the chagrin of his fellow officers, who generally felt obliged to follow his example.

The landlord of the *Fig Tree,* a comfortable establishment in the next street to Bonnet's billet was clearly grateful to Bonnet, and treated him as an honoured guest when he visited, keeping the best table and bringing out the good wine. Bonnet was not accustomed to this kind of treatment and wondered if senior officers got this all the time.

He was seated at his favourite corner table with his junior officers, drinking wine and playing cards when Señor Alba appeared, looking apologetic. "Your pardon, Captain Bonnet, but there is a man looking for you. Your servant, I think."

Bonnet groaned inwardly. He had left Pierre theoretically grooming his horses and baggage mules, which probably meant he had been lounging in the stables having bullied a Spanish groom into doing it for him. Bonnet got up, picked up his glass and drained it. He had deliberately not told Pierre where he was going. Pierre had no manners with the locals and Bonnet did not want the effort of kicking him out of his favourite tavern.

He found Pierre by the kitchen door, idly throwing stones at a cat which Bonnet had earlier seen sunning itself on the window ledge. Bonnet cuffed his servant hard around the head.

"Leave the bloody cat alone, you spiteful little shit, it's not done you any harm. Is there a message?"

"Yes, Captain." Pierre rubbed his ear resentfully. "Colonel Lacasse wishes to see all company officers in the parlour at nine o'clock."

Bonnet took out his pocket watch. He had another hour and a half. Dismissing Pierre, he went back to the table.

"Orders, sir?" Lieutenant Allard enquired, shuffling the cards and preparing to deal.

"I suspect so," Bonnet said, pouring the wine. "Still time to finish this though."

"Where do you think General Suchet will march next?" Sub-Lieutenant Duclos asked.

"Fuck knows. He gets paid to work that out." Bonnet saw the expression on Duclos' young face and relented a little. "Valencia or Tarragona. I'd heard his original orders from Bonaparte were to take Tortosa and then Tarragona, but that might have changed. We'll find out soon enough."

"Will Tarragona surrender do you think, sir?" Duclos asked, reaching for his cards.

Bonnet did the same and carefully kept his face expressionless. Unless he did something particularly stupid, he held a hand which would oblige Allard and Duclos to pay for the wine and still owe him.

"It will if it's got any sense, but they mostly haven't," he said. "I've not been to Tarragona, but I'm told it's likely to be a bastard of a place to take, and we're going to have the bloody Royal Navy trying to blow us to pieces every time we get too close to the coast. Still at least the weather is improving. It's your turn, Duclos. And let's get some more wine. It helps to be half-drunk for one of Lacasse's briefing meetings."

Chapter Five

There had been too much wine served at the regimental dinner and it had ended late. Afterwards, some of the Spanish officers of the garrison led an expedition into town. There had been more wine and drunken toasts and a rather dangerous attempt to balance on some of the harbour walls, which had been swiftly quelled by the officers of the watch who were stone cold sober and had no sense of humour about the matter. Captain Don Bruno Ángel Cortez could not exactly remember at which point in the evening he had acquired the girl or where she had come from. When he awoke, dawn was beginning to spill a faint light through the open shutters of her bedroom and she was beside him, soundly asleep and faintly snoring.

Ángel moved carefully, not wanting to wake her until he had his thoughts in order. He padded across the room to the water jug, filled a glass and drank, his eyes on his companion. She was fair haired and very pretty and from what he could remember, she had been an enthusiastic lover. Ángel had no idea what her name was or whether she was a prostitute.

This presented a social difficulty. Ángel thought about it for a while then decided to avoid the issue by removing himself before she woke up. He drank more water then splashed some on his face, wondering if breakfast might improve his thumping headache. Tiptoeing around the room, he collected his clothing and dressed as quietly as he could. After some thought, he dug out his purse and took out several coins, putting them on a small table beside her bed.

He was almost at the door when he heard movement and froze, hoping she was merely turning over. After a moment, however, she spoke:

"What is this?"

He had got it wrong. Ángel closed his eyes and cursed silently. Then he turned. She was sitting up, the sheet clutched around her. She was pointing at the coins but her eyes were on his face.

"It is a gift, querida," Ángel said. "Forgive me, I must go, General Contreras will be expecting me. I wanted to express my thanks and my appreciation…I thought you could buy yourself…"

"The courtesy of waking me up to say goodbye would have been a better gift. Cheaper and less insulting. Take your money and leave."

Ángel walked back and picked up the coins. "I am sorry," he said honestly. "I was very drunk. But I would still like to buy you a gift."

"Perhaps you should see if one of your friends can tell you my name first."

Ángel pocketed the money and gave a little bow. "I would prefer you to tell me yourself, Señorita."

"I would prefer it if you left."

Ángel decided he would prefer it too. He bowed again and went to the door. As he opened it, a flash of memory came back to him and he turned to look at her.

"As you wish, Señora Morata. Please give my regards to your husband when he returns from Gibraltar. He is a fortunate man."

As the door closed behind him, something crashed against it. Ángel buckled on his sword then ran lightly down the stairs and made his way through the streets to his lodging.

Cadiz was quiet, bathed in a pearly dawn light. It was not far to the house where General Juan Senen de Contreras and his ADCs were staying. The mansion belonged to a wealthy merchant and Ángel was enjoying a few weeks of luxury while Contreras attended endless meetings with both Spanish and British senior officers, the naval officer in command of the Cadiz squadron and the members of the Cortes, the temporary government of Spain.

Cadiz neither looked nor felt like a city under siege, although it had been invested for almost a year now. Ángel, who had spent a lot of time with both Spanish and British officers over the past few weeks, suspected that the French could sit outside the city for another year and be no closer to taking it. Cadiz was ideally placed to resist a siege, being situated at the northern tip of a sandy peninsula. With both the British and Spanish navies protecting the city from the sea and using it as a naval base, Cadiz went about its usual business while in the French siege lines some twenty thousand troops remained pinned down.

By the beginning of 1811 the garrison of Cadiz consisted of twenty thousand Spanish and approximately five thousand British troops and Marshal Victor's besieging army had given up hope of taking the city. Instead, it was the job of Victor's troops to protect the French in Andalusia from the British and Spanish forces in Cadiz, as a number of Allied expeditions had been launched from the city.

Ángel made his way to his room where he washed and changed before going down to the dining room. He found Contreras already seated at the table along with his other ADC. Lieutenant Don Óscar García was twenty-one, ten years younger than Ángel, and had only recently joined Contreras thanks to the influence of his father who was a member of the Cortes. Ángel had initially been somewhat scornful of the younger man's lack of combat experience, but he was beginning to thaw. García was intelligent, interested and most importantly very willing to take over the majority of the boring administrative tasks which had formerly been part of Ángel's duties.

"There you are, Captain Cortez," Contreras said pleasantly. "You were up very early. A fine morning for a walk."

"It was, sir," Ángel said, accepting coffee. Opposite him, García had his eyes glued to his plate, which told Ángel that he knew perfectly well that Ángel had not come back last night.

"And has it cleared your head?" Contreras said genially and Ángel looked up sharply. The General's shrewd dark eyes met his and Contreras gave a faint smile.

"Sir…"

"Do not trouble to excuse yourself, Cortez, you are a grown man and I am not your mother. I only knew because I sent a message to your room earlier. There is news."

Ángel put down his cup, realising that something serious had happened. "I am sorry, sir. What news?"

"The French have taken Tortosa," Contreras said. "Sir Richard Keats sent a message just before dawn to say that the *Blake* had sailed in with the news."

Ángel said nothing. He knew that Contreras was impatient for another posting and Tortosa was one of the places he had thought he might be sent. Ángel did not particularly care where he went next, as long as it was in the front line against the French.

He ate without speaking while the General shared what he knew of the French attack on Tortosa. Contreras had previously been posted to Galicia which was where Ángel had met him a year ago. He had been reluctant at first to accept the position of ADC in case it took him away from the fighting, but he quickly realised that Contreras would never willingly remain far from the action. Ángel admired the older man's energy and courage and they worked well together, but they were not close. Ángel was close to nobody and he preferred it that way.

When the meal was over, Contreras called for more coffee. "I have a meeting with the Marquis of Campoverde in one hour. He has recently been appointed to command the army in Catalonia. This news is a blow to all of us, but I hope soon to be informed where I am to serve. I will not need you this morning, but I would like a word alone with you, Cortez, before I leave."

García rose quickly and saluted. "I have finished, General, I will leave you to talk."

Ángel watched García leave, admiring the speed with which he whisked himself out of the danger zone. He accepted more coffee and waited until the servant closed the door behind him, than said:

"Is this about last night, sir?"

"Yes."

"I am sorry. I was invited to dinner by Captain Brummell of the Guards. I should have remembered how much the English drink. It will not happen again."

"I have no objection to you being drunk, Cortez. If they do not find me a command soon I may take to drink myself. I do not even object to you finding a woman, providing the matter is handled with discretion. But to go to bed with the wife of a prominent Spanish naval captain in such an obvious manner causes me to question your judgement."

Ángel blinked. "Is that who he is?"

"Did you not know?"

"No, sir, I swear it. I do not…my memory of last night is a little confused. There was the dinner and then we went to some public ball. I think that is where I met Jocasta. She left with us and there was more drinking. There were two or three other women there. She mentioned she was married and said he was away in Gibraltar. I didn't ask why. I didn't care and it was clear she didn't either. Did García tell you?"

"No, he did not. He came home very late and very drunk and went straight to bed. As it happened, Colonel Masters saw you leave with her and thought I should be aware, just in case Captain Morata finds out. I am hoping we will be away from Cadiz before he returns. I cannot have my ADC involved in an affair of honour."

Ángel's lip curled slightly. "I would not fight a duel over a woman like that, General."

"If you are challenged, you will have no choice, Captain, or he will brand you a coward. Hopefully the rest of them were so drunk they will not realise or remember what they saw. Have you arranged to see her again?"

"Good God no, sir. She would not wish it either. It was nothing. Too much wine and a moment of lust. I offer my profound apologies."

Contreras nodded. "I accept, Cortez. We were all young once. I hope you did not say that to her, incidentally?"

Ángel thought about it. "I may have implied it," he said honestly. "She behaved like a common prostitute, sir, she is a disgrace to her sex and to her husband. I shall not think of her again."

"Very well. If you should hear anything more of the matter, come to me before you do anything about it. No, sit down please. There is one more thing."

Ángel lowered himself back into his chair. "General?"

"Colonel Masters also tells me that you became involved in a brawl in the tavern with one of his officers."

Ángel felt himself flush slightly. "Once again, it was nothing serious. A matter of pushing and shoving. I am willing to apologise for my part in it."

"The Colonel has suggested you meet with Captain Martin-Jones to shake hands, in the spirit of co-operation between our two great nations," Contreras said. "I am not worried about a drunken brawl, Cortez, I am worried about what started it. He called you an Afrancesado. A traitor who welcomes the French invaders and fights for Bonaparte."

Ángel's jaw was tight with anger. Even remembering the insult, uttered in appallingly bad Spanish, made his hands curl into fists.

"He did, sir. And I should not have taken offence, since it was true."

"It was once true. And you were hardly the only one. For a time, we were allies of the French. Our ships fought beside theirs at Trafalgar. When Bonaparte broke every one of his promises to us and invaded our country three years ago, you were not the only Spanish officer stranded in Denmark with the Division of the North. You were not the only one who boarded Royal Navy ships and returned to fight for your country against the invaders. You were not the only one forced to make a dangerous retreat through the mountains after Espinosa. You have nothing to be ashamed of, Cortez, yet you behave as though you have taken the whole of our national error onto your shoulders. How old are you now?"

"I am thirty-one, General."

"You are still a young man, and you are one of the most courageous fighters I have ever seen. You will make a name for yourself in this war, and nobody will ever be able to say that you were anything other than a loyal Spanish patriot. Do not get yourself into trouble defending something that you have no need to defend. Have I made myself clear?"

"Yes, General."

"Good. Now you may leave. May I suggest either a brisk walk to clear your head, or a few hours sleep. I will speak to you later."

Ángel chose the walk, making his way down to the Alameda which was the main promenade of Cadiz. It was a wide avenue with views across the open sea and was lined with ornamental trees and shrubs. During the afternoons it was the favourite place for fashionable Cadiz to show itself, but this early in the morning there were few people about. Ángel took up a position leaning on the sea wall, gazing out at the shipping in the bay.

He was angry at himself for what had happened the previous evening and he was annoyed that it had been reported to Contreras. His General was a tolerant man and had asked very few awkward questions but Ángel felt like a schoolboy who had been reprimanded by his headmaster. He loathed sharing personal information with anybody and was never comfortable talking about his feelings, but above all he did not want Contreras to ask why he became so upset when anybody referred to his early service fighting for the French. He knew the General was right when he said that many Spanish soldiers had changed sides in 1808 and felt no shame. What Contreras did not know, and would never know, was that Ángel had fought for Bonaparte not from necessity but because he believed in him.

There was nothing original about the story, although at the time it had seemed to Ángel that he was the first boy ever to experience that overwhelming sense of anger and frustration. His parents were well-born but struggling financially, gradually selling off their lands to maintain a station in life that was well beyond them. A strategic marriage might have staved off the inevitable ruin and from the age of sixteen Ángel was thrust into the company of a series of girls, the daughters of wealthy merchants who might be persuaded to exchange an ancient name and the dubious privilege of blue blood for a hefty dowry and a promised inheritance.

Ángel resisted fiercely, although looking back he thought that it was his parents' attitude which had brought every prospective alliance crashing down. His father could never quite manage to hide his contempt for the men he was trying to woo and his mother's false warmth to her prospective daughters-in-law did not always conceal the curling of her lip at some social error. They had made Ángel despise them too, made him see the promised marriage as a penance he must undergo to shore up the failing fortunes of his family.

Ángel had rebelled by the time he was eighteen, rejecting their outdated values in favour of the new ideas of equality and enlightenment which had swept through Europe in the train of revolutionary France. He read everything he could find on the subject, sneaked illegal news sheets and political tracts into his bedroom, refused to go to church and dreamed of freedom. There were daily arguments with his father shouting and his mother crying and his young sister hiding bewildered behind her bedroom door.

In the end, Ángel took refuge in the army. His birth guaranteed him an officer's commission although he went without his family's blessing. Ángel did not write to them. His pride kept him going through the worst shocks of military life. He learned for the first time what it was to be cold and hungry and injured. He discovered courage in the face of the enemy and learned what it felt like to kill a man. He killed many.

When the shifting pattern of European loyalties unexpectedly drove Spain from the side of France into alliance with Great Britain, Ángel found himself returning to a country he did not know. Overnight, it seemed, the afrancesados who supported Bonaparte and wanted to pull Spain out of the middle ages into the modern era on his coat tails, were declared traitors. Joseph Bonaparte had been installed as king of Spain by his brother and those members of the Spanish nobility and bureaucracy who swore allegiance to him were despised by their countrymen who were rising up throughout Spain to fight the invaders.

Ángel hesitated, torn between loyalty to his company and his battalion which now fought against the French and his long-held belief that only Bonaparte could bring lasting change to Spain, breaking down the rigid structure of Spanish society, ending the power of the church and the corruption of the House of Bourbon. He might have slipped away quietly to take the oath himself to support the new regime but Romana's army, which included Ángel's battalion, marched quickly to join the Spanish resistance to Bonaparte and Ángel was swept into battle before he really had time to consider the choice.

Retreating through Spain amidst the consequences of Bonaparte's invasion broke Ángel's heart. He travelled through towns and villages torn apart by the French and the brutality sickened him. From the age of seventeen he had admired the Emperor, seeing in him the light of reason and progress. Now he saw civilian corpses littering the streets and people starving because the French had taken everything they had. Women were raped, men were cut down for trying to defend their homes and families and priests were hanged from trees or crucified in a grotesque parody of the death of Christ.

Ángel could remember walking through the burned out ruins of a convent, thinking of his sister, whom he had believed safe within religious walls. He did not know if she was still so, or even if she was still alive, though he knew his parents had both died several years earlier. It was too late to make enquiries about her and Ángel had too much to do. A few short months of war in his home territory had given him a new focus and a new passion. His hatred of the French burned deep within him, more fiercely he often thought, because their savagery felt like a personal betrayal. He had left his home and family in pursuit of an ideal, and the ideal proved to be nothing more than an illusion. All he wanted now was vengeance.

Ángel stirred, coming out of his reverie. He realised in some surprise that it had begun to rain. The few people taking the morning air on the promenade were turning back, scurrying towards the town. Ángel stood for a few minutes longer, looking out over the bay to the English warships. His headache had worsened and he felt chilled and depressed. He had tried to see these weeks in Cadiz as a much needed break after years of brutal war, but it was not working. If Contreras did not receive his orders soon, Ángel thought he might seek permission to apply for a regular commission in one of Campoverde's divisions. He liked Contreras, but he was not willing to spend any part of this war as a spectator. While the French occupied even an inch of Spanish soil, Ángel wanted to be in the front line.

The rain was getting heavier. Pushing himself off the wall, Ángel turned and retraced his steps back towards the town for a hot drink and an hour's sleep. After that, he would go in search of further news of the new French advance.

***

Faith had not really taken Mr Glinde seriously when he had warned her that she could expect a sudden influx of callers on her return to London and she was astonished to find that, if anything, he had underestimated the matter. The first week was quiet, but by the time Miss Caddick had been installed in the best guest bedroom and the dressmaker had agreed to rush through a large order for new clothing, the knocker was never still during visiting hours.

Miss Caddick proved to be a pleasant woman in her forties. She treated Faith respectfully, listened to her opinions and gave sensible advice when asked. After the first week, Faith admitted to herself that if Miss Caddick had been in search of employment she would have offered her the job. The contrast to the harsh voiced Mrs Irwin was almost comical and Faith found it easy to set aside her suspicions of Mr Glinde's sister-in-law and ask for help.

"I have no idea what to order," she said, in the carriage on their way to the dressmaker. "I cannot help but be delighted at being able to have some new gowns, but with father as he is…should I choose sober colours, do you think?"

"That is a very good question, and I don't know the answer, my dear," Miss Caddick said. "You certainly cannot go into full mourning with your poor Papa still alive, but I agree it should be considered. I suggest we ask Madame Colette what she thinks. She has been dressing the Ton for many years now, she must have come across such a situation before."

"I am not part of the Ton, ma'am."

"Perhaps not yet, but Mr Glinde is of the opinion that you might become so, should you choose," Miss Caddick said seriously. "At any rate, since you are well able to afford it, why not dress as if you are, even if only to please yourself?"

Madame Colette, a thin, elegant Frenchwoman in her late thirties, proved to have decided opinions on the matter. "But no. No mourning. There will be time enough for that when your Papa is indeed gone, Mademoiselle. For an older lady I would suggest more sober colours, but for a young lady such as yourself, there is no need; you will not be wearing anything too vivid. White, my dear, since you have the colouring to carry it off. Also I have a very pretty green which will look very well for day wear. Then we must think of evening gowns."

"Oh no, I will not be going out," Faith said quickly.

"But you must be prepared, Miss Collingwood, since you hardly know," Miss Caddick said firmly. "I do not think you need to trouble with a ball gown yet, since you are unlikely to dance, but to dine or to attend an evening reception, you must have something."

Faith hesitated. The dressmaker was calling to her assistants and bolts of cloth began to appear on the counter. The green was charming, but Faith was dazzled by a roll of old gold silk which seemed to shimmer as Madame pulled it out, catching the sunlight through the shop windows. Faith reached out to touch it and Madame laughed and lifted it, holding it against Faith's face and hair and turning her towards the mirror.

"Yes?"

"Yes," Faith said. It occurred to her suddenly that she did not need to consider what her father might say to a sudden burst of extravagance. Previous visits to the dressmaker had been filled with visions of his wrath if she overspent the amount he considered suitable for a young girl not yet out. Faith looked round at Miss Caddick and saw that she was smiling with a good deal of understanding.

"Indulge yourself a little, child. From what my brother-in-law has told me, you have earned it. And for a small bonus, I think Madame will be able to finish this order quickly? Miss Collingwood has been living in the country and has nothing fit to wear in London, Madame."

"That, I can see," Madame said briskly. "Very well. Day dresses, walking dresses, evening dresses, a riding habit…"

"I don't ride, Madame."

The Frenchwoman stopped at stared at Faith in astonishment, then looked at Miss Caddick. "Do you have charge of this young lady's debut? She must learn. You must see to it."

Miss Caddick studied Faith. "Would you wish to, Miss Collingwood?"

"I don't know. I have never thought of it, my father did not ride. But I…"

Faith stopped. She felt suddenly strange, as though she had opened a door and seen a path ahead of her leading to places she had never thought to go. There had been so many things that she had never done and never even been allowed to consider. Until last year she had never walked on a beach.

"Yes," she said abruptly. "Yes, I would like to learn. We will order the riding dress, Madame."

"Excellent," the Frenchwoman said warmly. "In this matter, I may be able to help you. There is a riding school which is run by a gentleman friend, it would be perfect for you. I will give you his card. Now – evening gowns. And we must look at your undergarments."

The first gowns had only just been delivered when Faith received her first callers. To begin with, most of them were people she knew: the wives and daughters of some of her father's City acquaintances. They came with ill-concealed curiosity, striving to discover as much as they could about Mr Collingwood's condition and likelihood of recovery without appearing to ask too many impertinent questions. None of them referred to Faith's very public disgrace and banishment and all of them spoke of her stay in Norfolk as though it had been a pleasant and entirely voluntary holiday.

Many of them brought an unmarried gentleman with them.

Before long, the list of callers had expanded. Aristocratic neighbours, who had never exchanged more than a distant bow with John Collingwood, seeing him as their social inferior, unbent to make a sympathy call to his daughter. Haughty matrons looked Faith over, taking in every aspect of her dress, her hair, and her company manners as if they were interviewing her for a job. They stayed the correct fifteen minutes and not a minute more and left with a stiff bow and a touch of the fingers in lieu of a handshake. Faith was relieved to see them go and astonished when many of them called again.

When they did, most of them brought an unmarried gentleman with them.

As Faith had not yet been officially brought out, she was safe from invitations to the balls and receptions that filled the days of fashionable London during the Season, but there were other activities. Ladies brought their daughters to call, and Faith found herself invited to walk in the park, to take tea under the eye of indulgent chaperones, and even to attend the opera as the guest of the Misses Partington. Faith loved the opera and would have thoroughly enjoyed the evening if she had not been persecuted by Lady Partington's son, a willowy young gentleman who had clearly been coached to pay court to the heiress although his eyes continually strayed longingly to a noisy crowd of his friends in the pit.

"I do not think I can bear much more of this," Faith told Miss Caddick the following morning at breakfast. "Really, I am beginning to wonder if I should go back to Norfolk."

Miss Caddick was laughing. "There is no need for anything so drastic, my child. Simply tell Mr Hudson you are not at home. You are too generous with your time, Miss Collingwood. Say no."

"I don't wish to be rude to anybody, ma'am."

"It is not rude at all, it will do them good. In any case, you will not have so much time now that you are becoming better organised. You have your riding lessons and your painting lessons and your singing teacher."

Faith laughed a little self-consciously. "My father would be so furious at the money I am spending on myself," she admitted. "I half expect him to awaken in the middle of Signor Farini's visit and come stomping into the room to demand to know why I am wasting my time on singing lessons."

"You have a beautiful voice, Miss Collingwood. And all these lessons are things that most girls in your position would have done as a matter of course. Your father spent as little as he could on your education, and it is a pity because you are an intelligent and accomplished young woman. I am very glad you are taking the opportunity to rectify some of his omissions."

Faith found herself blushing and drank tea to compose herself. "I am also aware that you must be wishing to go home, ma'am, and I am keeping you from your family. I'm so grateful, but I must make a push to find a more permanent companion."

Miss Caddick laughed. "As to that, do not worry about it. I have stayed longer than I intended, but to be honest I am enjoying myself. If I had been fortunate enough to marry, I would have liked a daughter, and I would have wanted her to be like you. You are so curious and so interested in the world. Another girl in your position would have done nothing but study her appearance and complain at the limitations of her situation, but you have so much enthusiasm to learn. I will need to go back to my sister, but I can stay a few more weeks."

"Thank you," Faith said with real gratitude. "You have helped me so much. I hope that when you do go, I will still see a great deal of you."

"You may depend upon it. I am deserting you this afternoon, however. I have promised to accompany an old friend to a church meeting."

"Of course. You make me feel very guilty, I haven't been to service since I arrived in London. I used to go to St Olave's with Miss Irwin before, but for some reason I cannot bring myself to go back there."

"Why do you not come to St Michael's with me on Sunday? Mr Stanton's sermons can be a little lengthy, I will own, but he is an excellent preacher. I usually attend with my friend, Mrs Dench, but you would be very welcome to join us."

Faith was touched. "Thank you, I would like to. Do you attend this meeting with Mrs Dench?"

"Yes. She is a widow and is involved in a number of charitable societies. Today's meeting promises to be very interesting."

"What is it about, ma'am?"

"Oh...well to tell you the truth, Augusta has become involved with a newly formed society which intends to lobby for the full abolition of slavery. There are several speakers, including two African gentlemen who are former slaves themselves."

Faith was intrigued. "Really? That does sound interesting, ma'am. I was still a young girl when the trade was abolished, but I remember reading some accounts in the newspapers. I did not know that there was progress towards abolishing slavery itself, but it makes me very happy to hear it."

"It is a very new group, Miss Collingwood, so I do not hold out a great deal of hope that anything will be achieved soon. But it is a cause in which I strongly believe. I would…I might have asked you to accompany me, but it would be dull for a young girl."

Faith studied her. For the first time ever there was something not entirely frank about Miss Caddick and it puzzled her. "I would not wish to intrude, Miss Caddick, but it sounds more interesting than waiting here for half a dozen vapid young gentlemen chasing my fortune to call. I hope you will tell me all about it."

"Oh my dear, you misunderstand," Miss Caddick said with quick contrition. "It is not that at all, I would be delighted if you would bear me company. It is just that with your father's history with the Africa trade, I did not know if you would feel comfortable."

Faith put down her tea cup. She felt an odd twist of discomfort in her stomach, which reminded her of how she used to feel when she realised that she had done something to displease her father. For a moment she could not speak, but she did not want Miss Caddick to feel any awkwardness. Striving for lightness, she said:

"That is even more interesting, Miss Caddick. Would it surprise you to know that I didn't realise that my father was involved in the slave trade?"

Miss Caddick regarded her compassionately. "No," she said gently. "I realised from the beginning that he told you nothing about his business, and as you have hardly been out into society you are unlikely to have heard from anybody else. Please don't allow it to distress you, my dear. Many, many families have connections with the trade. It has not always been seen in such a negative light, it is only a few years since it was abolished, and…"

"And it should have happened much earlier," Faith said flatly. "Ma'am, please will you excuse me? And will you tell Hudson that I am not at home to callers?"

"Oh, Faith, I've upset you. I'm so sorry."

"No. No, you haven't. All you've done is given me a piece of information, ma'am, and I needed to know it. I have no wish to cause discomfort, but if you will allow, I would very much like to accompany you this afternoon. After all, I should learn how my riding and singing lessons are paid for."

***

The meeting was held in an upstairs room in an old coaching inn and the room was crowded and hot. There were benches set out for the gentry and Faith sat beside Miss Caddick and Mrs Dench as the speakers shuffled their papers and talked quietly amongst themselves. There were two African men on the platform. At the end of the bench in front of Faith there was another African: a young woman seated beside a clerical couple. She wore a very plain gown, with her black curly hair tightly braided, and she sat still and quiet, her hands folded in her lap.

Throughout the speeches that followed, which told of unimaginable horrors, Faith realised that she was watching the girl. She wondered how it felt to hear her story told by other people. The two former slaves were very articulate and spoke powerfully of their ordeal. Around Faith, people were visibly affected, with tears in their eyes. Faith thought about her father and wondered what his involvement had been or still was, with the African trade. She felt almost as if she was here under false pretences, as though she had no right, coming from her background, to listen to these narratives.

Then again, she looked at the girl, and wondered what she thought about it.

There was a confusion in Faith's mind about the horrors she was hearing and the knowledge that somewhere, in a way that she did not yet understand, her father had contributed to them. That confusion at least made sense.

Alongside it, there was another sense of indignation, about the girl in the plain gown with the beautiful eyes, who sat silently listening to men speak. Faith was not sure why it made her so angry. She could not possibly understand how it might feel for an African woman who had experienced slavery to sit silently while both English and African men spoke of her suffering. But she knew, only too well, how it felt for men to speak on her behalf with no understanding of what she wanted, and she had never felt it so powerfully as now. She sat silently alongside the African girl and felt a shared sense of rage which was probably wholly imagined. Still, it gave Faith an illusory sense of solidarity which was oddly comforting. The speeches ended and nobody called on the girl to get up and, quite unexpectedly while Faith was watching her, the girl looked round and caught her eye. After a moment, she smiled.

Faith was temporarily embarrassed at being caught staring, but the girl showed no discomfort, so Faith smiled back. She felt warm and included, and suddenly part of what was going on in the room because of a brief connection with the other woman. The girl could not possibly know anything of Faith's emotional struggles and had no reason to care, but for the rest of the meeting, Faith felt better.

The meeting ended and people drifted outside. Some lingered in the afternoon sunshine, chatting to friends and acquaintances or trying to catch the attention of the speakers. One group gathered around Mr Benjamin Thurlow MP. Apart from Miss Caddick, Thurlow was the only person present that Faith had met before, though she did not think he had remembered her. She thought bitterly that given her father's participation in the slave trade she should not have expected to meet any of his associates at a meeting like this. Miss Caddick's voice interrupted her reverie.

"Faith, come and meet Mr and Mrs Stanton."

The Stantons made Faith think of a caricature. Reverend Stanton was very tall and thin while his wife was short and round. They both talked a great deal and very fast and once they had been introduced it took several minutes before Miss Caddick could find an opening to introduce the other couple in the group.

"Mr and Mrs Caldwell – Miss Collingwood. Mr Caldwell runs a bell foundry in Whitechapel and he and his wife are leading lights in the local Methodist society, my dear. Miss Collingwood is a young friend of mine whose father is sadly unwell. She is temporarily without a chaperone, so I am staying with her in Russell Square until a new one can be found."

"Delighted to make your acquaintance, Miss Collingwood," Mrs Caldwell said enthusiastically. "Are you interested in the cause?"

"Yes very, although this is the first meeting I've attended," Faith said. She was wondering why nobody had introduced the young African woman, who was standing on the edge of the group. "I was only a schoolgirl during the fight for the abolition of the trade, but I would like to know more of this new campaign."

"Well you have arrived at the right time," Mrs Caldwell said warmly. "This is a very new society. I realise that a young lady in your situation cannot formally join us, but you would be very welcome at our meetings, and should your father show an interest in the future…"

"My dear, your tongue runs away with you," Caldwell said firmly. "I do not believe Mr Collingwood is likely to be a supporter of our cause. Indeed I am surprised to see his daughter here. Forgive me for asking, Miss Caddick, but do you think it entirely suitable…"

Faith was mortified. She was also suddenly very angry although she was not sure why.

"I asked Miss Caddick if I could accompany her today, sir, and I am glad to have had the opportunity to learn more of a matter that I realise I knew very little about. But I have no wish to cause offence if my father's daughter is not welcome here."

There was a brief stunned silence. Faith could not believe she had said it and now that it was said, she had no idea where to look, so she looked straight ahead and found herself looking into the eyes of the other young woman. Faith was surprised to see a sparkle of amusement there. The girl glanced around at the group, checked that she was unobserved and then gave a broad, and clearly approving grin. Faith almost smiled back, it was so infectious.

"My apologies, Miss Collingwood," Caldwell said stiffly. "I meant no such thing. All supporters are welcome."

"You must be wondering about my maidservant," Mrs Caldwell said hastily, clearly searching for a change of subject. "Abi, come forward and make your curtsy to Miss Collingwood."

The girl did so, bobbing a polite curtsy. Bright, interested eyes studied Faith with such frank curiosity that Faith found herself smiling. "I was wondering why we had not been introduced," she said.

"I have made a point of bringing Abi to these meetings," Mrs Caldwell said. "As you see, her own situation is very fortunate now, but I think it a good idea for her to learn of the effort being made on behalf of those poor souls still labouring under the yoke of plantation slavery."

"We should be going, Faith," Miss Caddick said. Her voice was a little cool and Faith thought she was probably quietly furious at Mr Caldwell's rudeness. She would have liked to linger, to see if she could manage a conversation with Mrs Caldwell's unlikely maidservant, but she did not want to make her companion feel awkward, so she said her farewells, agreeing to attend service at St Michael's on Sunday and accepting, after a brief consultation with Miss Caddick, an invitation to a ladies' tea party during the next week.

Miss Caddick did not refer to the incident and Faith was grateful. The meeting had given her a good deal to think about, and she found herself thinking about it through most of a sleepless night. The following day she penned a brief note to Mr Glinde and sent a footman off with it. Faith had expected a note in return, but Glinde came in person, arriving just as Faith returned from her riding lesson.

"Mr Glinde. Thank you for calling so promptly, I hope I have not inconvenienced you."

"Not at all, ma'am, I wanted to speak to you anyway. How are you, you look very well?"

"I am, thank you. Give me ten minutes to change and I will join you in the back parlour."

Tea had arrived by the time Faith returned. Glinde was on his feet, studying one of the paintings on the wall. He turned and bowed.

"Miss Collingwood. I see you have been making changes."

"Very few. As I do not entertain, I cannot bear to be rattling around in that enormous drawing room, so I use this as my sitting room, and we dine in the breakfast room next door. This house has too many rooms."

Glinde laughed aloud. "It is a very fine house, though. You asked to see me."

"Yes. Please sit down, sir, and have some tea. Recently, I was told something about my father which I didn't know, and I would like to ask you the truth of it."

Glinde looked wary. "I will do my best, ma'am."

"Was my father involved in the slave trade, sir?"

Glinde did not answer immediately, which was all the answer Faith needed. She watched him trying to frame the response he thought suitable for a young female and decided that she did not want to hear it.

"I see. No – please don't give me a long explanation about how differently slavery was seen a few years ago, it will not help."

"I am sorry if you are upset, ma'am. At some point, I realise that we will need to go over the various components of your father's business interests. They are quite varied and…"

"Does he still own slaves?" Faith interrupted. She could hear a quaver in her voice, and she concentrated very hard on bringing herself under control since she was determined not to cry.

"No, ma'am. Your father was an outspoken opponent of abolition, but once the trade was formally outlawed, he gave instructions to sell his remaining West Indian interests. I do not think it was from altruistic motives…"

"You do not need to tell me that, Mr Glinde."

"No. Well. It was that…Mr Collingwood believed that once the trade was abolished, attention would turn to the plantations themselves. He once said to me that he believed it was only the ongoing war that stopped them making a serious attempt. He did not wish to wait until it became difficult to sell land and slaves because of the threat of abolition, so he had me liquidate all his West India assets."

"I am glad to hear it, sir."

"May I ask…"

"Yesterday I attended a meeting with Miss Caddick, of a newly formed society for the full abolition of slavery."

"Oh for God's sake," Glinde said irritably. "Foolish woman, what was she thinking to be taking you there."

"She is not at all foolish and I asked to go," Faith said frostily.

"It has upset you, and there was no need."

"I am not that fragile, sir. And there are some things that it is right to be upset about."

Glinde did not immediately reply and Faith allowed the silence to go on. She suspected that he was telling her the truth about her father having sold his West Indian interests, but with the horrors she had heard described on the previous day fresh in her mind, she did not want to enquire further. One day she would need to know the full story, but that could wait. Faith remembered suddenly that Glinde had mentioned another reason for his visit.

"You said that you wished to speak to me, Mr Glinde. What was it about?"

Glinde sighed. "I am reluctant to raise this now, ma'am, while you are already upset, but I received a visit from Dr Mercer yesterday."

Faith stared at him. "About my father?"

"Yes, ma'am. Dr Mercer was understandably reluctant to approach you and wanted to ask my advice about what you should be told."

Faith was furious. "I see nothing understandable about that, Mr Glinde. I believe you were present when I asked Dr Mercer to give me regular reports on my father's condition, particularly if there was any change. So far every one of his reports has said exactly the same thing, including the one he made yesterday. That there is no change. Am I to understand that he lied to me?"

"Miss Collingwood, if the doctor was less than frank, it is because of your youth and your…"

"It is because I am an unmarried female, Mr Glinde, and must therefore be considered too feeble-minded to hear bad news. The next time you speak to Dr Mercer, perhaps you might remind him who is paying his probably extortionate bills. Honestly, we could probably dismiss him and pay the nurses a higher salary, since they do all the work. What did he tell you? Is my father worse?"

"Dr Mercer believes so, ma'am. His pulse is weaker and there are other signs, other bodily functions…do you need the details?"

Faith decided that she did not, and relented. "No. Just tell me what he thinks."

"Nobody expected your father to live this long, ma'am, he has astonished us all. But Dr Mercer believes that his body is beginning to shut down. The nurses report they are no longer able to get him to take any nourishment and even getting him to drink water is becoming difficult. There is a method of inserting a small tube into his throat, which they are trying, but it is a dangerous procedure as it can cause…"

"Why was I not consulted about this?" Faith snapped, getting up. "He has no right to try these experimental treatments on my father without my consent."

Glinde did not speak for a moment. Eventually, he said quietly:

"Do you care?"

Faith walked to the window. She realised that she was close to tears. "Yes," she said. "Does that surprise you, sir? It surprises me too, since I promised myself after he last beat me that I was done with him and that I would never again care about him or try to make him care about me. But the thought of them pushing tubes down his throat or trying to force food into him…my father always wanted to be in control. He needed to be in control. He would hate this, and I find that I hate it too."

Glinde rose and went to the decanter on the sideboard. He poured sherry and took it to Faith. "Come and sit down, Miss Collingwood, and drink this. I am sorry. I realise that I am finding it very difficult to reconcile the view of your character and capabilities that I received from your father with the young woman I am coming to know. Sometimes I forget. Your compassion is a credit to you and considerably more than he deserves."

Faith sipped the sherry then searched for her handkerchief to wipe her eyes. "I think I would feel the same way about any man in his situation," she said honestly. "Mr Glinde, it would be very easy for me to step back and allow you and Dr Mercer to make these decisions on my behalf, but if I wish to establish myself as an independent woman, I cannot shy away from this. I will speak to Dr Mercer myself and I will talk to the nurses, but I believe I would like this to stop. If he can drink water then he will do so. If he cannot, I believe he should be allowed to die with dignity. I hope you will agree to that."

There was compassion in Glinde's expression. "I do, Miss Collingwood."

"Did the doctor say…?"

"Probably not more than a week or two."

"I see. Thank you. I believe that I should curtail my social activities for a while. I am committed to several gatherings this week, including another meeting with Miss Caddick, but after that I think I should remain at home with my father."

"I think that would be prudent, my dear."

"I have promised Miss Caddick to put some effort into finding a new chaperone and I will do so. Your poor wife must be missing her. Please tell her how grateful I have been; it has made this so much easier. As have you. Thank you, Mr Glinde."

Chapter Six

Durrell took a room at the *George Inn* for his brief stay in London. He knew that if he had asked, Mrs Thurlow would have happily accommodated him once again, but Durrell did not want to impose upon her hospitality. He liked the *George* which was a busy coaching inn on the south side of the Thames.

Durrell had deliberately not written to his mother ahead of his visit. He disliked feeling as though he was deceiving her, but he disliked even more the thought that he might not be able to entirely trust her. Durrell knew that his mother loved him, but since his brother Henry had improved his career prospects and his social standing, and made a very profitable marriage alliance, Mrs Durrell was firmly on his side in any possible family conflict. Henry made his mother a comfortable allowance and was willing to settle a substantial dowry on his younger sister and for that, Mrs Durrell was able to close her eyes to her older son's many faults.

His mother greeted him with surprised delight. Durrell and his brother had always had a difficult relationship, which had spilled over into open conflict during the miserable Walcheren campaign. Since then, Durrell had avoided Henry as much as possible. His illness and lengthy convalescence had provided a good excuse, and apart from a brief formal visit to congratulate his brother and to be introduced to his new sister-in-law, Durrell had stayed away.

Durrell made enquiries about Henry and his wife and listened patiently as his mother brought him up to date with family news at great length. He was delighted to discover that Henry was out of town for a few days.

"I hope you will still be here when he returns, Alfred. It is high time you spent some time together. Dreadful for two brothers to become estranged over the behaviour of a flighty girl…"

"My quarrel with Henry had nothing to do with Miss Collingwood, Mama."

"Henry said…"

"I cannot speak for Henry, but certainly on my part, our differences were over entirely another issue. However, it is in the past. I don't know if I will still be here when he returns, as we await orders to sail, and they may come at any moment. If I am, I will be glad to see him. I had hoped to see Abigail though, is she not here?"

"Yes, indeed, she will be back at any moment, I imagine. She is at the dressmaker's for a fitting."

Durrell frowned. "Are you really intending to bring her out this year, Mama? Surely it is a little late in the Season?"

"Did Abigail write to you?" Mrs Durrell asked, rather sharply.

"Abigail is a very regular correspondent," Durrell said, trying to keep his voice neutral.

"Indeed. Well it is hardly surprising, as she has had a great deal of time on her hands. One might say too much time. It is for that reason that dear Selina thinks it might be as well to introduce her into society a little before her formal debut next year. I have no intention of presenting her this year, Alfred, for as you say it is too late in the Season to arrange everything. But Selina believes it will do her good to be obliged to go out and meet people. Abigail is altogether too reclusive, too much inclined to hide away. Selina believes she has been kept too much a child and that it would be good for her…"

"Abigail is not yet seventeen, Mama," Durrell cut in. "It is not at all uncommon for girls to be presented far later. When I last spoke to you of this, you had no intention of bringing her out this year. Or indeed next year. What has changed?"

His mother sniffed loudly to indicate her disapproval of his interruption. "It is clear that you know all about it, Alfred. I collect that your sister has written to you to complain. She should not have done so; it is not at all the thing for a young girl to be setting herself up to know better than her elders, and I shall…"

"She did no such thing, Mama. She merely mentioned your intention and I was surprised. Are you telling me that Abigail does not wish to be brought out this year?"

"Did she not tell you that?"

"No."

"Oh." Mrs Durrell seemed nonplussed. "Oh. Well it has all been a big fuss over nothing. Perhaps you could talk to her Alfred and make her see sense. She has been behaving very badly and has put Henry all out of patience with her."

There was the sound of the front door. Mrs Durrell rose but Durrell was faster. "Let me, Mama. It's been a long time since I saw her."

His mother hesitated, then sighed. "I have letters to write anyway," she said. "But Alfred, please do not encourage her to be difficult."

"Mama, I've no idea what is going on here, but unless my sister is very much altered, I cannot imagine that she will be difficult at all. Thank you."

His mother removed herself to her private sitting room and Durrell went to the top of the wide staircase. His sister was ascending the stairs, untying the ribbons of her bonnet. She did not immediately see him and when she did, she stopped. Durrell could not help smiling at her astonished expression.

"Alfred?"

"I believe so, little sister."

"Alfred!"

Abigail ran up the stairs so quickly that Durrell was poised to catch her if she tripped. He held out his arms and she went into them, holding him very tightly. Durrell kissed the top of her head and noted that she clung onto him with something like desperation. Eventually, he set her very gently at arm's length.

"Let me look at you. My goodness, very elegant. Whatever happened to the little girl with the yellow braids and ink-stained fingers?"

In response, Abigail drew off her gloves and held up her hand. "Spotless, dear brother. My sister-in-law insisted that I soak my fingers in lemon juice and then cover them in rose balm to keep them white and soft. It appears that no gentleman will wish to marry a lady whose hands show the least sign of useful activity."

Durrell laughed and took her hand, leading her into the drawing room and closing the door. "She cannot know you, Abigail, your fingers will be black within a week."

"It is very unlikely, Alfred, since I am only allowed access to pen and ink three times a week for the purposes of correspondence, and then under supervision. At other times, I am to occupy myself with embroidery. They don't trust me with watercolours, I might try to write with them."

"I beg your pardon?" Durrell stared at her, looking for signs of levity. He was appalled when he realised that she was serious. Abigail's manner was not at all like herself. There was a brittle gaiety which spoke of something more serious than a fit of nerves about an early debut.

"I'm sorry," Abigail said abruptly. "Don't think of it again. You are here and knowing you, you only have a short time before you sail off again. I have no wish to spend the time complaining about my trivial problems. Alfred it is so good to see you. Where are you posted next and when do you sail?"

Durrell opened his mouth and then closed it again. Learning when to speak, and about what, had not come easily to him but on this occasion he decided that his young sister needed a sense of normality before she could bring herself to open up to him. Biting back a number of scathing remarks about his brother and sister-in-law, he summoned a cheerful smile.

"The Mediterranean fleet. A small squadron under Captain Codrington, off Menorca and Tarragona. The Captain is a good friend of Captain Kelly's so it should be a comfortable posting, I think. I have a few days here, Abigail, I am hoping we can spend some time together. Would you like to go to the theatre this evening?"

"I would love to," Abigail said fervently. "Just the two of us, Alfred. Mama will not wish to come, she does not enjoy it, and Henry is away from home. Unless you have other engagements…"

"None, apart from a few items of shopping, but you may accompany me to do those. I'm wholly at your disposal, Abigail."

"That sounds so lovely. I do hope they do not come home too soon and spoil it."

"Why should they spoil anything?"

Abigail shrugged and then grinned, suddenly looking much more like her usual self. "Well putting you and Henry in a room together is generally a recipe for disaster, Alfred. Besides, I want you to myself for a few days."

"That sounds like a wonderful idea."

"Are you staying here?"

"No, I'm at the *George*, but I'll be here as much as you want me."

Abigail's cheerful smile wavered a little. "I want you all the time, Alfred, but I can't have that."

"Let us make the most of this then," Durrell said firmly.

***

By the end of the week, Durrell was beginning to think that he had imagined his younger sister's unhappiness. With no other obligations, he devoted himself to her entertainment and enjoyed himself enormously. They went to the theatre and to the opera and Durrell hired a hack to ride with her in the Row. He enjoyed Abigail's sharp observations of their fellow riders and wished he could be present for her debut, since he suspected he would appreciate his sister's clear-sighted honesty in a way that his mother and brother would definitely not.

With his travel to Portsmouth arranged and most of his packing done, Durrell took Abigail to Greenwich Park for their last afternoon together. It was a beautiful day with a dazzling blue sky and the park was not crowded. Durrell and his sister strolled along leafy walkways and went in to the Greenwich Seaman's Hospital to admire the Painted Hall. They stopped at a refreshment booth with tables outside and Durrell bought lemonade and ices and managed to stop himself reminding Abigail that she should keep out of the sun for fear of tanning because he suspected she heard enough of such strictures.

"Do you leave early tomorrow?"

"No, the coach leaves at two in the afternoon. I was wondering if I should call in the morning…"

"No, don't. You've said your farewells to Mama, and I would rather say goodbye to you this afternoon, when it is just the two of us. I shall miss you, Alfred."

"I'll miss you too. Do you think you will be allowed enough ink to write to me regularly."

Abigail laughed aloud. "I thought you had forgotten that, as you haven't mentioned it. I should have known better."

"Can you tell me about it now? I collect you are not getting on very well with our sister-in-law."

"I loathe our sister-in-law," Abigail said frankly. "Does that shock you? I have tried to be charitable, you know, but I have given up because she is not charitable at all. She believes that the money she has brought to the family gives her the right to order all our lives exactly as she wishes. She has wholly taken over the running of the house from Mama."

"That is quite usual, Abigail, when a son marries."

"Yes, but one does not have to be so objectionable about it."

"What does Henry say?"

"Henry does not care a button for anything other than his parliamentary career and toadeating important men in the hope of a government post."

"I thought he already had a government post."

"He wants a better one. I think he would like to be a cabinet minister, and since my sister-in-law would love to be married to one, they suit each other very well. And I think Mama is happy, since all she has to do is drink tea with her friends and spend stupid amounts of money on new clothing. It is ridiculous."

"I gather Selina is at least generous."

"She can afford to be since they are obscenely wealthy. I believe her father owns half of Antigua or Jamaica or some such place. I know nothing of any of them apart from the fact that they are plantation owners and anti-abolitionists and you know how father felt about slavery."

"I know, Abigail. But Henry is not like father."

"Henry would not care how many people died to provide him with his London home and his club memberships. I despise him."

Durrell could see how upset she was and could think of nothing he could say to comfort her. "I'm sorry, Abigail. Have you not thought of going home to Hayes?"

"I have asked to do so, but I am not allowed. Henry talks of renting the house out, since he now has a magnificent country estate in Buckinghamshire. He even mentioned selling it, but Mama was so upset that he set the matter to one side."

Durrell did not speak immediately. He was surprised at the sharp pain he felt at the thought of his childhood home being sold. Abigail seemed to realise and squeezed his hand. "Don't worry, Alfred, I don't think he will do it. I suspect that once I am married, they will want Mama to retire there. They will not want her at Asterley Court while they are entertaining all their important friends."

"And do they want you there?"

"Only if I am married to one of them."

Durrell was angry but held it firmly in check. "Do they have somebody in mind for you, Abigail?"

"Yes, I believe so. I have not met him, it is another of the West India set. Very wealthy and on the catch for a wife."

"You don't have to marry anybody you don't want to, Abigail."

"I know. And I don't intend to. But I am under no illusion about how unpleasant this could be, for me, but also for Mama, since they will bully her in the hope that she will bully me."

Durrell was silent again, trying hard to think of a solution. He believed his sister implicitly. Abigail was very young, but she was formidably intelligent and a very good observer of people. Durrell was the only person she had allowed to read some of her writing, and he was impressed and rather taken aback at both the fluency of her prose and her talent for biting satire. If Abigail believed she was about to be coerced into an early and unwanted marriage, he suspected it was true.

"Is that why they are bringing you out early, part-way through the Season?" he asked, suddenly understanding.

"I believe so. They have told Mama that it will do me good to gain some experience of fashionable life before my formal debut next year. Because I am so awkward and shy in company. To do Mama credit, I think she believes them. But I do not. I think they are worried that once I am officially 'out' I might attract the attention of another gentleman and their friend will be cut out."

Durrell studied his younger sister thoughtfully. "I think they may be right, Abigail, you're very pretty."

Abigail snorted vulgarly. "They will not care a penny for that, Alfred. But thanks to my brother's fortunate marriage, I have an impressive dowry."

"That still doesn't give them the right to push you into a marriage you don't want, Abigail. I'm going to speak to Mama. And I think I need to delay my departure until Henry comes home."

"Don't," Abigail said fiercely. "Do not do so. It will not help in the least, because Henry is my legal guardian. All it will do is to stir up another huge row, which will result in my being forbidden to write to you. And I can't bear that, Alfred. If I am to do this, I will need your support."

Durrell looked at her and felt an immense sense of affection and pride. "Don't give in," he said. "They can't make you."

"I know they can't. I have a feeling it will be unpleasant, but short of kidnapping me, there is no possibility that I will marry a man I cannot like. Indeed, I don't want to be married at all."

"That might change."

"Perhaps it will. Do you think you will ever marry, Alfred?"

"I don't know. I think I would like to, but God knows when that will be, since I have neither the time nor the money at present."

"Well if you do not, perhaps one day we could live together. I could keep house for you and write novels and poetry under an assumed name. Do you think I could?"

"Keep house?"

"Become a novelist, idiot. Anybody can keep house."

"I don't know, Abigail, but I don't see why not. You're a very talented writer. Have they really banned you from writing?"

"Yes. Dear Selina believes it is corrupting my mind. It is driving me mad. She searched my room, you know, with the intention of destroying what I have written, but I guessed that she would and so I have hidden it. I removed the nails from one of the floorboards in my room and hid all my work there. I wish I had thought to hide my writing materials as well."

Durrell regarded her with something like awe. "I wonder if I was that inventive at your age."

"Well you were because it was you who gave me the idea. Can you not remember telling me that you fashioned a secret cubby hole at the back of the midshipman's area to hide your valuables because you were tired of the other midshipmen stealing from you? I must say, I thought it very ingenious. Did they ever find it?"

"No," Durrell said. "Have you finished? Come along. We have plenty of time."

"To do what?"

"To buy you an early birthday gift."

Ackermann's Repository of Arts was situated on the Strand, close to Somerset House. The hackney cab dropped Durrell and Abigail outside and Durrell saw his sister pause in the doorway, looking around her with an expression of pure happiness which made Durrell smile. He could remember coming here as a boy to buy writing supplies for his first voyage with the Royal Navy, almost too excited to speak.

Ackermann's shop was spacious, with high windows which Durrell thought he remembered were a legacy of the shop's former use as a drawing academy. These days, Ackermann published decorative prints, expensive colour-plate books, and fashionable periodicals. He also sold art and drawing materials and good quality stationery. The shop was a popular meeting place for fashionable London and Durrell's only concern was that another customer would recognise Abigail and report her purchases back to Selina or Henry. He was reassured to find that most of the browsers were gentlemen, either looking through prints or discussing the finer points of ink with the clerk behind the counter.

The walls of the shop were crammed with framed artwork, while behind the counter, tall cabinets held Ackermann's supply of stationery and artists' materials. Two women were seated on tapestry-covered stools at the counter, while a slim gentleman showed them a selection of watercolour paints. At the other end of the shop, a printer's apprentice wearing an ink-stained smock was discussing an order for some invitations with a young African woman in the sober gown of an upper servant.

"There is nobody I know here," Abigail said softly, echoing Durrell's thoughts. Durrell grinned.

"I suggest you make your selection then, little sister, before our luck turns. Here, allow me to show you something."

The clerk listened to his request and disappeared, returning with a leather bound book. Durrell took it with a smile of thanks. The book felt comfortable and familiar in his hands. He had been given the first one of these as a gift from Sir Home Popham during the Walcheren campaign. Popham had a collection of them, documenting his time at sea over many years and had suggested that Durrell begin the practice.

"What is it, Alfred?"

"It's a log book, we use them aboard ship. Some of them are pre-ruled, but this one is blank. When I'm away, I keep one of these and make notes in it every day."

"Like a journal?"

"A little. But not about my personal thoughts. I write about the ship and the coastline and the tides. About what I've learned and what I've seen. It's incredibly valuable. Sir Home Popham gave me the idea. I'm going to buy one for you. I'll get you some paper as well, but if you are serious in your intention to become a novelist, you will have to learn to document your ideas and observations of people and the world around you in the same way that I document my ship."

Abigail ran her fingers over the leather binding, then looked up at him with shining eyes. "Alfred, what a beautiful idea. Thank you."

"I will leave you with this gentleman to choose your paper, pens and ink. Get plenty, as it may not be easy to obtain more while I'm away. I am going to study that collection of military and navy prints and criticise the depiction of the rigging. Call me when you are ready."

Durrell stood regarding the prints thoughtfully. There was rather a good one of a battle between two frigates, but try as he might, Durrell could not make out how the second ship had not already been destroyed given her position in the water. He was mentally composing a letter to the artist when a voice said:

"Lieutenant Durrell."

Durrell turned in astonishment. The young woman standing before him was elegantly dressed in white muslin with a dark green pelisse and matching hat. Her attractive face was framed by chestnut brown curls and a pair of steady hazel eyes which held a lurking smile.

"Miss Collingwood!" Durrell was so surprised that he almost saluted, remembered at the last minute and turned it into an awkward bow. "How are you? I was surprised…I had not thought…I mean…"

Durrell broke off as her smile widened a little. He reflected gloomily that this was not the first time he had made a complete fool of himself in the company of Faith Collingwood. He also thought how well she looked.

"You thought I was still in exile, I imagine," Faith said quietly. "And I presumed you would be at sea."

"I leave for Portsmouth tomorrow," Durrell said regretfully. "But how are you? You look very well. I have so often wondered…"

He broke off as two gentlemen drew closer. Faith looked around her. At the back of the shop, beyond the print counter, was a shabby sofa: probably a relic of the art school. Faith motioned for him to join her and seated herself, indicating that he should do the same. Durrell did so, hesitantly.

"Are you with somebody, ma'am? A lady…"

"No," Faith said. "I am here, quite shockingly, completely alone. My chaperone is visiting her sister and my maid fell down the garden steps yesterday and twisted her ankle. I should probably have brought one of the housemaids with me, but it seems so ridiculous when they have more than enough to do. And besides…I wanted to see how it felt. I spent a good deal of time walking alone in Norfolk and nobody cared at all."

"How did it feel?" Durrell asked.

"Very uncomfortable," Faith said, and Durrell remembered how much he had always liked her frankness. "In a twenty minute walk, I have been stared out of countenance by at least a dozen men and been glared at by as many ladies. Luckily, I don't think any of them knew me. It was an interesting experiment, but I do not think I shall try it again."

"I have often wondered how it must feel to be so restricted and for so little reason," Durrell admitted. "How stupid that I can walk around London as much as I like, but you are subject to all kinds of judgements for doing the same. May I…that is, I am here with my sister, but I would like to offer you my escort home. I was intending to summon a cab and it would be no trouble to drop you in Russell Square first. Only, I am concerned that your father would be furious if he knew."

The girl's eyes widened slightly. "Oh…oh, you have not heard. Of course you have not, why should you? My father has nothing to say in the matter, Mr Durrell. I am afraid he is very unwell. He had a stroke and is wholly incapacitated, which is why I have returned to London."

"I didn't know."

"He is not expected to live, Mr Durrell."

Durrell said nothing. After a long, rather painful silence, Faith gave a very small smile. "Thank you. I am glad you did not offer me the usual sympathy. You are one of the few people who know how he treated me."

"Ma'am, I've thought of you constantly this past year, worrying about you. After what happened, I felt so responsible."

"You were not responsible, Mr Durrell, you did nothing wrong. Neither of us did anything wrong."

"My brother did something wrong, ma'am, and I cannot forgive him for it."

Faith shook her head. "It was very unpleasant, and I was horribly upset," she said. "But now that it is over, I realise that I am immensely grateful to Mr Henry Durrell, since I did not really want to marry him, and I think I should have been very unhappy."

Durrell was surprised and then realised he should not have been. From the start of their acquaintance, he had found Faith's tendency to speak her mind an attractive contrast to her shyness. Some of the shyness had gone now. She had grown up during this past difficult year and he liked her new maturity.

"I'm glad you didn't marry him, ma'am, since I think you deserve much better. But I was afraid your father would have treated you very harshly over our supposed intrigue."

"Yes, he did," Faith said honestly. " Lieutenant, you will not know this, but very recently, I have become interested in the abolitionist movement."

Durrell was a little confused by the abrupt change of subject. "Really? I had no idea. You may know that my Captain has become a little involved."

"Yes, I know. I have been told that he spoke at several meetings about his experiences in the West Indies. I wish I could have heard him, I have been hearing people singing his praises. Mr Durrell, when your brother broke our engagement with such dreadfully false accusations, my father sent me away to the Norfolk coast. Before he did, he beat me. He had done so before, of course, but never as badly as this. My former maid actually ran into the room to intervene, as I believe she thought he had lost control of himself and might not stop."

Durrell realised that she had not changed the subject at all. He was appalled.

"Oh no. Dear God, ma'am, I'd no idea. I'm so sorry."

"I am not telling you this because I require your sympathy, Lieutenant. Recently, I attended a public meeting, and I heard an African gentleman describe how often and how badly the plantation slaves are beaten. I looked around the room, at the men and women in the audience and it occurred to me that probably most of them had no idea how that felt. Perhaps they had been chastised as children. But to be beaten until you bleed...and of course it only happened to me once. Those poor, poor people, who live with it every day and under such terrible conditions. It should not continue and in my personal opinion, we should not even be discussing the matter with the West India planters who perpetrate this."

Durrell could hear the passion in her voice, but while he agreed with her entirely, he could not pull his thoughts away from what had happened to her.

"What of you? Are you fully recovered?"

"Me? Yes. Oh, yes. I do not think of it that much, especially now that he is never going to be in a position to strike me again. It probably seems wrong that I am here, pretending to care and waiting for him to die, but I have always been able to speak the truth to you."

"I hope you always will, Miss Collingwood. I wish I had more time, but I have orders."

"I am sorry to hear that, but so glad we have met again. Perhaps you would..."

"Miss Collingwood!" The voice sounded appalled, and Durrell turned to see a middle aged woman clad in sensible dove grey who was regarding them with a look of pinched disapproval.

"What are you doing here with a gentleman, Miss Collingwood?"

Faith did not flinch. "Mrs Stanton. How very nice to see you. Mr Durrell is an old acquaintance and we stepped over here to have a conversation. It is perfectly public."

"But where is Miss Caddick? Or your maid?" The woman's voice was almost a hiss. Durrell opened his mouth to speak when a voice from behind him said:

"No need to worry, ma'am, I am here with Miss Collingwood."

Durrell turned in surprise to see the young African woman, holding several wrapped parcels, smiling at Faith. The older woman looked startled.

"Are you? Are you, indeed?"

"Yes, ma'am. Miss Collingwood's maid is indisposed. Mrs Caldwell wanted me to arrange for some cards of invitation to be printed and Miss Collingwood had some shopping to do so my mistress asked me to accompany her."

Durrell had to remember to close his mouth. He had no idea who the girl was, although she clearly knew Faith, but her facility at lying was hugely impressive. Faith looked surprised as well, but she recovered quickly and turned back to the other woman.

"Thank you for thinking of me, ma'am, but I assure you all is well. I will see you at service on Sunday."

"Yes. Yes, of course." The woman sounded stiff, and slightly embarrassed. "My apologies, Miss Collingwood."

When she had retreated, Faith turned to the girl. "Thank you very much," she said. "I had no idea you were there."

"Sorry, ma'am. I was waiting for the printer to come back with the bill, and I couldn't help overhearing. I remembered you from the meetings and from church."

"Please don't apologise, I'm very grateful. As you saw, there was nothing amiss, but Mrs Stanton seems to think I am in need of a surrogate parent; she haunts me. I am sure she means it kindly enough, but it is not at all her business to monitor the company I keep. Still, you showed the greatest presence of mind and averted an embarrassing situation."

"No trouble, ma'am. Sir." The girl looked at Durrell and then flashed a sudden unexpectedly mischievous smile. "I'm right here and as deaf as Mrs Caldwell's grandma. You want to carry on with your conversation you go right ahead. I'm telling you, I would."

Durrell felt himself redden, and Faith blushed scarlet but she was also laughing. "That is very kind of you. I'm sorry, I'm very stupid, I can't remember your name although I know I've been told it."

"It is Abisola, ma'am. Abisola Danjuma. And it's no trouble."

The girl moved away and Faith turned back to Durrell. "When do you have to leave?"

"The day after tomorrow. We're sailing for Spanish waters to join a squadron under Captain Codrington."

"I remember him. I met him, I think, aboard the *Iris*. How is...oh this is too quick. I have so much to ask you."

Durrell took a deep breath. "May I call?" he asked. "It would have to be tomorrow. I have packing to do, but if I leave now, I could have all done."

Faith's smile told him he had said the right thing. "Please do. I promise, I will give them instructions that I am at home to nobody else."

The warmth in her tone made Durrell very happy. "May I ask who is taking care of you now, Miss Collingwood? Do you have a companion?"

"Not a permanent one, I need to employ one. I have dismissed my former companion along with my maid. Both were hired by my father to spy on me, and I refuse to have them about me. My father's man of business is in charge of his financial affairs and has employed a new maid for me."

"Do you trust him?"

"I have not always done so, but I think at the present we have common interests. I can speak more freely tomorrow. Please call if you can."

"I give you my word, ma'am. But you do need an escort home."

The African girl had been studying some of the paintings, but she turned and came forward. "Sir, if it's awkward, I'd be happy to walk home with Miss Collingwood. It would make my story look true."

Durrell hesitated, but Faith was smiling. "Abisola, that would be very good of you. Thank you. Mr Durrell, I will be very well taken care of and I hope to see you tomorrow."

***

Faith watched him go, his tall figure stooping instinctively under the door lintel as he escorted his sister from the shop. He had still been ill the last time she had seen him, and she remembered trying to hide her shock at how drawn and thin he was. He was back to his usual self now, although Durrell would always have a willowy figure. She thought he looked very much the same as when she had first met him aboard his ship in Walcheren, but his manner was different, with a quiet confidence that she did not remember. At the time, his boyish awkwardness made her less self-conscious of her own painful shyness, but Faith decided that this new, more adult Durrell was appealing. She wondered if he had noticed any difference in her.

Faith turned back to the other girl. She had no idea why Abisola Danjuma had intervened as she had, but she was grateful. The girl bobbed a little curtsy.

"Thank you again, Abisola. That is...do you mind me calling you by your first name? I am not sure..."

"Of course, ma'am. It's what Mrs Caldwell calls me."

"It's a very pretty name."

"Thank you, ma'am. It's my name. My real name. When I was little, in the big house, they called me Jane. My mama worked in the kitchens there, she came over on the ship from Africa. They called her Mary, but her real name was Ife. When I was freed, I wanted to use my real name, the one my mama gave me. The Caldwells were good enough to have me baptised with that name, though the vicar insisted I use Jane as well. I'm not sure he thought I could be a good Christian with an African name."

"And your surname? Is that African?"

"Yes, ma'am. It is a Yoruba name. My mama was a young woman when they took her, she could remember her life before. It was her family name. They said I could call myself Caldwell, but I didn't want to, and they didn't make me."

Faith opened her mouth to ask another question then closed it again, concerned that she was being intrusive.

"I'm sorry, I'm being very curious, aren't I?" she said finally. "I'm fascinated, but I don't want you to think you are obliged to tell me things which are none of my business."

To her surprise, Abisola gave another of her wide, relaxed smiles. "I don't mind, ma'am. In fact..."

She stopped. Faith felt a sense of fellow-feeling and she knew what the other girl was not saying. "You're curious too, aren't you? You were listening."

"I'm sorry, ma'am. I know I shouldn't have, but what you were saying...it's not what I'm used to hearing in Methodist circles."

Faith laughed aloud. "Have you finished your purchases?"

"Yes, ma'am."

"Are you sure you don't mind?"

"Not at all. It's a lovely day for a walk."

They left the shop and turned left, walking in silence for a few minutes. Faith was very conscious of how much better she felt walking with a companion and the fact both amused and irritated her.

"I didn't come this way," she said.

"If you went through Holborn, it's no wonder you felt uncomfortable, some of those streets aren't fit for a respectable woman, ma'am."

"I realised that very quickly. But then walking alone isn't respectable."

"It was a mad thing to do, Miss Collingwood."

Faith looked at the girl in some surprise and realised that Abisola was smiling broadly. She smiled back. "I just wanted to try it."

"You're not much like other young ladies, ma'am."

"This was good of you, Abisola. And I'm glad. I've seen you at meetings and at church and I've been dying to talk to you."

"Why, ma'am?"

"I have seen you several times now, with Mrs Caldwell, but I've never really heard you speak before. The men - Mr Nelson and Mr Andrews - speak very eloquently about their experiences of slavery. But surely you have a story to tell. Why have we not heard it?"

"Mrs Caldwell does not believe it would be proper, ma'am. Because I am a woman and young and unmarried."

"They have not said that to me."

"It's different for you. I am a servant."

Faith studied her. "And I am an heiress?"

"Yes, ma'am. I've heard the Caldwells talking about it. Sometimes they forget I'm there."

"Sometimes they forget I'm there," Faith said without thinking, and Abisola laughed. Her laugh was very infectious, and Faith found herself joining in.

"Oh, I'm sorry, ma'am. It's just so nice to talk to someone younger. All their guests are older and church people and they're so good and so kind to me. But..." She broke off, searching for words.

"You must feel like a successful project," Faith said. Abisola looked blankly at her. "I'm sorry. I didn't mean to be unkind. They are such good people. It's just that I would have liked to hear your story alongside the others. I suppose they wish to protect you. But that was the reason my father used to give for never allowing me to do anything. I discovered that he had no desire to protect me at all."

"Did he really beat you?"

"Yes. He thought it would teach me to behave better. All it taught me was to lie very well and to be terrified of him."

"Is he going to die?"

Faith nodded.

"Are you sorry?" Abisola's eyes widened and then she clapped her hands over her mouth. "Oh no. I'm so sorry, ma'am, I shouldn't have asked that. I forgot..."

"It's all right. It really is. You're right, it is very good to talk to somebody close to my own age. And in answer to your question, I am not sorry at all. But I will not say that to anybody else since they will think very badly of me."

Abisola walked quietly for a moment, then she looked up and the glint of mischief was back in her lovely dark eyes. "Nobody else?"

Faith could not help smiling. "Perhaps one. He is an old friend, and he already knew about my father."

"I think he looks very good, ma'am. Not so big and loud as some of the others, but he has *okan*, that one."

"*Okan?*"

Abisola frowned. "My mama used to say it, in her language. Our language. I don't speak it. Never had time to learn when I was a small girl, and then she died and all I had was what I remember she used to say. But *okan*...it means heart. Conscience. Strength, but inside."

Faith felt silly tears behind her eyes. "You are a very good judge of character, Abisola. Because you are right. He does have *okan*."

Abisola grinned. The imp was back, dancing in her eyes. "Of course, he doesn't look so bad either, and that don't hurt."

Faith laughed. "You seem to know a lot about me, Abisola, and I don't know anything about you. Tell me how you came to England."

They walked slowly back to Russell Square. When they arrived, Faith looked up at the house, then turned away and went into the square garden instead. Seated on a bench, they talked on until the light was changing, and Faith suddenly realised that she was very cold and that Abisola might well be in serious trouble. She got up.

"Into the house with you. I must have gone mad, I completely forgot about the time and Mrs Caldwell will wonder where you are. I'll write her a note explaining and I'll send you back in the carriage."

"There's no need, ma'am."

"Yes, there is. It will make my point. Abisola, thank you."

"It's no trouble, ma'am. I…I enjoyed talking to you."

"I enjoyed it too." Faith hesitated. She felt a sudden sense of certainty which she could not explain. "Abisola, this probably sounds like a strange idea to you, and I realise you will need some time to think about it. But I would like to offer you the position as my companion. I need to employ a lady to accompany me and I think you and I would get on very well."

Abisola looked at her for a long time. Eventually she said:

"Ma'am, I am a former slave and I've been working as a maidservant."

"You seem to be a very well educated maidservant."

"Mrs Caldwell saw it as her Christian duty to educate me, though I don't really use it much."

"Well I'm grateful to her since it makes you very well qualified for this position. Will you think about it?"

"I don't know how to behave in polite company, ma'am."

"Your manners seem perfectly good to me. Besides, you can learn. I won't be going into polite company much for a while anyway, as my father is about to die."

"I don't think I'll be a very good chaperone, ma'am."

"Good. I am tired of chaperones."

Abisola did not speak for a moment. Then she said abruptly:

"I wanted this."

"Did you?"

"No, you don't understand. I knew your situation and earlier in the shop, I saw an opportunity. I didn't expect it to work, but I thought I'd try. I did this on purpose."

Faith was astonished. "Abisola, that was very clever of you."

"It was dishonest of me, ma'am. And now I feel ashamed, because I like you."

"I'm not sure dishonest is the right word," Faith said, much entertained. "After all, you didn't lie to me. And you rescued me from an embarrassing situation with the greatest aplomb. I was very impressed."

"I can't use you to better myself, ma'am. It wouldn't be right."

Faith did not speak for a long time. Eventually she reached out and took Abisola's gloved hand, drawing it through her arm. "Let us be very clear, Abisola, about who is doing whom a favour here. This is not about me helping you. This is about you helping me. I need somebody under the age of forty to show me how to laugh again. Just think about it, will you? I'm very lonely."

"So am I," Abisola said unexpectedly. "I'm going to say yes, ma'am."

"Good," Faith said. "Now come inside and get warm."

Chapter Seven

The wind was brisk as the *Iris* made her way out of Portsmouth and Hugh Kelly stood on the deck looking up at the billowing sails with mixed emotions. In his younger days, the ocean had been his world and the decks of his ship were his home. He was never as happy as when he was at sea, feeling the rolling movement beneath his feet and seeing the wide horizon beckoning.

These days his happiness was tinged with sadness at leaving Roseen and his son behind. During the first year of their marriage she had travelled with him to his station off the coast of Gibraltar and she had seemed to love being part of shipboard life. But the birth of Alfred had made it impossible for her to continue on board. It was not just the danger of shipwreck or battle that Hugh feared, it was the constant stalking presence of fever: both aboard ship and in the ports he visited. Roseen had almost died of shipboard fever before their marriage and Hugh could not bear to risk her again.

Hugh suspected that left to herself, his intrepid wife might have taken her chances and joined him. She had found a compromise with a rented home in Chatham, which made it possible for her to see him whenever he was home even for a short period. It also meant she was within easy reach of London and Maria Thurlow, her girlhood friend. Roseen had proved to be a very adaptable navy wife and she was making friends in the service. Hugh missed her during their separations with an ache of loneliness, but he knew that however much they missed each other, she was safe.

Hugh's orders were to report to Admiral Sir Charles Cotton, who had replaced Lord Collingwood in command of the Mediterranean fleet after Collingwood's sudden death the previous year. Hugh had been upset at the news of Collingwood's death. He owed his current command to his capture of an escaping French prize in the chaotic aftermath of Trafalgar, but he knew perfectly well that courage and skill would not have been enough without a patron.

Hugh had been a junior officer, desperately looking for a way to get noticed, when he first met Lord Collingwood. He did not know why Collingwood had taken a liking to a young Manxman of relatively humble birth, but the liking was mutual. Collingwood was a down-to-earth, cheerful man with a good sense of humour and a way of putting his juniors at their ease.

Collingwood had taken Hugh under his wing and pushed for his promotion to command a series of small ships, culminating with the *Newstead*, an elderly but surprisingly fast frigate in which Hugh had made both his reputation and his fortune. After Trafalgar, Collingwood had taken the trouble to write letters on Hugh's behalf and the result was that command of the *Iris*, a 74-gun third rater had gone to an unknown Manxman with no other patronage at the Admiralty. Hugh would never forget what Collingwood had done for him and thought the navy poorer for his death.

Hugh did not know Sir Charles Cotton particularly well and had heard mixed reports of him. He knew that the Admiral's orders were to continue the blockade of the French fleet in Toulon, as well as conducting operations against French troops in southern Spain. Some of Hugh's friends considered that Cotton seemed slow to make decisions and reluctant to engage the enemy, but Hugh knew how easy it was to judge a man's actions from the comfort of an armchair.

"Captain Kelly."

Hugh turned to see his bosun approaching. Geordie Armstrong was in his fifties, a stocky figure of medium height with the comfortable gait of a man at home on the deck of a ship. With so much time ashore since Armstrong joined the *Iris*, Hugh had not had time to get to know him personally that well yet and was looking forward to doing so during this voyage. He liked what he had seen of the man so far.

"She's looking very good, bosun."

"Aye, sir, she's a fine ship and fast. French-built, wasn't she? The master tells me you took her yourself after Trafalgar."

"I did. One of the madder exploits of my career, but it's paid off. How are you getting on with Mr Manby?"

"He's a good man, sir. Been with you a long time?"

"He was a carpenter's mate on my first ship and worked his way up. I lost Mr Randall, my long-term master in a skirmish with a Danish man o'war and Mr Manby received his warrant then. I hope he's given me a good reference."

Armstrong grinned, acknowledging the hit. "Aye, he has that, sir. I won't disturb you now, but if you've time later on I'd like to talk to you about the rigging. I've got to know it pretty well in dock, but I'll need to see how she sails. Still, I've got some ideas about one or two changes."

Hugh was amused. "Have you spoken to the Master about this?"

"Aye, sir. He tells me you're a captain with a very good understanding of the rigging yourself."

"I was a topman when I was a boy. I thought for a time I'd end up with a bosun's warrant, but then I had some help along the way and here I am."

"You'd have made a fine bosun, sir," Armstrong said gravely, and Hugh burst out laughing.

"I'm happy enough with the one I've got so far. We'll talk about the rigging later."

At seven bells, Hugh was in his cabin setting out his accounts when the ship's master, Mr Manby appeared, indicating that he was ready to go on deck to take the noon sight. Hugh got up, closing his ledger with relief, and collected his sextant. It was the task of the master to ascertain the ship's position at noon each day and make a report to the captain. Hugh had served on ships where the captain showed no interest in being part of this daily ritual, but he had never lost his fascination for navigation and star-gazing and he seldom missed it.

The master's mates were expected to attend the noon sight along with all the midshipmen and any of the ship's boys with an interest in learning navigation, and the quarterdeck was crowded. Hugh ran his eyes over the earnest faces, busy with a variety of navigational instruments from basic wooden quadrants to gleaming brass sextants. The best position for taking the sight was a little nook at the end of the hammock netting near the gangway, and the midshipmen made way for Hugh. Hugh took up his position and Manby joined him, his eyes on the bright blue sky.

There was the usual buzz of chatter from the younger men and boys as they took their readings. There was a certain amount of jostling for position and banter amongst them. Hugh listened without appearing to do so. He liked this hour of the day, not just for the satisfaction of the calculations, but because it gave him an opportunity to spend time with the midshipmen informally. He knew some of them already, but there were a number of new faces. There were also seven boys under the watchful eye of the schoolmaster. Four of them were young gentlemen, sent to sea as class one volunteers, with the expectation of becoming midshipmen. The other three were ordinary volunteers, one of whom was Brian Murphy, Hugh's leggy Irish cabin boy.

Brian's thin face intent on his sextant. The instrument was new, a gift from Hugh after an exemplary report from the schoolmaster about Brian's progress. Hugh watched his servant with affection tinged with sadness. Brian had been with him since he was twelve and Hugh had watched him grow up. He was almost eighteen now, and Hugh knew that it was time for Brian to move on. He had already spoken to James Manby about taking the Irish boy as master's mate and Brian was overjoyed. Hugh realised he had been putting off the moment, not because he could not find another cabin boy, but because he was attached to Brian and would miss their daily interaction.

Hugh turned his attention to his sextant. It was a bright clear day, making the readings easy. Beside him Manby worked out his latitude in a small notebook and there was silence over the group of observers who were suddenly intent on their work. When the master had finished, he walked aft to where Lieutenant Baker, the officer of the watch waited. Baker accepted his report of noon along with the degrees and minutes of the latitude observed.

Hugh watched, hiding his smile, as Baker approached him to make the same report. Manby had needed to walk past him to reach Baker, but it would not have occurred to the master to report directly to Hugh and Hugh would not have asked him to do so. The daily rituals of shipboard life were important, not because of routine days such as this when Hugh was present and available, but for the one day when he would not be, and a crisis might occur.

Baker saluted, announced that it was twelve o'clock and gave the latitude which Hugh already knew. Hugh nodded.

"Make it twelve, Mr Baker."

"Aye, sir." Baker raised his voice to the mate of the watch. "Make it twelve, Sanders."

"Aye, sir." Petty Officer Sanders turned to the waiting quartermaster. "Sound eight bells."

The quartermaster stepped onto the ladder and called below. "Turn the glass and strike the bell."

As the first stroke of the bell rang out, Baker turned to where Geordie Armstrong waited, his whistle ready. "Pipe to dinner, Bosun."

Hugh stood watching as officers and men dispersed. The officers dined in the wardroom at one o'clock and then Hugh dined an hour later, theoretically in solitary splendour. In practice, if he had no other guests, Hugh dined with his First Lieutenant. He knew that one or two of his other officers during the past few years had looked askance at his close friendship with Durrell. There had been mutterings of favouritism, particularly after Walcheren when Hugh had stood by Durrell against all attempts to put him on half-pay.

Hugh could see Durrell now, his long form leaning against a grating. He was demonstrating something in a notebook to two of the midshipmen, waving his pencil in the air as he explained. Hugh had no idea what he was teaching them, but he knew it would be accurate, very well-explained and incredibly detailed. Hugh had received many such lectures from his junior and at times they had driven him mad, but he had also learned a great deal. He stood waiting for Durrell to finish, watching the midshipmen. Mr Clarke was staring into space, looking as though he would rather be somewhere else. His companion, one of the new boys by the name of Holland, was scribbling frantically in his own notebook, looking up every now and again with something like hero-worship at Durrell's oblivious form. Hugh made a mental note to spend some time with Mr Holland and came forward.

"Mr Durrell. As it's our first day at sea, I've invited the other officers to join us for dinner."

Durrell smiled. "We're very grateful, sir."

"I'm sure you'll be willing to act as my second host. And I'd be grateful if you'd do the same tomorrow when I'm hosting the midshipmen. I may need help with that."

Durrell laughed aloud. "I'd be delighted, sir. I'm sure the young gentlemen will be on their best behaviour."

"They'd better be." Hugh surveyed Durrell's two pupils. "Mr Clarke, I hope you're studying hard. Mr Holland, you're new to us. How are you enjoying your lessons?"

"Very much, Captain."

"Excellent. You were taking notes there."

"Yes, sir. Mr Durrell was explaining the difference between various instruments when making calculations and how they…" Holland stopped suddenly and blushed scarlet. "It was very interesting," he said lamely.

"It's fascinating," Hugh said, amused. "I applaud your ability to rein in your enthusiasm but don't do it with me, you're exactly the kind of young officer I'm looking for. I'd like to get to know you better; you'll sit beside me tomorrow at dinner. Now go and get your own dinner before your messmates eat it all."

He watched as the younger men raced away to their meal then turned to Durrell. "Are you sure you're ready to help me at this dinner tomorrow?"

"Of course I am, sir. There are one or two very promising men among the new midshipmen, but Mr Holland is my favourite so far."

"I can see why. If he's as good as he seems, why don't you find him some extra duties that will give you a chance to work with him?"

Hugh saw his First Lieutenant's eyes light up. "Thank you, sir. I'd like that."

"Excellent. I'll see you at dinner. As my clerk is struck down with sea-sickness, I intend to spend the next hour continuing to set out my accounts book."

Hugh heard the gloom in his own voice. Durrell laughed. "Would you like me to do it, sir?"

"Yes, but you're not going to, you take on far too many duties that are not yours, including schooling the midshipmen. I…"

Hugh broke off at the sound of raised voices from the gangway. Before he could move, Durrell was ahead of him. Hugh watched as his First Lieutenant crossed the deck and barked an order. Three boys scrambled up onto the deck and lined up before him and Durrell looked them over, unsmiling.

"Mr Oakley, Mr Bristow. Can you explain to me why you're brawling with Lewis when you should be on your way to dinner?"

"Not a brawl, sir. Just joking around."

Durrell said nothing. He let the silence lengthen until the boys were shuffling their feet. Hugh could feel their discomfort and he did not blame them. Durrell's withering expression was enough to discompose even the liveliest midshipman.

Eventually, Durrell moved his gaze to the third boy. Teddy Lewis was a wiry ex-pickpocket from Southwark who had been pressed as a landsman and had chosen to remain as a volunteer, acting as Durrell's servant. He was sixteen and smaller than most of the boys, but made up for it with a belligerent willingness to fight even the biggest of them. Durrell glared at Lewis for a full minute then looked back at the other two boys.

"Aboard a Royal Navy vessel, a midshipman is considered a young gentleman. I happen to know that you both qualify by birth, if not behaviour. Repeatedly picking on one who is both smaller and below you in rank because you think he cannot fight back is not the act of a gentleman or a future officer, it is the act of a snivelling coward. Please do not be under the misapprehension that because you joined this ship as midshipman, you will necessarily remain so. If you persist in bullying the other boys I will have you broken to common seaman, and you'll find that below decks the men will be unimpressed with your status. Now get to your dinner. I will see you at four o'clock after the watch is called and we will spend some time improving your mathematics."

"But sir, study time is over then," Bristow said in appalled tones.

"Not for you, Mr Bristow, since it appears that you struggle to find constructive ways to spend your leisure. Dismissed. Not you, Lewis."

When the other boys had gone, Durrell regarded his servant thoughtfully. "Are you hurt?"

"No, sir."

"Did they take anything?"

Lewis hesitated and Hugh could see him considering whether he could get away with a lie.

"I will find out, Lewis, and you will regret it."

"My lesson book, sir."

"Did you get it back?"

"It's spoiled, sir. In the animal pen, it's covered in shit…I mean dung, sir."

Durrell did not speak for a moment. When he did, his voice was pleasant and even. Hugh could tell that he was furious.

"Go to the purser after dinner and get another one, with my authorisation. When you're not using it, you have my permission to keep it in my cabin. The money will be deducted from their pay. In the meantime, Lewis, in addition to practicing your reading and penmanship, I would like you to practice walking away. If you spend your time defending every inch of your dignity you'll never rise above able seaman and that would be a shame, because you are more intelligent than either of them. Now go and get your dinner."

"Yes, sir."

Durrell watched him go then turned back to Hugh. "They bully him," he said, almost apologetically. "Sooner or later it will go too far, and it will be Lewis who is flogged. While I understand the need to maintain discipline and the separation between ranks…"

"You don't have to explain it to me, Mr Durrell, you're forgetting I started in this navy below decks. I know exactly how an over-privileged midshipman can treat a ship's boy. I also know how immensely satisfying it is when you pass them by on the way up. Would you like me to have a word with Lewis?"

"I think that would be very helpful, Captain. I, as you know, was an over-privileged midshipman."

Hugh laughed aloud. "I'd be astonished if you ever abused your position to bully a younger boy, fella. I'll see you at dinner."

A brisk wind sped the *Iris* on a southerly course. She rounded Brest and entered the Bay of Biscay, where the fine weather abruptly gave way to winter squalls. Hugh had sailed these waters many times and knew better than to underestimate Biscay. It was easy for ships to be driven into the bay by prevailing westerly winds and, close to the coastline, the Atlantic swell could quickly build up, making some of the ports dangerous to enter.

Having taken on supplies and water, Hugh chose the traditional route keeping far from the coastline and plotting a direct course towards Corunna. Their passage was fast but unpleasant, and those new crew members unaccustomed to long periods at sea suffered badly from sickness. Driving rain and unpredictable squalls made life a misery for everyone.

They were anchored off Corunna when the weather suddenly worsened, bringing Hugh from his bed halfway through the middle watch. He arrived on the quarterdeck to find Durrell already there, bundled into a waxed cape, his hat rammed firmly down on his head. The wind shrieked appallingly, and the violent flapping of the sails told Hugh that he was dangerously late to his duties.

"Where the hell did this come from? Why didn't you call me?"

"I was busy, Captain," Durrell yelled. Hugh knew he was not being aggressive; it was the only way to be heard. "I sent Madson with a message."

"Well he got lost," Hugh roared back.

"I am always astonished at how well you are able to sleep in poor weather, Captain."

"Well I'm awake now," Hugh said grimly. He ran his eyes over the rigging where men scrambled, buffeted by the wind. What Hugh had thought was rain was cold sleet, driving into his eyes and cutting through the thick layer of his cloak. The decks were awash with huge waves which slammed into the *Iris*. They crashed over her boats, which looked alarmingly as if they would be washed overboard.

"Secure those boats!" Hugh bellowed, and men scrambled to obey. Sleet and seawater soaked the decks again and again and the men lurched about their duties, clutching at anything that might steady them. Hugh stared up at the rigging, shielding his eyes, and realised that Durrell had already given the orders to take in sail. Men clambered aloft, clinging desperately as the wind buffeted them and the ship dipped dangerously from side to side. The noise was unbelievable.

Hugh stood watching anxiously as the men made their way up the rigging, unable to tear his eyes away. This had been his job as a youth and at the time he had had treated the danger as a challenge. He could remember racing his fellow topmen with no thought for his own safety or theirs. Twenty years on he had buried crewmen, some of them friends, who had fallen to their deaths on the deck or into a boiling sea. He was only too aware that his order could send a man to his doom.

The ship lurched violently again recalling Hugh to his duty. Another huge wave washed over the deck, drenching every man there. One seaman slipped and fell, sliding on his back across the deck until his progress was halted by a grating. The slam of his body made Hugh wince. One of his shipmates reached out a hand to haul him up. Durrell took one look at his bloodied face and dangling arm and ordered him below to the surgeon. Hugh turned and surveyed the rigging again.

In weather this severe, Hugh's priority was to minimise damage to the ship and to ensure the safety of his crew. He wished he had been awake when the storm broke but he knew that was illogical because Durrell was just as capable as he was. The wind had been brisk when Hugh fell asleep but with no hint of the approaching tempest.

After a brief yelled consultation with Durrell, Manby and Armstrong, Hugh gave orders to strike the topgallant masts and yards. The process required many of the ship's company to man the ropes, while the topmen scrambled into position. Their courage was breathtaking. Hugh watched them and could not imagine ever being that young and foolhardy.

Durrell was organising teams to go below and man the pumps. Currently the hull was undamaged, but the *Iris* was taking on water every time she was hurled from side to side by the wind and waves. Hugh turned his attention back to the sails. Their violent cracking in the gusts of wind sounded like gunshots. It was usual in a storm this bad to remove the top-weight and avoid damage to masts and rigging. This would help to reduce the motion of the ship and remove the stress on the rigging.

Under the supervision of Manby and Armstrong, the topgallant yards and masts were carefully lowered to the deck and the topsail yards were sent down, while the topmasts were reduced to the cap of the mast below. In good conditions, Hugh's experienced crew could achieve this in half an hour but it took a lot longer in this appalling weather and Hugh had to remind himself to breathe, watching the men scrambling about the rigging and the slippery decks. The air was heavy with moisture and Hugh could taste salt on his lips.

With all possible precautions taken, the crew of the *Iris* hunkered down and prepared to weather the storm. The men took turns at the pumps and ensured that the stores below were properly secured. Every man remained at his station, on edge and alert for new orders, knowing things could change suddenly.

Hugh remained on the quarterdeck with Durrell beside him. There was no possibility of rest and he wanted to be there, alert and ready, in case the storm grew worse and more drastic action was needed. Hugh had been aboard ships where it had become necessary to cut away the masts and jettison the guns. They were not there yet but he was alive to the possibility; to the lash of the spray on his face and the violence of the wind lifting his oilskin cape. The deck moved beneath his feet and Hugh concentrated with every fibre of his being on the *Iris*. He knew his ship well: knew the creak of her timbers and the rattling of the masts and the sense of her in the water.

"Mr Durrell, I want a report from below. Are the pumps holding up?"

"Yes sir. There is no structural damage and the stores are safe."

"Injuries?"

"Four men in the sick bay including Morton. All of them fell. Nothing serious as far as we can tell."

The wind continued to howl around them. Before dawn, Hugh gave orders for the young midshipmen and the ships' boys to rest below decks, although sleep was impossible. Their clothing was soaked and they shivered beneath wet bedding but it was not safe to light fires to dry out. Hugh ordered dry biscuits and the grog ration to be distributed to all. It was almost dawn but the sky was still dark and overcast. He wondered grimly how long this would last.

The rain stopped mid-morning although the sky remained heavy and grey and the white capped, gun-metal waves still buffeted the battered ship. Still, Hugh could feel the wind dropping. He realised he could speak without bellowing, although his throat was sore and his voice was hoarse from a long night of yelling to make himself heard.

Beside him Durrell stirred. "I think it's easing, sir. Permission to check below?"

"Granted, Mr Durrell. We'll give it some time, but I think the worst is over. Remind me to ask Sir Richard Keats when we get there whose idea it was to send us across the Bay of Biscay in the middle of fucking winter, will you?"

"I would like to know the answer to that myself, sir. I hope it was for a very good reason." Durrell lifted his face to the wind and spray and inhaled deeply, almost as if he was smelling the air. "It's a good wind for making up time though."

"Agreed. I for one will be glad to get there."

"You could go to your cabin, sir. There's nothing…"

"So could you, Mr Durrell, but we both know that's not where you're heading." Hugh raised his face to the wind also and felt more of a gentle salt spray than the razor sharp sleet of the previous night. "We'll give it a little longer, I think, then I want the galley fired up, stoves lit to dry out and a ration of grog. I think we've earned it."

**

It was supper time before the ship was set to rights and Durrell was bone weary, soaked to the skin and very hungry. Hugh had ordered the cook and his assistants to provide a substantial meal, to make up for the meals they had missed. It meant that the huge Brodie stove in the galley was alight far later than usual and as Durrell went below he observed a number of the men hovering close to it to dry their wet clothing. Generally Durrell would have sent them about their business but tonight he looked casually in the other direction and made his way to the sick bay.

There were four injured men, all in the main area of the sick bay. Able Seaman Jennings had broken his wrist and had a huge contusion on his forehead. He seemed to be asleep as Durrell approached, his face pale under the bandage. Two other men were awake, one with his arm strapped firmly across his body and the other with bandages about his abdomen and chest. The fourth man lay on his bunk with Dr Cavendish binding up what looked like a broken leg. Durrell waited for him to finish before going forward.

The patient was just a boy, his face white, and he was shivering violently, despite being wrapped in blankets. Durrell spoke a few words although he was not sure how much young Madsen absorbed. He was in shock and in pain and Durrell hoped Cavendish would give him something to make him sleep.

"How are they doing, Doctor?" Durrell asked quietly, moving with Cavendish away from the bunks.

"All right, I think. Jennings' wrist is cracked but I think his head injury is worse, he hit it on the corner of the grating. Dobbins fell down the ladder on his way to the pumps, he's broken his collar bone. Caine is a bit of a mess, he ended up under a splintered barrel below decks, but the wounds are superficial, he'll recover. Madsen you know, came down from the rigging earlier. Badly broken leg, that'll take a while to mend, poor little bastard."

Durrell looked around. "There were two of them. They came down in that first squall. Where is the other man, Doctor? He's one of the new men – Eliot, I think his name is."

Cavendish shook his head. "I'm sorry, Lieutenant. He didn't make it. Cracked his head on the rail and died before he got to sick bay."

"Oh no! Does the Captain know?"

"Yes, he was down here earlier speaking to the men. He's in his cabin, I think." Cavendish surveyed Durrell. "You should change your clothing, Lieutenant, and get warm. Can't have you getting ill again."

"I will do so shortly, Doctor, although I do not think a soaking in a storm is likely to bring on an attack of Walcheren fever. Take care of them and call me if I am needed, please."

As Durrell turned to go, he saw a trim figure bustling towards him, wrapped in a woollen shawl, and bearing a covered tankard. The woman bobbed a curtsy.

"Good evening, sir. I've just brought down a posset for young Joey. It will warm him up and help him sleep. Best thing for him now."

Durrell was inexplicably cheered. He had discovered that the Bosun's wife often had that effect on him. He remembered his younger self; rigid with disapproval at the custom of allowing warrant officers to bring their wives aboard. He had once spent fifteen minutes explaining to Hugh Kelly why the practice was against regulations. Durrell sometimes wondered why his Captain had not thrown him overboard during the early weeks of their acquaintance. He smiled at Janet Armstrong gratefully.

"The very best thing," he said. "I was going to speak to the surgeon about it, but I should have known you would think of it. Are you all right, Mrs Armstrong? That was a bad one."

"It was, sir, but not the worst I've known. I was down at the pumps for most of the night."

"That's exhausting work, ma'am."

"No worse for me than for the men. Mrs Manby joined me there, and her little girl brought drinks down for us all. How is the Captain, sir? He took it hard when young Eliot fell."

"He hates losing men, I've seen it before. I'm going to find him now."

"Aye, you'll know the way to comfort him. It's a good ship where a captain and his first lieutenant are as close as you are. My man is that pleased to have had this chance; he's never been happier."

Durrell watched for a moment as Janet Armstrong bent over Madsen, helping him to sit up, and wondered how many other boys had benefited from her practical good sense and infinite kindness during their time at sea. Recalled to his own particular responsibility, he went in search of his Captain.

He found Hugh Kelly in his great cabin. Hugh had installed a red velvet armchair in the corner of the room with a small chest beside it, which acted as a side table. He was seated with a glass of wine on the chest and at first Durrell thought he was asleep. A large tabby cat was draped elegantly across his lap, her head on his folded arm. She was snoring. Until he met Molly, the overweight and underworked ship's cat of the *Iris*, Durrell had never heard a cat snore. It was alarmingly noisy.

A second cat was stretched out along the back of the armchair behind Hugh's head. Orry was black and sleek and lean, and an expert hunter, keeping the rodents under control. Durrell had no idea where the cats had spent the long hours of the storm but strongly suspected it may have been under the covers of the Captain's bed.

Hugh opened his eyes and gave a weary smile. "I'm glad you've come. Brian is bringing supper in a while, will you stay?"

"Gladly, sir."

Durrell walked forward and scooped up Orry, settling him on his lap as he seated himself on one of the dining chairs. Orry grumbled a little then curled up philosophically under his stroking hand. Durrell had never realised the soothing properties of a cat until Hugh had pointed it out. The softness of Orry's fur under his hand was immediately comforting.

"We'll bury Eliot tomorrow," Hugh said.

"I'm so sorry, sir."

"So am I, Mr Durrell. But we survived and the ship is intact. Sometimes we just have to give thanks for what we have. Get yourself a glass of wine."

"I'm amazed the wine survived, sir. Or the glasses."

"They're packed around with sheep's wool. It was Roseen's idea. Not a single crack."

Durrell thought about it and began to laugh. "Manx sheep's wool?"

"From my own flock. Top up my glass, would you?"

Durrell got up, scooping up Orry. He set the cat down on another chair. Orry glared at him briefly then settled to sleep. Durrell brought the wine and poured for both of them.

"We'll make any emergency repairs tomorrow," Hugh said. "The Bosun tells me it's not that bad. Once we get into into Mahon, we can look at what's needed there."

They sat in silence for a while and Durrell appreciated the peace. Eventually he stirred.

"I was too slow," he said.

"I was asleep and I'm worried a man died because of it."

"Sir, that's not true."

"No, it's not. It was a bloody awful storm and none of us saw it coming. There are things we could have done but we didn't. It makes no sense to berate ourselves, fella. Let's learn from it and move on."

Durrell sipped his wine and thought of all the other captains he had served under since joining the navy as a boy. "I have to be the most fortunate first lieutenant in the Royal Navy," he said finally.

He knew that Hugh would catch his meaning. His Captain laughed and shifted Molly to a more comfortable position.

"I know what you mean, Alfred. We do all right together, don't we? Do me a favour and chase up that food, will you? I'm worried Brian has drunk his grog ration and dozed off in the galley."

***

Rear-Admiral Sir Richard Keats had returned to active duty in the previous July, hoisting his flag on the *Implacable*. He had been sent to command the squadron off Cadiz, with instructions to assist the defenders who were under siege by the French. Hugh met him in his dining cabin aboard the *Implacable* and was greeted warmly.

"It's very good to see you again, Captain. I understand you had an interesting voyage."

Hugh accepted a glass of wine. "It was fast and eventful. We've made emergency repairs, but I'll need to put into port for a week or so to ensure she's fully seaworthy. Whose idea was it to send me across Biscay in January, sir?"

"It was mine," Keats admitted cheerfully, waving him to a seat. "I'm very occupied here, as you might suppose, and I want a man to reinforce Captain Codrington. The French have taken Tortosa and we're not sure where they'll march next, but Tarragona is a strong probability. I've ordered Codrington and the *Blake* to take charge of a small squadron. I want you to join him."

Hugh studied the Admiral thoughtfully over the top of his wine glass, considering what had not been said. "As you say, it's a small squadron, and he already has the *Invincible* and the *Centaur*," he said finally. "Is it the extra firepower you're wanting, sir?"

"It may be useful if the town is under threat. They could close off Tarragona from the land quite easily with enough men, but we control the coast."

Hugh sipped the wine. He had served under Keats many times and smelled a rat. "And?"

Keats grinned. "And I want a cool head, in case it all goes badly wrong, Captain. Ned Codrington isn't particularly easy to work with, but you've proved good at it in the past."

"I don't find him difficult at all, sir. We're friends and Roseen is close to Jane. She and the boys stayed with us for a few days when they came back from Plymouth last year. What's your concern with Captain Codrington?"

"Captain Codrington is an intelligent man, Kelly, with a very good grasp of local politics. He's met most of the Spanish leaders and he gets on well with O'Donnell, but O'Donnell isn't a well man. He was injured in a recent attack on Palamós and has retired to Mahon to recover. In his place we have Campoverde. Codrington doesn't like him and doesn't think he's up to the job."

Hugh tried to imagine what Edward Codrington had actually said about Campoverde and grinned. "Well Ned isn't a military man, sir, but like you said, he's not stupid. He's probably right about him."

"That is hardly the point," Keats said sternly. "If Captain Codrington has a fault, it is his tendency to explode like a mortar shell when faced with any perceived incompetence. These people are our allies and we have to work with them. I need you to keep an eye on Codrington to ensure that he doesn't start a war with the Spanish alongside the one we're fighting with the French. And do it tactfully."

Hugh set down his glass. "Ned Codrington will know exactly why you've sent for me, sir. But it will be all right, he's senior to me and he knows I'm happy to serve under him. What happened at Palamós, I've not heard?"

"The Spanish General, O'Donnell led an attack, supported by the British under Fane and Doyle and it went very well. Unfortunately that encouraged them to return a month or so later with a landing party. Sailors and marines from the *Cambrian*, the *Kent* and the *Ajax* went after eight merchant ships carrying supplies for the French army at Barcelona. The ships were lying inside the Mole guarded by French troops, two 24-pounders, and a mortar in a battery on a hill. O'Donnell's men managed to sink six of the ships, but it went badly wrong on the withdrawal. We lost thirty-three men dead, around ninety wounded and about the same taken prisoner including Captain Fane. We've been trying to negotiate for his release, but the French aren't offering sensible terms."

"Oh bloody hell. I'm sorry, sir, I like Francis Fane. Who's in command of the *Cambrian* now?"

"Charles Bullen has moved over from the *Volontier*." Keats rose and went to his writing desk to collect several letters. "These are your orders. They say nothing about keeping Codrington on a leash for me. That does not need to be written down. There's also a letter there for Codrington. You should find him in Mallorca at present. He wrote that he intended to take on supplies at Mahon and make one or two small repairs."

"I'll join him there." Hugh studied the older man. He was not sure of Keats' exact age, probably around fifty, but he looked older and very tired. "How are you, sir?"

"Well enough, Captain."

"You turned down Malta because you didn't think you were well enough and now they have you shoring up the defences of Cadiz. I'm not sure that's going to aid your recovery."

"Probably not. But I am happier. I have discovered that idleness does not suit me, Captain. I suspect you are the same. I received a letter recently from Mr Hurt, by the way, singing your praises for the help you gave with the abolitionist society. Thank you for your contribution, it is very much appreciated, since I know you did it partly as a favour to me."

"In part, but not entirely, sir. It's a cause I genuinely believe in, the more so after hearing the stories of men who have personal experience of slavery."

"I am told that your friend Mr Thurlow has been very supportive."

"Ben Thurlow is his own man, sir, it was his choice. He's honest in his opinion that Parliament has no appetite to take on the West India interest at present, but I think he's right that all good causes must start somewhere. The campaign against the trade took many years and endless petitions to achieve its aim."

"I hope this does not take as long." Keats got up and Hugh rose as well. "You'll need to sail early tomorrow to catch the tide. Will you dine with me this afternoon?"

"Yes, thank you, sir."

Hugh had reached the door of the cabin when Keats said:

"Bring him."

Hugh turned, his eyebrows raised, and Keats laughed. "Your young firebrand. Bring him along. He may not be in favour at the Admiralty, but a man who has the integrity to call Sir Home Popham a liar in open court is definitely owed a dinner or two."

Hugh grinned. "Thank you, Sir Richard. He'll be delighted."

***

John Collingwood died during the night, slipping away so silently that the nurse who was dozing in the chair beside his bed did not notice until heavy rainfall woke her at dawn, and she realised that the rattling breath had ceased. After checking his pulse she made her way along the corridor to wake his daughter.

Faith stood beside her father's bed looking down at him. She was shocked by her lack of feeling and hoped the nurse would mistake her silence for grief, since she could not manage to cry. She had tried hard, these past weeks, not to long for this moment but she had not always succeeded. Now that he was gone all she could feel was relief and a sense of emptiness.

"Miss Faith, I'm sorry."

Faith turned to find that Abisola stood in the doorway. Unexpectedly the tears came and Abisola came forward and put her arms about her.

"It is done," she said simply. "Come back to your room and I will send a message to Mr Glinde. He will know what to do next."

Faith obeyed. She sat in silence in her room while Abisola penned a note to Glinde. Faith watched her and thought affectionately how quickly Abisola had adapted to her new role. She was passionately grateful for her companionship during these last weeks of her father's life. It was a relief to be able to talk to somebody who knew the truth about how Faith felt.

Faith received her man of business in the drawing room. She had no idea why she felt the need for formality, but it felt right. She observed, as Glinde made his bow, that he had taken time to don black gloves and a black armband.

"My sincere condolences, Miss Collingwood."

"Thank you. At least he is at peace now."

"I have spoken to my wife, ma'am, and to Miss Caddick. She has no wish to interfere but was wondering if you would like her to stay with you for a short time, just until after the funeral. I realise you are determined to maintain your independence, but there are formalities of which you may have little experience."

"Thank you," Faith said quickly. "I should be very grateful for Miss Caddick's assistance."

"I will speak to her, then. She can help with matters of mourning custom." Glinde swept a look over Faith's simple white muslin gown. "And with mourning clothes, of course."

Faith was aware that Glinde was deliberately not looking at Abisola, who had seated herself at a discreet distance with her sewing. Faith felt no need for a chaperone with Glinde, but she had begun to ask Abisola to be present during their meetings purely to make a point. Glinde had been appalled at Faith's choice of companion and had done his best to override her decision. Faith did not know if it was Abisola's youth or the fact that she was African that offended him and did not particularly care. She had eventually forbidden him to speak further of the matter and had warned him that she expected him to treat her new companion with courtesy.

"I have asked Abisola to arrange for Madame Colette to come to the house. I believe it is quite usual in a case of bereavement. As for the rest, I know Miss Caddick will advise me well. Once the funeral is over, I imagine we will have to look to matters of business."

"There is no hurry for that, ma'am. The business has been running smoothly during your father's illness and I will ensure that it continues to do so."

Mr John Collingwood was laid to rest in the churchyard at St Olave's. The funeral was well attended, mainly by City colleagues of the deceased, and the vicar spoke of Mr Collingwood's standing in the community, his excellent business reputation and the loss that must surely be felt by his orphaned daughter.

Faith did not attend. It was not unusual for ladies to decline to put their grief on show publicly and Miss Caddick assured her that nobody would think the worse of her. Faith was more concerned at allowing her lack of grief to show, so she accepted the excuse with relief and remained at home with Abisola, allowing Mr Glinde to organise the funeral as he wished. A hatchment was hung above the front door, the curtains remained closed, and the door knocker was swathed in black ribbon.

Faith remained within doors. She would be unable, for the early part of her mourning, to attend any social activities other than church and Miss Caddick advised against continuing her involvement with the abolitionist society for the time being.

"It is not exactly forbidden, my dear, since it could be counted as a church activity, but I am afraid that as your father's prior involvement with the West India connection is well known, it might be seen as disrespectful, at least during your mourning period."

"By whom?" Faith asked, somewhat mutinously.

"By society. It is only for a short time, but it would not be wise to give rise to any gossip which might affect your reputation. At some point in the future you will wish to take your place in society, and Mrs Glinde and I are agreed that if a patroness can be found, you might even be presented at court. You are a very pretty girl, Faith, with an excellent fortune, and you could do very well. Even a title."

"I am not sure that I want that," Faith said. "When I visited Walcheren with my father, I became acquainted with several titled gentlemen and their behaviour convinced me that a man may be born a gentleman but still have no idea how to act like one. I am not looking for an early marriage, ma'am."

Miss Caddick shook her head. "Child, what else are you going to do? You need somebody to take care of you; to advise you and to guide you. To run your father's business. I understand that your early experiences have left you with a disgust of fortune hunters, but you should not turn your face entirely against marriage."

"I'm not ready to think about it yet, ma'am. Will you advise me, please, what I am permitted to do and for how long I am so restricted?"

Miss Caddick looked a little discomfited but recovered immediately. "You may attend church, of course, and you may go out for walks, although I do not think you should attend any of the popular promenades during the fashionable hour."

"I never do so. What about my lessons?"

"Well I cannot see that anybody could reasonably object to those. In fact unless the servants gossip, they cannot possibly know what you are doing in your own house. You may attend the lending library and do any necessary shopping, of course. And you may accept calls. In fact, I am afraid you will be expected to accept calls of condolence and there may well be a large number of them."

Faith discovered that she was right. With the funeral over, it seemed to her that the door knocker was never silent. Neighbours, business associates of her father's and acquaintances from both church and the Society beat a path to her doorway. They paid fulsome compliments to her father, even though some of them had barely known him. They made vague offers of help although Faith had no idea what services they hoped to provide for her. They offered sympathy and condolences that she did not need, and some gave advice that she had not asked for.

"You will be going home to Surrey for a while, I imagine," Mrs Stanton said. "Now that your poor Papa is gone, there can be nothing to keep you in London. And I suppose your guardian will see to it that a proper chaperone is hired."

"Residing quietly here in London is undoubtedly the best thing," Lady Starling pronounced. "You will be in familiar surroundings with your friends about you. I do not approve of making too much of the mourning period. I know you have business advisors, but if you need advice on any personal matter, you should call on me. Or on my son, of course, if it is a matter where a gentleman is best suited to assist. I know he will be very happy to do so."

"Distraction, that is the thing," Mrs Thomas gushed. "While it cannot be proper for you to go out into society, you should not mope at home, dear Miss Collingwood. We hope to see you often in our home for some quiet evenings with music or games. No other guests, just one or two particular friends who understand, and of course dear Frederick, who will be delighted to dedicate himself to your entertainment."

"I shall go mad if this carries on," Faith said at the end of the third week. "I thought I was supposed to go into seclusion during this period and instead I find myself beset – no, persecuted – with callers. Especially callers with unmarried gentlemen in tow. I am not at home today, Abisola. In fact I may decide never to be at home again. Is this what it is going to be like from now on?"

Abisola laughed. "I will tell Hudson," she said. "All the same, Miss Faith, you cannot hide behind closed drapes forever. Perhaps you should think of going into the country."

"Perhaps I should." Faith set down her tea cup. "I've never really liked Barton Hall, our estate in Surrey. Father bought it furnished a few years ago because he thought a gentleman should have a country residence, but it makes me feel as though I am living in somebody else's house. Really, if it were in better condition, I preferred Wickham House, the place I went to in Norfolk."

"Does Wickham House belong to you?"

Faith stared at her. "I suppose it does. My father took possession of it in return for a debt. I think he intended to sell it, but it needs a great deal of work doing to it and he did not wish to spend the money. Abisola, do you think I could do so?"

"It's not my place to say, Miss Faith, but from what you've told me, you're wealthy enough to employ builders and workmen. You might need help doing it, though."

"I would have help," Faith said. She could feel her heart lifting at the thought. "Abel knows everybody. He'd know who would be best to employ and what to pay them. We could do this together, Abisola. We could decide on colours and furnishings and…"

Faith paused, remembering her first months in Norfolk. "It won't be very comfortable for a while," she said apologetically. "I got used to the discomfort."

Abisola gave a peal of laughter. "Where do you think I grew up, Miss Faith? I can cope with discomfort, and it would certainly keep you busy through your mourning period."

Faith had a sudden memory of Walcheren and the moment she had decided to throw propriety to the winds and walk barefoot on a beach with a young man she hardly knew. Through all the consequences, she had never regretted it for a moment. She had the same feeling of recklessness now.

"We're going to do it," she said. "I need to send a note to Mr Glinde."

Chapter Eight

The weather improved through the spring months which made marching and bivouacking less unpleasant, although still arduous. There had been little respite for General Suchet's army of Aragon through winter quarters this year. It was rumoured amongst his officers that Bonaparte had promised Suchet a marshal's baton should he successfully capture Tarragona and he was an ambitious man.

Supplies were a problem in areas already ravaged by years of war. The local farmers and peasants were hard put to feed themselves, let alone provide for an army. Suchet had the reputation of a commander who paid attention to logistics as well as tactics and he took time to build up his stores of food ahead of his march on Tarragona.

The 30th légère spent tedious weeks chasing partisans through the mountains around Valencia. They endured long hours of hard marching, chasing an enemy with the ability to vanish like smoke into the countryside. As Bonnet's men fought a series of pointless skirmishes, Bonaparte wrote endless letters regarding the reorganisation of the army and the importance of gaining possession of Tarragona.

It was April before General Suchet was ready to move on Tarragona and by then, Bonnet was heartily sick of the routine of march and counter-march after the elusive partisan bands. It was a relief to receive orders to join the main army at Zaragoza ready for the advance on the city.

By the time the 30th légère approached the manufacturing city of Reus, ten miles from Tarragona, Bonnet's mood had worsened. The weather was becoming warmer but it still rained a lot, particularly at night, and early marches involved squelching through mud along rutted roads. By midday, Bonnet could see steam rising from the men's uniforms as they dried in the sun and there were plagues of biting insects. To make it worse, Bonnet's feet hurt. He had acquired new boots from the stores in Zaragoza. It always took a long time to wear in new footwear, but these were worse than most. They had rubbed huge blisters on both heels and toes, which bled when Bonnet removed his stockings and they hurt even when he was on horseback. It made him bad-tempered. He was short with his fellow officers and irritable with the men.

There was a short stay in Reus as General Suchet awaited news of his siege train. Reus was a challenge for discipline because of the preponderance of wine shops. The city had grown prosperous through its textile and liquor trade and after three days Bonnet was tired of continually having to haul his men out of wine cellars and taverns, where they were demanding liquor without payment. It was a relief when Colonel Lacasse, who was billeted in the town, invited his company captains to dine with him and shared what he knew of Suchet's plans.

"Headquarters and supply depots will be established here in Reus and the men will carry rations when we march on to Tarragona," he said, indicating for his servant to refill the wine glasses. "Be sure that they do, gentlemen, since the land is barren and we cannot rely on finding food locally."

"How far is it to Tarragona, sir?" Captain Faure enquired through a mouthful of pigeon pie.

"Less than ten miles. We receive orders tomorrow. Are the men ready?"

"Eager for glory, Colonel."

"Ready to die for their Emperor, Colonel."

Lacasse looked at Bonnet. "Captain Bonnet?"

"Ready to loot the wine cellars of Tarragona, sir," Bonnet said, since he knew it was expected of him. His companions laughed and Bonnet gave a dour grin and raised his glass to them. He was in fact, not looking forward to Tarragona. A protracted siege with limited rations made it hard to hold discipline, and Bonnet knew that once the French army was inside the town, the Spanish civilians would suffer along with the garrison. He had been through a number of similar actions and he disliked them.

Marching out of Reus, the 30th bivouacked on the edge of a forested area six miles from Tarragona and settled down to await further orders. On the third night, Bonnet had barely dozed off when he was jerked into wakefulness by an unexpected noise. He lay still, wondering what the hell it was, until it came again: a woman's scream cutting through the evening air.

Bonnet lay silent for a moment, trying to work out where it was coming from and wondering if it would stop if he closed his eyes and pretended to be deaf. He listened, hoping to hear the sound of one of the other officers on his way to investigate, but instead he heard the voice of one of his men.

"What the hell was that?"

"Delain and Vannier are out on a spree. Sounds like they found a woman, lucky bastards."

"If she keeps screaming like that, Vannier will shut her up with his fists, he's got no patience."

Bonnet groaned, swore, and hauled himself out of his bedroll, reaching for his hated boots. Just putting them on was painful and did not improve Bonnet's temper as he stomped in the general direction of the noise, limping.

The screaming stopped suddenly as if cut off and Bonnet, who knew what he was probably hearing, broke into a run. There was a cottage, little more than a hovel, surrounded by a low stone wall. A neat garden had been planted to grow vegetables, but it was ruined now, the beds torn apart and wooden supports trampled and broken. The front door of the cottage stood open, its simple latch bent out of shape. Bonnet drew his sword and walked in, making as much noise as he could.

The cottage consisted of one large room with a ladder leading up to a sleeping loft. It smelled of wood smoke, some kind of stew and the pungent odour of unwashed human bodies which Bonnet attributed to the three blue-coated infantrymen making themselves at home. One had found a wine bottle and was seated astride a wooden bench drinking from it. A second was rummaging through a wooden pantry built into the wall muttering complaints about the lack of food. The third was administering a vicious kick to a prone figure on the floor. On the other side of the table a woman was struggling to her feet, her lip bleeding from a recent blow and the front of her shabby gown torn.

All turned to look as Bonnet entered. Bonnet looked back, wishing heartily that he had stuck his fingers in his ears and stayed where he was. If it had not been for the presence of the woman, he might have been tempted to remove himself and allow the men to get on with looting whatever meagre fare they could find, but Bonnet had been raised by his hard-handed Parisian mother to respect women and no matter how tired he was and how much his feet hurt, the lesson had stuck. He studied the thin faced Catalan peasant and decided that she had not been raped yet, probably due to the intervention of the man on the floor, but that she was definitely about to be. He sighed.

"If anybody had asked me which fat-arsed, evil-smelling lumps of pig turd I'd find out of camp and brutalising the locals I'd have put you three top of my list," he said. "Vannier, put that bottle down and get to your feet. Delain, get your head out of that cupboard, there's nothing in it. Fortin, if you kick him again you'll get the same from me. Line up, the lot of you."

They scrambled into a reluctant line, Vannier swaying slightly. Bonnet eyed them with distaste. "Mother of God, you stink. Where did you spend last night, the pig sty?"

"No, Captain, in the forest. There are pigs there though, the third company caught one and roasted it. They also caught an old man collecting wood and he told us of this place, said they had chickens and a goat." Delain indicated the man on the floor. "He would not tell us where."

"Look around you, Delain, and use your brain if you can find it. They've nothing here, the old man lied so you'd let him go. These lands have been crossed by our army and the Spanish for half a year, there's nothing left. Look at them, they're starving. They've nothing you want."

"She has," Fortin said with a leer.

"She's probably riddled with the pox, Fortin. You're bloody lucky I turned up or you'd be itching and burning for months. I told you, the army's been through here before, she'll have picked it up from a Gascon hussar. Now piss off out of here and get back to the lines. If I catch you doing this again I'll fucking cut your bollocks off." Bonnet surveyed them then shrugged. "You can take the bottle for your trouble. When you get up there, send Pierre down with my kit."

"You are staying here, sir?"

"I am. Inform Lieutenant Duclos. They might not have much I want, but they've a dry bed. Though if it turns out you've killed him, I'm getting you back down here to dig the grave, Fortin. Now fuck off."

Bonnet watched them go, cheerfully passing the bottle between them until the darkness swallowed them up. He turned back into the cottage and closed the door behind him, bending the metal latch back into place. The young woman was on her knees beside the man, running her hands over him to check for injuries. The man groaned.

"I see he lives," Bonnet said.

The woman jumped, looking up quickly, then got to her feet. She seemed to remember her torn gown and held it closed, staring at Bonnet from wide brown eyes. Bonnet looked back thoughtfully.

"Your husband?" he asked in Spanish.

"My father."

"Is he badly hurt?"

"I do not know. They kicked him."

Bonnet went to investigate. There was a good deal of blood from a cut over the man's ear, but Bonnet knew that head wounds tended to bleed alarmingly. The man's eyes were open now, the image of his daughter's wide gaze. He flinched as Bonnet bent over him. Bonnet held up his hands in mock surrender.

"I'm not going to hurt you. Let's get you up and see the damage."

He hoisted the older man to his feet, seated him on the bench and prodded him. Clearly there would be bruising and possibly a broken rib or two but Bonnet decided that it was unlikely to be fatal. He looked over at the woman.

"Is there wine?"

"They took it."

Bonnet assessed her thoughtfully. He judged her to be somewhere in her twenties, dark haired and underfed with the wariness of a wild animal. Bonnet did not blame her, but his interrupted slumber and sore feet did not make him feel particularly gentlemanly so he got straight to the point.

"We're here for a few days, then marching on to Tarragona. I'm Captain Gabriel Bonnet of the 30th légère. If you can feed me and give me a bed, I'll billet here until we march; my servant is bringing up my kit and my horses. Unlike my men, I don't insist you share the bed with me."

She flushed a deep red and the colour gave unexpected life to her pale face. "How do I know you will keep your word?"

Bonnet grinned, which was unkind of him, since he knew that the sabre cut he had received down the left half of his face at Wagram gave his smile a look of unintentional menace. "Well, I imagine you are going to find out at bed time," he said.

She flinched and turned away and Bonnet thought about apologising, then decided that it would not help. Over almost twenty years' service he had seen what the French army had done throughout Europe and he did not think that this skinny Spanish peasant girl would be interested in his apology. The best he could do for her was not to rape her and she was safe from that.

It was half an hour before his servant arrived with his two horses and baggage mule. Bonnet heard him swearing from inside the house. He had spent the time watching the girl tend her father's injuries, wondering if she was going to continue with her charade and deprive the old man of his supper rather than produce the food for the French to steal. Her performance kept him entertained. He got up at the sound of Pierre's arrival and went to help him with the animals. The cottage had a small byre attached to one end, with hay and a wooden trough. Bonnet moved his animals in without compunction, then left Pierre to feed and water them and find a space to sleep while he carried his kit through into the little cottage.

He had already explored the upper loft and decided that the fleas would be at their worst up there. Instead, he unpacked his bedroll and spare blanket, rolled up his army great coat as a pillow and settled it before the fire, then went outside in search of more wood. There was plenty on the forest floor and he dumped his pile on the stone hearth and bent to build up the fire again.

"I will do that."

Bonnet shrugged and moved away to allow her to work. Instead he went to his pack and rummaged for his rations. There were four hard tack biscuits, some cheese and a knob of salty bacon. Bonnet had not drawn rations for the march yet, so he spread his small feast out on the table, took out his knife and divided the cheese and bacon into three. He took his share along with two biscuits then pushed the rest towards the girl, gesturing at her father, and began to eat.

Neither of the Spaniards moved for a long time. Bonnet ate placidly, enjoying her struggle. Eventually, she came forward and took the food, placing it in front of her father. Bonnet looked up.

"No," he said firmly. "You will eat your share or I'll take it back."

"He is hurt."

"That does not mean he needs extra food. Eat."

After a moment, she sat down. Bonnet watched her out of the corner of his eye. She was clearly ravenous. The old man ate with good appetite, shooting resentful glances at his daughter which made Bonnet wonder how often she went without food for her father's sake.

When she had finished eating, she got up, looking at her father as if for permission. The old man merely grunted but she seemed to take it as consent and disappeared through the door. She was gone for some minutes. Bonnet studied the old man and then sighed and went for his tobacco. He begrudged wasting a perfectly good cigarillo but it occurred to him that the man had just been beaten to the ground apparently in defence of his daughter by Bonnet's own men, so perhaps he owed him a scratch meal and a smoke.

The old man visibly brightened at the first puff and by the time the girl returned the air in the room was rich with tobacco smoke. Bonnet stared in surprise at the sight of the bottle in her hand. She went to a shelf for pottery cups, setting them on the table. As she poured the wine, Bonnet said:

"Where the hell were you hiding that? Not in the garden, I could see they'd already had a good dig around out there."

She did not reply, merely handed him the cup. Bonnet sipped cautiously and then drank again.

"You're right, Señorita. Best not tell me, I might not be able to resist the temptation before we march. You make it yourself?"

"Yes. We farm a little patch near the village. Some vines, some fruit trees. We sell to the Spanish troops."

"Not the French?"

"The French do not buy, Señor. They take."

Bonnet said nothing because he knew that it was true. There were supposedly rules about looting the local population, but when supplies ran low the Emperor's troops were encouraged to live off the land. Bonnet, who had never bothered to read the regulations, thought it a contradiction designed to be exploited and he had watched his men exploit it through Austria and Prussia then into Spain. Without clear guidelines, most officers ignored their troops' depredations unless they affected discipline. Bonnet wondered if Bonaparte's occupation of Spain would have been easier if the Spanish people had less cause to hate his army. He drank more of the wine.

"Well if you've some to sell, Señorita, I've money to pay before I leave. I can see the uses of a bottle of that on a cold night in the siege lines."

She nodded, drinking from her own cup. They sat in silence which felt more comfortable now, until the girl noticed that her father was dozing over his wine cup. She woke him gently and helped him to climb the ladder into the loft. By the time she returned he was already snoring audibly. Bonnet reluctantly stoppered the bottle.

"Finish it," the girl said. She went to the fire and added the last of the wood. Bonnet hesitated then unstoppered the bottle and poured into two cups.

"Only if you will drink it with me."

She turned and studied him for a moment, then returned to her seat opposite him. Bonnet noticed that she had managed an emergency repair to her torn gown, tying it together with rough cord and draping a shabby woollen shawl about it. He presumed it was her only one.

"Can you mend that?"

She touched the gown, flushing slightly. "Yes."

"I'm sorry about them. Your father was brave to defend you."

"My father was a soldier all his life. Sometimes he forgets he is now old."

Bonnet gave a faint smile. "Fighting with us or against us?"

"Mostly with you," the woman said. "But these days he is angry at what your army has done to Spain."

"Your mother?"

"She died when we were in Tenerife, winter fever. My two brothers also. We used to travel with the army, but my father was wounded and could no longer fight. We came here to be with my uncle, but he died last winter. I wish we had stayed, it was better there. Here, we barely survive. Always waiting for the next army to take what we have."

Bonnet sipped the wine. "Is that why I have this?" he asked, lifting the cup. "Protection?"

"They will not break in with an officer here," she admitted. "They may come back after you have gone, of course."

"If they do, they'll be deserting, and they'll be sorry. But keep your stores hidden, just in case."

"We always do. Usually, I hide as well. They surprised me."

Bonnet had wondered. "Why are you not wed?" he asked abruptly.

"Who should I wed? There are no men in the village, only women and children and the infirm. Sometimes the Spanish forces come by. They try to take me to bed and tell me they will take care of me, but I say no. All they will do is leave me with an extra mouth to feed, and I have seen children starve to death. I do not wish to watch that happen to my own child."

"How old are you?"

"I am twenty-five. How old are you, Captain?"

Bonnet smiled at her impudence. "Thirty-eight. What's your name, I didn't ask."

"Bianca. My father is Diego Ramos. You speak Spanish very well, where did you learn?"

"As a young man I fought against the Spanish in the Pyrenees. There was a very pretty Spanish girl called Ava. She taught me my Spanish and I taught her never to trust the promises of a soldier. The Spanish has proved very useful through many campaigns. I hope my lesson was as useful to her."

"May I trust your promise?"

"Which one?"

"That you will not harm me."

Bonnet thought about it. "I am not sure I made you any such promise, Bianca. But don't be alarmed. Twenty years ago I would say anything to talk my way into a girl's bed. These days, I seldom have the time or the energy. You should sleep."

She got up, collecting empty cups and tidying the table. Bonnet shifted on the bench and bent to remove his boots, wincing with the effort. To his astonishment she dropped to her knees before him and took over the task, setting the boots before the banked fire to dry out. For a moment she stared at his feet then made a small sound of disgust.

"Take off the stockings."

Bonnet stared at her in astonishment. "Why?"

"They are wet and there is blood on them."

"Blisters. The boots are new."

"Wet, dirty and bloody. Your feet will rot away."

"Nonsense."

"It is not nonsense, how many times have you seen it? With your years on campaign, you should know this."

Despite himself, Bonnet grinned. "My servant generally acts as my mother on campaign. When he is sober."

"You are old enough to take care of yourself. Give me those stockings."

Bonnet obeyed then padded over to his bedroll.

"Here. You will be cold in the night."

Bonnet stared in surprise at the woollen stockings she held out. They looked hand knitted. "Señorita, you do not need to..."

"It is a loan, not a gift. Before you sleep, give me your laundry, I will wash it early and it will dry quickly in the sun. And I will mend what needs mending."

"Thank you, Señorita."

"Tomorrow, we will return your kindness and share our meal with you."

Bonnet hastily concealed a grin. "That is good of you."

"You have given us protection, Captain. I pay my debts."

Bonnet was too tired to argue so he sat to pull on the rough wool then removed his blue coat and hung it over the chair. As he blew out the final candle and settled to sleep he could hear her moving about for a short time in the loft above. The wine and the warmth and the pleasure of sleeping within walls made him drowsy, and he drifted into sleep laughing silently at how much he enjoyed even the fleeting sense of being fussed over by a capable and not unattractive woman.

***

During the first night that the French officer was billeted in the cottage, Bianca Ramos slept little. She was accustomed to the noise of her father's snores on the other side of the loft space, but they were nothing compared to the resonant sounds floating up from the fireside below. The snores were keeping her awake but she did not mind. Captain Bonnet was clearly sleeping very soundly, which reassured her that he was unlikely to pose any threat to her.

Bianca thought that Bonnet had probably been sincere in his promise not to harm her, but her narrow escape earlier in the evening had unsettled her. Raised in an army camp, she had always known the risks of being an unprotected woman when troops marched through and she was cynically aware that it did not necessarily matter which side they were on.

After the initial shock of Bonnet's casual appropriation of her home, Bianca decided she felt much safer with him around. His regiment remained camped on the edge of the village awaiting orders and she suspected that if Bonnet had not moved in, the three would-be rapists might well have come back.

Bianca had little to give in return for his protection, but she was determined to do what she could. He was out early the following morning, presumably to check on his men. He had not followed her instructions about his laundry, so she went through his baggage herself and carried the worn garments down to the stream to wash, along with her own linen and her father's spare shirt.

It was a fine day with a strong breeze. She draped the wet garments over the makeshift washing line which hung between two fruit trees in their garden, then went inside to mend her torn gown and shift. The fabric was so thin and worn it was not surprising it had ripped so easily. Bianca, who had no prospect of a replacement, seethed silently over her work, stabbing the needle in so fiercely that she managed to add a spot of blood to the other stains on the faded wool.

Her mending done, she swept and tidied the cottage, collected wood for the open fire, then went in search of supplies while her father, his face battered and a bandage around his injured head, dozed in a wooden armchair in a patch of sun. Bianca paused to study him as she passed. Her father had never been a big man, but during this past year since the death of his brother he seemed to be shrinking daily. He was no longer able to help her much with the daily tasks of tending their small patch of land or taking care of their animals. She was afraid that it would take him a while to get over the assault, not just physically but emotionally. His inability to protect her had upset him and she had heard him muttering during the night, restless in sleep. He had barely spoken since, although when she had mentioned that Bonnet was likely to remain with them for a few days he had looked up.

"Are you all right, child? I mean, he did not…?"

"No, father." Bianca shook her head firmly. "And he won't. This one isn't looking for a woman and even if he was, I'm not likely to tempt him. But if he's here, he'll keep the others away so I've said yes."

"Good. That's good. Can we feed him?"

"We'll manage something."

It seemed that several houses in the village had been requisitioned for the use of the French officers and a supply depot had been set up in the squat little church. Men in blue coats hung around with nothing to do but wait for orders, smoke cigarillos and ogle the local women. There were very few women about. Bianca presumed they were hiding in the cottages and quickly understood why. As she walked along the main street towards the patchwork of planted fields, there was a barrage of shouts and whistles from the lounging men. She spoke no French and was glad she could not understand their words but the gestures were expressive enough. She pulled her worn shawl up over her head and walked more quickly, her heart pounding.

As she approached the smallholding, Bianca's steps slowed in dismay. There were soldiers here too but they were more interested in looting than women. Trees were being systematically stripped of their fruit and two men had acquired spades from somewhere and were digging up garlic, carrots and turnips. Around the outside some of the villagers stood watching in helpless fury. She began to run, fear forgotten in her anger. The patch farmed by her and her father was an open strip of earth on the southern side of the field.

They did not grow many vegetables here, preferring to plant them in the sunny walled area outside the cottage, but there were vines and chestnut trees and a rickety wooden frame for beans and peas. The frame had already been stripped of everything ripe and not by the French. When news had arrived that Suchet's men were in the area, Bianca and her father had come down with two sacks and picked everything that could be eaten. They had done the same with their small garden and the bags of vegetables were carefully hidden. There were chestnuts though, and the almond trees were beginning to bear fruit although it was not nearly ready to eat. As she watched a soldier bit into one, then pulled a face and spat it out.

Bianca came to a stop at the edge of the field. Not all the villagers had thought to hide their stores of food. Señora Molina, who lived on the far side of the village was crying, her arms about her two children. She had been widowed more than a year ago and struggled to eke a living from her small plot. Close by, the elderly Senor Tevez held his sobbing wife in his arms. He was screaming insults at the Frenchmen over her head and one of them clearly understood too much Spanish because he broke off from his systematic looting to strike the old man with the butt of his musket. Tevez fell to the ground, blood streaming from his head, and his wife dropped beside him moaning his name, begging him to wake up.

Bianca ran to help her but before she could kneel, a hand grasped her arm. She whirled, pulling away and found herself looking up into the grim, scarred face of Captain Bonnet.

"Stop," he ordered firmly. "There's nothing you can do to stop them and it's going to turn nasty in a minute. Get these people back up to the village. I'll get a couple of my men to carry the old man. Which is your patch?"

"That one."

Bonnet turned and surveyed the field then raised his voice. "Chauvin, Descampes, get your boots off that field. Anything you find in that patch is mine."

"There is nothing left, sir, apart from the chestnuts. These almonds are bad."

"They're not ripe, you bloody imbecile. Leave them alone or you'll have bellyache for days. You can pick the chestnuts and bring them up to me and I'll give you some in payment. Pierre will show you the way. As for the rest of you, take what's edible but for fuck's sake don't destroy the rest. Most of this countryside has been stripped bare by us and the Spanish partisans. We might need to come back this way and they can't feed us if they've starved to death. Use your wits, if you have any."

Bonnet turned back to Bianca again. "Get them to go back to their houses, Señorita. It's for the best."

She nodded grudgingly and went to kneel beside Senor Tevez, who was trying to sit up groggily. He was able to stand with help and she helped the old couple back to their one roomed cottage. The other villagers followed slowly.

There was nothing more to be done. Walking back to her cottage, she felt sick at the thought of the coming months, frantically trying to repair the damage done by the French and coaxing another crop from the trampled fields and gardens, with winter looming ahead. The village was small and poor by any standards and none of the villagers had resources to spare. The French had rounded up any livestock they could find and butchered them for the evening meal. Bianca thought of her goat and chickens and the two pigs belonging to Señora Molina which were hidden with them and wondered dismally if they had been discovered yet. She could not believe they would not be.

When she arrived back at the cottage there was no sign of Captain Bonnet, although a bag of chestnuts stood in the middle of the table. Her father was outside in the little walled garden hoeing the churned up earth back into neat rows. There was nothing growing there as they had harvested the turnips early. She had a precious stock of seeds ready for planting but she had no intention of doing anything with them until the French had marched out.

"Where is he?" Bianca asked. "The Frenchman."

Her father straightened, leaning on the hoe. Even this small exertion seemed to exhaust him but she was glad to see him making the effort. Sometimes she worried that he had given up on life and would be happy just to doze in the sun until he did not wake up again. He wiped sweat from his face with one grubby sleeve and pointed towards the forest.

"He went that way."

"Was he alone?"

"Yes."

Bianca picked up her skirts and began to run. She knew it was illogical, because if Bonnet was determined to find her hiding place, no speed on her part would stop him. It was difficult to run in the woods, especially in bare feet, with fallen branches and logs concealed in the thick undergrowth to trip her. She stopped to catch her breath and then forced herself to slow down. It would be ridiculous to break an ankle trying to prevent the inevitable.

She saw him suddenly, making his way between the trees towards her in a leisurely fashion. He was carrying his hat and gave the impression of a man enjoying a pleasant stroll. Bianca stopped again, watching his approach. He was a big man, a little overweight and she thought his face must have been pleasant before the scar gave it such a menacing aspect.

Bonnet saw her and changed course a little to meet her. As he drew closer, she realised that he was carrying the hat a little too carefully and her stomach lurched in understanding. She said nothing, merely waited.

Bonnet reached her and held out the hat for her perusal. It was full of eggs. "A very good harvest," he said genially, in Spanish. "But I don't suppose you came out to collect them last night, did you?"

"No," Bianca said flatly.

"Can you cook omelettes?"

"Yes, very well. With wild herbs and garlic. And there is some cheese."

"Goats cheese, I imagine?"

"Yes."

"You make it yourself?"

"Yes. Also I help Señora Vasquez make butter."

"Is there a bread oven in the village?"

"Just one, in the big house. I think your Colonel stays there."

"Greedy bastard, I don't see him sharing much. That's all right, they've set up a supply depot in the church. I should be able to get some bread, or at least biscuit. I'll see what else I can scrounge. Colonel Lacasse says we'll be here five or six days."

"My people will have nothing left by then."

"The men have been told to collect their rations. It will slow down the looting though it won't stop it. I'm not going to set a guard on your secret farm because I don't trust any of them. That includes Pierre by the way, so we'll tell him I got these from the village."

She stared at him with dawning hope. "You will not tell the others?"

"No. I told you, Bianca: I'm a very simple man. I want food and drink and a dry bed. The laundry was extra and you didn't need to do it. I may buy these woollen stockings off you though, they're the most comfortable thing I've had on my feet for months."

"If you leave us our livestock, you may have them as a gift. I will cook and do your mending. And we could kill one of the chickens. Captain, thank you."

He smiled, which did not improve his scarred face at all, but she unexpectedly saw kindness in his eyes.

"I'll do my best, though I can't promise. But if I make it obvious I've searched the forest and found nothing, I doubt they'll look again. All the same, if they do, they'll take everything. You've sacks of vegetables up there. Did you dig them up when you knew we were approaching?"

"Yes. The French have been this way before."

"Clever girl. But if they find your hoard, you'll have nothing left. I suggest we bring everything but the livestock back to the cottage and hide it in the sleeping loft. Nobody will search there, they'll assume I've found whatever there is to steal. That way, if they discover the beasts at least you'll be left with something."

"I will do so now."

"Do it before Pierre gets back. I don't trust him not to sell the information to the troops."

Bianca gave him a puzzled look. "You do not trust your own servant?"

"Not as far as I can kick him."

"You should find yourself a better servant, Captain."

"I keep telling myself that, but I'm too idle. I'm going to find him and give him an errand that will keep him well out of the way for a bit. After that, I'll give you a hand. What the hell was that building by the way?"

"It was an old church. I think there may have been a convent or monastery but it fell into disrepair many years ago. They built the little church in the village and nobody ever goes out there now. My uncle used to use it when he was still alive, for hunting. He would hide in the walls and trap rabbits and hares and sometimes birds."

"That ivy is an effective screen, I practically fell over the place before I realised it was there. You might be lucky and get away with it. It depends on who else in the village knows you use it and how hard the soldiers lean on them. But we'll move the portable supplies just in case."

Bianca studied him for a long moment. "You are very good," she said abruptly.

"No I'm not. I want a comfortable billet and a few decent meals for the week, that's all."

"That is not all. Why do you not like it when I thank you?"

Bonnet rubbed a hand over his unshaven chin. "Because you'll bloody take advantage of it, just like they all do. I'm not an idiot, woman. Don't you have a pair of shoes?"

"Yes, but I cannot afford to wear them out so I use them only when I need to. I have no money for more."

"Well go and put them on before you start tramping through the forest, there are probably snakes in there."

Bianca felt an irrational urge to stick out her tongue at him. His tone reminded her of her mother.

"I always wear them in the forest. It is just that I was in a hurry to…"

She broke off and Bonnet grinned. "To see if I'd discovered your hiding place? I'm not sure what you thought you could do about it if I had. Look at the size of you. It would be like a kitten squaring up to a wolf."

"Cats scratch, Captain, and a wolf can lose an eye if he does not pay attention."

Bonnet turned to look at her in some surprise. She saw his mouth twitch into a smile which was unexpectedly different to his usual wolfish grin.

"I'll bear that in mind. Now go and put some bloody shoes on."

***

The *Iris* arrived in Port Mahon on the island of Menorca to find the *Blake* anchored peacefully and her Captain apparently ashore being entertained by the locals. Hugh thanked God that he had arrived too late to be included in the invitation. He requested his Master and his First Lieutenant to draw up a full list of repairs needed and ordered out his barge to make a courtesy call on Sir Humphrey Granville, the current British representative in Mahon.

The Port Mahon Dockyard had been established by the Royal Navy in 1708 following the English capture of the island of Menorca. Mahon had one of the deepest natural harbours Hugh had ever seen and the dockyard had proved a valuable asset to the British, although it had changed hands several times during the long wars of the previous century. It had been one of the principal ports of the Royal Navy Mediterranean Fleet until it was handed back to Spain during the brief peace of 1802.

Now that Spain was Britain's ally, the port and the dockyards were once more fully available to Royal Navy ships and a resident commissioner lived in one of the elegant houses overlooking the harbour. Hugh, who had been to Mahon many times, walked up the steep hill and waited in a white painted ante-room until a servant appeared to conduct him to Sir Humphrey's combined reception room and study.

"Captain Kelly. Welcome, sir, welcome. Come and have a drink. It's been a while, I think. Let me see, when did we last meet?"

"Gibraltar I think, sir, after Trafalgar. How are you?"

"Well, very well. And yes, I believe you are right. Wounded weren't you, and too damned stubborn to give up your prize to another man? Admiral Collingwood was very worried about you, he had a soft spot for you."

"It was mutual, sir, he's much missed."

"He is. What can I do for you, or is this a courtesy call?"

"It's both, sir. I've orders to join Captain Codrington's squadron, but we hit a storm in the Bay of Biscay, so she'll need some repairs before she's fit for regular duty. I've a letter from Sir Richard Keats."

Granville took the letter. "Thank you. Well you know the ropes, Captain, you don't need me holding your hand. I'll send a note to the Master-Shipwright telling him to expect your orders."

"I've left my First Lieutenant with the Master and the Bosun assessing the damage, they can liaise with him."

"Excellent. Now how are you, Captain? I understand you've married since we last met?"

With his social duties done, Hugh walked back down to the boat and gave orders to row out to the *Blake*. He was pleased to find that her Captain had returned, and a servant showed him through to the great cabin where he found Captain Edward Codrington taking his ease. He rose to greet Hugh and returned his salute.

"Captain Kelly. Is this a social visit or have you brought orders?"

"Orders. I've come from Sir Richard Keats. Although it's very good to see you, Captain."

Codrington opened the letter and waved a hand. "Get yourself a drink and sit down. Don't pour one for me, I'm stuffed full of rice, olives and Spanish wine, I may never drink again."

Hugh grinned and obeyed while Codrington read. Eventually he put the letter down with a snort of disgust.

"Bloody Keats. He thinks he's being subtle, but it's so bloody obvious what this is about. You're my governess, aren't you, Hugh?"

"Do I look like one? I think they're being cautious, Ned. They don't know which way Suchet is going to go or what will be needed. And they know we've worked together before."

"Stop being diplomatic, Hugh, it doesn't suit you. Although looking at these orders, you've got bloody good at convincing the Admiralty that it does. What did Keats say that he didn't write down?"

Hugh sipped the very good wine. "I told him you'd know perfectly well why they sent me to join your squadron, Captain Codrington. You're right of course, Keats was under the impression he was being subtle."

"Ha! Sir Richard Keats must lose every card game he plays, he conceals nothing. I've sat in a room and watched his lip curl every time the name Popham is mentioned, and he doesn't even know he's doing it."

"There's nothing wrong with that response," Hugh said. "Calm down about it, Ned. You command the squadron, I'm under your orders and I'm not going to interfere, though if I think you're about to let off a broadside in the wrong direction, I will tell you so. But you already know that, and it's never bothered you before."

"I suppose not." Codrington got up abruptly and walked through to his cabin. When he returned, he had covered his bald head with a neat green velvet cap. Hugh blinked in surprise and Codrington glared at him.

"Don't look at me like that, Kelly. Jane sent it to me, I was complaining how cold my head gets and I feel ridiculous sitting in my armchair with a bicorn hat on. A few more years of life in this navy and you'll be as bald as I am, and I'll be laughing at you."

"I'm not laughing at you, I've been known to sit wrapped in blankets like a grandmother on a cold night. Jesus, Ned, what is the matter with you, you've been snapping at me since I walked in here? Even if Keats did send me to make sure you don't do anything rash, what's the problem? It wouldn't be the first time they've given you a nursemaid and at least you and I generally see eye to eye on things."

"Clearly not everything," Codrington said shortly. Hugh did not reply. He sat looking at Codrington feeling genuinely bewildered. After a moment, the other man got up and went for more wine. He brought the bottle and topped up Hugh's glass without asking. Hugh sipped it and waited for Codrington to sit down.

"I don't understand," he said. "I'm not generally this slow, Ned, but I have no idea what I've done wrong here. You're going to have to tell me."

"Nothing. You've done nothing wrong. A man's political convictions are his own. But I can't help finding myself wondering how many times we've sat at table together and you've been biting your tongue to stop yourself blurting out what you really think of my family."

Hugh was beginning to wonder if Codrington was more drunk than he had realised, or possibly unwell. "The only members of your family I know personally are you and Jane, Ned, and we're friends. Or I thought we were."

"Not the kind of friends you would invite to dinner with Mr Worthington or the Reverend Caldwell though."

Hugh froze, staring at the other man. He realised that during his brief involvement with the infant Society for the Abolition of Slavery in British Dominions it had never occurred to him that his actions might cause a problem with Ned Codrington.

Hugh and Codrington had been friends for many years, with the casual affection of navy officers who might be stationed on opposite sides of the world for much of the time. They had served together several times and worked well together. Codrington was something of a firebrand, a well-liked and respected officer who nevertheless had a reputation for his willingness to take independent action more readily than most. Hugh liked that about him, and their friendship had become even closer when Roseen had become friends with Codrington's wife, Jane. The two women were close in age, both with young children, and had a great deal in common.

Hugh knew that Codrington was an absentee slave owner. Thinking about it now, he wondered why he had thought so little about it before. Jane had been born in Jamaica, although the couple had met in England and Hugh knew little of Jane's family background, but he supposed that he had always assumed that she too came from a plantation family.

It had not troubled Hugh. His own background was different from most post-captains in the navy. Hugh's father had been a farmer, renting land until his drinking had led to eviction followed by an ignominious death, lying drunk in the street in winter. Hugh had joined the navy as an escape and had discovered both talent and ambition, which had taken him far beyond his wildest boyhood dreams. He had learned to mix with all social classes during his time in the navy and judged a man by his actions in the present, not by stories of his past. Ned Codrington was a fine man, a brilliant captain, and a good friend. Hugh suddenly felt as though he had run into a brick wall.

Codrington gave a grim little smile. "Dear God, Hugh, you really didn't think about it, did you?"

"No," Hugh admitted. "But to be honest, I don't know much about your background, Ned, other than you'd an uncle who raised you and who left you some property, which came in bloody useful back when you were still a rising man."

"I was twenty-seven. My uncle was like a father to me. When he died he left his property between me, my brother and my sister. He had connections who helped me in my early days in the navy. He was a good man. A kind man. Gave generously to charity and gave so much of his time and energy to us. I loved him."

Hugh did not reply. He had seldom felt more uncomfortable. He could think of nothing to say that would help Codrington, but he also could not lie. Eventually, Codrington said:

"What would you have done, Hugh, if your father had left you property which included slaves?"

Hugh shrugged. "I don't know, Ned. My father died drunk on the quay in Castletown and left me nothing but a few debts at local taverns and a feeling that I needed to prove myself a better man than he. Which turned out to be a very good legacy. I did six weeks labour on the land to pay those debts before I joined the navy, so that when I finally came home I could do it with my head held high. I went home the owner of the land I'd worked on. I've been so bloody lucky, it's not my place to judge anybody about anything."

"When you got up at those public meetings, you judged me."

"No, I didn't. I told of what I'd seen and what I knew. I named no man, and I criticised no individual. I talked of a system, of an institution, that I hate and of people suffering, that I'd witnessed. I didn't think of you, or Jane. It didn't occur to me. But if I had, I'd have done the same thing. I'm sorry if that comes between us."

There was a long, painful silence. Hugh drank his wine and wished himself somewhere else. He had been looking forward to his reunion with Codrington.

Eventually Codrington reached for his glass and drank deeply. "I had too much wine at that blasted dinner," he said conversationally. "I didn't mean to say any of this to you."

"It would have been worse if you hadn't," Hugh said. "It would have sat between us. It might still, but at least now I'll know why."

Codrington did not respond immediately. Finally he said:

"You're a very principled man, Hugh, no matter how hard you try to pretend you're indifferent. I like that about you. I'm not sure I'm ready to talk about this yet."

"You don't have to, sir."

Codrington turned dark eyes onto him with an expression of utter disgust. "Don't you dare call me sir in here. Up on deck, that's who I am. Down here, between friends, you'll call me Ned. Or whatever the hell you like."

"Can I call you a stiff-rumped arsehole?" Hugh enquired pleasantly.

"Fuck off, Captain Kelly. We may need another bottle after all. I'm going to tell you all about Tarragona."

Chapter Nine

Durrell had been to Tarragona previously, during a spell on blockade duty off the coast of Spain, but he had not spent much time in the town. It had proved a thorn in the side of the occupying French for several years now. There had been attempts to besiege it in 1809 and again in 1810 but both had failed. The area surrounding the town had been poor even before the French invasion. War and bad harvests had further devastated it and the remaining Spanish peasants barely managed to eke out a living. It was impossible for a French army to live off the land in the area, so a besieging army would have to provide their own supplies.

The town was situated in a strong position on the coast, just beyond where the River Francoli met the sea. The natural harbour was protected by the mole which was a massive stone breakwater, flat topped to form a causeway stretching out into the Balearic Sea. The commercial centre of the lower town was centred around the port while the upper town was built on the cliffs and granite hills above the harbour. It was surrounded by formidable walls which were protected by a string of forts and redoubts.

Commodore Edward Codrington was in command of a small squadron of Royal Navy, ships along with a number of Spanish frigates and gunboats. His orders were to co-operate with the Spanish defenders of Tarragona and to make use of his guns to cause as much damage as possible to the French forces. Above all it was the navy's job to keep the town open from the sea to enable the free movement of supplies, weapons and troops. Durrell thought, although nobody had mentioned it, that they might also be expected to manage an evacuation if something went badly wrong.

On May 3rd the Marquis of Campoverde and his troops were defeated as they tried to reinforce the Spanish garrison at Figueras and Codrington announced that he was taking the *Blake,* with several other vessels, to Cadagues to collect supplies and troops for Tarragona. He left Hugh in command of the reduced squadron off Tarragona and Durrell had the sense that his Captain was relieved. Hugh and Durrell were invited to dine on the *Blake* the day before Codrington sailed along with the captains of the other ships currently under Codrington's command and Durrell thought he could detect a slight tension in Hugh and Codrington's generally easy relationship.

There were eight Royal Navy ships currently operating under Codrington's command; though the composition of the squadron was fluid with ships moving in and out as they became available. Durrell was slightly taken aback to discover that none of the other captains had brought their first lieutenant to the dinner. He wondered if Codrington had specifically included him in the invitation or if Hugh had just brought him along. He suspected the latter. Durrell was well aware of his Captain's determination to ensure that the debacle of the Walcheren inquiry had no lasting ill-effects on his first officer's career and Hugh's easy-going manner masked a surprising ruthlessness when he cared deeply about something.

Codrington greeted Durrell with a grin and a look at Hugh which strengthened Durrell's suspicions. He took his seat. The dinner was intended as both a social event and a briefing meeting before Codrington left and Durrell knew that his job was simply to listen, unless his opinion was directly asked. His younger self would have resented this, but now he understood how much Hugh valued his insights. Sitting quietly, Durrell could be overlooked and he was very good at watching the interplay between the other guests and picking up on nuances that Hugh might miss. He also had a remarkable memory and could have written detailed notes on the meeting if Hugh had asked him.

They ate roast beef and goat stew and drank local wine, while Codrington summarised what he knew of the current state of the war in the area. He was personally acquainted with most of the Spanish commanders and it was quickly evident to Durrell that his preference was for General Henry O'Donnell, who had still not recovered from the wound he had received during his triumph at La Bisbal. Codrington was less enthusiastic about the Marquis of Campoverde, who had recently taken over command. He was trying to be diplomatic about it, but Durrell could see Hugh was struggling not to laugh at the effort it was costing him.

Codrington made his dispositions. He had chosen to leave three ships off Tarragona under Hugh's command, with instructions to watch for any French movement and to take appropriate action if it could be done without risk to the ships. Codrington would move up and down the coast with the rest of the squadron, ferrying troops and supplies to where they were needed. It was clear that General Suchet was marching on Tarragona but the Spanish hoped that the strength of the town defences combined with the ability of both Campoverde's forces and the local partisan bands to harass them from the rear would cause him to reconsider.

"I consider it probable that he'll turn back and make for Figueras," Codrington said, as the servant came to clear the dishes and the port was brought out. "Losing it to the Spanish will have shocked the hell out of them and they'll want it back. If Macdonald has sent to Suchet for help, I don't see how he can refuse."

"What if Suchet doesn't see it that way?" Hugh asked, topping up his glass and passing the bottle to Charles Adam from the *Invincible*. "It's a while since I was in Tarragona, sir, and I'm sure they've improved the defences since then."

"The defences are good and with a strong garrison they should hold. The French have failed twice before here. All the same, Campoverde's local agents tell me that Suchet is making meticulous preparations with regard to both his siege train and supplies for his men. We shouldn't become complacent."

Durrell had a sudden idea and spoke without thinking. "Which road must they take, sir?"

Several of the company turned to stare at him in surprise and Durrell felt himself flush a little but Hugh immediately gave him his full attention.

"I don't know, Mr Durrell, I don't know the country that well. Why do you ask?"

"Only that in other parts of the coast, the best roads for heavy equipment run close to the sea where the ground is more level. Possibly within range of our guns."

Hugh looked over at Codrington who gave a faint smile. "As I shall be otherwise engaged for a few days, I'll leave it to you to give your orders, Captain Kelly. You'll have the *Sparrowhawk*, the *Termagant* and the *Cambrian* and I'll leave you three of the Spanish gunboats. How is your Spanish by the way?"

"Appalling," Hugh said cheerfully. "It doesn't matter though, as Mr Durrell is fluent and can translate if necessary."

"Most of the Spanish officers speak at least some English," Codrington said. "We'll sail with the…"

He broke off as his servant appeared in the doorway. "What is it, Bell?"

"Boat tying up, Commodore. Seems it's from the *Wren*, asking permission to board."

"The *Wren*?" Hugh said, and his tone of voice made Durrell turn to stare at him."

"Just dropped anchor, sir."

"Sir Charles Cotton has ordered her up from Cadiz. I presume it's Captain Winterton, Bell. Send him down. He's missed dinner but there's plenty of wine."

The man who presented himself in Codrington's dining cabin was a slight man of medium height, probably in his thirties, with a shock of dark curls barely contained by a black ribbon. He saluted to Codrington and the table at large, but his eyes were on Hugh and as Codrington waved him to a vacant chair, Hugh got up and moved forward to shake his hand. Both men were smiling broadly.

"Captain Winterton. I've been waiting to offer my congratulations in person, but you're a hard man to catch up with. Do they ever let you ashore?"

"Not that often, sir. It's very good to see you." Winterton lowered himself into the chair, looking around the table. "I'm sorry I'm so late, Commodore Codrington, the wind was not my friend."

"No matter, you're here now. I've no idea who else you know here, Winterton, so I'll introduce everybody. You know Captain Kelly of course."

Codrington made the introductions around the table and the seven other captains greeted Winterton, several of them offering congratulations on his promotion to post-captain. The newcomer smiled his thanks and bowed to each of them. Codrington paused when he reached the end. For an agonised moment, Durrell wondered if he should introduce himself. Winterton was looking at him enquiringly.

"Oh yes," Codrington said lightly. "And at the end there is your replacement aboard the *Iris*, Lieutenant Durrell. Captain Kelly seems unable to go anywhere without him these days."

Durrell felt himself flinch at what was undoubtedly a snipe at his presence although he could not decide if it was aimed at himself or Hugh. He bowed slightly to Winterton. The other man nodded back to him with a friendly smile and took his seat. Hugh said nothing to Codrington, which Durrell thought was probably the right thing to do, although he was in no doubt that his Captain had noticed the comment. Hugh never missed anything.

The conversation resumed with a discussion about tides and supplies and the recent news that Admiral Sir Charles Cotton, who commanded the Mediterranean Fleet, would shortly be returning to England to take over the Channel Fleet. The new commander in the Mediterranean would be Sir Edward Pellew and there was some talk about the two men and their different styles of command.

Eventually Codrington brought proceedings to a close and the various captains went up onto deck to await their boats. Hugh clapped Winterton on the shoulder.

"Do you need to get straight back to the *Wren*, fella? It didn't escape my notice that you weren't offered food there. Why not come back to the *Iris* for some supper first?"

Winterton smiled. "My penalty for a late arrival. I can get something aboard the *Wren*, Captain, but I'd love to join you if you've time. I have a lot of questions that I'm not sure the Commodore has the time to answer."

"Excellent. Send your boat back to the *Wren*; we'll send you back in ours later. Mr Durrell, will you wait with Captain Winterton? I want a quick word with Commodore Codrington before we leave."

Codrington had disappeared below deck. Durrell met Hugh's eyes and shook his head. "I would not, sir. It was a passing remark, I doubt he meant…"

"It was a snide comment and it had nothing to do with your presence at table, Mr Durrell. He knew I'd bring you and he's never objected before. It won't take long."

Durrell waited beside Winterton, feeling awkward. It was strange to be in the company of a man he had heard so much about and who had held the post of Hugh Kelly's First Lieutenant on a previous ship, while Durrell had still been a midshipman, studying hard for the lieutenant's examination. During their many conversations, Hugh had talked about a number of his previous officers but of them all he had spoken most warmly of Luke Winterton. Durrell felt unexpectedly young and gauche although he knew he was only a few years younger than Winterton. He also realised with painful self-knowledge that he was a little jealous, which was embarrassing.

Hugh took longer than Durrell had expected. There was a cold wind and beside him, Winterton shivered.

"Any idea what he's doing down there?"

Durrell hesitated. His instinct was to say nothing but he suspected that Hugh would tell Winterton everything over a glass of wine anyway and he did not want to appear churlish, so he said cautiously:

"I'm not sure, sir. I felt today that there was some coolness between Captain Kelly and Commodore Codrington, but I have no idea why as they are very good friends. I think the Captain was irritated when the Commodore made a remark about my presence at dinner. He should have let it pass, it was not important."

Winterton grinned. "You know him as well as I do, Lieutenant, you must know that when it's a matter of his officers or crew he never lets anything go. Though I wish he bloody would, we're freezing to death up here. Perhaps I…"

Winterton broke off as Hugh's tall form appeared. Durrell studied his face through the gathering dusk. His Captain's expression was reassuringly untroubled. Hugh put one hand on Winterton's shoulder and the other on Durrell's.

"Right, let's get going, it's bloody freezing up here in this wind. I've an excellent Portuguese red and a few years' gossip to catch up on. I also want to introduce you properly to my current First Lieutenant. You two have a lot in common. Let's go and get some decent food and some good wine."

Durrell felt his discomfort ease immediately and silently laughed at himself. He led the way to the ladder where their boatmen waited below to row them back to the *Iris*. Setting aside his moment of irrational jealousy, he was looking forward to getting to know Winterton. Hugh's former officer had been in command of two different frigates over the past five years and his success in single ship actions against the French was becoming legendary. Durrell's ambitions had suffered a setback after Walcheren but he had by no means abandoned them and he suspected that Luke Winterton would be a good man to know.

***

Bonnet spent a full week as the uninvited guest of Bianca Ramos and her surly father, while waiting for orders to march on Tarragona. It proved to be a surprisingly comfortable one, despite the simmering resentment against the French occupation which permeated the rest of the village.

After her initial awkwardness, Bianca seemed to relax in Bonnet's company. They spent little time around one another during the day. The 30th légère had received a draft of new recruits, marched in with some more experienced reinforcements from the battalion depot. Bonnet was faced with the depressing task of trying to bring twelve men into some kind of combat readiness in five days and he very nearly handed the impossible task over to his junior officers and went back to bed.

In the end he decided that he would use the opportunity to give the rest of his company some extra drill and skirmish practice. There was not usually much chance to train men on the march and Bonnet concentrated on the absolute essentials of getting the battalion into square at speed and making sure they understood how to fire, clean and maintain their muskets. Beyond that, they would have to learn as they went along.

Returning to the cottage at the end of a tiring and often frustrating day, Bonnet found it soothing to find Bianca busy about her work. There was hot food every day, which Bonnet was able to supplement from army stores. She was a good cook and could make a scratch meal surprisingly tasty using dried herbs or wild gleanings from the forests and meadows. Bonnet did not always know exactly what he was eating, but it tasted good.

He provided beef and mutton from the army livestock pens, bribing the quartermaster to give him a little more than his due. In return, Bianca washed and mended everything he owned to a standard well beyond anything Bonnet's idle servant could manage. She groomed and tended his horses and pack mule and even volunteered to cut his hair for him.

In the evenings, the officers of the battalion congregated in the priest's house where Lacasse was billeted, to drink and play cards. Bonnet walked up once or twice to join them but he preferred to remain in the cottage. Ramos usually fell asleep quickly after dinner and Bianca would settle him in the sleeping loft then return to sit with her mending or knitting. On cooler evenings they sat by the fire, but when it was mild they took their chairs out into the small garden, now repaired and ready for new planting once the French moved on.

They talked little at first but gradually, under his casual questioning, she began to open up and talked of her childhood following the army with her father. Bonnet told her stories of his early campaigns, careful to keep the subject matter light and away from his more distressing experiences. They spoke as friendly acquaintances, thrown together briefly by circumstances, but Bonnet enjoyed it.

Before bedtime he would walk with her through the thick tangle of the forest to tend her hidden livestock and to collect eggs. Bianca offered to kill a chicken one day but Bonnet declined. While Pierre saw him living off army rations supplemented by his hosts' vegetables and herbs he would not be suspicious, but the sudden appearance of roasted chicken was going to make him wonder where it came from. Bonnet did not trust him not to spread the news that the Ramos family had some hidden source of supplies. The French army presumed that they had already stolen what there was to steal from the villagers and had stopped looking. Bonnet wanted it to stay that way.

He came in for some heavy-handed teasing about Bianca Ramos from his fellow officers who assumed that his preference for her company meant that he was sharing her bed. Bonnet made no attempt to either confirm or deny the assumption. After too much home-made wine, one of the sous-lieutenants from Foulon's company went so far as to suggest that Bonnet might have forced the issue. Bonnet decided that was a joke too far and gave the younger man the simple choice of making an apology or taking an unanticipated swim in the river. Lieutenant Claudin apologised quickly and Bonnet let the rest of the banter flow over him. It could do no harm to Bianca who need never even know about it and if the men thought she was his woman she would be safe from further annoyance.

When orders came that the army was to march out the following morning, Bonnet went to find Bianca. She listened in silence to the news then gave a little nod.

"Your clothing is clean and mended, Captain, and your horses and mule are ready. We will eat early as you will need to rest before the march. Wait."

Bonnet obeyed, amused at her proprietary tone. She disappeared into the cottage and emerged with something folded which she handed to him. Bonnet shook out the stockings then looked up, startled.

"Is this what you've been knitting all week?"

"Yes. They are a gift, I will not accept payment. They are made from goat hair, I spin it myself. Very warm. Have your blisters healed?"

"Yes," Bonnet said. He realised he was having trouble with his voice and cleared his throat. He could not remember the last time he had been given a gift. "But you should not have."

"I wanted to. You have kept me safe this week and you have shared your food and protected our animals. I am grateful, Captain Bonnet."

"Bianca, you've waited on me hand and foot, I've lived like a prince. You don't owe me anything."

"It is a gift, not a debt."

"Then I will accept, with thanks. You've been good to me this week, Bianca Ramos. I hope you get some peace once we march out. You ought to, I think we'll be stuck at Tarragona for a while with no time to wander off on a looting spree."

Bonnet was up before dawn, chivvying Pierre to saddle up his horse and load up the pack mule. The mule was notoriously reluctant to get moving in the morning and bellowed his complaints so loudly that Bonnet thought it could probably be heard all the way to Tarragona. He had tried not to wake his hosts while he was dressing but they must be awake now. He was about to mount his horse when the door opened and Bianca appeared. She was wrapped in her ancient woollen shawl with her dark hair loose around her shoulders and she looked cold and tired. Bonnet handed the reins to Pierre, deliberately ignoring his servant's rolling eyes because he could not be bothered to chastise him, and went back to the house.

"I am sorry, Bianca, I was hoping not to disturb you. Take care of your father and I hope this winter hasn't been made the worse for your people by these thieving bastards."

Bianca raised her hand and uncurled her fingers. There were several coins in her palm. "What is this, Captain? You left this on the table. I told you I did not expect payment."

Bonnet gave a little smile. "It is a gift, not a debt. Thank you for everything."

"Wait."

She disappeared into the cottage and reappeared with a small cloth bag. Bonnet took it and opened it. Inside was a chunk of dark bread which must have been left over from the previous day's dinner and two eggs, boiled in their shells.

"For the march. You will be hungry long before you have the chance to stop. Goodbye, Captain Bonnet. Thank you for showing me that a Frenchman can be a decent man. I will try to remember the lesson."

Bonnet studied the thin face in the pale misty dawn light and felt a surprising twinge of regret that he would not see her again.

"Don't," he said abruptly. "Forget it. The next time you see a blue coat marching in, you do exactly as you've always done and run like hell to your forest hideaway. Don't trust any one of the bastards. Promise me, Bianca."

She gave her quick smile which always reminded him of some woodland creature. "I promise. Now you must go or you will be late."

Bonnet mounted his horse, glared at his braying mule then looked back at Bianca. She was laughing. He grinned back and pantomimed shooting the animal with an imaginary pistol, then turned his horse and made his way up to the road to join his battalion at the crossroads which led to Tarragona.

***

The French marched to Tarragona along two separate routes. Several divisions started from Lerida and took the Montblanc road but the siege train, as Durrell had predicted, took the road from Tortosa which ran for much of the way alongside the coast.

Hugh kept his small squadron on constant patrol and was rewarded by a shout from the lookout just as Lieutenant Murtagh, who was officer of the watch, had ordered the main topsail to be set. Hugh was in his cabin writing up his log when he heard the cry and he was already on his way to the quarterdeck when Midshipman Hastings came to summon him. Hugh found his first officer already on deck with his telescope to his eye. He passed it to Hugh without speaking and Hugh studied the shoreline and felt a little lift of satisfaction.

The French column was strung out along the road: a long train of carts, wagons, gun carriages and marching troops. Hugh moved the glass along, trying to get a sense of numbers, then lowered it and handed it back to Durrell. Numbers did not matter. From here, the road ran close to the sea for long stretches all the way to Tarragona and his ships would be able to shadow them all the way. Hugh did not know how close General Suchet was to reaching the outskirts of the town, but he was going to have to wait a while for his siege train.

"Mr Durrell, clear for action. Mr Clarke, I've orders for the squadron."

The ship came alive around Hugh as men raced to their allotted stations, following the shrill blast of the bosun's whistle. Hugh stood watching the shore for a few more minutes then beckoned to Clarke, who was his senior midshipman and signal officer, to follow him below. In the heat of battle his signalling orders would be given verbally, but at other times Hugh liked to write them down.

When Clarke had raced away to the poop deck to begin hoisting the signals, Hugh rose and walked to the large table which was scattered with maps and charts. One of them was a rough drawing of the Spanish coastline, marking cliffs, hills and the direction of the road. Durrell had worked on it from memory for most of the past few days. When it was as complete as he could make it, he had taken possession of one of the boats and had himself rowed between the various ships of Hugh's small squadron, taking the map with him. Drawing on the knowledge of the other four captains and their officers, many of whom had served on this coast over the years, Durrell had created a small masterpiece.

There was a sound in the doorway. Hugh turned to find that one of the Bosun's mates had arrived with a party to clear his cabin. Hugh left them to it and went up onto deck. The crew of the *Iris* had practiced clearing for action so many times that they could do it without need for further orders. Each man had his allotted task and station as listed on the quarter bill and the crew went about their work almost in silence.

Clearing the ship for action centred around five main areas. The decks needed to be cleared; the magazines had to be opened and powder and shot prepared; the surgeon needed to get his room ready to receive emergencies; the ship's guns had to be unleashed and dragged into position and the bosun and his mates needed to adapt the rigging and make preparations for potential damage.

Most of these preparations would not be required today, as Hugh could see no possibility of the French returning fire, but it was good practice for the crew and besides, once the guns were in use there was always a risk of accident or fire aboard ship. Some preparations were wholly unnecessary, such as slaughtering livestock or throwing surplus provisions overboard but for the most part, the *Iris* was fully prepared for battle.

Hugh stood on the quarterdeck, dividing his attention between the coastline and the movements of the other ships around him. Battle at sea had not the frenetic urgency of land combat and although once the enemy was engaged Hugh often lost all sense of time, the manoeuvring into position could seem painfully slow. Hugh watched the marching French along the shore and wondered what their commander was thinking and whether he was at all aware of what was about to happen. He was clearly making no move to get his men under cover.

A shout came from Clarke on the poop deck, then Midshipman Sandford came racing towards him. Hugh did not need the signals to tell him his ships were in position. He surveyed the shore once more then turned to his First Lieutenant who stood awaiting the order.

The first broadside from the *Iris* left every man on the ship with ringing ears. The lower gun deck bore the huge 32 pounders while the upper deck had recently replaced all its 18 pounders with the more formidable 24-pounders and the ship shuddered as the starboard guns facing the coast roared out. Below decks, the guns recoiled to the end of the breeching rope securing them and as they came to a halt the gun crew leaped into action again, sponging out the gun muzzle before loading the gun once more.

Hugh raised his glass to watch the French column and saw that it had come to a stop. The *Iris*, a 74-gun third rater was too large to approach any closer to the land than this and although the broadside had done some damage to the rocky shoreline, it had not hit the column directly. There had been some casualties from flying rock and it looked as though one of the heavy wagons had broken down. It rested at a crazy angle over its damaged undercarriage while men swarmed around it. Hugh wondered what it contained and hoped for their sakes that it was not powder or ammunition.

He could see movement on the water from his peripheral vision as he gave the order for a small adjustment of their position in the water, then another broadside. This one was more satisfying, since it hit a rock face just above a section of the unmoving convoy, bringing devastation to a cluster of blue-coated infantry just below. Even in his partially deafened state, Hugh could hear their cries and screams across the still water and a babble of panic as the French commanders tried to bring their troops into order and get them under cover.

Hugh could have told them it was far too late for that. He was waiting for the sound, and it came first from the 40 gun *Cambrian*. Under cover of the fire from the *Iris,* Captain Bullen had managed to move in very close and his guns raked the French convoy, completely destroying the already damaged wagon and blowing apart the escort currently trying to repair it.

Two further explosions of fire from aft told Hugh that the *Sparrowhawk* and *Termagant* were in position. Both were 28 gun sloops with far less firepower than the bigger ships; but they were fast and easy to manoeuvre and their fire was appallingly accurate, leaving bodies scattered on the ground.

Hugh turned to Durrell to give the order for the gunners to stand down. The *Iris* had no need to fire again. It had done its job of inflicting damage on the column and in neatly distracting the French from the fast smaller ships and he had another task for his crew.

"Good work, Mr Durrell. Send below to the gunners to stand down and secure the guns for sail but keep them standing by. They'll be needed again presently. Mr Clarke, send the next signals if you please."

Hugh paused in his orders as the 38 gun *Wren* came into view, tacking fast in towards the shore. The wind was light but variable and Winterton was making superb use of it, swinging in ahead of the *Sparrowhawk* which had drawn off after her last volley. Hugh watched for a moment as the *Wren* moved into position, waiting for her guns to fire. The explosion came at exactly the moment Hugh himself would have chosen.

Winterton had managed to get in further than either of the sloops and the *Wren* sailed parallel to the shoreline, raking the French column with cannon fire.

"He's a very skilled seaman, Captain."

Hugh turned in surprise to find the Durrell stood just behind him, his eyes on the *Wren*.

"He is, though I don't think he'll ever have quite your feel for the ship. What he does have, blast him, is recklessness. I've no objection to watching him land a few broadsides on an immobilised French column but I've heard accounts of a few of his actions and I wouldn't want to be there to see it: it would give me a heart attack."

Durrell gave a faint smile. "He's been remarkably successful, sir. He's very well thought of at the Admiralty. I'm not surprised he's made post-captain so young."

There was no hint of envy or regret in Durrell's tone. Hugh, who knew him, wondered how he was managing to conceal it so well. He moved to stand beside his first officer and put a hand on Durrell's arm.

"Luke Winterton is a brilliant officer and a good friend, Mr Durrell and I'm deeply proud of him. But you'll go further."

"I am not convinced of it, sir. I do not suffer from false modesty but I do not think the nature of my talent lends itself to a public glory. Nor do I have the personality to make up for that. But that does not mean I will not keep trying."

Hugh's heart ached for him. "I know you feel you've taken a step backwards, Mr Durrell, but I think you'll find…"

"No, I don't," Durrell said unexpectedly. "I find that I am exactly where I want to be at the moment, Captain. Perhaps I could achieve more glory in charge of a fast frigate, but I doubt I would be as happy. And every day I spend aboard the *Iris* with you, I'm learning more about seamanship. I'm not sure any early promotion could give me that."

Hugh said nothing for a moment due to an unexpected lump in his throat. Eventually he said:

"I know you don't believe me just now, Mr Durrell but your talents are exactly what this navy needs and at some point they're going to realise it. And if they don't, I'm going to find the opportunity to hammer it into their thick skulls. Set a north-west course, heading for Tarragona. We've done enough here and they're beginning to pull the convoy off the road into shelter. We can leave it to the smaller ships and the gunboats to keep them occupied. I've the perfect place in mind to delay them further."

The place was a curved headland where the road to Tarragona followed the exact line of the coast. Hugh spent the time below in his cabin studying the map alongside his First Lieutenant but was on the quarterdeck as the *Iris* came in sight of the promontory. It was difficult to gauge how long it would take the marching column to reach this section of road, especially given the damage already inflicted upon them, but Hugh did not think they would be able to do it for at least another forty-eight hours, possibly more. For some of their route the road ran further back from the coastline, out of reach of the Royal Navy's guns, but here they would be back within range for a short time.

Hugh studied the coast. The wind had picked up again and he could hear Durrell's voice giving orders to set the sails to bring the *Iris* round into easy range. There was nothing to oppose them here, not the slightest risk of field artillery or a stray musket shot. As the ship tacked down ready to deliver the first broadside, Hugh thought again about the careful lines of that map on his desk and glanced over at his First Lieutenant. Durrell's eyes were on the rigging, his thoughts wholly on the task in hand. Hugh gave a little smile and turned to where Midshipman Bristow awaited his orders.

"Guns at the ready, Mr Bristow?"

"Aye, Captain."

"Commence firing then."

Once again the guns roared out, one cannonade following another. The wind was picking up more and Hugh braced himself against the rise and fall of the deck, his eyes glued to the shape of the road. The first shots landed short and Durrell called orders to adjust course slightly. The next fell squarely onto the road and the third smashed into the rocks beyond it, bringing them down with a rumble which sounded muted from this far out but which was probably much louder on shore. The guns crashed again and Hugh studied the shore through a cloud of acrid smelling black smoke and saw, to his immense satisfaction, that the road was in ruins, blocked by a pile of rubble with dust rising up from it.

"That should slow them down a bit. Call a halt, Mr Durrell and we'll haul off and put the ship to rights. Let's get the galley fired up and the crew fed. The rest of the squadron should be able to join us tomorrow and then we'll wait for the convoy to reach us again."

"They may have decided to take another road, sir."

"Either way, it will delay them and make their lives more difficult, which is what we're aiming for. Mr Bristow, take the order below."

***

After several days watching General Suchet, his senior officers and engineers inspecting the defences of Tarragona, Bonnet was depressed and wondered if the ambitious General felt the same way. If Suchet genuinely hoped to win his Marshal's baton by taking this formidable coastal stronghold, he must be wondering by now if the prize was beyond his reach.

The 30th légère bivouacked on rocky ground two miles from the outlying defences and settled down to await the arrival of the siege train. This was considerably delayed, according to Lacasse, by the Royal Navy which had followed it throughout its journey along the coastal road, firing at the wagons when it was possible and bombarding the road when it was not. Bonnet was grateful that his battalion had not been sent along that route.

The countryside around Tarragona was bleak and barren and Bonnet knew that Suchet had made careful arrangements to ensure that his troops would not go hungry due to lack of supplies, since it would be impossible to live off the land. Suchet was making sure that his preparations for an effective commissary and good medical provision were very visible to his men. Bonnet approved both the arrangements and the intelligence behind them. In a protracted siege or a difficult assault, morale could make the difference between success and another ignominious failure. Bonnet usually had a good sense of the mood within the battalion and he thought that both officers and men were surprisingly optimistic about the outcome.

As the French advanced towards Tarragona the Spanish troops withdrew immediately within the defences and Suchet allowed his men time to rest and settle in while he toured the fortifications with his chief engineer and artillery officers. The southern front of the town was protected by the sea, and the northern and eastern fronts were either too steep and rocky or too difficult for the transport of artillery. Suchet spent another day studying the western front then gave orders for siege works to begin at the northern defences of Fort Olivo which would have to be taken before any further siege works could begin.

It was clear that some action needed to be taken to control the Royal Navy ships which currently lay in the northern end of the harbour. Codrington had a small squadron which seemed to vary in size as ships came and went, ferrying supplies and troops up and down the coast, but there were never fewer than two 74-gunners and two or three frigates as well as several Spanish gunboats. They were positioned perfectly to fire across the mouth of the River Francoli where Suchet wished to build his siege works and it was going to be impossible to make progress unless the squadron could be driven off.

The 30th légère spent three miserable days trying to protect Suchet's engineers as they raced to build a fort on the shore. Once it was completed, it could carry heavy guns with enough range to keep Codrington's ships at a distance. Lacasse's men could do nothing about the raking fire from the frigates other than take cover during the day, but the engineers worked frantically through the night. The new fort was taking shape despite the efforts of the ships to destroy it and Bonnet thought if they could hold on for another few days, the guns could be installed and Codrington would have to draw off or risk being hit by a barrage of fire from the French 24-pounders.

Lacasse had placed his men along a hastily constructed series of earthworks which had taken forever to build because the ground was so rocky and unyielding that extra soil needed to be brought in. The effort had been worthwhile though, as the solid earthen walls gave considerable protection from the ships' guns. Occasionally one would manage a lucky shot which cleared the parapet and there were a few dead and wounded but for the most part there was nothing to do but squabble over the most comfortable sleeping places and admire the engineers' frantic tenacity as they scrambled to complete the fort under cover of darkness.

The battery was finished on the 8th of May under a brutal bombardment from the ships. Bonnet supposed that Codrington, or whoever was currently in command, must have recognised that this was their last chance. He was relieved when Lacasse pulled his men back out of range.

There was nothing they could do to protect the workmen and it would be stupid to lose fighting men unnecessarily. At the same time, Bonnet wished they were a lot further away, too far to hear the screams of the workmen when the ships' guns found their target.

"Poor bastards," Allard said glumly. "I thought they'd got away with it quite lightly until now. Do you think he'll pull them out, sir?"

Bonnet shook his head. They were watching from a rocky ledge, well out of danger. The viewpoint gave an excellent view over the trenches and earthworks which led to the newly constructed battery.

"No, they're almost there. Another couple of hours and they'll have completed that trench and be wholly under cover. Those buggers know it as well. The minute they start hauling in the guns, he'll have those frigates and gunboats out of there, he's not stupid. I wonder who it is? It's not the *Blake*."

"The 74-gunner is called the *Iris*, sir. Captain Forget could read it through his telescope. He's keen on ships. He says she's new in these waters. They're obviously pulling in as many ships as they can to help the defenders."

"Well she can fuck off as far as I'm concerned," Bonnet said. There was another distant boom from one of the frigates followed by two more in quick succession. The larger ship could come no nearer to the shore but the frigates and gunboats were close in, raking the unfortunate engineers and their workmen as they struggled to extend the ditch to protect themselves. One cannonade found its mark and there was a cacophony of cries and shouted orders. Earth and broken rock flew high into the air and with it, a man's body twisting horribly before crashing down into the ruin of the ditch. Bonnet was not sure, but he thought the man had no legs.

It was frustrating to have to watch the slaughter and not be able to return fire. Bonnet glared out at the fast moving frigate. She was turning in the water, making a sweeping pass behind the other ships, tacking skilfully to bring herself about. The ships were acting together with remarkable co-ordination, firing and then retreating to reload. It enabled the small squadron to keep up a relentless fire on the hapless workmen and casualties were becoming heavy.

Bonnet watched as medical orderlies began to carry out the wounded. Some of them looked as though they would not make it to the hospital alive and Bonnet realised he was clenching his fists in impotent anger. He looked back at the frigates. He and Allard had been joined on their rocky perch by Captain Bergne.

"They're bringing down the guns from the siege park," Bergne said. "Another hour and they'll be ready to open up."

"I'm looking forward to seeing these bastards scuttling out to sea," Bonnet said grimly. "Although I really wish that one of them – that frigate for preference – would get stuck in a sudden calm for long enough for us to blow the fucker out of the water."

Bergne sniggered. "It isn't going to happen unfortunately. They'll pull them back the minute they see those guns coming down. It's certainly not going to happen to the *Wren*. About a dozen of our frigate crews could testify to how fast he can move. Or they would be able to if they weren't in a prison camp or at the bottom of the ocean."

"That's the *Wren*?" Bonnet said. He was not interested in naval matters and valued ships only as a means of transporting troops. Given how sick even a short voyage made him, he preferred to travel by land whenever possible. Nevertheless, even he had heard of the *Wren's* fearsome reputation in single ship actions during the past two years. "Then I really wish we could sink the arsehole."

Bergne lifted his face to the strong breeze. "Not a chance. The Captain of that 74 is standing on the quarterdeck watching our every move. He'll have them out of there in a heartbeat if he notices any change in the wind or gets a sniff of an approaching gun. I wonder where the *Blake* is? Probably picking up more troops up the coast to supplement the garrison here."

"He can bring in as many as he likes," Bonnet said. "If the Emperor has really offered Suchet a marshal's baton for this town, he'll throw half his army at it and he won't give a shit how many lives it costs. It's going to be a long bloody summer, Bergne, with a lot of dead Frenchmen."

"At least this part of it is over," Bergne said. He had turned and was looking inland, up the road towards Reus. Bonnet turned and followed his gaze. He felt a rush of relief at the sight of the gun carriages rumbling towards the shore, their crews marching beside them.

"I hope that bastard frigate doesn't manage to get off a lucky shot," he said.

Bergne shook his head. "He's not stupid. Even if he was, his commander won't let him. You can't move a man o' war as if it was a cavalry charger, he'll give himself plenty of time. You watch, he'll run up the signals the minute he sees those guns."

He was right, Bonnet saw. He wondered how long it took to learn the combination of little flags and how many of the ships' crews understood them. Signalling was a complete mystery to him and he saw no need ever to change that. He watched gloomily as the smaller ships and the gunboats set their sails and prepared to withdraw. They were so close in, that even without his telescope, Bonnet could see men swarming over the rigging of the frigates. The thought of clambering that high above the deck made him feel sick. Bonnet hated heights. He turned to look over at the walls of Tarragona and profoundly hoped that it would be full dark before Suchet finally ordered the storming parties in. In the dark it was difficult to see how far down it was to the bottom of the ladder.

"Well at least that's got rid of the fucking navy for the time being," he said. "And I'm hoping that's our relieving party marching up behind the guns. I'm going to be bored wherever they put us, but I'd rather be bored and comfortable."

Chapter Ten

Diego Ramos died in the early hours of the morning after an illness which had progressed with terrifying speed. Bianca had been dozing beside the dying remains of the fire, but some change in the laboured breathing must have reached her, jerking her awake. She was exhausted after a week of nursing him, snatching sleep or food when she could manage it.

When it became clear that her father's illness was much more than a minor episode of sickness, Bianca had brought his bedding down from the sleeping loft. Ramos was wretchedly sick, long after there was anything left to bring up. He also lost control of his bowels and the tiny cottage stank, despite Bianca's efforts to keep it clean and keep up with the endless laundry.

She had been hoping that this had been caused by something bad that he had eaten and that once his body had evicted the poison, he would recover. He did not. Instead, he seemed to shrink before her eyes, his wrinkled skin looking almost translucent. Since the previous day his bowel movements had consisted mostly of dark blood.

There was no medical man anywhere closer than Reus and Bianca had no money to pay for a doctor anyway. She walked up to speak to Señora Alonso who acted as midwife for several villages. She could also set bones and had some knowledge of herbal medicine. The older woman accompanied her back to the cottage and spent ten minutes examining the patient and questioning Bianca. Eventually she retreated to Bianca's little garden, taking in big gulps of fresh air.

"He has the bloody flux. I've seen it many times."

"What can cause it?"

The woman shrugged. "I've heard it said lying on damp ground. Or breathing in bad air, that comes off a swamp. I don't really know, I'm not a doctor. And I am not sure they know either, though for the right fee they will make something up."

"What can I do for him?"

Señora Alonso studied her with sympathetic dark eyes. "You can pray for him, child. Sometimes the illness burns itself out with the fever. I have seen men recover. But usually they are younger men than he. If I were you, I would think of a priest not a doctor."

Bianca felt sick with worry but found she was not surprised. Watching the terrifying speed of the illness, it seemed to her that her father had neither the strength nor the will to resist its inexorable pull towards the grave. He had not been well for a long time. Something had drained his strength, melting the once powerful body until she could feel his bones under her fingers when she helped him up into the sleeping loft. She wondered angrily if the injuries he had sustained from the French infantrymen had caused some internal damage, but if they had, it had merely hastened the process. Diego Ramos had been dying for a long time and all she could do was watch helplessly as he sank into unconsciousness.

The priest came and Bianca managed to rouse her father enough to receive the last rites. Once Father Moreno had gone, she washed and changed him again and walked down to the river to wash yet more bedding in a blur of exhaustion. After that she collected wood to keep the fire going into the night, ate a scratch supper and settled to the long night watch.

She awoke suddenly, her neck and back stiff in the wooden armchair and was immediately aware that his harsh breathing had changed. With each breath Ramos uttered a rattling snore which seemed to become slower and more laboured as she sat listening.

Bianca got up stiffly and settled herself on the earthen floor beside her father. She had brought straw to make a bed for him, which was easy to change when he soiled himself, and had managed to borrow two extra blankets from her neighbours. Even so his hand was freezing when she took it between hers and his skin looked mottled, with a bluish tinge. There was a strong odour which suggested that he needed changing again but warmth seemed more important.

For a while she sat with him, holding his hand, but the cold worried her. She rose and went to rebuild the fire using the remainder of the wood then went to the door. Dawn was still some way off and she could not go searching for firewood in this black darkness but as she had hoped, there was a pile awaiting her against the cottage wall. It was the job of the village children to collect wood and for the past few days they had clearly been told to leave some for Bianca. The small kindness brought tears to her eyes.

She carried the wood inside and went to bring the goats milk from the cold pantry. There was an iron bracket in the fireplace and she put the milk to heat in a pan then went to fetch the remainder of their meagre stock of bread. Bread and milk was the only food she had been able to get into her father. She wondered if she could trade some milk and turnips for more. She also wondered if she might be able to mash some egg into the bread and milk. It might give him some much needed strength.

Bianca reached for the pan and set it on the hearth then got up to collect a pottery cup. As she crossed the room she could hear the sound of her bare feet on the cool floor. Otherwise there was complete silence in the room. She froze, listening.

There was nothing.

Bianca turned slowly to look at her father. He lay in the nest of straw and blankets she had made for him. The rattling sound of his breathing had stopped. For a long moment, she could not make herself move. Eventually she went to his side and knelt down. Very gently she touched his face and the remains of his wispy hair. Finally she leaned over him and turned her face to one side so that her cheek was against his parted lips. She could not feel any whisper of breath. With a heavy leaden feeling in her gut, she reached for his wrist. It was frail and cold. She placed her fingers over the inside and searched for a pulse but she knew that she would not find one. He had died silently and peacefully while she had searched for ways of keeping him alive.

Bianca sat for a while, holding his hand. He had not been an easy man and had never seemed particularly appreciative of everything his wife then later his daughter had done to make him comfortable. Still, he had always been there, a steady figure in her life and when it mattered he had defended her fearlessly. He had refused several attempts to bully her into marriage with men she did not like and he had risked his life to save her from rape. In his own morose way, she thought he had loved her. In her own briskly practical way, she had loved him in return.

Eventually the room became lighter and the fire began to die again. Bianca got to her feet. She was stiff and sore and very cold and she discovered to her surprise that at some point she had begun to cry. There would be things to do, a body to wash and lay out and a burial to arrange. That would require money, but she had a little saved from the sale of eggs, milk and some of her vegetables. She also had the coins that Gabriel Bonnet had left for her. She would manage.

***

For a short time, the village closed ranks protectively around the bereaved daughter and Bianca was grateful. Señora Alonso and her daughter came up to help prepare Diego Ramos for burial and the priest agreed to hold the burial service for a very small charge. There were no young men in the village, they were all at war either with the Spanish army or with the bands of partisans who were encamped in the hills. The priest enlisted the help of some of the boys to dig the grave which needed to be deep as there was no coffin.

After the funeral, the priest opened his little house to the mourners and the village pooled its resources and brought wine and hard baked biscuits. Bianca accepted their condolences and tried to ignore their obvious curiosity about what she intended to do next, although she knew they were dying to ask. She took refuge in silence and hoped they would think it grief and not rudeness, but she could not have told them what she did not yet know herself.

When the last of them had gone, Bianca went through into Father Moreno's tiny kitchen to see if his elderly servant needed any help. It was clear that she was not needed, so she went back to the little church where she found the priest also about the business of tidying up. He straightened as she entered and watched as she made the habitual genuflection before the altar then came to join her as she sat on the plain wooden pew.

"A difficult day, Bianca."

"Yes. Thank you, Father, you've been very kind."

He gave a reserved smile. "I hesitate to speak of this on such a day, but I know I will not have been the only one to ask."

"What will I do next?"

"Yes."

Bianca took a deep breath. "I need do nothing immediately, Father. I have tended the land and the animals without help for the past year. My father has not been well enough to help me for a long time."

"I know. I have admired how well you have managed, my child. And you are right, you can have some time to mourn. But forgive me, I do not think you will be given very long."

"Why?"

"Child, you are a young woman and unmarried. You cannot live alone. People will think it strange and unwomanly and unseemly."

"There are many women living without a man in these times."

"Of course. But they are married, even if their husbands are away. Or they are widows. They have a man's name to give them respectability. You had that with your father but now? I know you have refused several suitors, but I think you must resign yourself."

Bianca was under no illusion that he was speaking theoretically and her gratitude was beginning to be replaced by a slow burning anger.

"Has somebody spoken to you, Father?"

"Yes, my child. Pedro Rodriguez from the village of Hernandez. He wanted to attend the burial but I persuaded him that you should have a little time. Still, with your father gone, you need the protection of a man."

She did not speak for a moment, picturing Rodriguez. He was a tall stooping man with a thick grey beard which did not quite conceal his pinched mouth.

"Father, he has two sons who are older than I am."

"Indeed he does. One farms his wife's land. The other has gone to join the army. Senor Rodriguez needs a wife to take care of him and to help him. He has a good farm, small but well tended and the house is bigger than you are used to. You're strong and of childbearing age and he has a liking for you."

"He wants an unpaid servant. He must be sixty, how can he want more children?"

"That hardly matters," the priest said inexorably. "You need a husband and there is nobody else. I have told him to wait a week or two and then I will invite him here and we will discuss the arrangements."

"What of my cottage? My livestock? My land?"

"You can take the beasts with you. As to the land, I do not think you will be allowed to keep it, Bianca. Probably the elders will give it to one of the men who…"

"They have no right to take what is mine. I am my father's daughter. He inherited the land from his brother and I from him."

"Do not raise your voice in anger in the Lord's house, Bianca. Marriage is the lot of women. You should be grateful that there is a man ready to take you. The alternative is to go to the hills to join up with the partisans and I know that some of the women in the village believe that is what you will do. They are always looking for women to help with domestic duties."

Bianca gave a derisive snort. "I know very well what those duties are likely to be, Father. It won't involve marriage, or even choice."

"I am relieved that you are not considering that option. Child, I know you are upset and this is a shock to you, but I believe when you have had time to think, you will realise that Senor Rodriguez is the best choice. The only choice."

Bianca did not reply. It was pointless. She knew that the priest genuinely believed that he had found the best solution for her. She also knew that he was probably right. She might manage for a few months, but in the end they would not allow her to live alone and free as an unmarried woman. Their kindness had touched her, but such kindness came with strings attached.

She thought about it walking back to the cottage. It was quiet in the early twilight and very clean and tidy. Her animals were back in their rightful place in the small stable and she fed and watered them, her throat tight around tears and her heart aching. She missed her father, not only for his taciturn presence in the cottage and in her life but also for the protection and respectability he gave her. Without him she was adrift in a world not designed for a young woman to survive alone, no matter how capable she might be.

She sat late into the night, staring into the fire, considering her options. She knew several of the young men who fought with the guerrilla bands and she knew that if she chose, she could seek their protection but it would not lead to marriage or even a lasting alliance and the thought of being passed around like some worn out garment was unbearable.

Rodriguez was unthinkable. She had disliked him when he had first applied for her hand and she did not think that he would have forgotten her determined refusal. She would live a life of constant gratitude and she had a feeling that Rodriguez would expect a great deal from a wife in return for his name and his protection.

There was no other man in the district likely or able to offer for her. Bianca supposed she could stay where she was and try to brazen it out, tending her plot and her livestock and surviving the long cold winter as best she could; but after the depredations of the French, the village would need to help each other to survive. A lone woman trying to live without male protection would be vulnerable both to theft and personal attack and she no longer trusted the people to take care of her. If her place in the village relied upon her willingness to fit in, then it was no place for her.

Bianca rose and went to the corner of the room. There was an area of loose earth which concealed a small cloth bag in which she kept her precious supply of money. She had hoarded it jealously, refusing to allow her father to spend too much on tobacco or brandy. This was their savings, against a bad harvest or a long winter. She tipped it out onto the table. There was more than her father had known, since she had never told him of the Frenchman's generous gift. It was enough to feed her for a while, even if they took everything from her and enough to buy lodgings on whatever journey she chose to take. It was might even be enough for a small dowry should she find a man to offer it to, but there was nobody she liked enough. Perhaps that should not matter but she was still able to remember her parents, before her mother died on Tenerife, and she knew that they had liked each other a great deal. She wanted what they had, or nothing at all. That was unreasonable and against all common sense.

The trouble was that she had found it, briefly and unsuitably, in the person of a big scarred Frenchman with a slight paunch and a ready laugh. She had only known Bonnet for a week but the memory of his smile, his casual kindness and his curious sense of honour had remained with her, warming her through the worst of her father's illness and the misery of his death. She wished that she had found a way to tell him during those few days, that she would not have minded if he had taken her hand one evening as they walked down to feed her hidden livestock and asked if she would stay a while in the dim forest with him, safe from prying eyes.

Bonnet was gone and the news from several fleeing citizens was that Tarragona was under siege and likely to fall into French hands. Bianca wondered if she made her way to the city, she would be able to find him in the siege lines. The idea was so daring that she was shocked at herself for considering it but once she had done so, she could not push it from her mind.

She had no idea if Bonnet would find a thin, exhausted Spanish peasant girl an attractive proposition to take to bed, but she had gained the impression that he had a low opinion of his chances with women and that might work in her favour. At the very least, he might be willing to offer her his protection until she could either find work in the city or a different lover. She was not beautiful but she was not ugly either and the French army was full of men without female companionship. She supposed the only difference between that and the guerrilla encampment, was patriotism and she felt no particular loyalty to Spain. Her country had done nothing for her, either under the Bourbons or King Joseph Bonaparte and she was cynically aware that some local man was just as likely to take advantage of an unprotected woman as a French infantryman. Bonnet, with all his opportunities, had not only respected her but had made sure his men did the same.

The risks of such a journey were enormous but balanced against the certainty of a miserable life married to a man she loathed they seemed worth taking. There was no point in lingering over her decision. She made an inventory of her few possessions and realised there was little she wanted to take with her. With no further need to save for the winter, she lived well for the next few days, eating properly and catching up on her sleep. She considered what to do with her livestock. A public sale would attract the attention of the priest and she had no wish to find Rodriguez on her doorstep trying to press his suit. Few of the villagers could give her much for the animals, but even a little would be better than simply abandoning them. After some thought, Bianca put on her shawl and walked up through the village to the substantial cottage inhabited by the Widow Alonso and her two daughters. Of all of them she thought that this woman, who had remained determinedly alone after the death of her husband, might understand or at least not make a fuss about it.

Señora Alonso listened to her proposition in silence, then went to bring wine and two cups. They were alone in the kitchen and Bianca sipped the wine, remembering how much Bonnet had enjoyed it. The kitchen doubled as Señora Alonso's still room and there were bunches of herbs drying on a wooden rack and a strong smell of wild garlic.

"I do not understand, Bianca," the older woman said finally. "According to Father Moreno, you will be taking the livestock as a dowry to Pedro Rodriguez when you marry him."

Bianca took a deep breath and raised her eyes. "I am not going to marry him. I am leaving the village."

"To go where?"

"To Tarragona."

"Tarragona? Child, are you mad? The French were marching on Tarragona. By now they'll have the city sewn up like a miser's purse. You'll never get through the siege lines."

"The siege will not last forever, Señora, and I may be able to find work within the city. Or possibly a man. A different man."

Señora Alonso studied her for a long moment. "Are you following that big Frenchman, child?"

Bianca felt herself blush. She took another sip of wine. "He may not want me, Señora. But if he does not, there will be somebody who will."

"If you are auctioning yourself to the highest bidder, you could walk up to the Spanish lines. At least they will speak your language."

"And I know very well the words they will use, if they bother to speak to me at all."

Shrewd dark eyes regarded her thoughtfully. "What of your Frenchman? Did he talk to you?"

"Yes. He was good to talk to."

"And has he a wife and family left behind in France?"

"No."

"How do you know?"

"Why would he lie to me? He was not…we did not…"

The midwife gave a splutter of laughter. "Girl, are you telling me you are following a man without even knowing if he wants you?"

"I know it will sound crazy to you, Señora. To everybody. But this…this may well be my one chance to have something different. If I stay here, I will have to marry Rodriguez and clean up his mess and warm his bed and I will die of it. I will shrivel up day by day until there is nothing left of me. I was not born to this. I did not grow up here and without my father I have nothing to stay for."

The older woman surveyed her with surprising sympathy. "I know you've never really fitted in, child. How could you, you were used to a wandering life. But so far you've had your father to protect you. This is different. You might make it to Tarragona and find your Frenchman. You might even persuade him to take you on. But you are just as likely to end as a raped corpse in a ditch."

"That could just as easily happen to me here, Señora, if I try to carry on alone."

The other woman did not respond immediately. Eventually she said:

"I wish I could argue that is not true, but I cannot. There are such men in every community. Rules keep them in check, though, which is why a woman needs a man to protect her and to give her respectability. You need a husband."

"I will not give myself to a man I cannot stand just to remain safe. My father, for all his faults, understood that."

Señora Alonso snorted and got up. "Your father should have beaten some sense into you while you were young enough still to listen. I will take the animals and any stores you must leave behind. I can give you something for them, although not much."

"Thank you. But please…I do not wish anybody to know, Señora."

"I have no need to tell anybody. I think Father Moreno would try to stop you for your own good."

"I think Father Moreno would try to stop me for Rodriguez' good," Bianca said cynically. "I wonder if he made a donation to the church in payment for the priest's good offices?"

"Very possibly. They are both men, after all. I will bring the money to the cottage later and collect the beasts on the day you leave. But I will require a proper bill of sale or these fools will accuse me of stealing them. Can you provide it? I do not know if you can read and write."

"I can but I have no paper or ink."

"Then I will do it here. Wait."

Bianca finished her wine as the other woman bustled about preparing the bill. She took the pen to sign it, trying to remember the last time she had needed to write something. It felt clumsy in her hand as she traced her name.

With the formalities over, Señora Alonso disappeared again and returned with the money. It was undoubtedly less than the market value of the animals but more than Bianca had hoped to get. She stowed the coins with the others in her purse and rose to leave.

"Thank you, Señora. I will leave early tomorrow. It is not a long journey but I intend to keep to the smaller roads until I know more about where the army is camped so it will take a few days."

"You should take food with you. The French will have taken everything in the villages close to the siege lines, they will have nothing to spare. Show caution with the soldiers, they cannot be trusted. Wait until you can approach an officer. Stay here, I have something for you."

Bianca wanted to say that she had considerably more experience of life in an army camp than Señora Alonso but she refrained. The older woman bustled about again and returned with a small bundle which she pushed into Bianca's hands.

"It is an old shawl. It was my mother's but it is warmer than that threadbare garment you wear. Take care, I have wrapped up some bread and some bacon. You will need food that you can carry with you."

Bianca stared down at the bundle feeling close to tears. "Señora, I cannot…"

"Take them. I cannot pay you what those animals are worth but I am glad you came to me. I am glad you trusted me. I will make sure you are well on the road before I collect them."

"Anything left in the cottage is yours, though there will not be much. Thank you for your kindness and your understanding, Señora."

Señora Alonso pulled her into a quick embrace. "I still think you are mad, Bianca Ramos. But I envy you your courage. I hope you find what you are looking for, in some form or another. Good luck."

***

Durrell thought that watching the steady progress of the French siege of Tarragona was like watching a ship being driven inexorably onto the rocks with no possible way of saving it. The Royal Navy squadron kept well away from the reach of the French guns and were in no danger, but they could do little to help the Spanish garrison apart from to carry supplies and fresh troops. According to Commodore Codrington this ought to have been enough, but Durrell thought privately that Codrington's obviously poor opinion of most of the Spanish commanders was a blind spot.

Durrell had been introduced to several of the Spanish leaders at dinner aboard the *Blake* and he wondered if Codrington realised how bad he was at concealing his impatience. The Marquis of Campoverde was new in post and gave the impression of a man scrambling to catch up with events. He commanded a disparate collection of troops and his senior officers were a problem: not because of any individual incompetence but because they were so suspicious of each other and so conscious of their own rank and position that they seemed to find it difficult to co-operate.

Hugh Kelly was better than Codrington at concealing his exasperation. Codrington had arrived back at Tarragona with a flotilla of British transports and smaller Spanish sloops and feluccas, bearing Campoverde and the four thousand men under his command who had been brought to augment the garrison. Landing the troops took some time and Durrell had the impression that Codrington would have been happy to dump them overboard before sailing off into the distance.

Durrell stood beside Hugh on the quarterdeck of the *Iris* watching the chaos unfolding around him. Hugh's expression suggested that he was enjoying it immensely. Two of the small Spanish feluccas had managed to collide, spilling several men into the water, and there was a cacophony of yelled instructions as the sailors attempted to haul them back aboard. Further in to shore, a lone Spanish frigate was preparing to load soldiers into the ship's boats but her master was screaming frantically to halt the process and

Durrell realised that she had come too far in and was in serious danger of running aground.

Hugh took out his telescope and inspected the frigate then turned his gaze onto the quarterdeck of the *Blake*. He grinned.

"I wish I could hear what Ned is saying. He's very red in the face and is yelling a lot. I'm surprised I can't hear him from here. I wonder if he'd like some assistance?"

Durrell breathed a wholly involuntary sigh of relief. Watching the landing operations falling apart was agonising. "Do you think he would be offended if I offered, sir?"

"I think he will probably try to offer you a permanent job, Mr Durrell. Don't accept it. And tell Commodore Codrington to get himself over here for dinner. They must be sick of him on the *Blake*, the mood he's in."

It took Durrell four hours and the use of most of the *Iris's* boats to complete the landing of the troops. He arrived back on the *Iris,* having missed dinner, with the thanks of a number of Spanish officers ringing in his ears. It had taken a good deal of manoeuvring to avoid their embraces and even more to avoid an invitation to dinner in the citadel but Durrell had managed it. He presented himself in his Captain's dining cabin and was surprised to find Codrington still there, looking considerably happier with a glass of port before him.

"Mr Durrell. Are you here to tell me the landings are complete?" Codrington said hopefully.

"Yes, Commodore. All the troops are ashore and I have organised safe anchorage for the Spanish ships some distance from our own squadron. I thought it best to do so as one or two of their pilots do not seem to know these waters particularly well."

"Some distance?" Codrington repeated. "A considerable distance, I hope?"

"I think it is far enough, sir."

Codrington sighed happily. "I have a very good first officer, Mr Durrell, but if you are ever looking to make a change I am sure something could be arranged."

"Mr Durrell, the Commodore has been drinking port and he's not accustomed to it," Hugh said firmly. "Ignore everything he says. Have you eaten?"

"Not yet, sir."

"Go and get yourself cleaned up and I'll get Brian...I mean Miles...to bring you something from the galley."

Durrell obeyed, masking his grin. Hugh had finally and reluctantly allowed his servant to take up his post as master's mate and had acquired a new servant in the person of Miles Randall, an undersized eleven year old whose late father had been Hugh's ship master. It was Miles' first time at sea since his father was killed in Danish waters and Hugh was watching him like an over-anxious mother.

Miles did not require that much anxiety in Durrell's opinion. He was an alarmingly intelligent child and considerably less clumsy than Brian had been. If Miles had a fault, it was that his brain seemed permanently on double speed and even Durrell struggled to keep up with him at times. It made him an excellent officer's servant and Hugh rather smugly informed Durrell that since making the change his possessions had never been kept in such good order. Durrell estimated that it took Miles about a quarter of his time to perform his duties and about a twentieth of his intelligence. Durrell sometimes worried what Miles was doing with the rest of it but he had decided to leave Hugh with his illusions for a little longer.

When Durrell returned to the dining cabin the boy was just setting a steaming bowl down at the table. Hugh indicated that he should sit and Miles produced cutlery, bread and a glass of wine with the air of a conjuror then whisked himself away. Codrington watched him go with a surprised expression.

"Where on earth do you find them, Hugh? I've been through half a dozen officer's servants and every one has two left feet."

Hugh grinned. The smug expression was back. "I can't take credit for young Miles Randall; his father was the original master of the *Iris* and he served with me on the *Newstead* before that. Miles was born at sea. His mother died a few years back and John left him with his brother's family: but he's been mad to join up and I was glad to give him a chance. He's settled in amazingly well. Very bright, the schoolmaster informs me. Eat, Mr Durrell, we dined earlier. We've been watching your efforts from a safe distance. Very efficient."

"I wish I'd had you at Mataro when I was loading them up," Codrington said morosely. "It took hours and I had to intervene personally or we'd probably still be there. The Spanish staff officers stood around smoking cigars and arguing about which men should go in which boat and whose job it should be to get them there, so I counted them off and ordered them into the cutters myself. I was tempted to leave the officers behind, but I remembered that Sir Richard Keats was mumbling about diplomacy and inter-service relations before I left Cadiz so I pasted on a smile and invited them aboard. My face is still aching."

Hugh was laughing uncontrollably. "I wish I'd seen it."

"If you'd been there, Captain Kelly, you wouldn't have been watching it, you'd have been doing it. Next time they want to use the *Blake* as a troop transport I may take your first officer with me. I like to delegate."

"You're awful at delegating, Ned."

"That's because you consistently refuse to allow me to steal your First Lieutenant. I cannot delegate to idiots. I must say your servant looks promising though. Can you train him to do what you do, Mr Durrell?"

Durrell considered the matter while chewing on a mouthful of mutton stew. "It is early to say, Commodore, but I believe young Randall shows a great deal of promise. Getting him to direct his intelligence may be a little harder, but give us a few years."

"I can wait. I'm tired of doing the work myself. Though I must say I'm pleased with young Lennox. I wasn't sure about taking a Duke's son but he's a thoroughly good lad. Hard working and not at all above himself. It's working out well."

"I never seem to get sons of the nobility applying for a midshipman's berth aboard the *Iris*," Hugh said regretfully.

Durrell finished another mouthful heroically, wondering how long the cook had stewed this mutton. It was like eating leather in gravy. "Possibly that is because you refuse to consider them, Captain. I believe you had a very flattering application from a connection of the Fane family for the position of First Lieutenant which you rejected."

"Just as well I did, or Commodore Codrington would have had to untangle his Spanish troops all by himself. I gather you were on shore with Campoverde last night, Ned, looking at the siege lines."

Codrington rolled his eyes again and took another sip of port. He was a moderate drinker by navy standards but Hugh could usually tempt him with a particularly good wine. Durrell thought that he looked as though he needed it today.

"Every conversation I have with that man confirms my opinion that he is not up to the job," Codrington said. "I was trying to explain to him that we can shoot as much as we like at the beach and we have the range, but now that they've completed their trenches it is a waste of shot. O'Donnell situated a battery on the shore, specifically to protect the Mole, that would be far more useful. We had a pointless argument about whether it was within range or not, then when I walked him down there I found he had no idea where it was and had made no attempt to find out."

"The French are digging out towards the Olivo Fort," Hugh said. "They're making more progress than I'd like. Ned, you've been very confident all along that this town can hold. I told you last time we met I wasn't as sure. What's your opinion now?"

Codrington's gaze fell to the wine glass on the table. He picked it up and swirled the remainder of the rich red liquid around, inhaled it deeply and took a small sip.

"The town ought to be able to hold," he said. "If we had O'Donnell here and proper support from the rest of the Spanish forces, I still think it could. But we don't. Hugh, are you happy with the command here? I need to go back up the coast for more supplies and I want to speak to Charles O'Donnell. I don't know him as well as I know his brother, but Henry speaks very highly of him. I'm half-supply ship and half-diplomat here and I'm feeling my way." Codrington hesitated. "It means a great deal to me knowing I have a man on the spot who is capable of taking whatever action is needed should events change suddenly. You're making my job a lot easier."

Hugh smiled. Durrell recognised the smile, not Hugh's usual flashing grin but something warmer, denoting both understanding and friendship. It was that smile that would make Durrell follow this man into hell and back if necessary.

"You didn't need a nursemaid, Ned. Nobody thought you did. You needed a second in command and a friend. I can be both of those."

"I know you can. Thank you. I should be getting back, I want to catch the early tide and I've some letters to write. Mr Durrell, thank you for your efforts today, I am exceedingly grateful. No, don't come up. I can find my own way to the boat."

Codrington stood up, draining his glass and went to the cabin door where he turned and smiled.

"Oh and Hugh?"

"Yes?"

"Sir Richard Keats definitely thinks I need a nursemaid."

Hugh looked back at him, his expression serious. "I think he may have used the term governess, sir. Or perhaps it was menagerie keeper, I can't quite remember."

Codrington laughed aloud, called him an impressively vulgar name and left. Hugh waved Durrell back to his seat and refilled his glass.

"Finish your meal, Mr Durrell. Thank you for today. Poor Ned really needed a break."

"I was happy to help, sir." Durrell pushed his plate away without regret and sipped the wine. "I prefer it when I am allowed to intervene when something is going badly awry. It is frustrating watching…"

He broke off, realising that he was about to sound appallingly conceited but Hugh laughed aloud and finished his sentence for him.

"Watching other men struggle with something you find very easy. I know, fella, it's painful to watch you."

"I thought today that Commodore Codrington seemed more relaxed, sir. More like his usual self."

"You mean less like a man with a poker up his backside? Yes, I thought that too. I'm glad. We had a brief conversation just before he left, so I wasn't sure how he'd be, but he's had time to think about it and it seems he's glad we're here. He asked me to apologise on his behalf for his rudeness that day on the *Blake*. I think he felt it would be too awkward to do it himself."

"It would, sir. I accept wholeheartedly, but I am not sure that his remark was aimed at me at all."

Hugh studied him and sipped his wine. "You haven't asked, Mr Durrell."

"I was not sure if it was a professional or personal disagreement between you and the Commodore, sir. One may be my business but the other is definitely not."

Hugh smiled. "We're friends, Mr Durrell, which makes it your business. It was more of a political debate…a clash of ideas, I suppose. You're aware that I had some involvement with a newly established abolitionist society while I was in London, of course."

"I attended a meeting with you, sir. I thought you spoke very well."

"I got involved at the behest of Keats: one of the young clergymen is a family friend. But it's a cause dear to my heart."

"But not to Commodore Codrington's?"

"It's more complicated for him. I don't know how he really feels about slavery because I've never asked. And that was deliberate because I know he owns a share of his late uncle's plantation along with his siblings. I'm not sure about Jane, but she was born in Kingston which probably means she came from a plantation family as well."

Durrell winced internally. "I see. I had no idea, sir."

"Well I had, but I admit I didn't think of it when I stood up on that platform and spoke. I'm not sure how he heard about it. It was reported in several newspapers, but there were also one or two naval officers present and they might have passed it on."

"He cannot hold your principles against you, sir."

"He doesn't. But he now knows what they are, which is uncomfortable for him." Hugh sighed. "It's very easy from where I stand to judge any man who owns a slave. And I have, in principle. But Ned pointed out to me that I might have felt differently if I'd received such an inheritance at a difficult time in my life. I want to say I'd renounce it, but would I have?"

Durrell gave a little smile. "I think you would have boarded a ship and gone to see what you'd inherited, sir. I've never known you to take on any responsibility that you don't fully understand. Unlike me, you have visited a plantation. Do you think you could have stood there and taken possession of such an inheritance?"

Hugh's lips curled in an answering smile. "No," he admitted. "No, I prefer my little green patch of Mann, Mr Durrell, where my farm labourers might be my dependents but they have the perfect right to tell me to piss off whenever they like. Although of course they live in tied cottages for the most part, so it might not be wise."

"I'm sorry things have been difficult with Commodore Codrington, sir, but it seems that he has reached an accommodation with the situation."

"He said that he isn't ready to talk about it. And I can accept that. He's not the only man I know who owns slaves, Mr Durrell. Half of London is built on the proceeds and before I get carried away about that, there's a mansion or two on Mann that came about the same way. I think Ned is uncomfortable talking about it because I think he's uncomfortable thinking about it. And I'm glad. Maybe one day we'll be able to have a different conversation."

"I hope that one day there will be no slavery, sir, and no need to have any conversation about it at all," Durrell said seriously. "I did not find time to mention that when I was in London, I met Miss Collingwood."

Hugh put down his glass and stared in astonishment. "You didn't find time? That's a matter of some significance, Mr Durrell. You know I've been concerned about the girl. How is she? Has her father forgiven her yet?"

"I'm sorry, sir. I am not sure why I did not tell you. She is back in London because her father has been taken very ill. He suffered a huge stroke and it is not thought that he will recover."

Hugh raised his eyebrows. "That's interesting," he said affably. "I suppose I should murmur some polite regrets, but as I met the man and I know how he treated that girl, I feel like writing a letter of congratulation. Is she all right? Did you get the chance to ask?"

"I did. We met by chance in Ackermann's but I called on her the following morning. It was a relief to finally be able to tell her how very sorry I was for my brother's appalling behaviour."

"Your brother did the girl a favour, Mr Durrell, though I know that wasn't his intention."

"That was what Miss Collingwood said," Durrell said with a faint smile. "We talked for a long time. Given her situation, her social activities are obviously limited, but she told me that she has attended several meetings of the Society for the Abolition of Slavery in British Dominions and had heard that you had been involved."

Hugh's eyes widened. "Really? Does she know that her father…?"

"Oh yes, sir."

Hugh laughed aloud. "Good for her. I wonder if she's staying in London. I'll mention it to Roseen when I write, I know she'd like to call when she's back in town."

"I think Miss Collingwood would appreciate that, sir. Most of her current visitors have an unmarried gentleman in tow."

Hugh's eyes gleamed with amusement. "Is she his sole heiress? I'll just bet they do. I hope they're not persecuting the poor girl, she's been through enough. Are you going to write to her, Mr Durrell?"

"I do not have permission, sir, it would not be suitable."

Hugh looked as though he would have liked to say more, but to Durrell's relief he refrained. Durrell finished his wine and rose.

"With your permission, sir, I'll make the rounds before…"

"Leave it, Mr Durrell. You've done enough today, you must be exhausted. I'll conduct the inspection tonight."

"Thank you, Captain. Goodnight."

Durrell retired to his small cabin where he seated himself at his tiny writing desk and took out his log book. He was tired, but the habit of making his daily entry was ingrained into him by now and there were some interesting points about the difficulties of the landing operation that he wanted to record. As he wrote, he reflected that this was the one legacy from his service with Sir Home Riggs Popham that he would never regret. Popham had given him his first personal log book and taught him the value of these daily records and however much Durrell had come to dislike the man, he was grateful for this. Durrell thought about Abigail and wondered if she was making good use of the book he had bought for her. He hoped their sister-in-law had not discovered her hiding place.

This led him to think about Faith Collingwood. When his entry was finished, he reached into his storage chest and took out a bundle of letters. For a moment he sat looking at them on his desk. They had come to represent all his frustrations about his friendship with Faith and the brutal way it had been cut short. He had written to her regularly this past year, sharing his thoughts and feelings and the day-to-day happenings of his life. He had never sent them and never thought he might do so.

Today the letters looked subtly different in the light shed by his closed lantern. They had not changed; the alteration was in him. Since their meeting in London, he had thought of Faith constantly, not with regret or guilt but with simple happiness. They had talked for an hour and said very little of consequence, updating each other with the story of their time apart. But he had found pleasure in her company again and he was quite sure she felt the same way.

Durrell could not be a suitor. He was not a pauper but as a younger son his financial position was embarrassing when set against the size of her fortune and he would not be yet another man trying to persuade her into marriage. But Durrell did not think Faith was looking for a suitor at all at this point in her life. She needed a friend, and Durrell thought he was very well qualified for that. He could not send these letters, but he sat to write the next one with a different hope that one day he might be in a position to write to her properly.

Chapter Eleven

Faith Collingwood's return to Wickham House caused a considerable stir in the neighbourhood which had still not died down after she had been there for a month.

Her business manager was appalled when she approached him about the move. Faith explained her reasoning carefully at first, then in more detail, and then finally with an edge of exasperation in her voice. Glinde's responses were a catalogue of reasons why she could not possibly go back to Norfolk. Faith stopped talking and listened for a while until eventually he appeared to have talked himself out.

"Is that everything, Mr Glinde?"

"It is more than enough," Glinde said. "I am sorry, Miss Collingwood, since I realise you had set great store by this project, but it is not to be contemplated. I hope I have helped you to see it rationally now. Now if you wished to spend some time at Barton Hall there could be no objection. Perhaps we can try to find you a more mature lady to act as chaperone and…"

"Mr Glinde, have you heard one single word that I have been saying?" Faith asked frostily. "I have no intention of going to Barton Hall. I have not yet decided what I wish to do with the place. I don't particularly like it, but I have taken your point that I may have taken against it because it was my father's choice. I think perhaps you are right that I should authorise Mr Cannock to rent it out until I have had a chance to reconsider."

Glinde bowed his head. "I think that would be a wise choice, Miss Collingwood. It is a fine house and an excellent estate and while it is far too large to be comfortable for a young lady alone, it may well suit you later on when you have a husband and family to consider."

"If I choose to do so."

Glinde drew his brows together. "I know it is very soon," he said gently. "It will take you some time to recover from…from the events of the past year or two. But with the sad loss of your father…I do not think you realise, Miss Collingwood, how much your world has opened up. I am convinced that with the right sponsor, we can achieve a presentation at court and a proper Season. You have beauty, fortune and excellent manners. There is no reason why you could not aim very high indeed, ma'am. Just see out your mourning period quietly and then..."

"That is precisely what I intend to do, sir, but I will do it on my terms not yours," Faith said crisply. "If I should ever desire to enter Society there will be time enough to consider a suitable chaperone. In the meantime I am perfectly happy with Miss Danjuma as my companion. I intend to return to Norfolk the week after next. That will allow me enough time to apprise the existing staff of my intention and to complete any necessary shopping here. I will…"

"Miss Collingwood, I must insist…"

"No you must not," Faith said in steely tones. Glinde froze, staring at her in astonishment.

"Ma'am?"

"I am beginning to think that I may be in need of a new man of business rather than a companion, Mr Glinde, if it is going to be this difficult to persuade you to do a simple thing like making travel arrangements. Once I am established at Wickham House I will request the assistance of Mr Turner in finding local builders and workmen to begin the renovations."

"Do you have any idea how difficult and how uncomfortable that will be?"

"Do you have any idea how uncomfortable it is to live in a house with moisture running down the inside of the walls and no means of buying warmer clothing for the winter months?" Faith snapped, her patience gone. "You have no idea what I have endured and no idea what I am capable of doing. Certainly I am capable of dismissing you from my employ and finding another business manager to replace you if you persist in treating me like an idiot or a child. Of course I will be uncomfortable for a time, but I will also be busy and interested and a long way from this parade of half-witted young men trying to marry me for my fortune. I do not propose to live the rest of my life in Norfolk, but it is where I wish to be at this moment. In the house that I own, with the companion that I have chosen. Is there anything about that which you do not understand, sir?"

Glinde's face was scarlet. "No, ma'am."

"Thank you. Please make the travel arrangements. I will ask Abisola to write to the housekeeper and we will look at hiring more staff when we get there. I'm sure Abel will help with that as well: he knows everybody in the neighbourhood. I will not take up any more of your time as I know how busy you are. Good afternoon, Mr Glinde."

Glinde bowed rather lower than usual and left. The door closed behind him very gently. Faith stood still in the centre of the room breathing deeply. For a moment she could not believe that she had won.

"Well you told him what for and no mistake, Miss Faith."

Abisola's tone was rich with amusement. Faith had almost forgotten she was there. She turned to look at her companion, putting her cool hands against her scarlet cheeks.

"Oh my goodness, I believe I just lost my temper."

"No reason why you shouldn't have, ma'am, he was asking for it." Abisola began to laugh. "You've got a rare turn of phrase when you're angry. I especially liked the part about the half-witted young men."

"Oh don't, I was so rude. And he is related to one of them."

"Doesn't mean he shouldn't hear the truth about it. Don't you worry, Miss Faith. You know what's right for you. Just stick to it."

"I will. Thank you, Abisola, for agreeing to come with me."

"I'm looking forward to it, ma'am. I like to be busy."

After two weeks at Wickham House, Faith realised that Abisola was speaking the truth. Her companion, given a task to perform, was like a small whirlwind of activity. She toured the house with Faith on the day of their arrival, observing the damp walls and peeling paint with thinned lips. Faith watched her anxiously, wondering if the other girl was regretting her decision.

"I told you it was a mess," she said apologetically. "Do you think it will be too much work to make it beautiful again?"

"No, ma'am. It's a good house: got good solid walls. I reckon new roof tiles and new window frames might fix that damp. Nothing wrong with this house that time and money can't mend, but I don't know why that means they can't keep it clean enough. I started out as a housemaid, I'd be ashamed to own this work."

She reached out and ran one dark finger over the surface of a small table, wrinkling her nose at the dust it picked up.

"We probably need more servants," Faith said.

"We'll start by getting the ones you have off their lazy bottoms and back to work," Abisola said crisply. "Then we'll talk to your Mr Turner and make some lists."

By the end of the first week, Faith had stopped worrying and apologising to her bewildered servants. She was too busy to do either. Under Abisola's ruthless supervision the house was cleaned from top to bottom. Every dusty corner was scoured and every piece of furniture polished. Bedding and drapes were washed and dried, mattresses thrown outside to air and carpets and rugs were beaten. The servants were harried from room to room and given no time to complain. To Faith's surprise, after the first few days they seemed to enter into the spirit of the project with enthusiasm.

Only the cook departed, her portmanteau clutched in her hand, after a spirited discussion with Abisola about undercooked meat. The kitchen maid took over the preparation of basic meals and Faith wrote to her housekeeper in London asking her to procure another cook. Afterwards she donned an apron and went to join her companion who was turning out the linen cupboards making little noises of contempt at mould on sheets and badly darned towels.

Faith spent hours with Abel Turner discussing necessary repairs and meeting a series of contractors. She wrote to London merchants for samples of wallpaper and curtain fabric and wandered through rooms she had never used, with colours and ideas spinning in her head. Recklessly she set up accounts with local tradesmen, hired more staff and sang at the top of her voice as she weeded the overgrown garden.

"How much is all this going to cost, Miss Faith?" Abisola asked her one morning as they watched the new gardener Faith had employed receiving his instructions from Abel Turner. "I hope you're really as rich as you think you are."

Faith laughed. "I am keeping accounts of every penny spent. Not that I need to, it's just a habit my father ingrained in me. When I first realised that he could no longer control my spending, Abi, I used to flinch inside every time I ordered a new gown. Now I have decided not to care. I'm not wasting this money I'm turning something that was badly neglected into something very beautiful. And to assuage my guilt, I have told myself that this is back payment for twenty years of neglect and bullying."

"And what does Mr Glinde say?"

"I think Mr Glinde is quite relieved that I am behaving myself and actually doing what I said I would do. Heaven knows what he thought I really had in mind. Something far less respectable than house renovation, I suspect."

Abisola laughed. "He doesn't trust me as a duenna, ma'am."

"He is seriously mistaken then. He should have seen you freezing out some of my more annoying suitors, it would have delighted him. You were very good at it."

"That wasn't hard at all, they were driving you mad, ma'am. All the same, I hope you'll make it clear when a suitor comes along that you don't want me to get rid of."

Faith smiled. "I don't think we need to worry about that for a long time, Abi. If at all."

"Not even your young navy gentleman?"

Faith closed her eyes, wishing she did not blush so easily. She opened them again and fixed her companion with a look. "He is not mine, Abisola, and I've no idea when I'll see him again."

"I'd say that depends on how long it takes him to get from wherever they put him ashore, ma'am."

Faith could not help smiling. "It could be years," she said a little wistfully. "His duty will always come first with him, Abi."

"Would that matter, ma'am, as long as you came a very close second?"

Faith thought about it and decided she was right. She also decided that she was not yet ready to have this kind of conversation about a man who had never offered her anything other than friendship.

"I don't know," she said. "At the moment, I'm more interested in what colour to paint my studio. Come and look at the samples again, Abisola and stop matchmaking or I'll send you back to London."

Abisola fell in beside her and they walked back towards the house. "I don't think you'll do that, ma'am," she said consideringly. "You like laughing at my efforts to learn the pianoforte too much to send me away."

Faith could not repress a grin and decided that her companion made a very good point.

***

With little to do but supervise his men's share of the siege works and complain about the poor quality of provisions, Bonnet amused himself by making a cautious circuit of the outside defences. He was by no means sure that Olivo could be taken by escalade and he thought Suchet would be rash to make the attempt. With the garrison augmented by Campoverde's extra troops, the Spanish seemed to take courage. General Harispe's division had taken two outlying entrenchments close to Fort Olivo but the French defenders were almost immediately subjected to several desperate attempts to retake them. The first failed but the second managed to drive the French back from their lines and destroyed a section of the siege works. It took the intervention of General Habert's men to chase the Spanish back into the lower town and there were heavy losses on both sides.

During the previous week, Suchet's artillery established four breaching batteries, which included one of four 24-pounders; one of three eight-inch mortars; another of three 16-pounders and the fourth of two howitzers to batter the fort on its right. Getting the guns to their various emplacements was a hideously difficult task. It proved impossible to use horses so the soldiers themselves were put in harness to drag the artillery into place. Colonel Lacasse provided two companies for the task, fortunately not Bonnet's, and the rest of the 30th watched from the heights in seething impotence as the men were cut down by grape shot. As they fell, others took their place and slowly and painfully the guns were dragged into position.

The light was beginning to fade. The walls and turrets of Tarragona stood out against a glorious sky streaked with gold fire as the sun sank over the distant mountains. Bonnet watched the shifting colours and listened to the crash of artillery and the crackle of musket fire, wondering how many men from the 30th would die before they could get the guns set up to return fire.

"When do you think they'll be ready to open fire, sir?" Allard asked, coming to stand beside Bonnet.

"Possibly later tonight," Bonnet said grimly. "Certainly tomorrow. And I can't fucking wait to watch them blow holes in that bloody fort. I'm sick of sitting here watching them cut down our men. I'm looking forward to giving them a taste of their own medicine."

"Yes, sir. How long do you think it will take…"

Allard broke off, listening. Bonnet heard it too, a sudden clamour of sound from the direction of the city. He turned to look and realised that there were troops streaming out from the gates, bearing down on the men working on the batteries with terrifying speed. It was impossible to make out details in the gathering dusk but Bonnet had the impression that there were a lot of men. This looked like a serious attack.

"They're making another sortie," Allard said. "It looks like most of the garrison. Sir, what should we do."

Bonnet swore and spun around, scanning the watching troops for his commanding officer. He found him immediately, apparently in urgent consultation with his adjutant. Bonnet sprinted to join them and the other captains of the 30th converged on Lacasse at the same time. Lacasse held up his hands.

"Colonel, we need to get the men on the move," Forget said urgently.

"Not yet, Forget."

"But sir, that's a major attack, we may be needed." Foulon sounded horrified.

"We have no orders," Lacasse said. "We can do nothing without orders, Foulon. General Salme is in command and knows where we are encamped, he will summon us…"

"We should march anyway, Colonel," Bonnet said forcefully. "That's a serious attack, they might well need reinforcements and we're twenty minutes away up here. It can't hurt to get them into position."

Lacasse glared at him. "General Salme is in command," he said again. "If we go marching off without orders, who knows what the consequences will be? We may be required somewhere else…"

"Where the fuck else are they going to want us?" Bonnet bellowed, completely forgetting his usual policy of not raising his head above the parapet with his indolent Colonel. "There's a battle going on down there, Colonel, and we should be in it."

"Enough!" Lacasse snapped furiously. "Form up the men in column immediately but do nothing else. You forget yourself, Bonnet. This is my battalion and I will not march them without orders."

Both Forget and Foulon saluted quickly and turned away. Bonnet stood for a moment, taking a long deep breath. His brain was telling him to walk away and not to make his already difficult relationship with Lacasse worse, but his soldier's instinct screamed at him to make the idiot man see that this was not the moment for the 30th to continue to take their ease and admire the view sitting on a hillside while men fought and died below.

"Sir, please," he said finally, between gritted teeth. "At least send a messenger to find out where we're needed."

"I will await my orders, Bonnet. It is high time that you learned to do the same thing. Back to your company."

Bonnet turned away. He needed to do so before the urge to punch his commanding officer became too strong. Returning to his company he mounted his horse and gave orders in a tone which sent his subalterns and NCOs racing to obey.

The wait was agonising, with the sound of the fighting below filling the night air. It was too dark now to see what was happening apart from the flash of musket fire. The artillery had fallen silent, as neither side could fire without risking hitting their own men. Much of the fighting below was now hand to hand combat and the clash of steel could be heard even up on the hillside.

The sound of battle had begun to die away before a message came, and Bonnet realised that his neck and jaw were aching with tension. He stretched surreptitiously and rotated his shoulders, watching as two riders approached Lacasse. One carried a closed lantern on a pole and Bonnet could see that all three faces looked strained in the dim light. There was no sound from the ranks and the voices carried easily in the still night air.

"Colonel Lacasse. Orders from General Habert, sir, your battalion will guard the artillery for the rest of this night and also provide men to help carry out the dead and wounded. You will remain in position until you receive further orders at dawn."

The man's tone was flat and Bonnet peered through the darkness trying to assess whether Lacasse was intelligent enough to recognise the faint undertone of contempt. He had still not decided, when several more horsemen approached. In the distance, the battlefield was growing quieter, with only the occasional groan of a wounded man or a shouted order. The orders were all in French so Bonnet guessed that the sortie had failed and the Spanish had retreated behind their walls again.

"Colonel Lacasse."

The newcomer's voice was quiet and carried a wealth of authority. Bonnet could not see him properly and did not need to. He had only met General Louis Gabriel Suchet a few times in person, but he had seen him frequently and had heard him addressing the troops regularly. Suchet was only three years older than Bonnet but his commanding manner made him seem older.

Lacasse seemed startled by the arrival of the Commander-in-Chief. He saluted awkwardly and his horse fidgeted as though aware of its rider's discomfort. Suchet reined in. Bonnet held up a hand to indicate that his subalterns should remain in place and walked his mount forward very quietly. He was dying to hear what Suchet had to say and he did not think anybody would notice him. The air was thick with tension.

"General Suchet. Has the action...did our troops...?"

Bonnet winced. Given Lacasse's own spectacular failure to engage, he would not have asked.

"The fighting is over, Colonel and our brave soldiers have triumphed, though at considerable cost. It was unfortunate that your battalion missed the action."

Something in Suchet's voice chilled Bonnet. He stroked his horse's sleek neck soothingly, although he was not sure if it was Apollo or himself in need of comfort.

Lacasse finally seemed as worried as he ought to be. "I had no orders, General," he said. "I have been here awaiting orders. You will see that my men are formed up and ready to go, but we received nothing. We heard nothing."

"I imagine that you heard the rest of your brigade fighting for their lives, Colonel, even from these Elysian heights."

"But orders, General. I did not know if we should join the fighting or if we might be required to march somewhere else…if we might be needed…"

"The time of need is over at present. I believe you have General Habert's orders."

"But General Salme, sir," Lacasse protested. "I had no orders from General Salme and I…"

"General Salme is unable to issue further orders, Colonel," Suchet said. Bonnet realised suddenly that under his calm exterior, the Commander-in-Chief was furious. "He did his duty and when the Spaniards attacked he had his reserves ready – or at least, those of them who were available. He led them forward with immense courage but was shot down and killed instantly. His men continued the attack, enraged at his loss, and pursued the Spaniards to the very walls of the fort. The General will be buried tomorrow, with full honours."

There was a long silence. General Suchet seemed uninterested in breaking it and nobody else dared. Bonnet realised suddenly that he was in a conspicuous position away from the head of his company and that it would be difficult in this painful silence, to get back to it unheard.

The silence was ripped apart by an enormous crash, followed by another and then another. Flashes of light from below denoted the position of Suchet's newly placed artillery. Bonnet saw his opportunity and turned his horse. As he was moving away, he heard Suchet speak again and froze.

"Colonel Lacasse, you will report to General Habert, if you please: he will give you your new orders. I will bear in mind your evident disappointment at missing this action and I will ensure that when we storm the fort, which I think will be soon, your men will have the opportunity to prove their courage and gallantry without risk of any further confusion about orders. Dismissed."

Bonnet touched his heel to Apollo's side and went to join his junior officers, no longer caring if he was seen or heard. Both Allard and Duclos were watching him anxiously and Bonnet noticed several of his fellow captains easing their way forward to listen in.

"What did he say, Captain?" Duclos asked. "Did he say anything about the Colonel not receiving his orders?"

"He looks angry," Captain Bergne said. "What do you think, Bonnet?"

"He lost General Salme in that attack," Bonnet said, pitching his voice as quietly as he could. "He's furious."

"Was that because we did not go to join the battle, sir? Could we have saved him?"

"No. The General said he was shot down in the first charge. But if we'd been there it might have been over more quickly and there'd be fewer losses."

"And our orders now?" Captain Garreau asked. "What happens next?"

Bonnet could hear the anxiety in their voices and wished he could offer some form of reassurance. If Lacasse was in disgrace it would affect his entire battalion. Suchet might even decide to court martial the man for cowardice, but Bonnet did not think he would. Trials were lengthy and notoriously bad for morale and there were better ways of dealing with an officer who failed to do his job properly.

"We're fucked," Bonnet said in matter-of-fact tones. "We're completely and utterly fucked. We're in line for every shitty duty and every suicidal charge that Suchet can come up with until Lacasse either does something impressive enough to wipe the slate clean or does us all a favour and gets his fucking useless head blown off. Lieutenant Allard, get them into column. Tonight, we're either going to go deaf guarding those fucking guns or we'll be wading through blood and guts to bring out the dead and wounded. And that's just tonight. Tomorrow will be a lot worse."

***

General Contreras sailed from Cadiz aboard the *Prueba*, a 40-gun Spanish frigate, and Ángel spent most of the short voyage on deck trying not to be sick. He loathed sailing. It was humiliating for a grown man and an experienced officer to spend his time huddled over a bucket in the corner of the great cabin and only marginally less so to spend it leaning over the ship's rail, but Ángel preferred the latter. It was easier to ignore the occasional snigger from passing crew members than to deal with the relentless teasing of the naval officers. Ángel knew he was over-sensitive but could not help it.

He had not been to Tarragona before and neither had General Contreras, although young García knew the city well. He stood beside Ángel as the ship approached the harbour, pointing out the various landmarks and trying to ignore the relentless crashing of the French guns as they battered the outer defences of the city. Ángel wondered how close they were to creating a breach. The officer who had finally brought orders from Campoverde had given a dramatic account of the progress of the siege but that had been more than a week ago. Siege warfare was unpredictable and progress could be brought to a standstill by difficult ground or a successful sortie.

The frigate signalled their arrival and received permission for them to land. As the boats were prepared, Ángel remained at the rail. The northern side of the town was concealed by a low cloud of black smoke and even from here, the acrid smell of gunpowder caught in his nose and the back of his throat. It was the smell of battle and Ángel felt his stomach tighten and his pulse quicken a little. He had known that they had come here to fight but he was beginning to think they would be in combat sooner than he had expected.

They were met on the quay by a harried looking ADC who led them quickly through the narrow streets to a tall house, close to the impressive Cathedral of St Thekla. The Marquis of Campoverde, who had overall command of the Catalonian forces, awaited them in an elegant salon lined with solemn portraits of Spanish grandees interspersed with enormous gilt-framed mirrors. It was weeks since Ángel had seen the Commander-in-Chief and he thought that Campoverde looked haggard and tired.

"General Contreras, welcome. You arrive at an opportune moment. You must know that we are under attack at Fort Olivo, one of the outer defences."

Contreras frowned, glancing at Ángel. "I can hear that we are under attack, my Lord, but the city is new to me and I was unable to find a map before I left Cadiz. It was not made clear to me what my command here is to be, under your…"

"No matter. There is much to discuss and I will want your opinion, General, but for now, I wish you to take command at the front, facing Olivo. This is Don Jorge Castro, one of my aides. I have asked him to be your guide to the city until you know it better. Soon there will be a meeting of my senior officers and the delegates of the Superior Junta of Catalonia, but for now you should go immediately to assess the situation at the fortress. Castro will guide you to the Rosario Gate and introduce you to the officers there."

There was a stunned silence in the room. Ángel looked at his General and decided he had never seen him look so taken aback.

"Immediately?" Contreras said.

"The need is dire," Campoverde assured him earnestly. "It is possible they will breach within the next few days. I want your opinion on the position by nightfall, General."

Contreras reached into his coat and took out his watch automatically, although Ángel thought that he probably had a very good idea of the time already. "That is less than three hours away, my Lord."

"Yes, yes. I have an appointment with the members of the Junta, but I know – everything I have heard of you – assures me that you are the man for this job. I have faith in you, General Contreras."

Neither Ángel nor García spoke during the walk down to the gate. They were surrounded by troops with smoke-blackened faces. There were wounded among them, some limping along helped by their comrades. A few were carried on stretchers, still and silent. This close, the guns from the French lines were deafening and Ángel could already feel his ears beginning to ring. He felt a slight hollow sickness in his stomach which may have been tension about the coming battle but which might also have been because he had not eaten. It did not seem to have occurred to Campoverde that his new General and his ADCs would require food after their journey.

The Rosario Gate was a simple arch set in one of the old Roman city walls. Captain Castro talked all the way, pointing out the various defences and the disposition of the troops. Ángel recognised his gabbling as nervousness but he still wanted to punch him. Contreras managed to remain polite, asking questions when he could get a word in, but Ángel could sense his unhappiness at being thrown into command without even knowing the ground he was defending.

This close to Fort Olivo, the roar of the French cannon was so loud that it was difficult to have any kind of conversation. Contreras was introduced to the officer in command of the gate and asked a series of intelligent questions which had to be shouted at the top of his voice. They stood on the parapet above the gate looking over at the fort.

Fort Olivo occupied a formidable position. Perched on a rocky escarpment to the north-west of the city, it was surrounded by broad ditches and protected by around fifty guns. Castro pointed towards the enemy's forward battery.

"Their engineers have been struggling to get the trenches close enough to the fort, but now that they've succeeded they're beginning to do damage. Our sorties have had some success and we killed one of their generals only yesterday but now they have that battery working, they will eventually breach."

"Eventually?" Ángel said, as the guns boomed again. It was difficult to see from here just how much damage they were doing but he suspected it was a lot. "The Marquis seemed to think it might be tonight."

"I was in the fort earlier, Captain. I do not think they can form a practical breach tonight, but unless we can capture that position, they may do so tomorrow."

Ángel did not reply. He listened as Contreras asked questions about the French siege works and what had been done to hinder their progress. As far as Ángel could see, it was not enough. The sorties described as successful had brought losses on both sides but they had not driven the French from their positions, which made them a notable failure in Ángel's view.

As darkness fell, the frequency and direction of the gunfire seemed to change. There were flashes up and down the French lines which seemed to come from musket fire as well as cannon. Beside Ángel, Lieutenant García stirred uneasily.

"What's happening, sir? Are they preparing to attack?"

"I think it is unlikely, García," Contreras said. "They are nowhere near ready for an attack on the city. Those are voltigeurs I imagine, just trying their luck with the sentries. They should conserve their ammunition."

"Our men are not returning fire," Ángel commented. All the firing was coming from the French lines and although he agreed with Contreras that it was unlikely anybody would be hit in the dark, it bothered him that the Spanish sentries were not even trying.

"They'll have orders not to fire just now, Captain," Castro said. "At nightfall the garrison of Olivo is to be relieved by the Almeria battalions. They will be marching in very soon."

"I imagine the regiments in the fort have had a difficult few days," García said with a sympathy which irritated Ángel.

"They can expect many more difficult days to come," he said scathingly.

García looked at him, then turned away without speaking. Ángel studied his profile, wondering if his junior had actually just rolled his eyes or if it was a trick of the light. He was trying to decide whether to reprimand him for showing disrespect to a senior officer when Contreras said:

"That sounds like the relieving troops approaching."

Ángel turned to look. It was fully dark now and the approaching battalions were just moving shapes but he could hear the rhythm of their feet marching over the rocky surface. Along the French lines, the sporadic firing of muskets was steadily increasing while the battery had fallen silent. Further along, the batteries near the Francoli Fort began a steady fire on the lower town. The sudden burst of activity was bewildering. Ángel watched the mass of men approaching the fort and felt a sudden, inexplicable frisson of danger though he had no idea why.

Further along the parapet he heard Contreras say:

"How many battalions did you say were coming to relieve the garrison, Castro? And where are they coming from? Who are those men…"

The musketry rose to a thunderous roar, drowning out the marching feet, and it was only gradually that other sounds began to drift from the ground outside Fort Olivo. Ángel heard it first, the metallic clash of steel on steel. He leaned forward trying to peer through the darkness. Castro gave a sudden cry.

"They are French. The French are making an attack. General, I think they have run into the relieving force on the way. What should we do?"

Contreras did not speak for a long moment. The sounds of battle were growing louder.

"There is nothing we can do from here but watch and wait, Captain Castro," he said softly. "And pray."

***

Bonnet had no faith in the power of prayer, but he was tempted to murmur a few words to the God his mother had taught him to believe in, as he stood at the head of his men waiting for the order. Behind him, the men were unusually still, with none of their usual banter. Bonnet did not blame them. He had stormed a fortress before, but he had never been selected to be first over the breach because his Colonel was an imbecile.

Bonnet thought the attack was madness. No practicable breach had been made, so Suchet had ordered an assault by escalade. He was clearly in a hurry and Bonnet suspected he knew why. Suchet's army was cut off from any likelihood of reinforcements and if Campoverde managed to get the Spanish army organised to begin harrying the French rear, Suchet might be forced to raise the siege and march to the rescue. The General had taken an enormous risk when he refused to march to Figueras in support of Macdonald and needed a success to justify his actions to the Emperor. Bonnet understood Suchet's motives but resented being the sacrificial lamb on the altar of the General's ambition.

Suchet planned to attack on two fronts. The first assault column consisted of the 7th ligne and was to attempt the partial breach on the front right-hand side where the aqueduct entered the fort. The second column comprised the 30th légère and the 16th ligne who were ordered to move around the fort under cover of darkness and attempt to force entry through the gorge at the rear. Lacasse received the orders with a black scowl, summoned his officers and made his dispositions. He placed the carabinier and chasseur companies to protect the flanks while the central companies, led by Bonnet's men, were to make the assault.

Bonnet spent the remaining daylight hours surveying Olivo from the highest point he could manage. The gorge appeared to be made from solid rock. There were several entrance gates, joined by a wall and a palisade. The French guns could not reach this side of the fort so there was not even an imperfect breach but Bonnet surveyed the wall thoughtfully. It was difficult to assess from this angle, but he did not think the wall was particularly high: perhaps ten feet or so. There were often problems with ladders being too short to reach the top of a wall but Bonnet thought that here, the problem would be to find a place level enough to set the ladders down.

As they waited in the darkness for the order to set off, Bonnet's men were joined by Captain Papigny of the engineers and thirty trained sappers armed with axes and ladders. Lacasse had given strict instructions to wait in silence but given the thunder of muskets and artillery from the feint attacks along the line, Bonnet thought that if his men were in better spirits they could have sung a rousing chorus of the Marseillaise without the garrison of Fort Olivo having a clue that they were there.

When the order was given, Bonnet led his men forward at a steady pace, skirting the outside of the fort. The track was surprisingly well-lit by lanterns from the ramparts and palisades surrounding Olivo. The lights were both a blessing and a curse. Bonnet's men were less likely to break an ankle on the rocky uneven ground but would also be more vulnerable to musket fire. Bonnet was astonished that so far the Spanish had not fired at all. Either their sentries were both deaf and blind or they had been wholly distracted by either the feint attacks or the attack on the partial breach, which should just have started.

It turned out to be neither. As Bonnet led his men around the edge of the fort into the gorge he was astonished to find himself face to face with a solid phalanx of men. For an insane moment, he wondered if the other storming party had somehow mistaken its orders and made an encircling march similar to his own around the other way, but he immediately realised this was not a French battalion. These men were Spanish and the face of the officer at the head of the column wore an expression of horror which Bonnet suspected was reflected on his own.

"Retreat!" a voice called out from behind Bonnet. "They are making a sortie. Bonnet, pull back your men."

Bonnet raised his sword and pointed it at the ranks of the Spanish. "Advance!" he bellowed, trying to drown out the voice of Lacasse. "Charge the gate, it'll be open."

What ensued could not have been called a charge but it was definitely a forward movement. The Spanish reinforcements had almost reached the postern gate when Bonnet's men came upon them and although fully armed, had not been expecting to fight. The French, on the other hand, had been wary and on full alert for the order to attack and perfectly ready to engage.

Thankfully there was no musket fire from the parapet above and Bonnet, slashing his way through the enemy with his sword, prayed that would last. Friend and foe were hopelessly entangled in savage hand to hand fighting and neither side could hope to use firepower without shooting their own men. The only way to the gate was through these Spanish reinforcements and he needed to get there fast. Nothing he had seen from the Spanish garrison of Olivo so far suggested that they were commanded by an idiot, and their officers would quickly realise that the only way to keep out the French was to close the gate and shut out their own men. Bonnet would have done the same but he also suspected they would leave it to the last minute to try to save as many as possible.

The two sets of troops were so closely mingled that it was difficult to wield a sword or a bayonet. but Bonnet could see that his men were managing it very effectively. He could see nothing of Papigny and his engineers and he hoped they had had the wit to get their ladders and equipment out of the firing line and wait for him to do his job. He also had no idea where his Colonel was, but given how well they were doing he knew that at least Foulon and probably the other captains of the centre companies must have followed him in. If his company had been fighting alone they would have been slaughtered by now.

There was still a danger of that. The press of men was pushing Bonnet inexorably towards the postern gate and the palisades. He could see little apart from the men immediately around them but his nostrils were filled with the smell of blood, sweat and the smoke which hovered above the battle from the artillery and musket fire along the line. His hand was sweating inside his leather glove as he swung the sword, cutting down a Spaniard with a brutal slash across his neck and shoulder. As the man fell, another appeared behind him and Bonnet raised his sword and then froze, managing to stop himself stabbing one of his own men. The blue jackets of Spanish and French infantry were different enough close up to make the distinction obvious but in poor lighting and the heat of close combat, Bonnet wondered how many men tonight would fall under the bayonets of their own comrades.

"They're closing the gate, sir," Duclos yelled.

Bonnet swore loudly and cleared a space around him by the simple method of spinning around with his sword arm fully extended. Men leaped out of the way of the lethal blade, including one or two of his own, and Bonnet could see over the heads of the fighting men that several Spanish guards were struggling to force the postern gate closed. They were hampered by their own troops, who were still streaming in, pushing past them in panic. They were doing quite well, Bonnet thought, and there were fewer and fewer Spanish troops still fighting as more of them broke away from combat and raced to safety. The men manning the gate hesitated. Bonnet stepped in to cut down a Spanish officer who was screaming orders to the last of his men to get inside the fort. The officer fell, blood spurting from his throat, but his men had heard him and were sprinting to the postern.

The sentries stood ready to close the gate as the last of the Spanish entered but they were too late. Bonnet's men charged in pursuit and as the gate was almost closed they slammed into it, driving the sentries back. Bonnet began to run. He had no idea where Lacasse was, or any of his fellow officers but if his men got inside that fort they would need somebody to command them once they were there. He could see that some of them had already made it, a confused mêlée of French and Spanish pressed up against the rapidly closing gate.

For a moment it looked as though the gate was closed and then Bonnet saw the gap widen again. The final dozen Spaniards still on their feet scrambled through and with them went Sergeant-Major Belmas and his men. The gate flew open for a moment, and Bonnet saw a glimpse of the courtyard beyond and the Spanish guards, their eyes bulging with terror, their mouths wide. A Spanish voice screamed orders to close the gate and every man close enough hurled himself onto it. Bonnet bellowed to the rest of his company to follow him and charged towards the narrowing gap. He was so close when it finally closed that the men immediately behind him could not stop and slammed into him, driving him against the rough wood with a bruising thump.

Bonnet was still for a moment, unable to move. As his men pulled back he could breathe again and he took a long gasp of air into burning lungs, then spun around. He thought that between twenty and thirty of his men were on the wrong side of that gate and if they did not break in soon, every one of them would be dead, though knowing Belmas, he would make a hard fight of it.

Around him, the rest of the 30th were looking about them, taking stock. A tangle of men lay on the ground, some clearly dead and some wounded. There were probably an equal number of Spanish and French uniforms. Beyond Lacasse's battalion were the rest of the attacking column which was led by Colonel Ravel of the 16th ligne. As Bonnet watched, Ravel ran forward to join Lacasse and Bonnet felt a treacherous rush of relief that his commander would be outranked by the appointed leader of the column. The 16th had taken a lot of damage in the siege works on the previous day and Bonnet suspected that despite their depleted numbers, they were out for revenge.

Ravel spoke briefly to Lacasse then yelled orders. Bonnet called his men back from the gate and the sappers moved in quickly, making a concerted attack on the gate with their axes. The noise rivalled the cacophony of sound from the artillery and musket fire along the lines and splinters of wood flew up, but something about the dull thuds made by the axes suggested to Bonnet that the gate was solid and would not easily yield.

There was no time for a protracted attempt, given that the defenders of the fort had gathered their wits now that their troops were safely inside. There was clearly some confusion within, probably caused by the rampaging Belmas and his small band, but it was not enough to stop the Spaniards from directing their muskets onto the sappers. At such a range it was impossible to miss and several of the sappers fell. Bonnet, whose company was entirely exposed, knew that his men would be the next target and shouted orders to pull them in closer to the defences in the hope that that the rocky slope would give them some cover.

Captain Papigny appeared enraged by the attack on his men. Bonnet heard him shouting instructions to move back from the gate and take cover, then before anybody could stop him, he had raced forward to a lower section of the palisade. Bonnet swore as Papigny reached up with the obvious intention of scrambling over to open the gate from within. It was a suicidal attempt without proper support. Bonnet yelled at him to pull back and could hear Ravel doing the same thing. It was too late. As Papigny reached the top of the palisade, Bonnet saw him stop, his whole body jerking backwards as the musket ball took him squarely in the chest. For a moment he seemed to hang suspended in the air, then he fell, crashing to the rocky ground. Bonnet had barely known the man but he could feel bile in the back of his throat. Mentally he saluted the engineer for his courage while berating him for his stupidity.

Ravel was fully in command now, ordering the sappers to bring up their ladders. Bonnet heard his name called and peered cautiously forward to find Garreau making his way sideways like a crab along the wall under the parapet.

"He wants cover," he called out. "We're to get them loaded up and do our best to return fire."

"Fuck that," Bonnet said loudly. He did not think he would be heard over the constant crackle of musket fire from above but he did not really care if he was. "We're going to get our heads blown off before we get off a shot. Wait."

He looked around him and after a moment found what he was looking for. There was a rocky outcrop further along the palisade which could provide some cover for his beleaguered men.

"Garreau, can you cover us while I get them over there?"

Garreau looked around him. "Give me one minute. I'll yell when we're ready."

Bonnet spun about, shouting orders. Within the promised minute, his men were formed up with loaded muskets in the shadow of the fort and at Garreau's signal he led them in a charge towards the rocks. A grunt behind him told him that somebody was hit but the rest of his company made it to their makeshift defences.

Bonnet flattened himself behind the rocks then peered cautiously around. He felt a surge of sheer exhilaration as he realised that this was a far better position than he had realised. There were footholds and crevices and numerous placements behind crags and outcrops and all of them were within range.

"Fire at will!" he shouted.

The words released them to do what they did best and they were away in seconds, swarming over the rocks into every position they could find and opening fire onto the parapet. Bonnet could see the faces of the Spanish defenders registering shock as they stared wildly around them, trying to identify this new source of danger. The pause enabled both Garreau and

Foulon to get their men into a better firing position and the men on the parapet began to fall.

Further along the scarp, Ravel had taken command of the sappers and some of the grenadiers and was doing a rather better job than the enraged Papigny had managed. There was a section of the scarp without a ditch and with covering fire from the 30th, the sappers had raised their long ladders and the grenadiers were scrambling up fast, disappearing over the parapet. Bonnet fixed his eyes on the gate and realised he was counting the seconds, while around him his men fired and reloaded, fired and reloaded; a deafening wall of sound which he knew would leave his ears ringing for several days.

Abruptly there was a surge among the men of the 16th who were clustered in front of the gate, and Bonnet realised it was opening. He watched for a moment to be sure that it was not some piece of trickery by the defenders but it was clear that the French were inside. Bonnet straightened and raised his voice to a bellow to be heard over the guns.

"There's your invitation, boys! Best not be late."

They were moving before he had finished the sentence, leaping and bounding down the rocks. There was such a rush that they became briefly entangled with the 16th and the rest of the 30th trying to get through the gate. Then they were through, bayonets raised. Bonnet followed them at a loping run, his sword ready. He paused at the gate where Lacasse seemed to be catching his breath.

"Any news of the other assault, sir?"

"It too has succeeded, but the garrison have not surrendered yet, Bonnet."

"Well God help them then," Bonnet said. He thought that Lacasse looked drawn and tired with none of his usual irritating good cheer and wondered if his threatened disgrace had robbed him of sleep the previous night. Bonnet thought that today might have improved his Colonel's prospects and hoped he learned from it. He was not sure who else had heard Lacasse's panicked order to retreat when they had first run into the Spanish reinforcements, but Bonnet had definitely heard it and had filed it away as a piece of information he would not forget.

Chapter Twelve

Inside, the fort was utter chaos. The other storming party had made it into the fort via the aqueduct just before Ravel's men opened the gate. They were racing along the parapet, killing any Spaniard they could catch. The Spanish garrison fled before them. Their commander had drawn them down to the left side of the fortress into some kind of defensive order but they were hampered by their sheer numbers. Nevertheless they were putting up a fierce fight.

Above them, the entrenchment and the platform still held contingents of the enemy. Bonnet began to ruthlessly cut his way through a group of desperate Spaniards who were trying to make their way up to the platform to reinforce their comrades. Some of the French troops were yelling in triumph; their victory cries so loud they could probably be heard in both the town and the French camp. He thought they were premature; this battle was not over. The French, struggling to overwhelm the remains of the garrison, were caught between two firing lines and those still advancing were tripping over the bodies of their comrades. Bonnet dodged back out of range, shouting a warning to the rest of the 30th before they got themselves slaughtered at their moment of triumph.

He could see no way up to either the escarpment or the firing platform from here, or certainly no way that would not see him shot down as Papigny had been. There were sounds from outside though, which gave him fresh hope and he dodged between fighting men towards the front line of battle and was rewarded by the sight of more troops racing down towards the breach. Bonnet, who felt he had probably done enough, stepped to one side and let them pour past him, both French and Italians. They fell savagely upon the Spaniards' desperate last stand and the defenders were pushed backwards, fighting for their lives.

Another column charged the entrenchment and in a short, brutal attack managed to force their way onto the platform. The firing was immediately silenced and broken bodies lay strewn across the ledge. Bonnet, having caught his breath, returned to the battle, finding a group of his company cutting down the overcrowded Spaniards without mercy. Bonnet did not try to restrain them. Even if he had managed it, the rest of the French army was in the grip of bloodlust and would simply push past and finish the job. He was under no illusions that if the Spanish had managed to gain the upper hand they would have slaughtered his men just as readily.

Orders were eventually shouted down from the platform where Colonel Mesclop, commanding the reserves, had managed to stop the carnage. Firing and resistance were beginning to die down and Bonnet decided it was possible that his men would be able to take an order again. He made the experiment with the soldiers closest to him and was gratified when they immediately lowered their bayonets. Bonnet thought they looked faintly surprised that he was still alive. He was surprised himself.

Quarter was finally being given to any enemy who surrendered, and the Spaniards were doing so. Mesclop called together the various battalion colonels and began to give his orders. Bonnet drank from his water bottle, cleaned his sword on the coat of a dead Spaniard and waited for further instructions. He was always willing to take the initiative during the heat of battle and frequently found himself doing so, but he had long ago discovered that once the fight was won it was safest to retreat behind his usual vaguely unco-operative façade.

Fort Olivo was a charnel house. Bonnet was exhausted and knew the men felt the same way, but they could not afford simply to sit back and rest. The garrison was gone: either dead, wounded or prisoners but there were plenty of reinforcements in the town and the Spanish had shown their willingness to make sorties to recover lost ground. Bonnet collected his weary company together and ordered a quick roll call to find out how bad it had been. Of the one hundred and twelve men under his command he had lost ten dead and another fourteen wounded, several of them seriously. Most of these were among the men who had made it into the fort before the gates closed.

Belmas had survived, to Bonnet's astonishment. He felt a lift of sheer happiness at the sight of the big NCO clambering over a damaged palisade to join him.

"Sergeant-Major Belmas, I'm pleased to see you. How the fuck did you survive that?"

"Captain Bonnet, I am happy to see you too. I could not save them all, but I saved more than half of them, though some are wounded."

"You did better than I thought you'd do. What happened?"

Belmas shrugged his broad shoulders. "We are the 30th légère. We fought. We were willing to fight to the death, which would not have taken long, you understand, because there was only thirty of us and hundreds of these Spanish bastards. But suddenly you began to return fire and they were distracted and then there was firing from the opposite side of the fort where the other column was breaking in. So I thought about what you would tell me to do and I did it."

Bonnet grinned. "You hid."

"Of course I hid, Captain, I am not an idiot. There is a store room just to the right over there. As soon as they stopped killing my men for a moment, I made for the door and got them all in. Apart from those who had already fallen. We barricaded the door and listened. At first they tried to break it down and threatened to set fire to it, but I knew they would not. Very quickly they lost interest. Soon we could hear it was safe to come out. Well, not safe exactly, but better."

"I'm proud of you, Belmas. Well done."

"Thank you, Captain. Afterwards I went to find the officer with the yellow hair and whiskers. He was with his men and I stabbed him many times."

Bonnet blinked in surprise. "Any particular reason?"

"Young Chardin, Captain. He was wounded but not dead. I looked back when I was closing that door and he was trying to drag himself along. I thought I might make it back for him but that yellow-haired son of a Spanish whore was onto him. He stabbed him – oh many times. Over and over. But he did it slowly, in places not meant to kill. Chardin screamed and screamed."

Bonnet felt his stomach twist in horror. "The fucking bastard," he breathed. "What was he, seventeen?"

"Sixteen, Captain. He was a good boy, I liked him."

"Did you find his body?"

"Yes," Belmas said, and his voice silenced further questioning. "He is dead and he is avenged. What are our orders now, Captain?"

"The usual bloody housekeeping, Belmas. We're on prisoner duty, which isn't quite as bad as removing the corpses and makes me hope that our spectacular if unplanned assault means that Colonel Lacasse is forgiven."

Belmas pulled an expressive face. "If he is so, sir, it will be because of what you did, not what he did. But they may not know that."

Bonnet studied his Sergeant-Major narrowly. "If they don't know it, let's keep it that way, eh Belmas? I'd rather Lacasse took the credit if it means we're no longer wriggling at the end of General Suchet's freshly baited hook. Come on, let's see what we've got."

During the rest of the night the prisoners were conducted to the camp, the wounded taken away and the dead thrown into the ditches. There were over a thousand prisoners, both officers and men, including the commandant of the fort who was badly wounded. While Lacasse and his men dealt with the garrison, Suchet's engineers and their labourers set about making the fort secure. This included building steps on the breach, bridging the ditch, creating defences against any attack from the town and organising a garrison under the command of General Ficatier, who had taken over General Salme's brigade.

A number of the Spanish reinforcements had escaped. Bonnet knew nothing of numbers and heard everything from two hundred to a thousand quoted by knowledgeable officers. They had managed to retreat from the chaos outside Olivo and make it back through the Rosario Gate into the city. Bonnet applauded their good sense. If more of them had taken the same course and not effectively obliged Fort Olivo to keep its gates open, there might have been fewer Spanish dead.

Those dead lay reeking in the ditches. According to Colonel Lacasse, General Suchet had sent a message to the city offering a four-hour truce for the Spanish to collect their fallen men but Campoverde declined, so Suchet gave orders for the bodies to be burned. Bonnet wondered about that decision. On the one hand it seemed brutal for the Spaniards to leave their dead to be so mishandled by the enemy but on the other hand he understood how physically exhausting and emotionally draining it was for troops to have to spend hours burying hundreds of their dead. It suggested a surprising ruthlessness by the Spanish commander but Bonnet rather respected his choice.

Suchet inspected his new fort by lamplight and announced that it would be newly named Fort Salme after his deceased General. He appeared pleased with progress and delighted by the number of captured guns and the amount of stores and provisions the fort held. Bonnet, who was newly in possession of a very good bottle of brandy liberated from the store room where Belmas and his men had hidden, wondered if Suchet had any idea just how much food and drink the men of the 30th had managed to steal from the stores before the officers stepped in to secure them. Even Bonnet was impressed as he accepted his share. His company was relieved just after dawn and went back to camp to eat, drink and rest while Suchet planned his next move.

***

Commodore Codrington was not present during the savage assault on Fort Olivo, having taken the *Blake* and several of the other vessels to collect supplies and to ferry reinforcements to where they were necessary. He left Hugh to watch over the town along with several Spanish gunboats and Luke Winterton with the *Wren*.

By the time Hugh received a letter from Campoverde telling him about the attack on the fort, he had already worked out for himself what was happening. There was nothing he could have done to help. The French batteries made it necessary for the ships to keep a safe distance but even if he could have got closer, the Olivo was on the far side of the town, well away from the sea and Hugh's only view of the battle was the flashes of artillery and musket fire through the darkness. It was extraordinarily loud even from this far out and there was a strong smell of smoke in the air.

Hugh stood beside Durrell on deck, looking out over the town. It reminded him of other occasions when they had been bystanders to the action, particularly the appalling bombardment of Copenhagen more than four years ago. Hugh had not been on particularly good terms with his First Lieutenant at the time but he could still remember a sense of joint helplessness at the misery they were witnessing.

"Have you written to Commodore Codrington, sir?"

"No. I'll write once I've had news from Campoverde. There's no point in giving Ned half the tale, there's nothing he can do from Valencia which is where he was last time I heard. I'd love to know what the devil Campoverde is doing though. He should keep me informed."

"Perhaps he is busy just now, sir."

Hugh grinned at his junior's tone. "Stop being reasonable, it's infuriating. I'd be happy if he was busy standing at the head of his army but I've a suspicion that if he's doing anything, it will involve politics rather than an honest fight. I thought Ned was being hard on the man when I first arrived, but I'm coming round to his point of view. I think Campoverde cares more about his position and scoring off his enemies than defending this town."

"That's very harsh, sir."

"It was meant to be. I wonder how they're doing over there? The racket they're making, it sounds as though they're assaulting the entire bloody town."

"It's confusing isn't it, sir? I wonder if it is intended that way?"

Hugh shot his junior a sharp glance. "Feint attacks, you mean? You might be right, Mr Durrell."

They remained at the rail for a long time, until the crash of artillery fire began to die away and all that was left was the sound of musketry from the fort. Hugh was just beginning to think that too was becoming more sporadic when he heard the swish of oars through the dark water and saw the wavering light of a boat's lamp approaching the *Iris*.

"I believe this may be a message from the Marquis of Campoverde, Captain."

"About bloody time," Hugh growled. "I'm getting cold. Get the boatmen aboard for a drink, Mr Durrell - the Bosun will see to them - then bring the letter down to my cabin. I'm going to thaw out."

Hugh found Miles Randall in his dining cabin, diligently polishing wine glasses. He sprang to attention as Hugh entered, completely unnecessarily. Hugh regarded him blankly.

"Randall, what on earth are you doing here at this hour?"

"You were still up, Captain. I thought you might need something."

Hugh grinned and shook his head. "My hours are a bit erratic, lad, if you're going to mimic them you'll be sleep-deprived. Since you're here, you can bring me some wine. Pour one for Mr Durrell as well, will you, he'll be here in a minute. And then get yourself to your hammock."

"Yes, Captain."

Randall passed Durrell on his way in. Durrell turned to watch his speedy departure and shook his head.

"He is going to be very unpopular if he bursts into the sleeping deck at that speed and making that much noise," he said. "What was he doing here at this hour?"

"Cleaning my glassware apparently," Hugh said, taking the letter. "Sit down and have a drink while I read this."

Durrell did so, looking around the room. Hugh opened the letter, briefly admiring Campoverde's elaborate seal as he did so. As he began to read, Durrell gave a little snort. Hugh looked up.

"What is it?"

"Cleaning glasses is a new excuse," Durrell said. He rose and walked over to Hugh's mahogany desk and touched the surface with one finger. It came away black. Hugh was so surprised that he rose and went to look.

"Ink?"

"Ink."

"What in God's name was he doing?"

"Studying," Durrell said. "Last time, he claimed to be mending, but I watched him and a small rent on your trousers took him almost a week to finish."

"Why is he in here studying?" Hugh asked, genuinely bewildered. "Doesn't he get enough study time during the day?"

"There is never enough time for Miles. I suspect he considers the days unreasonably short. He can't read or write in his hammock, there's no light. Your cabins are the one place that are guaranteed to be well lit, at least until you go to bed. I'll speak to him, Captain."

"No, I'll do it. I admire both his dedication and his ingenuity but he'll addle that brain of his if he can't learn to take a day off. Were you this bad?"

Durrell gave a reminiscent smile. "Probably," he admitted.

Hugh returned to his chair and the letter. He read it through in silence then looked up and passed the letter to Durrell.

"I'll forward it to Codrington," he said briefly. "You can read it for yourself, but to summarise, the French have taken Fort Olivo and most of the garrison are either dead or taken prisoner."

Durrell scanned the letter. "It doesn't say how," he remarked. "Did they breach? When I was last there it did not seem possible for those defences to fall so quickly."

"I don't know, but I'd like to find out. We may well do so tomorrow. Campoverde has called a meeting of all his generals and senior officers, as well as those members of the Superior Junta of Catalonia who are present in the town, to discuss what should be done next. As Commodore Codrington is absent, I am invited in his stead. I'd like you to come with me, Mr Durrell and if you wouldn't mind acting as secretary, I'd appreciate it. I'm sure they'll have a clerk of their own taking notes, but I'd rather like to have my own set of very detailed minutes of this particular meeting."

He saw a gleam of understanding in Durrell's eyes. "I think it would be very wise, sir. I'd be happy to oblige. One thing I learned from those endless meetings with Sir Home Popham during the Walcheren campaign was how to take notes."

"It's nice that he had his uses. Unlike him, I promise not to use them to try to bring down the government. I just want a record, for my sake and for Ned's. We'd best get some sleep. Will you roust out those boatmen while I write a quick reply?"

Durrell got up, draining his glass. "Certainly, Captain," he said, raising his voice unexpectedly. "As for the letter, you may give it to Randall to take to the boat when you are ready. You'll find him right outside your cabin door, awaiting your instructions."

Hugh was halfway to his desk. He looked round in surprise to see Durrell open the door abruptly and reach for the boy, who was sitting with his back against the store cupboard door. There was a squawk of surprise and a brief scuffle, then Durrell led Miles Randall across the cabin by one ear and planted him firmly before Hugh. Hugh regarded him blankly. Randall looked back from wide, innocent grey eyes. Hugh forced his face into stern lines, though he could feel laughter bubbling just below the surface.

"Miles, were you eavesdropping on my private conversation?"

"No, Captain." Randall's voice was a masterpiece of outraged indignation. "I would never do that. I simply thought you might need something. And I'm not tired, really I'm not."

Hugh's lips twitched despite himself. "I do see that, Miles," he said gravely. "But have a thought for Mr Durrell here, he's exhausted with having to keep an eye on you."

Randall turned his gaze onto Durrell. "He's awfully good at it, sir," he said, with genuine admiration. "I can never catch him out. But there's no need, I promise. I'm just trying to do my duty and learn as much as I can, as fast as I can. And the best way to learn is to listen…"

He broke off, seeming to realise he was halfway through a confession. Hugh gave up and guffawed aloud. Durrell rolled his eyes, shook his head and departed in search of the boatmen.

***

The Superior Junta of the Principality of Catalonia was an autonomous governing body which had been set up in 1808 as part of the Spanish effort to fight the French invasion. The Junta dealt with both legislative and judicial matters in Catalonia and was responsible for collecting taxes to finance the war and for raising armies. Theoretically, the areas of Catalonia occupied by the French were annexed to the French Empire but French administration in the area was patchy owing to the ebb and flow of the war.

Durrell had met several of the delegates at dinner aboard the *Blake* over the past weeks. He was also acquainted with most of the Spanish generals, although none of them gave him more than an indifferent nod as he took his seat at the back of the room, his notebook open on a small table in front of him. There was, as Hugh had surmised, a Spanish clerk hunched over a desk in the corner, busily sharpening his quill. He gave Durrell a puzzled look and Durrell nodded pleasantly to him as the men began to settle into chairs or on the long benches around the big table.

There were three men present, all in uniform, whom Durrell had never seen before. The oldest of the three was a stocky man in his fifties; with dark hair sprinkled with grey and an impressive moustache. His two companions were considerably younger and Durrell suspected were there in a similar capacity to his. One was probably in his early twenties, slender and dark with a ready smile that he offered to Durrell as he sat down and took out an elegant leather bound notebook of his own. The other was older and taller. He sat beside his companion and surveyed the crowded room with barely concealed contempt.

The meeting began with a flurry of courtesies and introductions which threatened to go on forever. The stocky man was introduced as Lieutenant-General Juan Senen de Contreras who had arrived in Tarragona from Calais the previous day and looked to Durrell like a man still in shock. His two ADCs were named as Captain Don Ángel Cortez and Lieutenant Don Óscar García. Hugh introduced Durrell and García shot him another friendly smile.

"I am pleased to meet you, Lieutenant Durrell," he said in heavily accented English.

Durrell opened his mouth to reply but was cut off by Cortez, who spoke in blighting tones in rapid Spanish.

"Your English is so bad, García that you will have to communicate with hand gestures if you want to make a friend of the Englishman. He will assuredly not speak Spanish, they never bother with anything other than French."

Durrell saw the younger officer flush a little though he said nothing. Across the room, Hugh had clearly heard the exchange. His Spanish was very limited but Durrell suspected he had understood the sense of the remark. Durrell thought that his Captain had the air of a man already bored and ready to watch an entertaining side show. He gave Durrell a little nod. Durrell accepted it as permission and turned his cool gaze onto Cortez.

"As a matter of fact, Captain Cortez, I speak your language fluently although I might struggle with the Catalan dialect as I have only just begun studying it," he said in Spanish. "You are correct in your assumption that I speak French and I have also studied Portuguese and German, as it seemed to me that those would be the most useful languages for my service. I have recently begun to study Urdu but that is purely for my own amusement, although it might possibly be useful should I ever be posted further afield. As a scholar, I am merely entertained by both your prejudices and your bad manners. As First Lieutenant of a Royal Navy ship, however, I am your senior officer by a considerable difference in rank and if I were General Contreras, I would find the time to educate you a little so that you do not inadvertently insult Lord Wellington should you run into him at some point. Fortunately your General seems to have a junior ADC with a better understanding and far better manners. I will accept your apology whenever you are ready."

Durrell paused to take a breath although he did not really need one. Cortez had flushed a deep red and Durrell thought that he was clenching his fists out of sight under the table. Durrell met his eyes. They were an interesting colour, cool grey with the faintest hint of blue. Durrell wondered if the man ever smiled. He was certainly not smiling now. Durrell did not look away. His younger self would have felt his dignity demanded an apology from the Spanish officer. These days, Durrell thought less and less of his dignity but he decided that an apology would do Cortez a great deal of good. He suspected that Cortez had not been made to apologise nearly enough during childhood and it was time somebody rectified the omission.

Durrell was just wondering if he was going to have to repeat himself and was considering his words when Cortez got to his feet and gave a stiff little bow. "My apologies, Lieutenant Durrell. I did not intend to be so rude, I did not think."

It was not gracious but it was definitely an apology. Durrell gave a nod. "Accepted," he said. "Try to think in future. How in God's name did you think I was going to take notes at this meeting without a word of your language?"

Cortez' face could not go any redder. He bowed again and sat down. Durrell glanced over at Hugh who was looking amused. He had probably not understood what Durrell had said but he was clearly enjoying the effect.

Campoverde called the meeting to order and Durrell bent to his task. It was difficult to keep track of who was speaking, but Durrell knew enough about the situation to be able to sift through the lengthy speeches and arguments; to summarise the key points which Hugh would want to convey to Codrington to be passed on to London. It was why Durrell was here. Hugh had a perfectly competent clerk but he could not do what Durrell could do. This was not a First Lieutenant's duty but Durrell was very accustomed to taking on duties that were not his. It made for an interesting life.

His Captain had moved across the room to sit beside him. Hugh's Spanish was limited to polite social greetings and the odd vulgar swear word picked up from Spanish speaking crew members, but he could read over Durrell's shoulder very well and would occasionally ask a low-voiced question. What he was very good at, was reading the room and Durrell knew that when they discussed the meeting afterwards, Hugh would be able to accurately pinpoint a lot of the cross-currents that Durrell needed language to understand.

As the meeting progressed he had to force himself to concentrate. Tempers were running high and there was a sense of rising anxiety among both the army officers and the Junta, but it quickly became clear that the main tension was between Campoverde and his newly arrived subordinate. The two men fundamentally disagreed about the best way to defend Tarragona and it was obvious to Durrell, if not immediately to Contreras, that it was an argument that Campoverde was going to win, purely on the basis of rank.

Campoverde proposed leaving Tarragona with a substantial garrison under the command of General Contreras. The Marquis would depart immediately to join the Catalan forces and concentrate them into an army which would then attack Suchet's forces from the rear, forcing them to raise the siege.

It was a bold plan, but Contreras seemed appalled at the idea. He tried hard to interrupt Campoverde several times without success and by the time he was finally allowed to speak, Durrell could tell that the Junta delegates had been swayed by the Marquis' eloquence. Contreras rose and threw out his hands dramatically.

"I cannot agree that this is a good idea, my lord. I am but newly arrived in the town. I do not know its defences or its people. I do not know the surrounding countryside and I have not even been able to find a plan of the area. I have had no time to get to know the officers and I have no idea how the civil authorities work. How should I raise money for the defences? How do I...?"

"You underestimate yourself, General," Campoverde said soothingly. "All this can be learned from the excellent officers I shall leave with you. I know of your courage at Talavera and at Badajoz and your excellent work as Captain-General in Galicia. And I am told that you were good enough to give advice to the Cortes in Cadiz about how to remedy some of the difficulties in governing Spain. For such a man, this task is not too great."

There was a frozen silence. Contreras flushed, threw up his hands in a dismissive gesture and sat down. Hugh glanced at Durrell who gave a very small shrug. He had no idea what Campoverde was referring to but it was obvious that Contreras did. After a moment, Campoverde said:

"All you must do is hold out, General. I will return with an army in six to eight days and the town will be saved. I have faith in you. The Cortes has faith in you."

Contreras bowed his head. Durrell had not taken a liking to the Spanish General's bombastic manner but he felt a twinge of sympathy for him. Contreras looked defeated.

"I know well of the Cortes' faith in me, my lord. I will do whatever is in my power to hold this city, even at the cost of my own life." The dark eyes lifted to look at Campoverde. "But from the little I have seen of how it stands, I think that may well be the cost."

The meeting broke up at ten o'clock. Durrell closed his notebook and began to pack up his writing materials while Hugh went to speak to Campoverde about the arrangements to transport him to join his army. They had not eaten before leaving the *Iris* early that morning and Durrell was thinking longingly of a late breakfast when a voice spoke very softly:

"I think you were wondering what the Marquis meant by his remarks to General Contreras."

Durrell turned in surprise to see García regarding him. "About the Cortes?" he said, equally softly. "Yes, I was."

"When he commanded in Galicia, the General achieved many great things. He believed his system could be applied to the rest of Spain so he sent a memorandum to the Cortes in Cadiz, setting out his ideas and offering to implement them. The Cortes refused and some...many...were offended."

Durrell felt as though several things had fallen into place. He studied the younger man with considerable interest. "Were they? I wonder if was the ideas or the presentation that offended them. Or possibly the requested promotion to...what would it have been? Captain-General of all Spain? That's a big jump for any man."

García glanced around and moved towards the door to ensure they would not be overheard. "Very big," he said. "My father is a member of the

Cortes, Lieutenant, which is why I have this elevated post at this very young age. According to him, it was not tactful. But even if it had been, there are so many generals vying for position here. Sometimes I think it obscures what we are trying to do, which is to drive out the French."

Durrell was intrigued and more than a little impressed. "That kind of jockeying for position is not unique to Spain, Lieutenant García. My brother sits in the House of Commons, I have seen it all my life."

"I believe you, sir. But unlike us, you do not have Bonaparte on your doorstep to exploit your differences as weaknesses."

"García, what are you whispering about in corners?"

Cortez' voice was harsh and angry. Durrell turned to stare at him, lifting a supercilious eyebrow, and continued to stare silently until Cortez dropped his gaze, going red again. The Spaniard looked as though he wanted to hit him and Durrell did not really blame him. He knew he was deliberately baiting Cortez but the man had annoyed him.

"Lieutenant García and I were talking of our families, Captain Cortez," he said finally, when he felt Cortez had squirmed for long enough. "It has been very good to meet you both. I am sure we will meet again."

Durrell and Hugh walked down through the town towards the shore where Hugh's barge awaited them. As they arrived, Durrell heard the sound of activity up in the town. It sounded like large scale troop movements. He turned, shielding his eyes in the bright sunlight, staring up at the walls of Tarragona which stood out against a brilliant blue sky.

"Do you know what that is, sir?"

"A sortie against the recently lost Fort Olivo," Hugh said grimly. "Campoverde ordered it just as we were leaving. Some observer has told him the French have evacuated the fort."

Durrell turned his startled gaze onto Hugh. "Surely that cannot be right?"

"Well if I were in command here, I'd need more than a casual word to convince me the French have walked out of an essential bastion that they've spent blood capturing not twenty-four hours earlier. Let's hope Campoverde has got this right, for the sake of Colonel O'Ronan and the fifteen hundred men under his command. Let's get out of here, Mr Durrell. I've an unpleasant taste in my mouth that has nothing to do with the lack of breakfast. What was young García talking to you about?"

"He was giving his opinion about why General Contreras has drawn this particularly foul short straw," Durrell said, holding the edge of the barge steady as Hugh stepped aboard. As the rowers pulled away from the shore, he told Hugh the story. Hugh's eyes gleamed with amusement.

"Poor old Contreras. I'll wager he's wishing he'd kept his ideas to himself. I can't wait to tell Ned this one. No wonder Campoverde is leaving him up to his neck in it."

"Yes, sir, it seems like a harsh punishment for simply writing a memorandum, especially if his previous service is as admirable as it seems. All the same…"

Durrell hesitated, trying to put his thoughts into words. Hugh studied him for a moment. "Not an admirer of General Contreras, Lieutenant?"

"I know nothing to his detriment, sir, but there is something about his manner that is a little boastful. To tell you the truth, he reminds me rather of…"

"Popham," Hugh said with satisfaction. "It hit me half way through the meeting and I struggled to keep my face straight. I didn't dare whisper in your ear, you wouldn't have been able to concentrate afterwards."

"I'm glad you restrained yourself, sir. I'm not sure how much of the meeting you were able to follow, but it seems to me there is a risk that the command of the city will become divided."

"Is that what young García was talking about?"

"Yes, sir, although he implied that it's part of a larger problem in Spain. General Contreras has been given command of the garrison here, which he does not at all want, but the office of governor has been given to Colonel José González who is the brother of the Marquis of Campoverde. Meanwhile General Sarsfield has been given command of the port and the Spanish ships."

"That sounds like complete chaos."

"I thought so. It makes me glad that Spanish politics are not our problem."

"They are Commodore Codrington's though, to some degree. I wonder what he'll make of all this? I wish he'd get himself back here, this is all moving very fast. And well done for tearing a deserved strip off Captain Cortez, by the way. That is definitely a man in need of a surprise dip off the harbour on a cold day."

Durrell grinned. "Is that so, sir? I will find the opportunity of advising the Captain to avoid you, then. I've seen your tendency to follow through on that particular threat."

Hugh laughed and turned his head to watch the looming bulk of his ship as the barge moved smoothly through the water.

***

It was a relief to Ángel, after the long weeks of inactivity in Calais, to find himself busy again. He had come to realise that his temper improved when he had little time for reflection and in the days following Campoverde's departure from Tarragona, General Contreras kept his two ADCs fully employed.

There was too much to do, but Contreras thrived on a challenge and despite his reservations he threw himself into his new command. He was immediately engaged with the French, as the sortie to recapture Fort Olivo sent out by Campoverde was driven back with the loss of twenty men. Ángel, who was at the gate when the battered and bloody troops streamed back into the city, thought they were lucky it had not been worse. He stood beside his commander as Contreras received the report from Colonel O'Ronan, who confirmed that the French were fully in control of Olivo and already making the necessary improvements to use it against the town.

Campoverde had left a garrison of eight thousand men and his promise of a swift return. Contreras clearly did not believe him but set about improving the organisation of Tarragona with the same ruthless efficiency he had shown during his time in Galicia. The troops were re-organised and Contreras set up a military police force to deal with disciplinary problems. Ángel could not believe that had not already been done.

Turning his attention to the citizens, the General formed all able-bodied men into companies of civilian militia and organised the women of the city to make cartridges, lint and powder bags as well as to provide food and drink for the troops. He established a second hospital in one of the convents near the cathedral and set Ángel and García to checking supplies and making sure the city was ready for a protracted siege with its inevitable casualties.

Tarragona had already lost many of its wealthiest citizens as those who had the money to travel and somewhere to go had bought passage away from the city. Many of them had failed to pay their taxes before they left and Contreras was ruthless in seizing funds from those found to be in debt.

Ángel moved between supervising the clerks and book keepers, checking the repairs on several sections of the walls and helping to unload the weapons, ammunition and supplies being brought in regularly by the Royal Navy and Spanish frigates. He had plenty of opportunity to assess the morale of both the garrison and the citizens and he found it high. It was clear that, despite recent reverses, the people of Tarragona were wholly committed to defending their city. Ángel thought that if Campoverde could manage to pull together enough of an army to draw off Suchet's besieging force, the garrison would hold this stronghold through another campaign. He was painfully aware, however, that his commander did not feel the same way and he was concerned that Contreras was allowing his doubts to show. Ángel did not mention his concern to anybody and hoped that nobody else would notice.

Having taken control of Olivo, Suchet's forces turned their attention to the Orleans Bastion. Much of the work of digging the trenches was traditionally carried out at night; to minimise the enemy's opportunity to bombard the labourers and the troops guarding the works. However, Suchet's need for speedy progress meant that the men were working in two shifts through both day and night.

The Orleans Bastion was to the west of the city and dangerously close to the coast, which meant that Captain Kelly's small flotilla was able to keep up a destructive fire onto the hapless workmen. They were also under fire from the Spanish guns from the town. Ángel, who had walked up with García to the wall one morning to survey the works, could see a scattering of bodies. French troops were carrying away their wounded. Ángel thought it looked as though it had been a costly night for the enemy and felt a fierce satisfaction.

"It must be terrifying in those trenches," García said. "All they can do is keep digging and pray that they don't get hit. They have no way to defend themselves."

"Good," Ángel said shortly.

"Many of those workmen are our countrymen, Captain."

"Then they're traitors, taking French pay and they deserve to die."

"I cannot help wondering how many of them really chose this, Captain," another voice said from behind them. "The war has brought such poverty to these lands. It may well have been a choice between starvation and working for the French."

Ángel turned to see Lieutenant Durrell, immaculate in his blue uniform coat, his eyes on the distant siege works. He was trying to decide whether he was obliged to salute and hoping he could get away with it, when García did so. Ángel gritted his teeth and did the same.

"I think you are right, Lieutenant," García said, looking back at the trenches. "Some of them were probably just rounded up and marched away."

"They should have chosen to starve," Ángel said. "Or be shot. If every Spanish man and woman chose death over submission, the French would be gone by now."

Durrell looked surprised. "Surely that is too much to expect, Captain? These people are farmers and artisans, not soldiers. They have families to return to, lands and businesses to tend. This was not their choice."

"They could choose not to bow their heads and be slaughtered like cattle," Ángel said. Somewhere in the back of his brain, a small voice was imploring him to shut up and stop making this supercilious Englishman a present of his bitterness, but he could not help himself.

Durrell did not reply. There was an awkward silence, unexpectedly broken by an enormous broadside from the guns of the *Wren*. It was devastatingly accurate and several men caught outside of the trench were mown down. Those who escaped made a desperate scramble towards the half-dug trench for cover.

"Were you looking for General Contreras, Lieutenant Durrell?" García asked.

Durrell glanced around at him and smiled. "Yes. I'm sorry, I did not explain myself, did I? I was distracted. We do not have such a good view of the works from the ship and I was interested. I was present in the siege lines at Flushing a few years ago and I found the experience very bewildering, but of course I was on the outside then. I'm here because Captain Kelly sent me to invite your General to dine today. We have had a message from Commodore Codrington and he will be back in a day or two with more troops and supplies. Captain Kelly thought it would be useful if he was fully up to date when the *Blake* arrives so that he can brief the Commodore."

"And he sent you as his messenger?" Ángel said. He was finding it difficult to conceal his dislike of Kelly's first officer and he suspected he was failing when García shot him a startled glance. Durrell showed no sign of noticing.

"I volunteered," he said. "As I said, I was interested. This must be very difficult ground to dig, it's so rocky. At Flushing the trenches were easy. I have a friend in the army and I remember him telling me that there was no problem digging them out, the difficulty was to prevent everything from collapsing. It rained incessantly and then the French cut the dyke. We were wading through water up to our knees during the bombardment. All the same, they seem to be making surprisingly good progress here."

"Too much progress," Ángel said grimly. "They have good equipment and Suchet seems to be incredibly well organised with supplies, though it must be difficult given how barren this area is. The last time I was involved with a siege our spades broke all the time and we only had three pickaxes for the entire battalion."

"I imagine that did not go well," Durrell said dispassionately and despite himself Ángel grinned.

"Not at all well. How much can you see from the ship?"

"You can see for yourself later if you come to dine with your General. We could see nothing of the works beyond the Olivo. We have a better view of this, but nothing like as much as you can see from here. Why do they cut the trenches in that zig-zag pattern?"

Ángel shot him a glance but could read nothing but curiosity in the other man's expression.

"The whole idea is to prevent successful sorties from the garrison and to protect their troops from artillery fire while gradually moving closer to the walls. They build a series of trenches parallel to the fortress. They've completed that, we call it the first parallel. Theoretically, that should be built out of the range of any artillery but they can't do anything about your guns, which is why this is so costly for them. I have to say, Lieutenant, your ships are doing an extremely good job."

Durrell gave a faint smile. "We're doing our best, although as they move forward it is becoming more difficult because we cannot risk hitting your walls by accident. Our shots are not that accurate and that fortress – Francoli, isn't it – will very soon be in our firing line."

"General Contreras believes they will be in a position to attack it within days," García said.

"We'll do our best to delay them."

"Once the first parallel is completed they'll use it as cover to dig a series of forward trenches towards the town," Ángel went on. "They dig them in that zig-zag pattern to avoid them being taken in enfilade by defending fire. Once they are within artillery range, they dig the second parallel trench and fortify it with gun emplacements."

"I see. Presumably once they have guns in place they can use them to cover any further entrenchments until they are close enough to the walls to begin breaching fire?"

"Yes. They'll also dig more trenches to enable attacking troops to get close enough to exploit the breaches once they're made. Generally speaking, this is accompanied by repeated requests to surrender."

"Is that what General Suchet is doing?"

Ángel nodded. "General Contreras has refused all such offers and will continue to do so. He is willing to defend this city with his last breath, Lieutenant. But…"

He stopped speaking. Durrell waited politely for him to continue. Ángel realised with some exasperation that he had almost blurted out his anxiety about his General's gloomy outlook. He had no idea what had made him speak so freely to the naval officer, given that he did not even like the man, but Durrell's air of genuine interest was difficult to resist. Ángel clamped his jaw together and resisted.

"General Contreras will be at his desk, Lieutenant," he said instead. "If you will accompany me, I am sure he will be glad to meet with Captain Kelly. And he will be happy to know that supplies are on the way. If the attack happens…if they breach…we are woefully short of ammunition."

Durrell accepted the change of subject without comment. They made their way down the stone steps from the parapet and through the narrow streets of Tarragona towards Contreras' headquarters. Durrell was asking questions about the deployment of troops and the improvements in the defences. Ángel left it to García to answer. As they emerged from a dim alleyway into the sunlit square, Ángel looked up at the cathedral and thought how beautiful it was.

"That's a lovely building," Durrell said beside him. "I'm told you're using it as a hospital. I wonder if it's a comfort to the wounded men to feel closer to God? I suppose it depends how badly hurt they are."

"Or whether they believe in God in the first place," Ángel said.

"Don't you?"

"I've been fighting since I was eighteen, Lieutenant. Nothing I've seen during that time has given me any reason to believe there's a God. Or if there is, that he gives a damn about any of us."

Durrell gave a faint smile. "It seems you have one thing in common with Bonaparte then, as he has no respect for the church. Although unlike you, he claims otherwise."

Ángel felt his hands curl into fists. "I have nothing in common with that creature. I loathe him; he is not human."

They were at the door of headquarters. Durrell turned to look at him. "Do you think so?"

"Do you not?"

"I've never seen the man, Captain. At home they tell stories of him to frighten their children into good behaviour. I'm not sure he is that much of a monster."

"If you are a sympathiser, Lieutenant, I would rather not know it."

"I'm not. I just find myself wondering about him at times. On the surface, his achievements are extraordinary of course, but it seems to me that he lacks an understanding of the need to stop."

"Stop?"

"Yes, stop. How can he expect to continue doing what he does indefinitely? Were he to stop and search for an accommodation with the other European powers which suited both sides, I believe he could establish the dynasty he is hoping for. But he seems incapable of seeing what is obvious to me, that if your only method of getting what you want is to bully and overpower and humiliate, you give people no reason to trust you and every reason to oppose you. He finds reasons every time to go back to war, as though war itself is his purpose. But the longer he spends at war the more probable it is that he will suffer defeats, and how likely is it that England and Austria and Prussia and their allies will attempt to make a workable peace with a man they cannot trust to keep his word? He makes war as if it is the only thing he knows how to do. Perhaps it is."

Ángel could not speak. He could not remember hearing anybody express such a detached opinion about Bonaparte within his hearing for many years. Part of him wanted to lash out at the naval officer but the other part was fascinated.

"That is interesting, Lieutenant," he said when he could find the words. "Is that the general opinion within your service?"

Durrell laughed aloud. "I have no idea, Captain. I expect there are as many opinions as officers. I have only discussed it with my own Captain and his views tend towards the practical. Bonaparte is the enemy and it is our job to defeat him. After that we can allow the politicians to argue about the peace."

"I am not sure I could ever be that dispassionate about it, but I envy your Captain the ability."

"Captain Fenwick, my army friend, once told me that there is a difference between our services," Durrell said. "Generally speaking we in the navy do not see what they do to the people in the towns and the countryside. We leave that to the army. If I had seen what you have seen, Captain, I might feel as you do. After all this is your country and these are your people."

García reappeared in the hallway. "General Contreras will see you, Lieutenant Durrell."

Durrell entered the room Contreras was using as his office and sitting room. Ángel stood looking at the closed door for a long time, feeling curiously unsettled. He had never spoken of his French service and subsequent disillusionment to anybody and he was certainly not going to share such personal information with an Englishman that he did not even like. He did wonder what Durrell would think about it. The thought of having that impersonal intelligence focused on his own personal demons was frankly appalling and for some reason it was rather worse that Durrell could manage it in perfect Spanish.

"What an interesting man," García said, coming out of the office and closing the door. "Do you think…"

"We have work to do," Ángel snapped. "We should also both strive to improve our command of the English language. It is humiliating to be so far behind an Englishman in both application and ability. If we are to fight as their allies we should speak their language better."

García regarded him from surprised dark eyes. "I agree, sir," he said. "The General wishes us both to accompany him to the *Iris* later on, which will be an excellent opportunity to begin. Do you think Lieutenant Durrell would be willing to help me while he is here? I…"

"I have no intention of asking him," Ángel said. "I have books, I will do this myself. In the meantime, you should speak to the superintendent of hospitals about the shortage of bandages and dressings. Tell him that I have sent a request to the English for medical supplies and find out what else he needs. I am going over to the San Juan Bastion."

Outside the sun was dazzling and Ángel paused to allow his eyes to get used to the light. Two nuns, one in the habit of a novice, were climbing the steps to the front door of the cathedral. Ángel watched until they disappeared inside. He wondered if his young sister had survived the long years of war to take her final vows and if so, where she was now. So many religious houses had been destroyed; their inhabitants either dead or fled to safer houses in more remote regions.

Ángel preferred not to dwell on thoughts of what might have happened to his sister, since there was nothing he could do about it, but he thought of her now. She had been a child when he left his family home, too young to understand the intricacies of politics and war. Ángel wondered if she had ever known the truth of why he left and whether she would despise him if she did. As always, when she entered his mind he saw her as she had been then, a pretty child with soft brown hair and grave brown eyes. Ángel tried to work out how old she must be now. He thought she might be twenty-three or twenty-four. Was she safe in some convent still, anonymous in a dark habit like the two women he had just seen, or was she dead, a victim of war? Ángel felt his stomach clench, remembering some of the things he had seen done to priests and nuns by the French.

Such thoughts did no good and Ángel had no time to be maudlin. He shook his head as if to clear it and set off with long strides towards the San Juan Bastion, dragging his mind back to the task in hand.

Chapter Thirteen

Bianca's journey took longer than she had expected. Partly this was due to her decision to stay away from the main roads where either the French army or the Spanish guerrillas might send out patrols. Partly it was because she did not know the way and despite stopping frequently in villages and small hamlets to ask for directions, she got lost several times.

Her shabby leather shoes were not sturdy enough for this amount of walking and were quickly worn through. Bianca tried walking barefoot, but the tracks were stony and left her with a painful cut on her left foot. Eventually she put the shoes back on, wrapping her feet in strips torn from her petticoat to protect them. By the time she reached the edge of the French lines, she was limping badly.

Her confidence drained away with the miles and the sight of the army almost made her wish she could turn and go back. It was not possible. Her cottage would be empty, her livestock gone and the remains of her land and crops probably shared out between the villagers. Rodriguez would not marry a girl who had run off alone to the French lines. There would be nothing left to do but throw herself on the mercy of the Spanish army or the local guerrilla bands and that would feel just as terrifying as this.

As she drew closer to the town, Bianca could hear the French guns in the distance. She had been told by several people along the way that the French were already besieging Tarragona and it sounded as though the attack was well underway. It would make her search for Bonnet more difficult as he might well be at the front. Bianca was trying not to think about what she would do if something had happened to him. In all her imaginings, Bonnet was whole and healthy, if surprised and possibly displeased to see her. She had not considered the possibility that he might have been killed or wounded in action.

Thanks to her childhood following her father in the army baggage train, Bianca had a good idea of how to go about her search, and her most urgent need was a safe place to stay. Turning up at the campfire in any one of the French regiments would certainly produce a number of offers but

Bianca was not yet ready to take that particular step, although she accepted that it might come to that. She needed to find shelter and some measure of safety in order to continue her search.

There was a tiny village, little more than a hamlet, just at the outside edge of the siege lines. It consisted of half a dozen houses and a tiny church. Most of the inhabitants had fled ahead of the advancing French but when Bianca approached the church, she saw a black-robed figure in a small garden beyond the little graveyard, wielding a hoe. The garden reminded Bianca of her own tiny garden back in the village and she could visualise her father weeding the vegetable beds. The thought brought tears to her eyes and she paused to wipe them away before crossing the track to the garden wall.

The priest looked up as she approached and stood leaning on his hoe. He was younger than she had expected, probably not more than thirty, with a thin tired face and bloodshot blue eyes. Bianca bobbed a curtsy.

"Good day to you, Father. I'm glad to find you here, I thought the place was deserted."

"If you are looking for the villagers, my child, I am afraid they left weeks ago. The cottages are used by French officers as billets."

"They are not here now."

"They are at the siege lines. I have heard that General Suchet has called in all his troops in readiness for the attack. It will be soon, I think. Were you looking for somebody?"

"I am looking for directions, Father. I am alone after the death of my father and am seeking work. It seems I cannot reach Tarragona."

The priest frowned. "There is no possibility. And forgive me, child, it is not safe for you to be wandering through the French army lines alone. These men have no honour and they will not respect yours. Have you no other family?"

"No," Bianca said truthfully. "I will not trouble you, Father, I know you have nothing to spare. But I must live. If I cannot find work in Tarragona, perhaps I can find work for the French. My father was once a soldier and as a child I used to help my mother nurse the wounded. Is there an army hospital nearby? They always need nurses and I will work for food and a corner to sleep until this is over and I can look for something else."

The priest studied her for a long moment. Abruptly he leaned his hoe against the church wall.

"It might answer," he said. "I do know where the nearest hospital is, Señorita and I know they were looking for help. A man came here to look but I told him the people had gone. He asked if I would go but I have my church to take care of. He did not try to force me. But you…it is no guarantee, but if you work for them, you will have some standing and it may keep you safe."

Bianca felt a little lift of hope. "Can you tell me where it is? Is it far?"

"Two miles, in the Monastery of St Francis Xavier. The monks fled before the French arrived. They asked me to go with them but I wished to remain with my church. The people will return when they can and I should be here."

"Are you not afraid?" Bianca asked curiously. "I have heard that in some places, they have killed priests."

"I have heard it too. And sometimes I am afraid, Señorita. But this is my place and this is my work. To run from it would disappoint the Lord." Unexpectedly the priest smiled. "Are you not afraid?"

"Yes," Bianca said honestly. "But not every Frenchman is wicked, Father."

The priest studied her for a moment then beckoned. "Come into the church. My house has been commandeered by the officers but I am comfortable enough in the vestry. I have bread and some wine and once you are rested, I will go with you to the hospital. My presence may keep you safe on the way."

***

The difficulties in getting the siege train to Tarragona and problems with getting the artillery into place meant that the early weeks of Suchet's investment dragged miserably, but once the guns were in place events began to move with terrifying speed. Bonnet suspected that Suchet was working with a sense of suppressed panic; keeping one eye on Campoverde's roaming Spanish army and an even more anxious eye on the distant figure of Bonaparte, awaiting news of his progress.

Within a few days of successfully storming Fort Olivo, Suchet ordered a series of attacks on the rest of the outlying works, beginning with Fort Francoli. Bonnet had given up hope that the 30th légère would be released from its invariable position at the front of the worst-placed attacking column. He was almost beginning to get used to it and approached each new assault with a grim determination to come through it alive with as many of his company intact as he could possibly manage. It was a strategy of sorts, and although Bonnet was exhausted, he was not bored.

The next stage of the siege works was placed under the supervision of General Rogniat and Colonel Henri of the engineers, along with two-thousand labourers and more than a thousand trench guards. By now, Bonnet's men were very experienced and knew the exact moment to take cover along with the sappers when either the garrison or the Royal Navy opened fire on them. Sometimes there was no cover to be found, but losses were surprisingly few.

The new trenches were connected at the rear to the stone bridge over the Francoli. Because the bridge was so exposed, Henri gave orders for the construction of a bridge upon props close by to give cover for the troops coming from the camps to the trench. A redoubt was built to the left; and the right was shielded by two existing batteries. Some of the trenches ran through solid rock and the miners and sappers had to use pickaxes to dig through. It was back-breaking work, under constant heavy fire and Bonnet admired the stoical courage of the engineers and artillery men who laboured both day and night, not faltering as many of their comrades were carried away: either to the hospitals or to the mass graves. The batteries on the right bank near to the mouth of the River Francoli were fully operational now and proved very useful in keeping the Royal Navy at bay.

On the night of 6th June there was a successful attack on a Spanish post below the Bastion of the Canons and several more batteries were constructed. Three companies of the 30^{th,} including Bonnet's, joined half a battalion of light troops led by Captain Auvray who was one of Suchet's ADCs. The attack was a success with only one man killed and a few wounded among the French troops. Auvray instructed that the post should be dismantled to prevent its reoccupation by the Spanish and Bonnet gave orders to his weary company.

"Do you think they will give us some time to rest tomorrow, Captain?" Lieutenant Allard asked. "The men are very tired. If this continues they are going to make mistakes."

"If this continues, I'm going to start making fucking mistakes, Allard," Bonnet said grimly.

"Why is it always our company?" Allard asked. They were watching the men breaking up a wooden sentry post. Bonnet had ordered them to set the wood aside to be taken back to camp. There was a chronic shortage of firewood for the troops cooking fires and he had no intention of allowing anybody else to get their hands on this and was prepared to instruct his men to fight for it if necessary.

"Because Lacasse dislikes me," Bonnet said honestly. He thought that Allard had probably worked it out and that the question had been rhetorical but it would not hurt to be honest. "I'm sorry, Lieutenant, you have drawn the short straw. Lacasse is in trouble with Suchet, which is why he's being told to send men from the 30th to every shitty posting in this campaign. On the principle of kicking the next dog in line, Lacasse is giving the worst of that to me. I suppose it makes him feel better."

"I did not know he disliked you so much, Captain." Allard hesitated. "In fact, we all thought that he treated you as…well, as a bit of a joke."

Bonnet shot him a glance and managed a tired smile to show that he was not offended. "He did. And I've cultivated that, it was nice and safe. But during this campaign I've opened my mouth a few times on the matter of his incompetence and I've given orders that should have come from him. He needs a punching bag and I'm afraid I'm his man. Sorry. It's rough on you and Duclos as well as the men. If the chance comes up for a transfer to another company, you should take it."

"I am happy to remain in your company, sir."

Bonnet thanked him, reflecting that there was not really anything else Allard could have said. He thought over the conversation through the remaining hours of the night. Bonnet went to report to Captain Auvray before returning to camp to snatch a few hours rest. Auvray thanked him absent-mindedly and gave him leave to go. Bonnet turned to leave then on impulse turned back.

"Captain Auvray. In your position as ADC to the General, you must be more aware than most of us of any vacant opportunities in other companies, in other battalions. I was wondering…"

Auvray, who was several years younger than Bonnet, raised his eyebrows. "You are looking to change regiments, Captain?"

"Not me, sir. I was thinking of Lieutenant Allard and Sous-Lieutenant Duclos. Both are very good officers and this company is not the best place to be during this campaign. It occurred to me that their talents might be more valued elsewhere. Just if you heard of anything."

"Have they asked this of you?"

"Good God no, they're very loyal. I'm just concerned for them."

To Bonnet's surprise, Auvray gave a faint smile. "I thought as much," he said. "I will do as you wish, Captain, but if either of your officers were to ask my advice I would tell them that there are worse places to be. It is hazardous to be at the front of every charge but it is also an excellent place to be noticed. I am surprised that your Colonel Lacasse has not realised that and placed himself there rather more often."

Bonnet was so surprised that he could not speak for a moment. When he found his voice, he blurted out:

"Is that what the General is waiting for him to do?"

"With increasing impatience, Captain. Unfortunately for the Colonel, every time General Suchet searches for him, he finds you in his place. In the long term, that may not be to the advantage of both you and your officers."

Bonnet was silent for a moment, watching his company form up ready to march back to camp. "They're exhausted," he said abruptly. "They've not had more than a couple of hours rest for over a week. That's not the way to get the best out of your men."

"Your Colonel should be rotating his companies for duties such as this. He is not a stupid man, Bonnet, he knows this."

"It's not stupidity, Captain."

"I see. I will speak to the General and suggest to him that the 30th légère might improve for a day's rest. It will be no more than that, we are very close to an attack on the lower town, Captain."

Bonnet turned a surprised gaze onto the ADC. "You would speak to the General?"

Auvray smiled a little. "General Suchet understands the value of keeping his army fit and healthy, and so far he has been surprised and a little impressed at the performance of the 30th légère. He will not wish to lose it because it is too tired to fight. Take your men back to camp."

"I will, Captain. Thank you."

***

Bianca found the work at the army hospital surprisingly simple. She had been welcomed with surprised gratitude by a harried medical officer. Dr Tellier showed no interest in her sudden appearance. He barked a number of straightforward questions about her nursing experience, lifted his eyebrows at her admission that she had been raised in an army camp and took her to the kitchen to introduce her to Madame Savary, the cook, who was married to an artillery sergeant and who appeared to act as general manager for the few Spanish orderlies who worked at the hospital.

The building, like many army hospitals on both sides of the conflict, had once housed a religious order. Bianca, learning her way around the maze of open wards and individual cells, wondered where the monks had gone and if their departure had been voluntary. Madame Savary, who spoke good Spanish, explained her wages and ration allowance then surveyed Bianca's thin, travel-stained figure for a long silent moment and sighed.

"The men sleep in one of the barns with our medical staff but that won't do for you, child. Not that we have any trouble like that around here, they're all working too hard and besides, I wouldn't allow it. Nor would Dr Tellier, he's a good man. Still, best not put temptation in their way. You're not married, are you?"

Bianca shook her head. "I lived with my father but he died. I'm alone."

"And what made you come to the French lines?" Madame asked shrewdly.

Bianca looked back with wide eyes. "Safety," she said succinctly. "When the army – any army - marches through the villages a woman alone is not safe. Here, there are officers to keep an eye on them. I thought it might be safer. It is not patriotism, Señora, if the British or Spanish army were here I would be working for them."

Madame gave a throaty laugh. "Clever girl. And you're right, there's no point in trying to get into Tarragona, it will be in French hands before a month is out. Well, if you work hard and behave yourself you will be safe here. You will sleep in the kitchen: I will find you bedding. I have a small room off the scullery. My husband joins me when he is able. Which is never at the moment, he is manning those guns under heavy fire all day and all night. God willing, it will be over soon and he'll come back safely. Come, I will show you around. There is a chest in the kitchen for blankets. You may keep your possessions there."

There were no set hours of work on the wards and Bianca's work often continued until the doctor on duty noticed her falling asleep on her feet and sent her to bed. She slept warmly by the dying embers of the kitchen fire and took meals at the scrubbed table with the orderlies and assistant surgeons. The long exhausting days meant she slept, when she had the chance, without stirring or dreaming.

The main abbey was a sprawling building set around a central courtyard which was planted as a herb and vegetable garden. It was tended by a skinny Spanish boy of thirteen whom Sergeant Savary had rescued from a beating by two Gascon grenadiers by the roadside several months before. Manuel did not talk much but seemed grateful for Bianca's interest in his work and impressed by her knowledge of the plants and herbs. It was an excellent excuse for Bianca to spend what little free time she had in the cloister garden.

She had arrived at the hospital knowing little French other than what she had picked up from Bonnet during his time at the cottage. For the first two weeks she was often bewildered by shouted instructions in a mixture of French and appalling Spanish but it was definitely the quickest way to learn. By the end of the third week, Bianca realised she was beginning to understand more and more of the conversations around her and could communicate basic information and ask questions with both the medical staff and patients.

Wounded men were housed in the abbey and the adjoining church while the staff were billeted in two farm cottages and a big barn. There was a separate building which Bianca thought might have been some kind of guest-house which was used as a fever ward. It was an unpopular duty but Bianca quite liked it and volunteered whenever she could. She had recent experience of nursing a fever patient and knew the routine. It was quieter than the main wards and the patients seemed grateful for any kindness.

The hospital was one of a number set up around the outskirts of Tarragona and as she settled in, Bianca was impressed with how well organised and well supplied it was. Dr Tellier, who had served in Spain for several years and spoke good Spanish, explained that General Suchet was known for his efficiency in logistics and for his care for the welfare of his men. He had visited all the hospitals personally at least once and insisted on regular detailed reports.

Initially, Bianca's duties mostly involved serving food and water, cleaning the wards and surgery when necessary and helping with the mountain of daily laundry. After a while she began to assist with basic nursing tasks such as washing the patients and helping the surgeons on their rounds. The hospital day consisted of dull, repetitive tasks interspersed with sudden explosive action when a skirmish occurred and the wounded men poured into the hospital. The attacks on the various outposts often happened at night and Bianca grew accustomed to being called from her bed in the early hours to help dress wounds, give wine or water to exhausted, filthy men, and far too often to lay out the dead ready for burial. Grave pits were dug half a mile away and wooden carts trundled backwards and forwards bearing their grisly burdens.

There were few Spanish wounded brought in and those were quickly transported to a temporary prison camp at the back of the French lines which had its own hospital. Bianca was glad. She felt no particular guilt about working for the enemy but she suspected that some of her countrymen might have made themselves unpleasant about it if they had the opportunity to do so.

She told nobody of her hope of locating Gabriel Bonnet. This was not the time to be searching for him. Once the siege was over, one way or another, she could make enquiries from a far stronger position now that she had found herself a place with the French army. Already the men who worked alongside her were growing accustomed to her. Most of them treated her with casual kindness and in their free time they helped her to practice her French. In return, Bianca took on small mending tasks and delighted them one afternoon by offering to trim their hair and tidy their moustaches. One or two of them seemed inclined to flirt a little but Bianca kept a firm distance. She suspected that both Madame Savary and Dr Tellier had given instructions about how she was to be treated and so far their word held good. It would not do to encourage familiarity.

Bianca awoke in the early hours one night to find Madame Savary shaking her arm. The kitchen was dimly lit by the glow of the banked fire and a branch of candles on the table. Bianca sat up, blinking away sleep.

"Am I needed?"

"You will be. They just sent a rider out from the camp, there is fighting at Fort Francoli. They have sent out the hospital wagons."

Bianca got up quickly and turned to fold her blankets. She shoved her feet into her recently repaired shoes and searched for hairpins, twisting her long hair up into a hasty knot while Madame Savary set to work on the fire and went around lighting oil lamps.

By now Bianca knew the routine of these night-time alarms. She gulped down a mug of weak ale in the kitchen and ate the remains of a chunk of bread and hard cheese. Around her, orderlies and doctors came and went on the same errand. When she was ready she went through into the wards to check on her existing patients. They were awake and restless, calling out questions in both French and Spanish. Bianca gave reassurance where she could and distributed watered-down wine.

The surgeons had set up their tables in what had once been the Abbot's dining room, a long panelled apartment with tall windows at each end. Bianca found Dr Tellier supervising his assistant who was laying out his surgical instruments on a wooden side table.

"Bianca, there you are. I have assigned you to Verany and Trichet. As they bring the patients through, you will find beds for them and ensure they are properly settled." Tellier cocked his head, listening intently. "There is a wagon approaching. Go down now and direct them where to take the men. Assistant Surgeon Joubert is in the tiled hallway making the assessments. Madame Savary and two of the cantinières will tend to minor injuries in the kitchen, she'll call you if she needs help."

Bianca went through into the wide front hall of the main convent building. The two orderlies were already there, propping the big oak door open. The crash of artillery and musket fire was deafening and, even from here, Bianca could smell the smoke and see flashes of light splitting open the darkness of the night sky. Bianca took up position at the top of the shallow steps leading up to the convent, while on the packed earth of the driveway, several men began lifting the wounded soldiers down onto sturdy stretchers. As the first man was carried towards the house, Bianca took a deep breath and stepped forward.

Within thirty minutes the tiled hallway was full of prone bodies and the air was thick with the stench of blood and sweat. Bianca had been joined by two other women, both of them French cantinières. As wounded men were brought in, the assistant surgeon hurried to examine them to determine how serious their wounds were. Those who could walk and needed only dressings were taken through to Madame Savary and her assistants in the kitchen. Others were placed in a grisly queue to be taken through to the surgeon. A third, and mercifully small category were carried to a side parlour. These men were judged unlikely to survive and would not be seen by the surgeon until all the others had been treated.

Bianca found the system harsh and yet she had to admit that it probably saved lives. She made a point, when she could, of slipping into the parlour to give wine or water to any of the men who were able to drink. Most of them were unconscious: their laboured breathing lending truth to Dr Joubert's assessment. One, a stocky bald guardsman with a horrific stomach injury grasped the wine bottle like a drowning man, gulping it down. Bianca let him drink until he fell back exhausted. His face was grey beneath streaks of blood and she suspected that he would not live through the night. If the wine helped him to endure his painful death more easily she did not begrudge it to him.

She returned to him for the last time just as dawn was beginning to send faint streaks of light across the sky above Tarragona. The flood of wounded men had become a trickle and the tiled hallway was finally clear. Bianca went to stand on the steps again, breathing in the cool air which had cleared a little, though it still smelled of smoke. Over at the lower town the Spanish guns still thundered out with monotonous regularity and Bianca wondered what was happening in the lines. At times she felt a confused sense of guilt that she was here tending to the French while behind the walls of Tarragona her countrymen fought and died. At the same time she was aware that these men had taken her in when she was desperate, given her work and kept her safe in a way that her village had not. Perhaps she had not given them enough of a chance, but if marriage to a man she disliked was the price of acceptance, Bianca preferred to make her own way.

On her return to the parlour, there were several gaps in the two rows of men and Bianca's stomach gave a little lurch as she realised they had probably been removed for burial. The grenadier lay still and silent on the wooden boards. Bianca went to kneel beside him and reached for his hand. It was already cold, his unseeing eyes staring up at the ceiling.

Bianca reached out and very carefully closed the man's eyes. She stood up, realising for the first time how tired she was. There was no hope of going back to her bed with the kitchen full of wounded soldiers but Bianca wondered if there was any chance of a hot drink at least. She was stupidly tired and was surprised to find her face wet with silent tears.

Out in the hall again she found the assistant surgeon and told him of the man's death then headed back to the kitchen. The chaos had cleared a little, with only half a dozen men, all sporting bandages or dressings, sitting around the big square table, hands wrapped around cups of bitter black coffee. There was a jug of it keeping hot on an iron shelf in the fireplace and Bianca rinsed a used cup and went to pour herself a drink. There was very little conversation in the room. Madame Savary was stoking the fire. She gave Bianca a weary smile and disappeared into her pantry, emerging with some of her precious supply of sugar for Bianca's coffee. Bianca smiled back through her tears. She found space at the end of one of the benches and sat sipping her drink; trying to think of nothing at all. In the distance, the guns boomed on.

There was the sound of voices in the hallway, indistinct at first but then growing louder. Bianca was not really listening. They were speaking French and she was too exhausted to practice her language skills tonight. Instead, she decided to silently will the men to leave the kitchen either to go back to the lines or to find a bed on a ward, so that she could sleep. If they did not move soon she might simply unroll her mattress and lie down. She thought she was tired enough to sleep through the murmured conversation around her.

The voices outside grew louder again, forcing her to take notice. She was just trying to push her tired brain into translating the words when one of the men at the table stirred as if coming out of a trance.

"That's the Captain," he said.

"Oh fuck," his companion groaned. Bianca had learned that particular word during her first few days assisting the surgeons. "Surely he can't be here to round us up and drag us back."

His friend said something that Bianca did not understand and both men laughed. It had piqued her curiosity enough to make her listen properly and as she did so, she realised with a sudden shock of alarm that she recognised one of the raised voices and not from her time at the hospital.

Bianca drained her coffee cup and rose, going to the door. Madame Savary looked up.

"Bianca, if you go out there they will give you a job to do. Stay and rest, you have done enough."

"I will be back very soon," Bianca said and slipped through the door before the older woman could argue. The hall was lit only by an oil lamp hanging from a hook by the front door. Two men stood arguing just inside. One was Joubert, the assistant surgeon. The other, a big man in a stained blue jacket, was Captain Gabriel Bonnet.

"You must come to the surgery," Joubert was saying. "You are wounded and you must be treated before you return to camp."

"It's barely a scratch and I'm not here for that. Six of my men were brought up here and I want to know how they are. Mother of God, it can't be that difficult, even for a French army hospital, to work out what's happened to six men. Don't you have anybody here who has a clue what's going on?"

Joubert made an exasperated sound and Bianca decided that he had been through this conversation several times already. "I told you, sir, the returns will not be made up until tomorrow. Then your Chef de Battalion will be notified about…"

"My Chef de Battalion hasn't a fucking clue who these men are and cares less," Bonnet bellowed, apparently losing his temper. "They're my men. I want to know. There has to be a doctor here who is treating these men, doesn't he have a list? Even a scrap of paper with a few names scrawled on it? It can't be that difficult."

Bianca could not bear it. She stepped forward into the light. "I can probably help you," she said in Spanish.

Bonnet turned. Bianca saw his dark eyes fix upon her and then widen in complete astonishment. She was not sure what she had expected from this first meeting because she had not imagined it would happen under these difficult circumstances. She had hoped to find him in camp, during a quiet time between the fighting, where she would have the chance to try to explain to him why she had left her village. So far, Bianca had not even tried to rehearse what she would say. She realised, rather too late, that she should probably have planned for an unexpected meeting.

"You cannot possibly know anything about this, girl," Joubert said dismissively. He turned back to Bonnet. "She's a Spanish begger, works in the kitchen and helping out with the nursing, Captain. I assure you…"

"If she works here, she's hardly a begger, is she?" Bonnet said, somewhat acerbically. "As it happens, I know her, though I've no idea what she's doing here. Bianca?"

Bianca met Bonnet's bewildered gaze. "Two of your men are in the kitchen," she said apologetically. "They heard your voice."

Bonnet's lips twitched into a half smile. "That doesn't explain why you're out here telling me about it instead of them," he said in Spanish. "And it certainly doesn't explain what the bloody hell you're doing here. Where's the kitchen?"

"It's this way."

Bianca led him through the short service corridor into the kitchen. One of the ward orderlies was there, apparently allocating beds to the remaining wounded men. As Bonnet entered, the two men from his company straightened up and gave a wary salute. Bonnet looked them over thoughtfully.

"Prevel, Rostan. Are you all right?"

"Yes, Captain. I was shot through the arm. Prevel here took a bayonet in the back."

"It's not deep though, sir. They have put some stitches in but I think I am fit to come back…"

"Don't be a fucking idiot, Prevel. The idea of stitches is to let it heal, that's not going to happen if you're scrambling through ditches full of stinking stagnant water. You'll stay here until the doctor says you're fit for duty." Bonnet looked around the rapidly emptying kitchen. "It looks all right here. Better than a lot of army hospitals I've seen. Have you any idea what happened to the other four that came up?"

"Rigal and Soulier are on one of the wards, sir. Both went down in that bayonet charge. Soulier looked a mess but he's still alive."

"Good. What about the others?"

"Thibault isn't here, sir. I think he got taken to a different hospital."

"And Tisseur?"

"Tisseur didn't make it, Captain," Prevel said sombrely. "They were amputating what was left of his leg but he died on the table."

Bonnet did not speak for a minute. Bianca could see Dr Joubert hovering in the doorway, his eyes on Bonnet's bloodstained jacket. Eventually she said:

"I am very sorry, Captain. But will you not allow Dr Joubert to tend your own wound, now that you are reassured about your men?"

Bonnet stirred as if coming out of a trance and looked down at her. Bianca felt as though she had forgotten how big he was. His face was filthy, the white slash of his scar barely visible beneath the black layer of gun smoke and mud. He was also soaked through, which puzzled her because it was a fine dry night.

Bonnet looked over at his men again and then at the orderly. "Find them a bed and look after them," he said. "I could do with them fit to fight again, I'm rapidly running out of men in this fucking campaign. All right, Doctor, lead the way. I'd like Señorita Ramos to come with me, though. We need to have a conversation."

Joubert looked baffled but did not ask. Bianca suspected he just wanted to examine his patient and then get to his bed. It was full dawn now and through the long arched window of the surgery, she could see the walls and towers of Tarragona bathed in the rose pink glow of the sunrise.

Behind her, Bonnet gave a squawk of pain. Bianca turned quickly and felt her stomach lurch at the sight of the ugly wound on his shoulder. It was very swollen and bleeding sluggishly. She went to bring water and a dressing as Joubert probed at the wound. He was not particularly gentle and Bianca could see that Bonnet was gritting his teeth.

"What in God's name caused this, Captain? It doesn't look like either shot or a bayonet?"

"It was a piece of wooden fencing," Bonnet said. There were beads of sweat on his dirty face. "I have to give the Spanish bastard credit for improvisation. We came up out of the ditch on their flank and he'd clearly lost his bayonet in the first rush. A lot of the palisades have been smashed to pieces by our artillery over the past week. I was bearing down on him and he used what he could grab. It was fucking effective as well, it stopped me dead."

Joubert grunted. "Six inches lower and you would have been dead," he said. "I can't put stitches in this, it's too wide. I'll bandage it up and…"

"Would you like me to do it, Doctor?" Bianca said quickly, her eyes on the wound. "I have been learning with Dr Tellier and you are very tired."

Joubert glanced at her and gave a snort. "I think I know what he'd prefer," he said. "You should rest that as much as you can, Captain. Not that you will. Bianca, when you've finished, you can show the Captain to one of the empty cells and get him some blankets. At least he can get a couple of hours sleep before going back to his company. If he'll stay. And feed him."

When Joubert had gone, Bianca took a deep breath. She was suddenly so terrified that her hands were shaking and the bowl of water she was holding was in danger of spilling. She set it down quickly and turned to the side table in search of lint and bandages.

"I'm glad you volunteered," Bonnet said conversationally. "I've a feeling you'll be more gentle than the good doctor. He thinks I'm a bloody nuisance turning up here at dawn when he was on his way to bed."

Bianca realised that she was trying not to look at him which was ridiculous. She set down the dressings and forced herself to look directly at him. "He is very tired."

"I imagine you all are. I'll need to sit down or you won't be able to reach me."

"I am not that short."

"You're not that tall either." Bonnet hooked his foot around a wooden stool and sat down. Bianca surveyed him critically and sighed.

"I will have to remove your shirt as well as your jacket. I will try to be gentle but I wish to look again to be sure the doctor has not missed anything. Wood can splinter and it will not heal well if there is something left in it."

"If anybody could miss something it'd be Dr Joubert," Bonnet said, shrugging his way painfully out of his wet jacket and shirt. "Thank you for this, Bianca. I wasn't going to bother, but…"

"That would be very stupid," Bianca said crisply. "Here, let me take those. They are soaked. What on earth happened, did you fall into the River Francoli?"

"Not so much fell as waded," Bonnet said tiredly. "The usual bloody mess. We stormed the fort in fine dramatic style only to discover they'd already left it."

Bianca bent to her work, cleaning the ragged gash as gently as she could. "Then why are so many of your men injured, and you also?"

"Because my men are fucking idiots," Bonnet said flatly. "We were only ordered to take and hold the fort but once they were in there and met no resistance, they got carried away."

"I still do not see how you got so wet."

"The 30th were with the right-hand column; we were sent in across the mouth of the Francoli to attack the fort from the sea side. It's deeper than you'd think in places: we were wading up to our waists. But it wasn't just that. When we were in, Saint-Cyr Nugues tried to call them back but he lost control of the 5th and our men just followed them. They raced to the San Carlos Bastion yelling that they were going to take the town. Stupid bastards got cut down by musketry fire from both the bastion and the Spanish troops in the defences beyond. It was bloody."

"And you went with them?"

"I went to get them back. Saint-Cyr Nugues was doing his best but thank God Colonel Henri from the engineers came up to see what needed to be done to hold the fort and he managed to call them in, though we took some losses. But it involved scrambling through one or two ditches full of muddy water. Hence this mess."

"Did you manage to hold the fort?"

"Yes. We've spent the rest of the night dodging enemy fire and preparing for an attack; which means cutting trenches, building up the parapets and making a temporary bridge over those bloody ditches. We've been under fire the whole time, I lost two men as well as poor Tisseur. Needless to say the 30th has now been given the job of defending the fort which has just become the target for every piece of artillery that can reach it, including the Royal fucking Navy. Ouch."

"I am sorry. I think it is clean. I will put a dressing on it and bandage it, but you should try to rest it. Can you not remain here and let your officers…"

"No. I'll rest it when this is over and that bloody town is taken. Hopefully by then, General Suchet will decide he's had enough of tormenting the 30th légère and we can all have a night off."

"Why do you think he is…"

"I'll explain another time," Bonnet said firmly. "Since I do have to get back, Bianca Ramos, I'd like to know what the devil you're doing here nursing enemy soldiers miles from where you should be."

Bianca had known he would not leave without an explanation but she struggled to find the right words. While she was still thinking about it, Bonnet said quietly:

"Where's your father, Bianca?"

"My father is dead," Bianca said. She was surprised at the tremor in her own voice. "He had the bloody flux. He was too old and too weak to survive it, he lasted only a few days."

"Oh no. I'm sorry, Bianca. How did you get here?"

"I walked."

"Mother of God, you're lucky to have made it in one piece." Dark eyes studied her face and Bianca was warmed by the concern in them. "You did make it in one piece, didn't you? I mean…"

"Yes, of course. I was very careful, Captain and I am not stupid. I was born in an army camp, remember?"

"A Spanish army camp, not a French one."

"Do you think they are so very different?"

"Probably not. But it doesn't explain why you're here."

Bianca took hold of her courage in both hands. "I could not remain," she said. "It is a small village with small-minded people, Captain. An unmarried girl cannot live alone. It would not be permitted."

Bonnet studied her thoughtfully for a long moment. Eventually he got up and went to retrieve his filthy, torn shirt. He shrugged it on, tucking it in to his waistband. Bianca wondered if he was giving himself time to think or whether he was suddenly embarrassed at sitting half naked.

"I think I understand. Did they have somebody in mind for you?"

"The priest tried to make a match for me, a man from a neighbouring village. He is old and mean and spiteful and I will not chain myself to such a man for the rest of my life."

"So you came here. I have to tell you, Bianca, that there are spiteful men in the French army as well as in a Spanish village."

"I know that, Captain. Also in the Spanish army and probably the British as well. But at least here I have a choice. Here, I can leave if I wish."

Bonnet sighed. "It was a mad thing to do, Bianca. You'll be all right until the end of the siege but at some point they'll close this place down and after that your only choice will be to attach yourself to some man. You must know that."

"I do know it. There are a lot of men in this army. I am not much, but I will find one to take me on. For a time, at least."

"A Frenchman?"

"Unless the Spanish win, in which case it will be a Spaniard," Bianca said with brutal honesty. "I cannot afford to be patriotic, Captain, I have to survive. But I do not want...I am not a prostitute. If there is a man, I will take care of him. I can cook and mend and do all that he needs and I will be loyal to him while he wants me. I cannot bear the thought of being passed around from one to another like a thing. That is why I ran away."

Now that she had said it, she did not want to see his expression. She turned away but Bonnet reached out and caught her hand. She tugged to release it, but he held on firmly.

"Keep still for a minute, would you? Every time we've tried to have a personal conversation you get up and clean something or mend something or tidy something."

Bianca stared at him in surprise. "Do I? I did not know that."

"I stayed with you for over a week, it was difficult to miss. Did you come here to find me, Bianca Ramos?"

Colour scorched her face which was ridiculous given that it was exactly what she had done. For a moment, she considered denying it but immediately realised how stupid that would be. He would not believe her anyway.

"I should find you a room, the doctor is right. If you will not take sick leave you should at least sleep a little before you return to your battalion."

"You walked ten miles, dodging French patrols to come and find me, Bianca. Bloody well keep still and speak to me."

"I do not know what to say." Bianca met his gaze warily. "Captain, I do not know you and you do not know me, so I cannot come here to ask if I can stay with you. But you were kind to me for those few days so I came to ask...to ask if I could remain with you until I found a man who would take me on. I do not know how long that might take, but..."

Bonnet gave a splutter of laughter. "Bianca, if you weren't under the protection of the medical staff here you'd have been hard put to fight them off."

Bianca waved her hand, indicating the room around her. "This is temporary, you are right," she said.

"And after that, you're willing to join the French army as a camp follower? I can introduce you to my men, Bianca, but not until after the town is won. Before then I don't have the time to stop them from killing each other over you. Bad for discipline. You might do better with an officer."

"One of your officers?"

"Well, you don't stand a chance with Lieutenant Duclos, he's only a year married, and he is a very faithful husband. And Sub-Lieutenant Allard has never had a girl in his life as far as I can tell; he worries me. I could introduce you to some of my fellow captains. They'd thank me for it."

"That would be very good of you, Captain."

"Gabriel."

"Gabriel?" Bianca felt her heart beat a little faster.

"It's my name and there isn't a man in the army that uses it. They call me Bonnet. Or something worse. I would like you to call me Gabriel."

Bianca stood staring at him. She was still not certain if he had understood what she was trying to ask him and if she did not manage to blurt out the words soon he would be gone and she would be left in this uncertainty. Suddenly she saw her quest as the madness it really was. She had followed him into the unknown based on nothing more than casual kindness and an attractive smile.

"Gabriel," she repeated, for something to say.

"That feels like a good start," Bonnet said. "Have you done this before? I mean...been with a man."

Bianca blushed again, her eyes widening.

"Yes. A long time ago. His name was Pedro and he rode off to fight the French and never came back. Luckily, he did not leave me pregnant."

"How old were you?"

"Sixteen."

Bonnet studied her for a moment then grinned. "Woman dear, you must be even more out of practice than I am, I hope we can remember enough to get by."

Bianca stared at him with dawning hope. "Are you saying that you will...that you wish to..."

"I should tell you that I don't get much chance to bathe and I fart in bed," Bonnet said apologetically.

"I will heat water for you to wash, and all men pass wind when they should not."

Bonnet laughed. "A very practical viewpoint. Look, Bianca, I can't...I need to get back to my men. This is not the time."

"I know. Of course I know. I understand, it is why I did not come to seek you."

"You'd never have found me, I've been on duty every day since I can remember. Our Colonel managed to piss off General Suchet which means we're getting the worst of this campaign. But it won't be much longer. We'll have taken the rest of the external defences by the end of this week and we'll be in the city the week after that."

"You're very certain."

"Sometimes you can be. What I can't promise is that I'll survive it."

"I hope you do, Captain."

"What did I just tell you?"

"I'm sorry. Gabriel."

"Let's assume I will. I'm very good at dodging. I'll come and find you and you can stay with me until...until you find a man more to your liking."

Bianca felt suddenly very shy. "I was afraid...I am afraid that you will not like me enough."

Bonnet was halfway through pulling on his damp jacket. He stopped and turned to look at her in apparent surprise. "You?"

"There are prettier women in search of a protector, Gabriel."

Bonnet walked forward and raised a hand to cup her face. Her hair brushed the back of his knuckles and he closed his eyes for a moment as if revelling in its softness. Eventually he opened them, leaned forward and kissed her. Bianca moved closer to him, reaching up to put her arms about his neck. She felt ridiculously awkward. The kiss was very gentle, almost diffident and she wished it had lasted longer.

"I like you enough," he said very softly. "I'm more worried that I won't be able to get you to like me."

In response, Bianca reached up and ran a hand through his still damp hair. "Does that matter?"

"Yes. Yes, it matters very much. I want…I mean, I don't want...oh fuck, I sound like an idiot."

Bianca realised abruptly that under his blunt manner, Gabriel Bonnet was shy. The relief was overwhelming. "I like it when you sound like an idiot, Gabriel. And I like very much that it matters that I want you too."

"I'm not much to look at, little bird, you could do a lot better in this army."

"I like the way you look. You have very kind eyes."

Bonnet lifted a strand of her hair and tucked it behind her ear, observing her face intently. "I'll settle for that for now. If you'll say it in French."

Bianca blushed. He was smiling, waiting. Hesitantly she repeated the compliment in his language, wondering if she was saying it right. His smile broadened and he leaned forward and kissed her again, very lightly.

"I think you have the prettiest accent I've ever heard. Keep practising. I'll see you as soon as I can. I must go. Where do you sleep?"

"In the kitchen."

"Come, then."

He led her by the hand and they found Madame Savary alone in the big room, banking the fire. She looked at Bianca in astonishment and then at Bonnet. Bonnet gave a little bow.

"I think I have seen you before, Madame, your husband is with the artillery, is he not?"

Madame bowed politely. "He is, sir. You know Bianca?"

"We met several months ago." Bonnet jerked his head towards the town. "I must leave her, Madame, but should there be any difficulty, make sure they know that any man who so much as looks at her the wrong way is answerable to me. Bianca, take care and keep safe. And get some sleep, you're exhausted."

He was gone before Bianca could recover from her surprise. She looked over at Madame Savary, feeling suddenly shy. The older woman was studying her. She looked amused.

"Bianca, ever since you arrived here I have been thinking that there was no sense to your story about coming here to find work. It was idiotic and you are not an idiot. Have I just discovered the rest of the story?"

"Yes," Bianca said baldly. Given Bonnet's very public display of possessiveness there was no point in prevaricating. "Only I was not sure…"

"I think after that you can be sure," Madame Savary said. "Come, bring your mattress. You should sleep in my room for a few hours. You'll be disturbed in here and you will need your sleep for later. My husband tells me there will be no let up, now that they are so close."

Bianca turned to look out of the window and gave a little shiver. "Those poor people in the town. They must be so afraid."

Madame Savary put her hand on Bianca's shoulder. "We should thank God that we are here and not there," she said soberly. "There is nothing you can do, Bianca. And by the look of things, you have chosen your loyalties. Come and rest."

Chapter Fourteen

As the days passed and the French lines inched steadily closer to the walls of Tarragona, Hugh Kelly felt as though he was watching a boat being driven slowly onto the rocks without any possibility of going to the aid of her crew. It was agonising.

Codrington's squadron was giving every assistance that they could manage. As more and more Spanish troops were wounded, the boats and launches from the various Royal Navy vessels were in constant use, ferrying injured men out to the ships to be transported up the coast to safety. Supplies and ammunition were regularly brought in and the men of the squadron spent their spare time making sandbags which were ferried over to help the Spaniards shore up their battered defences.

"Is there any news from Campoverde?" Hugh asked Codrington. They were standing at the ship's rail of the *Blake*, watching the small boats taking a contingent of wounded men out to the *Centaur* and the *Sparrowhawk*. Codrington's squadron seemed to have expanded to include several ships which were not originally part of it. Codrington assured Hugh that he had written to Sir Charles Cotton for permission to detain the ships. Hugh suspected it would be retrospective permission but he doubted that Codrington's superiors would complain. The squadron was doing a fine job of assisting Contreras and annoying the French.

All the same, Hugh doubted they would be in a position to do the latter for much longer. As the French lines drew closer to the city walls and more batteries were built and equipped, the ships had been pushed further and further out. It would soon become too dangerous to enter this part of the bay at all, which would make it hard to keep the town supplied.

"I receive regular news from Campoverde and none of it is reassuring," Codrington said grimly. "The man is a fool and I'm not sure he isn't a coward. He's been snapping at the rear of Suchet's besieging forces for two weeks now but he refuses to take a chance on a pitched battle. The Valencian forces won't throw in their hand to attack the French depots and the guerrillas can do nothing more than annoy the occasional supply column.

It's as if they can't see the urgency of relieving Contreras. He feels abandoned and I don't know what to say to the man."

"Lieutenant Durrell says he's close to despair," Hugh said in neutral tones. "He's of the opinion that Contreras is working as hard as he can to shore up the defences but he's losing all the outposts one by one and he's losing too many men. As you can see." Hugh waved a hand at the boats, one of which was just tying up at the *Centaur*. "He's also losing officers. According to Durrell, some of them are passing themselves off as sick but others have just begged passage in the Spanish ships with no justification whatsoever. Including one or two fairly high-ranking gentlemen."

"Well I don't have control over the Spanish army, but I hope Contreras has written requesting their arrest and court martial," Codrington said grimly. Hugh thought he looked tired and drawn. "Your First Lieutenant seems to be a mine of information. Where is he getting it all from?"

"He's struck up a friendship with Contreras' ADC. I've been using Durrell as my liaison officer so they've spent a bit of time together over the past week or two. He's a useful source of information."

"Not Captain Cortez, surely?"

"No, the younger one. García. He's a nice lad, very intelligent and amiable. He's been to dinner on the *Iris* a couple of times." Hugh shot Codrington an amused glance. "You're not an admirer of Captain Cortez, I perceive."

"Arrogant young whelp," Codrington said dispassionately. "He's another Campoverde in the making. He despises everybody; it's difficult to tell the difference in his attitude towards the French, the Royal Navy and his own Spanish soldiers."

Hugh laughed. "That's just his upbringing, Ned. You must have encountered it before. I once had a captain's servant who was the son of a member of the current government. He seemed genuinely shocked when he realised he actually had a job to do."

Codrington choked with laughter. "I know who that was. Left after one voyage, didn't he?"

"With my blessing. I believe his father then bought him an expensive commission. I lost track of him after that but it's the hope of my life that he ended up on a battlefield under the command of my good friend Colonel Paul van Daan."

"You make some interesting friends, Hugh. What does young García say about Contreras?"

"Nothing to me. But he's told Durrell that both he and Cortez are worried about the man. He's taking a very gloomy view of the town's prospects and is furious about being landed with a job he wasn't ready for, while Campoverde skipped off into the hills to play hide and seek with the French."

"What about General Sarsfield?" Codrington asked. Hugh gave him a sideways look.

"I know you're a big admirer of Sarsfield, Ned, but I'm not sure he's helping. Contreras has given Sarsfield effective command of the lower town, the port area and the Mole, which is the current target of the French attacks. Sarsfield is good with his men according to young García, and ready to fight to the death but he and Contreras don't get on and the tensions aren't good for morale." Hugh shrugged. "It's frustrating. Their command problems shouldn't be our business but it feels as though they are."

"They're certainly my business," Codrington said glumly. "The *Prueba* came in this morning with letters from Campoverde both for me and for Contreras. Mine told me nothing at all useful. I'm hoping to hear from Contreras with better news but I'm not optimistic. This is going badly wrong, Hugh, and I'm concerned we're going to have to manage an evacuation."

"Then we'll manage one," Hugh said equably. "With your agreement, I've suggested to Contreras that he start sending as many non-combatants to safety as possible. We can land the women and children further up the coast. The locals will take care of them until it's safe to return and there will be fewer mouths to feed and less risk to the vulnerable if the French break through."

"Has he responded?"

"Yes, I had a letter yesterday. The gist of it is that he will do his best but some of the women don't want to leave their homes and their husbands. Still, I've written back to ask him for numbers. Depending on how many there are, I can get Winterton to load up some of the transports."

"Best not take all of them in case we need them for the garrison. But it's a good idea to get as many away as we can." Codrington shot Hugh an enquiring look. "So is young Durrell generally this friendly, or is he running his own intelligence service?"

"Are you asking me if I sent him to spy on our allies, Commodore?"

"Did you?"

Hugh grinned. "I sent him as liaison officer, Ned. I didn't give him any particular instructions because I knew I wouldn't need to. Durrell's intelligence is formidable and he's constantly thinking ahead. I actually think he likes García, but he's definitely making the most of what information we can glean."

"Bloody good job too," Codrington grunted. "I'll come over to the *Iris* in the morning and have a chat with him myself. Before long it won't be as easy for him to spend time ashore with them, but let's make the most of it while it lasts. Didn't he act as some kind of liaison officer for Popham in Walcheren?"

"I'm not sure what his job was there, Ned, apart from to make that snake Popham look good. But he managed to make friends in the army while he was doing it. He's good at this."

"He already had friends in the army, Hugh. The Earl of Chatham called in every favour he could still manage, including royalty I believe, to ensure the Admiralty didn't go after your boy after his performance at the Walcheren inquiry. He has a knack of inspiring loyalty in surprising places. You did well to hold on to him though I wasn't so sure at the time."

"Did he really? I'm glad to hear it, because Durrell was willing to put his career on the line for Chatham. I should get back, Ned. Come to breakfast tomorrow and you can talk to him then. Will you speak to Winterton about the refugees?"

"Yes, once I've worked out how many there will be and how many transports we can spare. And where the hell we're going to take them."

"Write to Campoverde. That's his problem, not yours," Hugh said firmly. "Our problem is to work out the best place to send in the boats if we do need to get the garrison off in a hurry. If they take the lower town we won't be able to get to the beaches at all. I might take my barge out this afternoon for a little reconnaissance. Best to be prepared."

Codrington surveyed him with grim amusement. "Are you advising me to stick to my job, Captain and mind my own business?"

"Not advising exactly. Maybe just a hint. You're better at politics than I am, Ned, which is why I'm happy to leave it to you. Just don't get yourself dragged in to this mess politically, will you? We can't fix the problems of the Catalonian high command or the Cortes of Cadiz."

"And you said you weren't here to be my nursemaid," Codrington said with heavy irony. "I approve of your reconnaissance though. Let me know your findings. And thank Mr Durrell for me; I can see I will live to be glad that he remained your first officer. I'll see you at breakfast tomorrow, Hugh."

Over the next few days, the ships of Codrington's squadron moved steadily from their policy of watching and waiting into more direct action. Hugh was accustomed to the sudden switch from inactivity into full battle with very little notice. Life in the navy often meant months of boring routine interspersed with short periods of frantic activity.

After Hugh's initial reconnaissance, he joined Codrington in the captain's barge from the *Blake* in a close survey of the rocky coastline to the east of the city. Once the French guns made it impossible to use the harbour, transport in and out of the town would have to be along the inhospitable shore of Milagro Point and Codrington wanted to be prepared.

At some point during the week, the Commodore had finally lost patience with his Spanish counterparts and had detached junior officers and crews from the various ships of his squadron to take over the small fleet of Spanish gunboats. Hugh was not sure about the diplomatic aspect of this action but applauded its results. As the French siege works and batteries moved forward at speed and the final Spanish outworks fell one by one into French hands, Codrington employed the gunboats and every available ship's launch at night, with as much firepower as they could carry, to harass the working parties in the trenches.

It was exhausting work. The boats could only be used at night when it was difficult for the French to return fire. Both Hugh and Codrington took personal command of their respective barges, with Durrell in charge of the *Iris's* gig. It was cold out on the water and the roar of the guns left Hugh with ringing in his ears each morning. After a few nights he was partially deaf for most of the time.

The French working parties were suffering badly but reinforcements had arrived as Suchet called in troops from the outlying parts of his army.

Contreras had no more reinforcements to call upon but the Spanish hung on grimly, supplementing the fire from the navy boats with a constant bombardment of the French works. Hugh wondered what the trenches must look like each morning as the boats hauled off leaving the French to collect up their dead and wounded and survey the night's work. It was brutal, bloody warfare at its worst and Hugh wondered if Suchet would reach the point where he could no longer justify the loss of so many men.

"I think not, sir," Durrell said soberly when Hugh raised the issue over a late breakfast in Hugh's dining cabin on the morning of the 21st. "García tells me that they have taken some French prisoners and all tell the same tale: that General Suchet looks for glory and probable promotion from this assault. More to the point, he took the risk of throwing his all at Tarragona when he could have marched to assist Macdonald at Figueras. If he does not take the town, his career could lie in ruins."

"And for that he'll let his troops be slaughtered in those bloody trenches every night? I'm not sure he deserves that promotion, Mr Durrell."

"Possibly not. But he has sent repeated demands for surrender to General Contreras, sir, and they've all been turned down. When the French break through there will be no mercy. Is that any worse?"

"Would you surrender? If the crew of the *Iris* was at risk?"

Durrell smiled slightly. "If I thought there was no hope of fighting our way out of it, sir, I hope I'd have the sense to do so. I'd willingly sacrifice the ship, as much as I love her, but I find it hard to contemplate giving up Miles Randall and Teddy Lewis and Bosun Armstrong to the slaughter to satisfy my sense of honour. Though I might possibly be willing to hand over Mr Oakley and Mr Bristow without terms or conditions."

Hugh choked on his ale. "Are you still having trouble with them, Mr Durrell? A night in the boats might settle them down."

Durrell shook his head firmly. "They're too young, sir. They'll learn in time, but I wouldn't choose to put them in a situation where their high spirits and lack of experience might endanger either themselves or their men."

"Nor would I," Hugh said regretfully. "It's a shame though."

"I think Randall found his excursion interesting though."

Hugh choked for the second time, this time more seriously. Durrell waited solicitously until he had stopped coughing and managed to compose himself. Hugh mopped his streaming eyes and sipped again more cautiously.

"What did you just say? Are you telling me that my servant managed to get himself into one of the boats?"

"Last night, sir. Oh, not my boat. I had no idea until Petty Officer Carling approached me this morning to say that although he thought Randall was a little young to be placed in such a situation, he had conducted himself very coolly and managed his oar surprisingly well. He was under the impression that I had authorised it."

"Did Miles tell him that?"

"When I asked Carling, he admitted that he couldn't exactly remember what Miles had said, although he gained the impression that he was there with permission."

"I'm going to kill him."

"That would be a pity after he has managed to survive the night in a launch under fire from the French. I have, however, instructed the Bosun to take charge of him when the boats launch tonight and not to release him until after we have left."

"What did Armstrong say?"

"He laughed a great deal, sir and promised to do so. He said something about not having had to deal with this kind of situation for thirteen years. I'd quite like to know the story behind that, but I hadn't the time to ask him."

"When we've time, I'll invite him and Janet to dine and we'll find out. And bloody Miles can practice his serving skills and learn from the tale as well. Jesus, those guns are getting louder. What in God's name is going on out there? Have you finished, Mr Durrell? Let's go up and have a look."

On deck, Hugh went to the rail to look over towards the town. The sound of the French guns seemed to have redoubled since the previous day and Hugh stood staring, trying to peer through the clouds of smoke which were already enveloping the walls of the town.

"They've opened up another battery," Durrell said beside him. "Possibly even two."

"They have," Hugh said grimly. "And they're trained directly onto the walls of the lower town. Order up my barge, Mr Durrell. I'd like you to accompany me over to the *Blake*. It might not happen tonight, but it's going to happen soon. I think they're going to breach and if they do, we need to know Commodore Codrington's final orders about bringing out the garrison. And Mr Durrell?"

"Yes, sir?"

"Before we leave, find my servant and make sure he's under guard. I'm going to have enough to worry about today."

"Yes, sir," Durrell said, and went to give the orders.

***

Even from the upper town, the noise of the guns was unbearable. Ángel had spent the night on the parapets with the artillery, his ears ringing and his eyes sore with peering down into the French lines. The Spanish guns were doing a lot of damage to the sappers and labourers and the Royal Navy launches managed to blow away half a company of infantry on its way up to relieve the trench guards. The screams of some of the injured men had been clearly audible up in the town. Ángel concentrated on being glad about it but privately he did not blame García for covering his ears. It could be difficult to remember how much he hated the French while listening to their agony.

Ángel found General Contreras in his private parlour, seated at his desk writing letters. He wondered if Contreras was writing to Campoverde or to the Spanish government in Cadiz. As the situation in Tarragona deteriorated, Ángel suspected that his General's attention was beginning to focus on what would happen when the siege was over, and his own actions and reputation were called into question.

"You wished to see me, sir?"

"Cortez. Yes, come in. I gather you were up for most of the night, I'm surprised you're not still in your bed."

"I'm surprised anybody can sleep with this noise," Ángel said. His commander gave a twisted smile.

"I am not sleeping well for a number of reasons," he said. "I've sent García to try to get some rest, he looks like a ghost and we may not have much chance over the next few days."

"Any news from the Marquis of Campoverde, sir?"

"Nothing useful. In fact, far from sending me assistance he is about to rob me of one of my few remaining generals. He is requesting that I send General Sarsfield to join him immediately."

Ángel swore and then apologised. Contreras shook his head.

"I share your opinion, Captain. Sarsfield is a difficult man but he has done an excellent job in the lower town, I would rather keep him. However, I will obey the Marquis. I have written a letter explaining his orders and a passport for Sarsfield. General Velasco can take over in the lower town. Would you take this down to Sarsfield please, while I write the orders for Velasco."

Ángel saluted. "Yes, sir. Have you asked him to report to you before he leaves?"

"No, but you can mention that I'd like to speak to him. It will take some time for him to find a ship, since I do not think Commodore Codrington will allow any of his frigates to leave at this time, in case…"

He broke off, looking down at his desk. Ángel knew what he was thinking and was suddenly angry at his reluctance to say the words.

"In case he needs to help evacuate the garrison of the lower town before the end of the day," he said. Contreras looked up but did not speak. Ángel thought that he looked exhausted. Generally Contreras possessed the energy of a man half his age but this past week seemed to have worn him down and he looked older and somehow smaller. Abruptly Ángel wished he had not said it. Contreras made no comment about his outburst however, merely nodded dismissal. Ángel left, feeling relieved. He had always been on good terms with Contreras, but the General's despondent mood currently made him a difficult companion and Ángel knew he was inventing excuses to avoid him.

Ángel made his way down to the lower town. It was becoming an increasingly hazardous enterprise. French batteries kept up an incessant fire at the bastions and town walls and seen close up, Ángel was shocked at the damage already done. He had heard Contreras talk of the possibility of the French making a practicable breach the following day but he was beginning to think it might come sooner.

Knowing that the attack, when it came, must hit the lower town first, Contreras had sent reinforcements. Sarsfield now commanded six thousand men from a garrison of eight thousand. Everywhere Ángel looked he could see men working on the defences, shoring up gaps with sandbags. A few daring souls under the command of a young officer were even trying to fill in one of the partial breaches using some of the debris from the shattered walls.

Ángel paused to watch, keeping well back from the corner of the bastion. He realised that the men were setting up a mine in the breach. It was a ridiculously dangerous enterprise and the men were wholly exposed to French fire. Twice, as Ángel stood watching, the men scrambled for cover just in time to avoid being blown to pieces. Glancing up at the turret, Ángel realised there was another officer up there watching the French gunners through a telescope, calling out a warning whenever they were ready to fire. The lookout was even more vulnerable than the men in the breach and Ángel stared hard for a moment. Then, abandoning his quest for Sarsfield, he broke cover and bounded up the steps towards him.

"García, what in God's name are you doing down here? The General told me you were resting."

García did not turn or lower his telescope. "The General treats me as if I were a child," he said placidly. "He is a very worried man just now, it seemed better not to argue with him. I cannot take a siesta while the French blow up this city around me."

Ángel did not respond. Abruptly, García lowered the telescope and swung around. "Take cover," he bellowed and Ángel jumped, despite knowing the warning was coming. He was astonished at the volume and wondered if García realised how useful that voice was going to be on a battlefield.

"What are you doing here, Captain?" García said, turning back to survey the guns again.

"Looking for Sarsfield, they said he was up here."

"He's just on the other side of the tower. Be careful as you go round it, they have a howitzer trained on it and it's more accurate than I'd like. We lost two messengers this morning. But you'll be all right if you run."

There was an enormous crash over to the right and Ángel spun round in time to see a section of the parapet toppling in on itself. García did not look around. His concentration was absolute.

"Lieutenant, you have a target painted on you up here," Ángel said. "Sooner or later they're going to realise what you're doing."

"At that point they'll have to realign the guns: I'm not within musket range. I'll see them doing it and believe me I'll run for cover like a spring hare. They're about to fire off that second battery. Once it's done, you've got about three minutes to sprint, sir."

Ángel turned and surveyed the narrow track, waiting. As García had warned, the guns boomed out. They grazed the edge of the tower and a number of roof tiles clattered down onto the track but no major damage was done.

"Now," García shouted, and Ángel sprinted down the dirt track, jumping over a pile of fallen masonry and skidding slightly on the loose shale. He did not lose his footing though, and within a minute he was past the danger point and ducking into cover inside an arched doorway which led into the bastion.

He found Carlos Sarsfield with two young ADCs, surveying the second breach. From up here the damage was more obvious and Ángel peered over the edge and caught his breath as he realised how close the breach was to being practicable.

The General was a thin-faced dark man of around fifty. He was of Irish ancestry, descended from a family who had fled Ireland after the wars of the seventeenth century. Ángel had not met him before this campaign and rather admired Sarsfield's air of focused determination. His ability to organise and motivate his troops was impressive and even under the brutal battering from the French guns, the men of the lower town remained surprisingly calm.

Sarsfield looked around at his approach. "Captain Cortez. Have you come to observe or do you have a message for me?"

Ángel saluted and handed the letter to Sarsfield. The General moved over to one of the narrow arched windows where the light was better and began to read. Ángel watched his expression and saw his dark brows draw together and his lips tighten. He seemed to read the orders twice, then he looked up at Ángel.

"Do you know the contents of this letter, Captain?"

"Yes, sir. I was with General Contreras when he wrote it. I think he wanted to speak to you…"

"Don't trouble yourself, Captain, I'll give him my final report myself." Sarsfield glanced at his two aides. Ángel had the impression that he was quietly furious and did not blame him. For a man like Sarsfield, being replaced at such a crucial point in the campaign must feel like a personal affront.

Ángel wished he knew what his General had written and hoped he had made it clear to Sarsfield that this reassignment was not his choice. Privately, Ángel thought that in Contreras' shoes he would have quietly forgotten about Campoverde's orders until the matter of the lower city was decided and left Sarsfield in place. He could easily have found a reason why it had not been possible to deliver the orders on the brink of battle. Ángel knew that Contreras had based his decision not on the current exigencies of war but on how his actions might look in the future, should there be an inquiry. That told Ángel more than anything else that Contreras thought Tarragona was already lost and was looking ahead.

Sarsfield looked again at the letter then up at his ADCs. "I will need to speak to Colonel Don Jose Carlos. Moreno, go and find him immediately, I will meet him at Headquarters."

"Yes, General Sarsfield."

"Lopez, I need you to get down to the harbour and find me a boat which can row me out to one of the Spanish frigates. I don't believe we need to trouble Commodore Codrington or his squadron just now, they are fully occupied. Come and find me when it is arranged."

"Yes, sir."

"Captain Cortez." Sarsfield turned to Ángel with a ghost of his usual charming smile. "Before I speak to Colonel Carlos, allow me to give you a brief tour of the works here. You may be of some help to General Contreras in the coming days."

Ángel frowned. "I am willing to learn, sir, but surely the General should hear it himself…"

"Oh he will be fully informed to the best of my ability. But as you are here…ah and here is your young friend. Is the mine in position, Lieutenant García?"

"It is, sir. I thought I'd better come down though: that last cannonade only just missed me. They're getting very accurate."

Ángel noticed that García appeared to have lost his hat. There was a small graze and a swelling bruise on his temple. García appeared completely unperturbed by his near-miss. Ángel swore.

"It looks as though your heroics nearly got your head blown off, García, and given that I'm not sure General Contreras even knows you're down here…"

"Lieutenant García asked permission of me, Captain and I gave it. He is a courageous young man and has given good service. García, will you join Lieutenant Moreno at headquarters, if you please, I have a final job for you before you return to your post."

"Yes, sir. Thank you."

When García had gone, Sarsfield turned shrewd dark eyes onto Ángel. "A very good officer, Captain. You must be proud of him. Come, this way. If we scramble around the back, it will give us cover from their batteries. Unless of course they manage to bring the entire curtain wall down."

Ángel managed to stop himself saying that it had never occurred to him to be proud of Óscar García, he was merely thankful for the younger man's help with Contreras' correspondence. He followed Sarsfield to the top of a section of the ruined wall where the General perched perilously, pointing out across the French siege works. Ángel felt himself flinch as a shot hit the wall so close that he was showered with dust and broken stonework. Sarsfield barely seemed to notice.

"See there. They call it their number twenty battery, it consists of four 24-pounders. It opened fire at dawn, the signal for all the other guns to begin firing." Sarsfield glanced at Ángel with a small grim smile. "Did you hear the explosion first thing?"

"It would have been impossible not to."

"The battery powder magazine went up, a lucky shot from one of our howitzers. It was a good start to my day, the entire battery collapsed and buried some of their men. A short lived triumph, sadly. Their engineers are very skilled. Two hours later they had it up and firing again. We could hear their infantry cheering them on. They think they're getting in here tonight."

Ángel could not take his eyes from the broken walls. "They may be right, General."

"Possibly, although I may not be here to see it. It is hard to be ordered to abandon my post in the middle of a battle. It has never happened to me before. This way, down this scarp. They have nothing trained on this, you will be safe enough for now, although we can go no further. It will give you a better view of the second breach."

Ángel followed him, aware of a sense of unreality. Sarsfield was behaving like a tour guide in the middle of the destruction of the city walls, pointing out the various French batteries and the damage to the bastions and fortifications. Ángel had no idea why he was getting this tour. He was beginning to wonder if the destruction and bloodshed had affected Sarsfield's brain. He suspected that under his urbane manner, the General was furious at being recalled at such a time and Ángel did not blame him. He wished again that Contreras had waited until after the French assault to deliver Campoverde's message.

It was a relief when Sarsfield apparently decided that it was time to end the tour and announced that he needed to return to his headquarters. Ángel thanked him politely and wished him luck. Once he had gone, he wondered if he should have offered to accompany the General to his debriefing meeting with Contreras. He decided to wait for Sarsfield. It could not possibly take long to pack his kit and give orders to his temporary commander. Sarsfield had indicated that he had no real faith in General Carlos but presumably once he reached the upper town, General Velasco would be despatched immediately to take over.

Ángel wondered suddenly if that had been the point of Sarsfield's strange behaviour. Was he going to suggest to Contreras that Ángel, and possibly García, be seconded to Velasco for the duration of the French attack on the lower town? If so, the flood of information he had tried to impart made a great deal of sense. Ángel felt his pulse quicken, both at the sudden prospect of immediate combat and at the possible advantage of the posting. It occurred to him that Contreras would probably not want to send both his ADCs and it had been Ángel, not García who had been in receipt of Sarsfield's personal briefing.

There was still no sign of the Irish General emerging from his headquarters but the sentries were still on guard. Ángel thought that Sarsfield was probably taking the time to write to Contreras and possibly to Velasco, as well as giving verbal instructions to Carlos. With the probability that he would be present during the French storming, Ángel decided to improve his knowledge of the defences and the location of the troops.

Ángel moved into the lower town, weaving his way through the narrow streets lined with houses, shops and, closer to the waterfront, the huge bulk of the red-brick warehouses, most of which were now filled with military stores. Every time he came across a body of troops he paused, his note tablets in his hand to document their position and numbers and, where possible, the name of the officer commanding them. Most of these troops were in companies, commanded by senior captains. They greeted Ángel with grim goodwill, answered his questions once he had established his credentials and gave him the impression that despite their desperate situation these men were ready to fight.

Around them the guns still thundered out defiance to the French, but some of them had already been silenced, their gun crews blown away and the guns damaged. He could feel the rising tension of the men as the afternoon wore on. It was looking more and more likely that the French would attack tonight.

There was still no sign of Sarsfield. Ángel paused, looking out over the batteries situated on the Mole. He could see the various ships of Codrington's squadron, safely out of reach of the French guns, presumably waiting to find out if they would be needed. Sarsfield had told him that most of the women and children who lived in the lower town had been evacuated, either to within the walls of the upper town or further up the coast to Villanueva, where the local people had made generous provision for refugees from Tarragona. Privately, Ángel thought that the Governor should have insisted on a compulsory evacuation of the town while there was still time, but Contreras had informed him that he had no authority to force people from their homes.

It was getting late. Ángel took out his battered pocket watch and realised in some surprise that it was approaching four o'clock. Every crash of the French guns was now followed by the rumbling of falling masonry. Ángel moved away from the shore and made his way back through the narrow streets of the town towards Sarsfield's headquarters. It could not have taken the Irishman this long to pack his kit and write a few letters and orders. Either Ángel had missed his departure and he was even now meeting with General Contreras to formally hand over his command to Velasco or he had assessed the disastrous state of the defences and decided that he could not leave his post at such a crisis moment. Ángel suspected it might be the latter.

The sentries were still on duty outside the building. They admitted Ángel with only the briefest challenge, directing him to the salon which Sarsfield used as his office and briefing room. Ángel knocked and waited. Nobody called to him to enter but he could hear loud, angry voices inside which suggested that some kind of meeting was in progress. Presumably Sarsfield had received reports that the French were about to breach and was giving orders for the positioning of his forces for the defence. Ángel knocked again, more loudly, and when there was still no response he opened the door.

There were a dozen officers in the room all talking at once and Ángel stopped in the doorway, absorbing the immediate sense of panic. He ran his eyes over the men and recognised only two of them. Colonel Don Jose Carlos, currently the most senior officer serving under Sarsfield, looked like a startled rabbit while around him his officers gabbled updates on the French assault and recommendations for action. Carlos looked like a man unable to act at all. His slightly protuberant blue eyes darted from one to the other and Ángel thought he seemed frozen by uncertainty.

Beyond the group, standing a little to one side, stood Lieutenant García . The swelling on his temple had already darkened to a horrendous bruise and Ángel thought that he looked like a man with a bad headache who had no idea what he was supposed to do in this wholly unexpected situation. He caught sight of Ángel and immediately looked relieved. Ángel skirted the mêlée and joined him.

"García, what in God's name are you doing here and where's General Sarsfield?" he demanded. "I've just been looking over those breaches from the top and I think they're through."

"They are. Several of these officers just arrived to make their reports. General Sarsfield has gone."

"Has he? Damn, I must have missed him. I was going to go up to Contreras with him to see if I could…"

"He didn't go to the upper town, Captain. I mean he's gone. He left in a boat at about three o'clock to join one of the Spanish frigates. By now I imagine it's out of sight."

"He didn't report to Contreras?" Ángel said, almost whispering. "But…I don't understand."

"He left a letter for him and another for General Velasco and ordered me to remain until Velasco arrived, when I was to offer him every assistance. But Velasco's not here, sir, and I'm not sure they know he's gone. Or how serious this has become." García lowered his voice even though Ángel thought there was no possibility of being overheard with the competing voices in the room. "He handed command to Colonel Carlos, but I'm not sure the Colonel really knows what to do. I'm not sure he's right for this command."

"He isn't, and Sarsfield knew it, he virtually told me so," Ángel said. He felt slightly sick, his previous admiration for the Irish General seeping away with the understanding of what had happened. "Sarsfield was furious about being replaced and I think he blames Contreras; you know they don't like each other. But to abandon his post before a competent replacement has arrived…look, you need to get back to headquarters and tell the General what's happened. At the very least, he can track down Velasco and get him down here to resolve this chaos."

"My orders were to remain here, sir."

"I'm issuing new orders, Lieutenant, as your immediate superior. And you're going to obey them because you're a very good officer and you know it's the only sensible solution."

García's resistance visibly melted. "I should have gone before. I'm sorry, I knew this was wrong."

"It's not your fault," Ángel said. He was perilously close to losing his own temper and he did not wish to do so until he was face to face with the French. Experience had taught him that other officers did not respond well to his lordly manner and visible contempt and although he had never managed to find another way to command, he had at least learned to keep it in check during a crisis. It occurred to him that this was probably the first time he had ever complimented García and he felt a little ashamed. Given the likelihood that at least one of them might be dead before tomorrow morning, he put his hand on the younger man's shoulder.

"You did the right thing, Óscar. You couldn't have countermanded Sarsfield's orders yourself. And at least you being here means you know exactly what's going on, so you can brief Contreras properly. I've just come from the defences and it's bad. There are two workable breaches in the San

Carlos and Orleans Bastions and the curtain wall in between has a hole in it that you could pass a cart through. There's also a lot of damage to Fort Royal on the other side of the wall; the guns there are completely out of action. I think, though it's hard to see, that he's getting his troops ready to storm the town."

"Oh God."

"I'm going to stay here and see if I can persuade these officers to stop squabbling and get back to their men in time to put up a fight. Take those letters and get to Contreras before the assault starts and they can't let you through the gate. Go to the San Juan, it's the closest."

García saluted, his young face very white. "Yes, sir. Please try to take care of yourself as far as you can. General Contreras needs you."

Ángel gave a faint smile and returned the salute. "Not as much as he used to, boy," he said. "Which is why you should get going. We can't have both of us trapped down here."

Ángel was relieved when nobody noticed García slip away, since it meant that nobody tried to stop him. He stood listening to the chaos of Carlos' briefing meeting in silence for a while, wanting to give his junior plenty of time to get clear. It also gave him time to work out what he was going to say.

Ángel knew that he was a good soldier, courageous in battle and with the ability to think quickly in a crisis, but he had been told many times that his weakness as a commander was his relationships with his fellow officers, and most of all with the men. Ángel had tried to dismiss the criticism over the years but there was some small part of him, carefully hidden from the world, which recognised that there might be some truth in the complaints.

Ángel did not make friends easily, having spent his younger years in a constant state of rebellion and his adult life on campaign. He could sometimes feign a camaraderie that he did not really feel with his fellow officers; though he knew that his impatience showed through far too often. He had never really bothered to try with his men. It was his job to command them and their job to obey and beyond that Ángel did not much care.

His position as ADC had removed some of his difficulties and he occasionally wondered if that was why he had been recommended to Contreras. Ángel knew that he needed to break up this pointless meeting and get the officers back to their men in case the French broke through before a new commander arrived. In this room, he had no authority to command and no idea at all how to persuade but he recognised that he was going to have to try to learn very quickly. Ángel threw up a prayer for help to the God he no longer believed in and stepped forward, trying to keep his voice calm and reasonable.

"Colonel Carlos, gentlemen, I need you to listen to me for a few moments. Please."

Chapter Fifteen

By four o'clock there were three passable breaches in the Spanish defences and Suchet gave orders for General Palombini to take command and storm the lower town.

Very few of the Spanish guns were still in any condition to fire, although one or two still stuttered out defiance. Bonnet stood at the head of his company in the deep ditch, listening to the roar of the French guns which would continue to pound the walls until the last possible moment to prevent any attempt by the Spanish to make repairs. In front of him stood Colonel Lacasse, his sword drawn. The whole of the 30th légère would be involved in this attack which meant that the Colonel would fight at the head of his men. To Bonnet, who had invariably been given command of any detached companies during these past weeks, it felt strange not to be in charge.

The assault was ordered to begin at seven o' clock and Suchet had drawn up his men in five columns. Three of them would make co-ordinated attacks on the Orleans Bastion, the San Carlos Bastion and Fort Royal while the other two advanced from the right. It was a formidable force and Bonnet wondered dispassionately why the Spanish did not simply turn and run.

They showed no sign of doing so. When the signal was given, the French guns fell silent and the 30th advanced with the second column along with men from the 1st and 5th légère and the 42nd ligne. It was becoming cooler after the heat of the day and there was a pleasant breeze coming in from the sea which made Bonnet long for a quiet table outside a tavern on the quay. Instead he gripped his sword, looked over his shoulder at his men and yelled back the order to advance.

They attacked at a run, covering the ground towards the San Carlos Bastion at terrifying speed. It was rough, rocky ground, pitted with holes and craters made by the constant shelling of the past weeks. A few men stumbled and one or two fell. Bonnet was briefly amused at the volley of vulgar epithets from Corporal Gerard who twisted his ankle so badly in a hole that he was unable to continue his run. His bellows of angry encouragement to the rest of his company could be heard in the distance as Bonnet's men reached the steep slope up to the breach and began to climb.

There was no artillery fit for use left in the bastion, but there were plenty of muskets and the first group of men who surged up the slope were blown backwards by a tremendous volley. Bonnet threw himself flat, hearing screams of pain around him, but as soon as the volley was done he was up on his feet again, clambering onwards. A second volley took down several more of his men and a few of the 5th who climbed beside them, but the French were too fast and as they reached the top of the breach there were more screams, this time from the Spanish who were bayonetted before they could get off a third volley.

It was close quarter fighting with very little shooting, although as the Spanish were gradually pushed back into the bastion some of Bonnet's more experienced light troops managed to get off a few shots at any of the enemy who tried to retreat. Few of them did. The Spanish put up a stubborn resistance over heaps of rubble and broken walls within the bastion. The structure had been almost completely destroyed within by the relentless pounding of the French artillery.

The piles of brick and stone gave the Spanish cover to fight back and some of them were beginning to make use of their muskets again. Stone flew up from a broken column where Bonnet and several of his men had paused to take cover and reload and Bonnet heard Private Dupont swear as a sliver of rock caught him squarely in the side of his face, drawing blood. His companions stepped out, returning fire, and Dupont ignored the pain and reloaded at speed.

Gradually, painfully, the French light troops pushed on. Bonnet could hear some of his fellow officers yelling encouragement to their men. He had stopped doing that himself, partly because it seemed superfluous since it was perfectly obvious what he wanted his men to do and partly because the steep climb directly into a fierce fight had left him out of breath. He saved his energy for the fight, slashing and cutting his way through the Spanish lines.

There was no opportunity to take prisoners and Bonnet did not try. The Spanish troops were showing no sign of surrendering. This was a desperate fight to defend their city and they looked depressingly like men willing to fight to the death. Bonnet applauded their courage and wished they had less of it because he loathed this kind of brutal bloodshed, but it was his life or theirs so he killed without hesitation while silently damning their commanders and his.

By the time the 30th reached the far side of the bastion, Bonnet was bathed in sweat and splattered with the blood of the men he had killed. He knew men who kept a mental count of the enemy they cut down and had even come across one or two who kept a tally using notches on their muskets. Bonnet disliked the idea and thought there was something wrong with a man who celebrated the men he killed. War was war and men must die but afterwards Bonnet preferred not to dwell on it. He paused to catch his breath on the far side of a broken stone wall and realised that the Spanish officers were trying to pull their men together for another stand.

At their head was a young officer in a bloodstained coat who was shouting orders along the straggling line. Bonnet decided he did not care how bad that line was, it was still a line and it had muskets. He bellowed an order of his own and heard it echoed by several other officers close by. Then he dived for cover behind the wall and heard his men scrabbling around him for similar protection. Most of them had already seen the danger and started moving before Bonnet yelled. The Spanish muskets thundered out their defiance against the French but did very little damage. Behind broken walls and piles of stone, the French light troops reloaded quickly and the Spanish line turned into a target. Bonnet's men stepped out as if at a hidden signal and fired.

It broke the Spanish resistance and they ran, their officers screaming at them to come back. Bonnet heard Colonel Lacasse urging the 30th into full pursuit and decided he did not need to call them back. Baccarini's grenadiers were coming up from the right, appearing from the ditch of the Prince's Lunette like demons and Bonnet could hear the third column approaching from the rear. The French were wholly in command of this section of the assault so he allowed his men to have their head.

They surged forward with a primitive roar, bayonets lifted, heading for the lower town. The Spaniards gave way and fled towards the winding streets with the French column in close pursuit, leaping over the defensive ditches and kicking down the palisades. Bonnet went with them, wholly caught up in the madness of battle.

A Spanish soldier was racing towards an overturned cart on the broad road which led down to the Mole. Sensing Bonnet close behind him he turned abruptly and lunged forward with his bayonet which was already stained red. Bonnet fell back, parrying with his sword. The Spaniard backed away slowly, around the edge of the cart with Bonnet moving steadily forward. He watched the man's face, wild-eyed with desperate terror, and saw the moment the Spaniard decided to run. Bonnet stepped forward to administer the final slash and found, to his astonishment, that his sword clashed on the steel of another blade.

Bonnet jumped back, falling instinctively into a defensive stance. He saw his original quarry turn and begin to run again. The man he was facing made no attempt to follow him. Instead he raised his sword, almost in a salute, and then stepped forward to attack.

It was immediately obvious that the Spaniard was a swordsman and a good one. There was seldom time for elegant fencing in a battle, especially during a retreat like this, and as Bonnet frantically parried the Spanish officer's swift, lethal attack he cursed his luck for finding himself face-to-face with the kind of arrogant sprig of the Spanish nobility who thought it more honourable to engage in a fencing bout with an overweight under-practiced opponent than to concentrate on getting as many of his men away alive as he could. Bonnet was furious with him and hoped that after his death, this elegant gentleman ended up spitted on the end of Private Claudet's badly cleaned bayonet for his pains. He thought it very likely. Ahead of him, the Spanish had clearly managed to pull together a final desperate defence of the harbour and the batteries on the Mole, but behind him he could hear more of the French reserves advancing into the fray. The Spanish were routed and if he did not run soon, the fair-haired officer was going to be stabbed or shot in the back once he had finished off Bonnet.

There was a sudden deafening flurry of musket fire and several shots hit the upturned wagon, sending wooden splinters flying. It distracted the Spaniard for a few vital seconds. Bonnet was too experienced to look away and was fairly sure the shots were an attempt by some of his men to stop him from getting his throat cut. He appreciated it but was too busy to thank them. Instead, he took ruthless advantage of his opponent's temporary lapse in concentration and surged forward, driving the Spaniard backwards more by brute force than skill.

With his rhythm broken, the younger man could do nothing apart from parry desperately. He was remarkably good at it and for a few moments Bonnet was not sure even now that he was going to be able to break through his guard. But the French were charging forward now and the Spanish retreat had been cut off by the other columns coming in on the right. It had turned into a full scale rout and the only hope of survival for the Spanish forces was to run and hope to make it to the gates of the upper town. Bonnet doubted they would be open.

His opponent's guard dropped finally. Bonnet lunged forward and felt his sword make contact. The other man made a small sound of pain, quickly bitten back. Bonnet withdrew and saw blood spurt from the Spaniard's right arm. It was a deep wound and Bonnet was astonished when his opponent set his jaw and raised his sword again, even though his arm was shaking badly with the effort. Bonnet could not decide whether to be exasperated or impressed.

"Oh for fuck's sake, you arrogant whelp, you can't fight me one handed. Surrender or I'm going to slit your throat. There's a fight going on down there and I need to be with my men."

Bonnet spoke in Spanish and saw the other man's light grey eyes widen in surprise. For a moment, Bonnet thought he was going to lower his sword. Then he straightened, though it was clearly an effort, and took the hilt of his sword with both hands, raising it high again.

"I would rather die here, choking on my own blood, than give up my sword to a French pig," he said. It was Bonnet's turn to be surprised at the Spaniard's crisp, colloquial French. "Your mother was a filthy whore in the stews of Paris and your father could have been any one of the stinking Jacobins who fucked her for pennies. As for you…"

Bonnet lost patience. He slashed again, accurately, and the Spaniard screamed and dropped the sword. He clutched his left hand to his chest, trying to stem the bleeding from a gash across his knuckles so deep it had reached the bone. Bonnet kicked the sword away from him, mainly to stop him trying to pick it up and getting himself killed. He kicked out with the brutal thoroughness of a Paris street urchin, catching the Spaniard on the knee. His opponent went down as if felled by an axe. Bonnet stepped forward and put the point of his sword at the other man's throat.

"I have no fucking idea why I've not killed you yet. Maybe I think you're still young enough to learn. Maybe I've just killed my quota today. You'd better fucking hope so. To set you straight, my late father was a very skilled leather worker who made the best horse tack in Paris and my mother still runs the best bakery on the Rue de St Jean. They couldn't afford fencing lessons for me, but they did teach me not to bandy words with a fucking idiot in a fancy uniform. Now stay down until the rush is gone and then get yourself out of here and don't waste all my hard work."

Bonnet flicked the sword briefly and saw a thin red line open up across the fair skin of the Spaniard's right cheek. It was very satisfying. He stepped back, checked that the other man's sword was well out of reach, then turned and set off at a run to find his company.

The scenes around him sickened Bonnet. He supposed that some of the Spanish must have made their escape but those who had found themselves trapped in the lower town had been ruthlessly slaughtered. Their bloody bodies lay scattered through the narrow streets, along the harbour, in some of the houses and right up to the town gates, where they had tried to make their escape.

Bonnet's company, along with the rest of the 30th légère, had drawn up within sight of the gate but out of musket range and Bonnet could see why. The French and the fleeing Spaniards had arrived in a bloody tangle up against the San Juan gate. It was impossible for muskets to fire either from the ramparts above the gate or from the attacking French without each killing each other's troops.

As Bonnet had expected the gates remained firmly closed but there was Spanish infantry up on the ramparts of the town. Initially they were as handicapped as the French by the entanglement of the troops, but somebody was in very effective command up there and Bonnet could hear him shouting orders.

The Spanish troops responded quickly and very efficiently. Under the command of a middle-aged officer they drew up quickly in battle order, managing to separate themselves from the French. By the time Bonnet rejoined his company, Colonel Lacasse had followed their example and called the 30th back into line. Bonnet skidded to a halt beside Duclos and Allard, swearing.

"No, no, no! What the fuck is that imbecile doing?" he raged.

Allard shot him an alarmed look and shushed him. "The Colonel will hear you, sir."

"No he won't. After the past few days of constant artillery fire, he's as deaf as the rest of us. Get the men ready to make a fast retreat, we're about to get mown down by musket fire from those Spanish bastards on the ramparts now that they can tell us apart from their comrades. We should have stayed close in with them and slaughtered them, it was the only thing to do. Allard, who fired those shots to save my skin just now?"

"Belmas, Chauvin and Roche, sir."

Bonnet looked around and found Belmas looking at him. He raised a hand in a casual salute and Bonnet returned it with a smile. As he did so he heard the Spanish General yell the order and he spun around, not waiting for Lacasse.

"Back!" he bellowed. "30th pull back. Out of range…"

His men, already warned, were beginning to move before the first thunderous volley of musketry and grape shot blew apart the French who were still milling around the gate. Bonnet did not stop to see how many of them were from the 30th but concentrated on driving his men back out of reach of the muskets, yelling at them to move faster.

When he turned to look back he could see that not all the French had moved fast enough and the ground was scattered with dead and wounded. Bonnet could not see any of his men there. Most of the French had pulled back out of range but a small group of grenadiers under a young captain that Bonnet did not recognise had ignored the order and rushed on to attempt to force the gate. They were within two paces when the muskets crashed again and both the officer and his drummer fell. The rest found themselves entangled with a much larger force of Spanish troops who bayonetted them without mercy. Bonnet looked away feeling queasy. His own recent brush with death had left him feeling oddly unsettled. Around him, the French commanders were beginning to call their troops back down into the streets. Bonnet summoned his company and followed Lacasse to receive their orders.

As they marched through the lower town Bonnet took out his watch and stared at it. For a moment he wondered if it could be wrong then he realised it was working perfectly well. The French attack had taken just over an hour. It was half-past eight and Fort Royal, the Bastion of the Canons, the San Carlos Bastion, the Mill battery and the whole of the lower town, were in French hands. The Spanish were either dead or had managed to flee to the upper town, leaving eighty pieces of artillery in enemy hands.

Bonnet had been told that most of the Spanish civilians had already fled to the upper town before the storming and he assumed that any who had been stupid enough to remain would have raced up to the gates clutching what valuables they could carry as the French moved in on the breaches. He was so shocked to find that he had been wrong that he failed to act fast enough at the sight of two men, clearly townspeople, being driven out of one of the houses at the points of bayonets.

The soldiers were not Bonnet's men but he yelled at them to stop anyway and broke away from his company, racing down the street with his sword drawn. He was not fast enough and by the time he reached them, both Spaniards were dead, bayonetted on the doorstep while French grenadiers ransacked their house for valuables, food and wine.

Around him, the orderly movement of troops was beginning to break down as men realised that there was looting to be done. Bonnet could hear Colonel Lacasse calling out orders and further up the untidy column, other officers were doing the same thing. Some of the men obeyed but more and more of them were falling out, heading into the houses, shops and warehouses of the lower town to see what they could loot, break or burn.

As Bonnet stood irresolute, trying to decide what to do, he saw Lacasse approaching at a jog. Approximately half of the battalion had drifted away but Bonnet was surprised to see that his own company seemed mostly intact. He was also impressed to note that Lieutenant Allard and Sub-Lieutenant Duclos had their pistols drawn. So did Belmas but Bonnet would have expected that.

"Captain Bonnet, we have orders from General Palombini to take up a position at the front of Fort Royal."

Bonnet ran his eyes over the rapidly disintegrating French column. "He'll be lucky, sir. For a couple of hours, at least."

"I want you to remain here. Choose a small party of reliable men. General Suchet wants the civilians protected if at all possible. You may join us when things are under control."

Bonnet did not salute or acknowledge the order. All his concentration was on not uttering the vulgar response he wanted to. Lacasse did not seem to notice. He turned away to return to the column. Bonnet took a deep breath and found that it didn't help at all. He waited until Lacasse was out of reach and therefore temporarily safe, then went to where his junior officers were watching him anxiously.

"You're in command, he wants me to stay here and save the citizens of Tarragona. Belmas, I want you with me. Ten men, hand-picked. Tell them they're about to be heroes."

Belmas snorted. "If we are to try to stop these greedy bastards we will be dead heroes and I do not think they will bother with a medal."

"Nor do I. So tell them if they can round up the citizens and get them to safety, under a reliable guard, I'll let them take what they want from the wine shops and stores with no repercussions. Will that help?"

Belmas drew himself up and saluted smartly. "Immeasurably, Captain," he said, and swung around, shouting out names.

***

It was morning before Bonnet was free to return to his company and by then he had no inclination to do so. He had been joined in his impossible task by a contingent of Italians and half a company of the 42nd ligne. The Italians abandoned any pretence at policing the looters within twenty minutes and joined in with enthusiasm. The 42nd were sullen and resentful but under a hard-eyed captain with a gravelly voice and a borrowed bayonet, they reluctantly began to escort the battered and terrified civilians from their houses, some of which were already on fire.

Bonnet had found a makeshift shelter for the refugees in a solidly built warehouse on the quay. This area of town was dominated by the harbour and most of the buildings had some mercantile function. Many of them had been requisitioned by the army for military stores and General Palombini, with an eye to the shortage of food in the area, had set guards on these buildings with orders to shoot potential looters out of hand. Bonnet decided these sentries would not stop to ask if the drunken troops were after rum, bread or women which was exactly what he wanted.

There were very few women or children among the terrified

refugees. Two or three families, local tradespeople reluctant to abandon their premises, scuttled through the streets under guard clutching small bundles and bags. The women were crying and the men looked as though they wanted to. A gaggle of wide-eyed, grubby children clung together. Bonnet wanted to say something reassuring to them in Spanish but decided that being addressed by a big Frenchman with a scarred face, armed with a pistol, might not reassure them at all so he desisted.

Not every civilian was as fortunate. They found bodies in some of the houses, a dozen men of various ages, probably those who had tried to fight to defend their property. In one house close to the docks, it was obvious that the householder had died trying to defend his wife. She was dead too and Bonnet looked away quickly. There was no need to check to see if she lived. They had raped her then cut her throat. Bonnet did not want to think about her last terrifying moments. He hoped that somewhere, she was at peace. He also wished there was some way of knowing which of Suchet's marauding troops had violated and murdered her so that he could slit their throats in turn, but he knew it was a vain hope.

All the same, it gave him a new determination to do what he could for the miserable citizens of the lower town. By the time he and his men trudged over to Fort Royal to join the rest of their battalion, the sun was already making its first tentative appearance over the rugged coastline and the men were tired and hungry, although well laden with the promised spoils of war.

Bonnet had barely lowered himself to the ground beside his officers when his servant appeared. Bonnet was astonished. He had not seen Pierre for over a week and was beginning to wonder if the man had finally absconded with his horses and pack mule. He was too tired to remonstrate but managed a glare with a lifted eyebrow which he hoped would replace any questions.

"I have a message for you, Captain."

"A message? Who the hell thought to give a message to you, you useless bastard? I've not seen you for a week. Are my horses and baggage still in one piece?"

"Yes, sir. I have taken good care of them. I found a billet with a stable and…"

"Never mind. Just make sure whichever poor unfortunate Spaniard is having to house you doesn't have cause to complain to me afterwards or I'll kick you into the Francoli. And I know you can't bloody swim. What's the message?"

Pierre handed him a note and Bonnet read it in bewilderment. Nodding dismissal to Pierre he hauled himself to his feet and went to find Colonel Lacasse.

"I need your permission to leave the lines, Colonel. I've received a note from General Suchet asking me to visit him at headquarters."

Lacasse made a spluttering sound. "The Commander-in-Chief? Let me see that note."

Bonnet handed it over although he was tempted to say that it was personal. He waited while Lacasse read the note twice. Eventually his Colonel nodded grudgingly and handed it back.

"Very well. Make sure you do a proper hand over to your officers."

Bonnet did not bother to point out that he had not yet had time to take back command. He saluted, spoke briefly to Duclos and Allard then went to find Pierre who had brought up one of his horses. Roland was the older of the two and not really suitable for battle these days but he was strong and steady and a good horse for a long slow march. Bonnet saw no reason to hurry and walked his horse up to the straggling hamlet where Suchet had established his headquarters in a solidly built farmhouse.

He found the General in a long, dim room furnished with a dining table and chairs. Suchet had dark hair and expressive, heavy-lidded brown eyes and might have been handsome had it not been for his tight mouth and dark brows which seemed to permanently frown. He was standing before the table studying what looked like a plan of the city but when Bonnet was shown into the room he straightened and came forward immediately. Bonnet rather liked that. In his experience most senior officers liked to show how important they were by ignoring their underlings and making them wait. He saluted more politely than usual and Suchet returned the salute gravely.

"Captain Bonnet. Thank you for coming. I understand you have been awake all night, you must be very tired."

Bonnet was astonished and tried to hide it. "I'm well enough, General. There hasn't been that much sleep recently, I'm not the only one."

Suchet's lips twitched into a smile and Bonnet was surprised at how much it altered his face. "I'm well aware you have been very busy, Captain. I asked to see you because I have received a report from General Palombini regarding your conduct."

Bonnet's heart sank. He had not really expected anything else but in all his years of official reprimands and minor complaints he had never before been hauled up before such a senior officer. It was disappointing. Bonnet racked his brain, trying to work out what he had done wrong during the past forty-eight hours.

"General Palombini regrettably struggled to control his troops during our attempt to restore order in the lower town," Suchet said neutrally. "He is naturally very embarrassed about this. However, when I discussed the matter with him earlier, he brought to my attention the efforts of Captain Ferdon of the 42nd and of yourself with a small party from the 30th légère. He informed me that the slaughter of civilians in the lower town would have been much greater without your intervention. I wanted to express my thanks personally. While I consider that the refusal of the Spanish to surrender placed their people in jeopardy, I dislike the murder of innocents and I am grateful for your efforts."

Bonnet was temporarily bereft of speech. Eventually, because something was clearly expected, he murmured his thanks and some nonsense about doing his duty. He hoped it would be enough. He was starving and thirsty and almost asleep on his feet and although he appreciated Suchet's praise more than he cared to admit, he mostly wanted to get back to the lines to eat and sleep if that were possible.

Unexpectedly, Suchet's smile broadened and Bonnet thought that it made him look ten years younger.

"There, we have completed the formalities. There is a room upstairs. Go to it. I will have them bring you some proper food and then you should sleep. I have heard very promising things of you, Captain Bonnet, and some I have observed for myself. I hope to get to know you better in the future."

Bonnet was stunned. He stood staring at the commander, once again struggling for something to say. This time the words came more easily and as he said them, he realised that Suchet would probably think him mad.

"I would be very grateful for breakfast, General. And thank you again. But if you would permit, I would like to ride up to visit the hospital at the Monastery of St Francis Xavier. Several of my men are there."

Suchet drew those thick dark brows together. "You wish to visit your men at the hospital? That is unexpected, Captain. But surely by now you have men scattered around various hospitals."

Bonnet took a deep breath. "I do, sir. I'd like to know how my men are doing but that's not why I want to go. There's a woman. A young Spanish woman working there, tending our wounded. I know her…I was briefly billeted with her and her father before he died. I feel some responsibility and after what I saw in that town tonight…"

Bonnet managed to stop himself speaking. He had not realised until this moment his frantic need to see Bianca Ramos and assure himself that she was safe and well. The image of the raped and murdered woman in the lower town was burned into his brain and he could not erase it. He could tell none of this to the Commander-in-Chief so he bit the inside of his lip and forced himself to remain silent.

After a long, bewildered pause, Suchet stirred. "Of course. Go. Collect food from the kitchen first, there is plenty. Once you have reassured yourself that she is safe, feel free to return here and rest. I am granting you twenty four hours leave, Captain, I will write to Colonel Lacasse. We will not breach before then and you have earned it. When you return I will instruct my adjutant to show you to your room."

Bonnet's throat was tight. He could not speak, so he saluted instead, then left the room and went in search of Bianca Ramos.

He found her, as he had expected, immersed in the blood and death of an army hospital in the aftermath of a battle. Despite the overwhelming French victory, which had left Suchet master of the lower town and the harbour and in an excellent position to begin his assault of the upper town; the French had almost as many wounded as the Spanish. Bonnet was not surprised. Some of the early assaults had been costly for the French, and the Spanish had benefited from the breakdown in discipline in the lower town. While the Spanish civilians had died as the French troops ran wild, the Spanish garrison had taken the opportunity to escape. Wounded from both sides had been carried out to the various hospitals and by the time Bianca was free, she was white-faced and exhausted, her gown splattered with blood and her eyes shadowed with tiredness and the horrors of the long hours working at the hospital.

The brown eyes widened as she emerged from the ward and saw Bonnet waiting in the hallway. She came forward uncertainly and Bonnet got up and moved to greet her.

"Bianca. They said you're off duty."

She gave a tired smile. "They think I'm going to collapse if I carry on."

"You look as though you might. Have you eaten?"

She shook her head. "I don't think I could. I need to sleep. I'm sorry, I'm not much company. But I'm glad you came, I've been worrying about you."

It had not occurred to Bonnet that she might worry about him and the thought gave a little lift to his depressed mood. "I came because I was worried about you. I had a bad night, helping the Spanish in the lower town. I needed to make sure you were safe."

She looked up at him and he saw, with surprising clarity, the light in her eyes at his concern. "That's good of you, Captain. I'm fine. While I'm here, I'm well protected." She gave a twisted smile. "They don't see me as a female, just as a useful pair of hands. Which is good for me."

"It's very good," Bonnet said fervently. Now that he was here he was wondering if it had been foolish to come. She seemed so independent and so competent that his anxiety seemed excessive. Still he was here and she had agreed to see him so he lifted the woven bag he had brought from headquarters. "I've been up all night as well and I've not eaten. I'm going back there to sleep: I've got some unexpected leave. But I thought you might want to join me for food…only if you're not too tired."

Unexpectedly the thin face softened into a smile which made his heart skip a beat. "I should probably eat something. Thank you, Captain."

They took the basket out to the monastery gardens, where a smooth lawn ran down to the fish ponds which stocked the Abbot's table. It was dry and brown at this season, but still cool this early in the day and there was a wooden bench overlooking the still water.

Suchet's cook had provided a loaf of fresh bread with goat's cheese, cured ham and a spicy sausage. There was also a flagon of wine and two pewter cups. Bonnet poured for them both and they broke the bread and shared the food, too hungry to talk for a while. Eventually, their hunger satisfied, he asked her about the wounded. In return she asked about his long night in the town and he told her, skimming over the details but not lying to her about the brutality her people had endured at the hands of his army.

She was quiet for a while and then unexpectedly moved closer to him, took his arm and wrapped it firmly about her shoulders.

"That is not you."

"No. But if you weren't here, it could have been you. I want to kill the bastards but I don't know who they are."

She turned her head to look up at him. "You cannot save everybody, Gabriel."

"Finally, you have remembered my name."

She gave a little laugh. "I will not forget it, I promise you. Thank you for this, I feel better."

"So do I and it's not just the food."

"I am happy that you came. But you should get back and sleep. For now, at least, we both have work to do."

"I know. And I will. But I wanted to see you."

She gave a broad smile. "I wanted to see you too."

Bonnet had no idea if it was true but even the idea of it delighted him. He tried to hide it. To cover his sudden shyness, he said:

"You're right, we both need rest. But Bianca…if anything happens, please promise me you'll give them my name and tell them you're under my protection. Even if not…even if you decide you don't want to…it might keep you safe."

Bianca stood up. "Are you saying that I should tell them that I am your woman, Gabriel?"

Bonnet felt himself flush. "Yes. I'm sorry. But it might stop them."

The brown eyes studied him for a long time until Bonnet was almost squirming, wondering if he had somehow insulted her. He wished, not for the first time, that he had some of the easy fluency with a woman that he observed in one or two of his fellow officers. Then again, they were not flabby around the middle with a scarred face. It was a relief when she finally spoke.

"Gabriel, I am not sure if I have made it clear to you, but I came here knowing that I must seek the protection of a man. When the army moves on, they may well send the wounded back to France and I will not be needed here. I have been lucky to find this work. It keeps me fed and gives me a measure of protection, but it will not last beyond this siege and a woman like me cannot survive alone."

"I know, cherie."

"What I am saying is that you do not have to be so careful with me, I will not be offended by plain speaking. If you want me I will stay with you for as long as you wish. I will take care of you and I will share your bed. If you decide you do not like me enough, I trust you not to throw me out until I have found another protector. You're a kind man."

Bonnet's throat was so tight that he could hardly breathe. He stood up and stepped towards her.

"I'd never do that. And I can't imagine wanting to. I think you're crazy, you could do a lot better than me. I'm not young, I'm not rich and I'm not good-looking."

"Nor am I, Gabriel. But you make me smile. Now go and sleep."

"Can I kiss you first?"

"Yes."

Bonnet reached for her, drawing her into his arms. She looked momentarily worried and he realised with a spurt of amusement that she was indicating her bloodstained gown and apron. Bonnet stepped back and held out his hands to display the appalling state of his blue jacket and filthy trousers. After a startled look, she giggled. It was very attractive.

This kiss was longer and much more satisfying. Bonnet took his time, hoping that it would convince her that he was serious about his willingness to take her under his protection. He was baffled by her choice but he had every intention of making the most of it for as long as he could.

When he finally, reluctantly, released her, she stepped back still holding his hand. "Keep safe, Gabriel," she said softly and the sound of her voice sent a shiver of longing through him.

"You too, Bianca. I'll come back when I can. If anything does happen to me, I'm going to leave a letter with one of my fellow captains to tell him to let you know. Garreau will make sure you're all right, I trust him. He's the reliable one. Go and get some rest, you look exhausted."

***

As the sun rose on the morning of 22nd of June the French troops were in full possession of the lower town, the harbour and the Mole. It was a disaster for the Spanish, given that the port was now effectively closed to them and their British allies. As the French dragged guns into position, the Royal Navy ships set sail, followed by the Spanish frigates and gunboats, passing along the shore from the great redoubt and beyond the Mole, out of the range of the French cannon.

The ships did not go quietly. As they sailed by they fired broadsides into the French camps, the trenches, and onto the lower town. The French scrambled to take cover in the ditches and siege works or in what was left of the buildings and defences of the lower town. Very little damage was done by the cannonade, which seemed more a gesture of defiance than a realistic assault.

From midnight until the early hours of the morning, the surviving Spanish troops struggled into the upper town, mainly through the Cervantes Bastion and the Rosario Gate. By dawn there were no more in sight and the gates were closed, barred and fully guarded. The shocked citizens of Tarragona came out onto the streets in search of news. They hung around in small worried groups, asking questions of the passing soldiers. Most of them gave no sensible answers.

Ángel had no idea how long it had taken him to reach the Cervantes Bastion. It felt like hours. He lay in the street after the fat French officer had inexplicably spared his life and wondered for a while if it might be better just to stay there. His right arm burned with pain but his left hand was worse. It lay across his chest and he could feel the warm blood soaking through his shirt. When he tried to move it, he found that it was impossible and it occurred to him in sudden panic that his fingers might have been cut off.

It was that which made him open his eyes and lift his head. His hand was still there, but it was a mangled mess with a huge cut across the back which gaped open. Both wounds were bleeding badly. Ángel forced himself into a sitting position and then realised that might have been a mistake. He looked around him quickly. It had grown dark but there was plenty of light in the embattled streets. Several houses were already on fire.

There were no French troops close by and Ángel supposed they must have run past him, assuming he was dead. Looking down at himself he did not blame them for the mistake. His shirt and coat were drenched with blood, making it look as though he had been shot or bayonetted through the chest. He could feel blood trickling down his face as well and with an effort, raised his right hand to feel the wound then winced. That too was deep. Ángel remembered that the Frenchman had borne a jagged scar. He wondered if that was why he had chosen to mark his enemy.

There were rising sounds of violence around him which told him that some of the French were already looting the town. At the same time, the thunder of musketry ahead suggested that the Spanish reserves were still putting up a fight at the San Juan Gate. Ángel knew they could not save the harbour and the Mole but it might be possible for them to keep the French busy while the rest of the garrison, those who had survived the slaughter in the lower town, made their escape.

Escape was Ángel's only option since he was clearly in no condition to fight. Using his injured right arm he grasped the overturned cart and dragged himself to his feet. He was shocked at how weak he felt, and stood hanging on to the wooden boards for a long time while the street seemed to shift beneath his shaking legs. Once again he considered letting himself fall to the ground again. Eventually he would either bleed to death or be bayonetted by the rioting French troops. Either might be easier than this.

Oddly enough it was the thought of the overweight Frenchman that finally spurred him into movement. The man had left him with a civil recommendation to get himself off the battlefield. At the time Ángel had heard savage mockery in his tone, but thinking about it now he decided that the Frenchman had actually been serious in his advice. He could have killed Ángel several times over and he had chosen to let him live. Ángel had no belief in the intervention of a benevolent God and even less in the goodwill of his enemy but he had been give a chance and it did not make sense to throw it away.

He took some time to search for his sword. He did not think that the Frenchman had taken it, he had a distinct memory of the clanging sound as the man kicked it to one side. Sure enough, after an agonising ten minutes scrabbling around in the dark, he found it in the shadows beside a doorstep. Ángel picked it up and after a few fumbling attempts managed to push it back into the scabbard. In his present condition the sword would be utterly useless but he had worn it since he first took up an officer's commission and he could not bear to leave it behind.

His progress through the streets was erratic. Partly this was because he kept coming across French troops and needed to duck into the shadows until they had gone. Some of them were marching in an orderly fashion but many were roaming the streets in search of drink or loot. Watching their movements, Ángel thought most of them had already found the drink. Their inebriation made them dangerous but it also made them easy to avoid.

His progress was also slow because it was difficult to keep on his feet. His left hand was useless and Ángel was worried about the amount of blood he was losing. He managed to arrange his left arm across his chest with the hand tucked inside his coat for some protection, holding it still with his right hand. The pressure on it was excruciating but Ángel hoped it might stem the bleeding a little.

He made his way through the streets, staggering from door to door. Occasionally he saw other Spanish soldiers, alone or in small groups, performing the same agonisingly slow retreat. Ángel followed them. Many of them were wounded and some were helping limping comrades. They glanced incuriously at Ángel but seeing him on his feet and more or less able to walk, they ignored him. Ángel did the same. This was no time for conversation or sympathy. They moved in silence, slipping through the shadows.

Beneath the pain, Ángel could feel humiliation burning into him. He was an expert swordsman. As a boy he had been taught by a Spanish master and as a man he had spent years training: honing his skills. He had been faced by a commoner who had probably never had a proper lesson in his life and he had been beaten because of a moment's distraction. When the shots were fired he had flinched and looked around, while the big Frenchman had not hesitated for a second. The Frenchman should have been dead on the ground. Instead, he had walked casually away leaving Ángel in agony. He had not even bothered to kill him.

Personal humiliation was made worse by the poor performance of the Spanish garrison. Once the breaches were gained, the garrison had made no real attempt to defend the lower town. The only determined fight had been led by General Velasco, who had arrived to take up his new command to find his troops either dead, wounded or fleeing incontinently from the triumphant French.

Velasco was appalled, having had no idea that Sarsfield had already left. He found his officers in confusion with Ángel desperately trying to persuade them to make a better stand. It had not worked. Ángel had no authority and was junior to most of them. The troops were already broken and the best Velasco could do was to take personal command of the reserve, with Ángel beside him, and make a doomed attempt to defend the harbour and the Mole. For a time his determined stand had halted the enemy progress but once the French reserves swept down into the town, there was no option but to retreat or die. A lot had died.

Ahead of him, Ángel could see the looming shape of the bastion. The French, distracted by looting and murder in the streets of the lower town, had not reached this far. Spanish troops were limping up to the gate and being admitted, while infantry with loaded muskets lined the parapets above the gate ready to shoot down any approaching French. Ángel realised with a flood of relief that he was going to make it into the town. He had no idea how much further he could manage.

It was chaos within the walls and for a moment Ángel had no idea what to do next. He stood, shaking and bewildered, as the troops streamed around him going in search of food and shelter and the rest of their battalions. Ángel knew his way to headquarters but he was suddenly terrified that if he let go of the wall he was hanging on to, he would collapse to the ground and be trampled. Dimly, he knew that he had lost too much blood and was about to pass out, but he clung on, maintaining his feet through sheer stubborn willpower.

A voice penetrated through the babble around him. It was a familiar voice and Ángel thought how impressively loud it was. He had a vague memory of thinking that before. It was calling his name. Ángel turned his head but could see nothing. His vision was blurry and all he could see was soldiers hurrying past him to get to shelter. After a few moments, he decided to give in and lie down. He had just uncurled the fingers of his right hand from the stone wall when a strong arm went around him, supporting him.

"I've found him," the voice called. "He's here. He's alive, though only just, by the look of him. Rubio, get up to the hospital and find a stretcher; I don't care who you have to kick to do it. He's not going to make it on foot. I'll stay with him."

The man lowered Ángel carefully to sit on some steps. A worried face peered at him from below curly dark hair. There was a massive bruise on the smooth olive forehead which jogged Ángel's memory.

"García? What are you doing here?"

"I've been looking for you," García said. "General Velasco finally made it back; he is giving his report to General Contreras now. He said you fought with the reserves but he was worried that you might have been killed or wounded. The General sent me down here to look for you. He sent his servant to the other gate."

"How many made it back?" Ángel asked.

"We won't know until tomorrow. He's ordered a general muster, we'll find out numbers then. I should have stayed."

"You did your duty, Lieutenant, and you did it bloody well. Sarsfield..." The name was like ashes in Ángel's mouth. "Fucking Sarsfield did this."

"He obeyed orders, sir."

"He stormed off like a scorned maiden," Ángel said. He intended it to be savage but his voice was weak and he sounded whiny instead so he stopped talking.

Two men appeared at a run through the thinning crowd with a sturdy stretcher between them. Ángel was momentarily confused then realised that he must have lost consciousness for a while. García was still there, his arm supporting him. Ángel wanted to say something to him but could think of nothing to say.

"Thank you," he mumbled finally.

"It's all right. We need to get you on this stretcher. Every time you stand up, your knees give way. Come on, I'll help you. The surgeons have set up in the cathedral, they're waiting for you."

Ángel lay back on the canvas stretcher then the sense of the other man's words reached him and he tried to sit up again. "No," he said. "No."

"You need medical help, Captain," García said patiently.

"They'll take my hand. I know they will. They don't have enough doctors so they'll just amputate. I'd rather take my chances."

"Captain, you're going to die if you don't let them treat you," García said, sounding exasperated.

"I'd rather die. Leave me here. Or get me back to my room and I'll tend to myself."

"Sir, is he coming or not?" one of the soldiers said. "We've dozens of wounded men needing help here. If he doesn't want…"

"He's going to the bloody doctor, if I have to knock him out," García said. "Captain, stop struggling or I'm going to punch you. I'll stay with you. I won't let them do…"

"They'll take my hand," Ángel sobbed. The stretcher tilted dangerously as he tried again to get up. García put a hand on his right shoulder.

"I'm sorry," he said apologetically. It was the last thing Ángel heard before something hit him in the face with the force of a club and he fell into blessed unconsciousness.

Chapter Sixteen

Hugh spent the two nights following the fall of the lower town leading out his ships boats to take off some of the wounded soldiers. It was a difficult and dangerous task. Codrington's squadron had anchored in the roadstead off Milagro Point, an open but sheltered body of water under the steep, rocky southern face of the city. The ships would be reasonably safe from rip currents, tide or ocean swell in the roadstead but there were no quays or harbour facilities and it was impossible to land at all in rough weather.

When it was relatively calm, however, boats could come into the shore and, under cover of darkness, those wounded Spaniards able to scramble down the rocky paths could be taken off and loaded aboard a selection of Spanish merchant vessels and traders who were heading to safety in Villanueva, Menorca or Valencia. The Royal Navy squadron brought every one of its boats into play and by the end of the second night the last of the refugees had departed and Hugh took Durrell to dine aboard the *Blake* to confer with Commodore Codrington.

Hugh was worried about his friend. Over the past few days, Codrington had barely slept and looked ten years older than when Hugh had first joined him at Menorca. Like Hugh, he had been up all night manning the boats but unlike Hugh, he had not slept through the day being engaged in writing letters to his superiors, to London and to the Spanish commanders. He was drawn and tired and for the first ten minutes of the meal pushed food around his plate as though he could not be bothered to eat.

Hugh watched him for a while and eventually interrupted Codrington's account of his previous night's adventure when an unchancy wave had almost overturned his captain's barge into the roadstead.

"Ned, I'm enjoying the story, but if you can't talk and eat at the same time I'd rather watch you eat. You've lost ten pounds in the past month; your face is grey and if I take you home to Jane in this state she's going to shoot me in the head. Eat something."

Codrington looked at his plate with mild surprise as if not expecting to see the food there. After a moment he gave a twisted grin and took a forkful of chicken.

"Sorry. I'm too tired to eat really."

"You need food and you need rest. This is a shambles, but you're taking it too hard. It's not our shambles."

Codrington looked up and met his gaze. "It should be," he said. "We should have troops in here, shoring up the garrison and stiffening the spines of some of these Spanish jellyfish. Sorry, I meant generals. Contreras is complaining about Sarsfield, about Carlos and about the poor showing of the garrison in the lower town, but what the hell does he expect? They were left without proper leadership when they needed it most. If Sarsfield had to leave, he should have gone down there himself, not written orders to Velasco. How the hell can men serving within a mile or two of each other not manage to communicate? It's bloody ridiculous."

Hugh grinned. "It is," he admitted. "I think these rivalries have a lot to do with why this has gone so badly wrong."

"The town is going to fall, Hugh, unless Campoverde manages to pluck up the courage to attack Suchet. And he's not going to. I had a letter this morning and he's withdrawn again."

Hugh blinked. "I thought you told me he was intending to make an attempt."

"That's what I was told. He divided his army into two columns under Miranda and Sarsfield and they marched to their allotted place and were supposed to co-ordinate a sortie from Contreras and the garrison. It's hard to untangle his various excuses, but from what I can tell from his letter, Miranda flinched at the sight of the enemy and withdrew. Campoverde should have taken his command off him and gone up himself with the second column, but instead he meekly accepted Miranda's assessment and both divisions retired without a shot being fired."

Durrell, who had been quiet so far, gave a little snort of disgust then quickly apologised. Codrington, who seemed to be wholly reconciled to his regular presence at Hugh's side merely smiled.

"No apology required, Mr Durrell, I agree with you. Since then Campoverde is blaming Miranda and Caro and they're both blaming him and each other. He's now demanding that Contreras send him his two best regiments with General Velasco to command them. At this rate by the time the French attack we needn't worry about the garrison because there'll be none left to defend the place. They'll all be hiding in the hills with Campoverde."

"It is rather more complex than you may realise, Commodore," Durrell said in precise tones. "It appears that the Marquis of Campoverde is now making attempts to depose General Contreras from his command. He has written to the remaining senior officers within the walls telling them that if the General shows any sign of surrendering to the enemy they should arrest and confine him."

Both Hugh and Codrington turned to stare at him. Durrell sipped his wine and looked back, appearing wholly unabashed.

"How the bloody hell do you know that, Mr Durrell?" Hugh demanded. He was running over the events of the past twenty-four hours in his head, trying to work out what his first officer had been up to. If a letter had been delivered he would have known and besides, Durrell would have brought it directly to him. It was clear that Durrell had been pursuing his own intelligence sources. Hugh gave him a look. Durrell gave a faint smile which reassured him a little, but not much.

"It is not as bad as you think, sir, I've not been absent without leave. At least, not for very long. I was commanding the last boats early this morning. It was just as the sun was coming up and when we arrived at the rocks below the Cervantes Bastion, I found Lieutenant García waiting there, hoping to be able to speak to me. There were only a few people to bring off, three or four wounded men and two women with a child. They were very distraught, it was upsetting. Anyway, all of them were able to fit easily into the launch with Mr Hart, so I sent them off with him and went ashore for a short time, telling Mr Hastings to come back for me in two hours, or sooner if the wind looked likely to pick up."

Hugh looked at him for a long time. "That was bloody rash, Mr Durrell. If things had gone wrong, you might have got stuck there."

"Not for long, sir. Even if the weather had turned suddenly, I only had to wait until it dropped again. Hart and Hastings knew where I was and I gave them leave to tell you immediately if it was not possible to bring me off as planned. I am sorry. I was already there and it was a good opportunity. There was no time to ask your permission, or I would have done so."

"And when you came back?" Hugh said ominously.

"I'd barely reached my cabin to change when you sent the message for me to join you here. I could have told you in the boat but then I'd have had to tell the same story twice. And also, I thought Commodore Codrington should be the first to hear it."

Hugh was exasperated, not for the first time, by his first officer's faultless logic. He glared at him, trying not to laugh.

"You haven't heard the last of this, you impudent young mutineer. But since you've a story to tell, let's hear it."

"García tells me that General Contreras feels beset on all sides. To the credit of his remaining officers, they told him immediately of the Marquis of Campoverde's attempts to undermine his authority. García says that it has added to his despair. He has no desire to surrender, but he is in an impossible position now. He has chosen to pretend to Campoverde that he knows nothing of the plot. He has agreed to send off the Almeria Regiment by sea but refuses to send the Iliberia as it will deplete his garrison too much."

"Yes, he's written to me asking if we can get the Almeria away in the boats tomorrow," Codrington said.

"How many did he lose in the lower town, Ned?"

"About five hundred, I believe," Codrington said. "I'm amazed it wasn't more."

"García says it would have been more on both sides if the garrison had made more effort to stand," Durrell said.

"Didn't they? Was García present?"

"No, although he'd been with Sarsfield earlier in the day, helping to mine the breaches. It didn't help though, the mines failed to detonate at the correct time. He had his information from Captain Cortez. He was in the lower town and fought under General Velasco when he came in with the reserve. He was badly wounded."

Hugh lifted his eyebrows. "Will he be all right?"

"I don't know, sir. He has a wound on his right arm and a slash across his face which will both heal but there is a great deal of damage to his left hand. The surgeon apparently wanted to amputate but Cortez was insistent that he did not want that, so García stopped them doing it. I think he feels a weight of responsibility if that was the wrong decision."

"It's hardly his fault if he did what Cortez wanted, Mr Durrell," Hugh said. He could see that Durrell was genuinely concerned. His friendship with General Contreras' young ADC may well have begun as an intelligence gathering mission but it had clearly moved to a closer bond.

"I have told him that, sir, but I don't blame him for worrying."

"Are they friends?"

Durrell gave a small, grim smile. "Not really. I think Óscar…I mean, Lieutenant García…has tried. Captain Cortez is very conscious of his dignity and his superior experience and doesn't make friends easily. They're very different. But they've worked closely together and at present, García seems to be the only person he trusts. He's very weak and feverish and they're short of pain relief and medicine of all kinds."

"We can probably help with that," Codrington said abruptly. "I'm very well stocked here. Speak to my surgeon, Mr Durrell, tell him what you know of the injuries and he'll supply you with everything the Captain might need. I'm sending a boat in with letters this evening, they can take it."

"Commodore, thank you, that's very good of you."

"I'd send my surgeon, if I thought we could guarantee to get him out again, but we can't. Contreras has asked me to arrange to transport this regiment out tomorrow to join Campoverde. I will tell him it will depend on the weather but I will do my best."

Hugh studied his friend. "It's looking fairly calm, Ned."

"I don't give a damn how calm it's looking, I'm not taking more troops from Tarragona to send to a man who will simply show them where to hide. I have already decided it will be too rough to send those troops, I'll write to Campoverde myself. The army doesn't understand tides or weather anyway."

***

Durrell was on deck when the lookout called the approach of unidentified vessels, then almost immediately declared them friendly. As they hove into view Durrell stood watching them draw closer, puzzled. The flotilla was led by two Royal Navy frigates, followed by a variety of troop transports and Durrell had no idea who they were or where they had come from. He was fairly sure, given their conversation of the previous day, that

Codrington would not know either. Catching sight of Hugh's servant diligently washing shirts, he waved to him to come over.

Miles Randall approached, smelling strongly of soap. The front of his shirt was soaked through and his arms were still wet but he stood to attention as if in dress uniform. Durrell managed not to smile.

"Get yourself below and find the Captain, Randall. There's a squadron approaching and he'll probably want a message sent to Commodore Codrington. And Miles?"

"Yes, sir?"

"Dry your arms first."

The boy grinned and snatched up a towel which lay beside the wash tub. Durrell turned back to watch the ships which were anchoring at a safe distance from the shore. The wind was beginning to pick up and the surf was becoming more choppy. Durrell reflected that Codrington's mendacious claim that he would be unable to take off the regiment as requested by Campoverde looked as though it would prove true after all.

By late morning, when a message arrived from the *Blake*, it was clear that no boats could approach the shore without danger of being driven onto the rocks. Hugh received the letter during the punishment hour when the last of a sentence of ten lashes was being administered to a resigned Italian sailor for drunkenness. As the crew was dismissed and the Master prepared to take the noon sight, Hugh opened the letter, skimmed it quickly and lifted his eyebrows.

"The plot thickens, Mr Durrell. Now we have the British army to contend with. Join me for a drink before dinner once I've taken the noon sight and I'll tell you everything. Miles, where are you? Go and get your sextant and your notebook or the sun will have moved on and you'll have no clue where you are or what you're doing. Run."

Durrell watched the boy racing across the deck. Since young Randall's wholly unauthorised excursion in one of the boats bringing off refugees, Hugh appeared to have stepped up his interest in his newest cabin boy. Miles took lessons daily with the schoolmaster but Durrell noticed that Hugh had begun to take him away from the mundane chores of his day and around the ship with him. Durrell approved although he was not sure if it was because Hugh had only just noticed his servant's remarkable intelligence or if it was simply a way of keeping an eye on him.

When the midshipmen and other boys had been dismissed for their dinner, Durrell joined Hugh in his cabin and accepted a glass of wine. It was not Hugh's usual quality and Durrell sipped cautiously, then looked up to find Hugh grinning and realised his expression had betrayed him. Hugh laughed aloud.

"Sorry. It's the best they could get in Menorca apparently. Blame Winterton, he did the last supply run."

Durrell drank again, smiled and put the glass down. "It improves after a few sips."

"And we won't care by the end of the bottle." Hugh set his own glass down, sat in his armchair and stretched out his long legs. As if in response to a silent signal, a fluffy shape appeared at the door in the partition between Hugh's bedroom and his dining cabin. Molly strolled nonchalantly across the deck and leaped onto Hugh's lap. Hugh stroked her fur.

"The flotilla is led by the *Regulus* and has brought troops from Cadiz, it seems. A few reinforcements from Valencia and Murcia, not very many. And then we have Lieutenant-Colonel John Byne Skerret in command of just over a thousand British infantry and half a company of artillery."

"Why?" Durrell asked blankly.

"That is a very good question, Mr Durrell. It appears the Spanish authorities in Cadiz have been putting pressure on to General Graham, who commands the British forces there, to send aid to Tarragona. This is his response."

"What good are a thousand men when the town is about to fall to the French?" Durrell said scathingly. Hugh gave a twisted smile.

"Another good question. I suspect the answer is not much at all. Ned writes that Skerret has been given specific orders from Graham not to put his troops at risk. He can do anything to help providing there is no chance of his men getting stuck in the city and either getting slaughtered or having to surrender. Apparently he's asked Ned that if he sends them in, can he guarantee he'll be able to get them out again if it all goes badly wrong."

"And what did Commodore Codrington say?" Durrell asked.

"I'm sure it was relatively polite, although that will have been an effort. Ned has told him bluntly that given the poor conditions for landing along this coast, nobody can promise anything."

"Has he even been able to get a message to Contreras in this swell?" Durrell asked.

"Well he couldn't send a boat in," Hugh said. "Which has the merit of making true his refusal to embark Campoverde's requested regiments. He managed to send off a letter though, it was carried by one of Winterton's master's mates who can swim like a fish."

Durrell realised that his mouth was hanging open and closed it. "Did he make it back?" he asked. Hugh laughed.

"Your face is a picture," he said. "It's not nearly as bad as it sounds. I know Elijah, he used to serve on the *Herne* when Winterton was my first officer. He was Luke's servant for a few years, they're very close. Luke would never have allowed him to go if he'd not been certain it was safe. He's back with a reply. Not surprisingly Contreras wants to meet with Skerret as soon as it's safe to land him. Ned is hoping to meet with them both tomorrow and he'd like both of us to join him. I suspect he's rather impressed with your source of inside information."

Durrell sipped the wine again and decided it was not as bad as he had thought. "When I joined the Royal Navy I did not imagine it would lead to a career as a spy," he said mildly. His Captain grinned.

"You didn't befriend that young man in order to spy on him, Mr Durrell, you did it to annoy Cortez. Does this bother you?"

Durrell returned his smile. "No," he said honestly. "I like him. It would bother me if I thought either of us was passing on information that could do any harm, but we're not. This is information we should be receiving as a matter of course and would be if there wasn't so much tension between the various Spanish leaders. To tell you the truth, Captain, I think Óscar knows perfectly well what he's doing and I'm sure he weighs up what he tells me in exactly the same way I weigh up what I tell him. It's what intelligent men do in wartime. Otherwise we'd never be able to speak to each other at all."

Hugh studied him in silence for a while. Eventually he said:

"You were so wet behind the ears when I first met you, Alfred Durrell, I was astonished you were so damned good at your job. Somewhere along the way you became very wise."

Durrell felt a little lift of pleasure at the compliment, since Hugh did not give them easily. "Thank you, sir, but I have a feeling you might have helped with that. Should I join the others for dinner…?"

"Good God, no, stay and dine with me. Winterton might have brought dreadful wine but my larder is well stocked again which means my cook is no longer so depressed. I wonder how they're doing for food in the city."

"Well enough so far, sir, although prices are sky high. But it's going to be difficult for us to keep them supplied if everything has to be taken in by a longboat in a choppy sea. They're going to struggle if this goes on for much longer."

Hugh regarded him sombrely and topped up their wine glasses. "I don't think that's going to be an issue, Mr Durrell."

***

By the following morning the rough sea had abated enough for Hugh and Durrell to land without difficulty. They arrived at Contreras' headquarters to find Codrington already there. He was accompanied by the captains of the other three ships currently with the squadron, Adam, White and Winterton. There were a number of both British and Spanish army officers present. Skerret had brought his officer of engineers and his senior artillery officer. Across the room, Durrell caught the eye of Óscar García who responded with a very slight smile.

The discussion was confusingly held in a mixture of Spanish and English. Durrell had wondered if he might be expected to translate between those parties who could not understand each other but he was saved by the presence of General Charles Doyle, a British officer currently serving in the Spanish army. Doyle seemed to have no difficulty in managing the conversation although Durrell thought that his translation skills were no help at all with the subject of it.

The meeting broke up with General Contreras suggesting a tour of the city, to show Skerret his arrangements for the final defence. Durrell, who had toured the defences very recently thought that Skerret was unlikely to be impressed and was relieved when García approached him as the men filed out of the door.

"Lieutenant Durrell, I am not required to join the General today. I am walking over to the cathedral to see Captain Cortez and I was wondering if you might accompany me."

Durrell shot a look at Hugh who nodded immediately. He and García waited until the room was empty before making their way out into the sunlit square.

"How is your Captain? Is he recovering?"

"He is much better than he was but not nearly as well as he thinks," García said with a little smile. "The fever seems to have abated but he is still very weak. The surgeon bleeds him daily and has said he must rest. If it had been possible, the General would have sent him by ship to Menorca to recover, but now it cannot be done."

Durrell gave his companion a sideways glance. García looked grave and Durrell understood.

"It seems that General Contreras believes they will begin their assault tomorrow."

"It is certain that they will," García said. "All morning we have been watching the progress of the breaching batteries. They will be finished by then and Suchet has been fortunate so far not to be attacked to the rear by our forces. He will not risk waiting."

"What do you think General Contreras will do?"

"He does not believe the town can stand against an assault, as he has said to Colonel Skerret. When the walls are breached, he will lead his men out of the Barcelona gate, and to try to join the forces of the Marquis of Campoverde. He hopes that as the French are busy storming the western side of the city they will not be prepared for a sortie on the eastern side. He would like Colonel Skerret to land his men and take part in the sortie. Or, if he prefers, he can choose to help defend the town from within. He will ask the Colonel to make the choice for himself."

Durrell felt heavy with misery but he could not bring himself to dodge the issue. "I don't think Colonel Skerret will choose either of those options, Óscar. He's been told not to risk his men."

García glanced at him and his expression told Durrell that this was not news to him. "If he cannot risk his men, he cannot land them."

"I know."

"I do not wish to seem ungrateful for the help your General Graham has offered us, Lieutenant, but I wish they had not come at all. The people see the British transports and hope they have come to save the town. Now they must watch them sail away and do nothing."

"I'm sorry. It's too little, too late. If the troops had arrived before the loss of the lower town, they might have made a significant difference. Does Captain Cortez know what is going on?"

"Yes. I saw him this morning. The talk at the hospital is of nothing but the arrival of the British, but the Captain is not optimistic. Like you, he thinks this is too little, too late."

The cathedral had been turned into a hospital, with rows of wounded men laid out in every available space. Durrell had not been inside the building before and wished he could have seen it before its transformation. It was an elegant structure with the original Romanesque building overlaid and extended in the Gothic style. Durrell had a liking for old churches and did his best to disguise the fact that he was gazing around him like a tourist, in case it seemed disrespectful for the sick and wounded men.

There were a number of small chapels around the edge of the cathedral, closed off by wrought iron gates or in some cases, embroidered curtains. These had been set aside for some of the more serious cases or possibly for the more senior officers. Presumably Ángel Cortez warranted special treatment as ADC to the commander of the garrison. He had been allocated the Chapel of St Francis, a tiny space on the right-hand side of the cathedral with the privacy of a curtain. García called out softly and peered around the curtain then to Durrell's surprise uttered an exasperated oath.

"What are you doing out of your bed?" he demanded furiously. "The surgeon said you needed to rest, that you would be weak from this wound and that you should…"

"I am weak from his constant blood letting," Cortez said irritably. "The fever is better, I do not need it, but every time he comes here it is to look at my hand and ask if he may yet cut it off. I have told him not to come back."

"Good. Excellent." García's voice was heavy with sarcasm and Durrell decided that his former polite deference to his senior officer had been yet another casualty of war. "Here, why don't you come outside where there is more space and we will practice fencing together. Better still, you should join General Contreras who is showing the British officers around the city. I am sure it will not tire you at all."

He threw back the heavy curtain and Durrell was surprised to see Cortez on his feet. He was in shirt sleeves, without his boots on and in his right hand he held his sword, as though he had been practising. He looked astonished at the sight of Durrell and quickly lowered the sword. Durrell bowed politely.

"I beg your pardon, Captain Cortez. I asked Lieutenant García to show me the hospital provision and to obtain numbers for the wounded. It would be useful to know in case we have to attempt an evacuation. I didn't mean to disturb you."

Durrell half expected a rude response. To his surprise, Cortez' rigid stance relaxed a little.

"You did not disturb me, Lieutenant, it was my idiot subordinate who did that. He is right, of course, I was ordered to rest. I wanted to test my strength, to see if it will be possible for me to get out of here if I need to. I am still weak but I would rather die fighting than be slaughtered in my bed when they break through."

Durrell felt painful sympathy for the sentiment. He knew he would have felt the same way. The man looked terrible. His face was pallid with dark circles of pain and exhaustion under the pale grey eyes and the blond hair which was usually scrupulously neat was pulled into an untidy knot on his neck. His right arm was heavily bandaged and there was a jagged scar across one cheek. The left arm was in a sling and what Durrell could see of his hand was bound and splinted.

Durrell could think of nothing to say, so fell back on simple courtesy. "I'm sorry you were so badly wounded, Captain. I spoke to General Velasco and he tells me you gave good service at an appallingly difficult time; he has been singing your praises. Has the surgeon given you his opinion on your hand?"

"The surgeon would like to remove my hand, Lieutenant, so that it would be less trouble to him." Cortez shrugged. "The fingers are broken. He believes the muscles were cut so badly that I will never be able to use it again but we will not know that until it begins to heal and I can try to move it."

"Lieutenant García is right, you know. You should rest." Durrell hesitated. "I don't know how difficult this would be, or even if it would be possible, but when we return to the ships later on, I would like to ask my Captain if you could come with us. Our surgeon is young but very experienced and a second opinion might be useful…"

"No."

Durrell studied the drawn face with compassion. "Captain, if the French break through we will try to get the garrison away but it will be difficult. Realistically, we will not be able to get the wounded out unless they can get to the boats themselves. You're injured, you'll be no use in a fight. Why not make our evacuation a little easier and come now?"

Once again he awaited an explosion of anger. Again the Spaniard surprised him. Cortez gave a very faint smile.

"Thank you. I know you mean well, Lieutenant, and I know you speak sense, but I cannot. I will not run from the French. They will either kill me or take me prisoner but I cannot desert my post for safety while these men lie here and await their fate."

"You know that makes no sense, don't you?"

"It is a matter of honour, Lieutenant. And although we are not friends, I feel somehow that you would do the same thing."

For a moment, Durrell was assailed by a flash of memory. He was on a beach on the island of South Beveland, surrounded by sick and dying men during the disastrous Walcheren campaign. All he had needed to do that day was find a Royal Navy ship that would take him and leave the army to manage its own fever patients. Instead he had stepped in, taken charge and ended in a fever ward himself. His insistence on taking responsibility for a crisis that was not his had almost killed him. He felt once again an uncomfortable kinship with this arrogant Spanish officer.

"Perhaps I would," he said.

"Perhaps you have. One day, if we both survive this, I would like to hear that story."

It was an olive branch. Durrell's smile widened a little. "Willingly, Captain. Although I warn you, it is not a particularly exciting story. You should lie down. If you do need to get out of here in a hurry, you'll need your strength. I must find Captain Kelly and the others. I hope this goes well for you. Good luck."

It took all afternoon for Contreras to complete his tour of the city and it ended as Durrell had expected. The General was tight-lipped as he finally escorted his visitors down to the shore. Durrell did not blame him. He thought that Codrington and Skerret had made the right decision not to land the British troops, given General Graham's very specific orders, but privately he agreed with García that it might have been better if Skerret had not come at all. It felt as though the British were about to sail off leaving the garrison and people of Tarragona to their inevitable fate. Durrell thought about García's white, set face as he returned to his chosen place directly facing the likely direction of the French assault. He thought of Cortez, injured, helpless and furious in the cathedral. Durrell liked García but he also felt a painful sympathy for Cortez in all his wounded, stubborn pride and he hated the feeling that he might well be leaving them to die.

It was very dark as they made the last scramble down onto the rocks where the boats awaited them. A wide flat rock projected out over the water. They had landed with ease that morning but the sea was much wilder now, with a heavy swell and there was no visible moon. Hugh called out and there was an answering cry from Hagley, coxswain to Codrington's boat. Hugh and Durrell stepped back to allow Codrington and the army officers to go first.

The surf was washing high up, above Codrington's knees and even reaching Durrell who was standing well back. Durrell could see the Commodore peering into the darkness. Durrell had good night vision and could clearly see the shape of the bobbing boat, but it was obvious that Codrington was struggling.

"Hagley, I can't see you. Tell me when to jump, I can't see the boat."

Codrington's voice carried across the water and Durrell felt himself flinch internally. Beside him he heard Hugh's voice in an anguished whisper.

"For fuck's sake, Ned, why not light a guiding beacon for them at the same time?"

"Jump now, sir." Hagley's voice was equally loud. Durrell closed his eyes and uttered a silent, agonised prayer.

There was a scramble and a crash and Codrington swore loudly. A babble of voices made enquiries about his safety and the Commodore called up cheerfully, reassuring them that it was nothing worse than bruised shins.

"Oh, I don't believe this," Hugh breathed softly.

As he said the words there was a crash and a shell fell harmlessly into the water. It was followed by another. Flashes of light exploded from the batteries along the Mole and the shore as the French guns boomed out into the darkness. There was no shelter on the bare rocks and Durrell could sense the panic of the army officers. Presumably they were accustomed to being in a position to at least attempt to find cover under enemy fire. Durrell, who had stood many times on the quarterdeck giving orders while a French ship aimed broadsides and enemy marines fired muskets down from the rigging felt rather sorry for them as shells rained down around the boats.

"You'll need to jump," Codrington yelled. "Follow my voice, it doesn't matter if you land on me."

The army officers moved forward to the edge of the rock just as a huge wave swept up and over them, drenching them in cold salt water.

"That was a big one," Codrington called out cheerfully. "Everybody all right? Come on then, you first, Colonel."

"Is there room in your boat, sir?" Winterton asked Hugh quietly.

"Yes. Adam, White, why don't you let the Commodore take care of the army and you can come back with us."

"Much more of this and you'll be in charge of the squadron, sir," Adam whispered. "They think we're landing troops, don't they?"

"The racket we're making, they probably think we've brought in Wellington with half the Light Division," Hugh said grimly. "Keep back under the cliff until they're away…oh no…"

Durrell stared through the darkness. It was easier to see the boat now because of the flashes of light from the French guns. Skerret and the other officers had jumped down into the boat but the combination of their weight and the increasing swell of the sea had driven the boat forwards and her stern had become caught on the rocks. There was a babble of voices as Codrington instructed the officers to sit down while the coxswain yelled orders to the oarsmen to try to push the boat off. Durrell glanced at Hugh.

"No," said his Captain flatly. "If you get blown apart by a shell trying to rescue them from this debacle I am going to shoot Codrington myself, the bloody idiot. Stand down, Mr Durrell and that's an order. The rowers will push them off in a minute. Either that or a wave will pick them up…"

He broke off, catching his breath as another shell came in. Durrell could hear it whistling through the night air. Somehow it sounded closer and with more purpose than the previous shots, though he knew that was his imagination. The men in the boat must have heard it too and felt the same because they fell silent as if waiting for it to hit. Durrell realised he was holding his breath.

There was an ominous plop, so close by that Durrell closed his eyes, not wanting to see the disaster unfold. The shell exploded in the water with a peculiar gurgling sound followed by a muffled bang. There were exclamations of consternation from the boat but no cries of fear or screams of pain. Durrell opened his eyes. Through the darkness he saw the stern of the boat rear up as though thrown up by an enormous wave. When it came down again there was a huge splash and water surged up over the rock, but the boat was free.

"Bloody hell," Hugh breathed. "Ned Codrington has the luck of the devil. That shell just went off under the boat and pushed it off the rock. Back against the cliff, gentlemen. We will remain here nice and quietly until that lunatic is on his way back to the *Blake*. I'm hoping that my barge is commanded by a man with a brain and we don't bring the rest of the French artillery down on our heads."

They stood quietly for several minutes as the French guns fired intermittently and then eventually stopped. Another few minutes passed.

Adam and White were restless and anxious but Durrell observed that Winterton, who had served under Hugh before, did not seem worried.

There was a whispering sound, the faint noise of oars through the water. Durrell glanced at Hugh who nodded. He moved forward into the cold spray of the waves and saw the dark shape of Hugh's barge moving close in to the rock.

A man stood up and leaped and Durrell reached out his hands to catch the slight figure. He was surprised to realise it was his servant, Lewis, a thick rope wrapped around him. Durrell steadied the boy and caught the rope, helping Lewis haul it in. He lifted a hand to wave Hugh and the others forward. Steadying the boat with the rope he watched as they clambered aboard. No word was spoken and no more shots were fired. Durrell doubted the French could see their target and they had no reason to waste shots in the darkness. When the other officers were settled in the barge, Durrell motioned to Lewis who flashed him a toothy grin before jumping nimbly down into the boat, to be caught and steadied by Fletcher, Hugh's coxswain. Durrell wound up the rope and followed more sedately and the barge cut swiftly through the waves out towards the waiting ships.

Nobody spoke until they were well out into the bay, closing in on the *Wren*. Captain White stirred.

"Well that was easier than I thought it would be," he said, in matter of fact tones.

The rest of the barge dissolved into suppressed laughter. The French heard nothing and no more shells were fired.

***

The guns from the breaching batteries opened fire at dawn.

Ángel heard the opening salvo from his uncomfortable pallet in the St Francis Chapel. He had not slept much, disturbed both by pain and the constant comings and goings of an army hospital. At the sound of the guns he got up and dressed. It took a long time because of his injured hand but Ángel knew if he asked for help he would be shepherded back to bed.

The cathedral had an octagonal bell tower above the smaller southern apse. It consisted of two floors: the first of which had windows. Above it was a small temple-like structure which housed the bells. Climbing stairs was difficult because Ángel was still weak. He was trying to disguise his weakness from García and the medical staff but there was nobody to watch him here, so he paused often in his climb. The tower had a spectacular view over Tarragona and the coastline. He could see the French lines and the smoke rising from cooking fires as well as the belch of black smoke coming from the cannon as they began their relentless bombardment of the city walls.

From here it was easy to see which section of the walls they intended to breach. The guns were trained on two areas: one to the left of the San Pablo Bastion and the other to the right, close to the San Juan. Both were having an immediate effect on the old walls and Ángel could see dust rising from sections of falling masonry. It was not going to take long.

He stood watching for a while, then turned his gaze out to sea. The transports bearing Colonel Skerret and the British troops had already sailed. The ships of Codrington's squadron remained, along with their gunboats. Sunlight sparked brilliant light off the water which looked surprisingly flat and still from here. Ángel was not deceived. He could see white capped waves close to shore and he knew that getting refugees away in boats would still be a dangerous enterprise.

By now, he could have been on the *Iris*, watching the guns fire on the city from the safety of a 74-gun third rater. Ángel thought about the coming hours and wished miserably that he had felt able to go. He knew that Contreras would have jumped at the chance to send his wounded ADC to safety and he was fairly sure that if Durrell had made the request, his Captain would have acceded. Ángel had not known the English lieutenant for long and was still not sure that he liked him but he had the impression that Durrell did not make promises that he was not sure he would be able to keep.

Ángel tried to imagine what it would have been like to watch the city fall and the garrison die defending it and knew that he had made the right decision. His sense of honour and duty, rigidly instilled into him from childhood, was an essential part of who he was. At times he felt as though it was the only thing holding him together. To lose that would have been to lose himself again and he had only just begun to recover from the blow of learning how badly he had chosen the wrong side during the early years of this war. He could not bear to let himself down again.

There were sounds from below; running feet through the streets as Contreras sent his troops to their final positions for the storming. Ángel held on to the parapet with his good hand and wondered what he should do. His instinct was to go in search of the General, to do what good he could and to die in battle as he had always intended. He was aware, however, that his presence might be a distraction and that a wounded man might be more of a nuisance than a help.

Eventually he compromised and went carefully back down the steep winding staircase. Food was being distributed and Ángel collected his portion of bread and strong goat's cheese. He went out into the cloister garden to eat it, away from the odour of sweat and blood and suffering that permeated the air of the cathedral. Perched on the edge of a stone fountain, he ate his breakfast and drank a measure of watered wine. García had brought him the wine late the previous night along with the latest news. They had sat here in the darkness, passing the bottle backwards and forwards while the younger man shared the General's plan and Ángel listened and tried not to despair.

Contreras, having hovered for too long over his favoured options, had chosen a muddled combination of the two. He had decided that if the French guns managed to breach the walls during this first day, he would only attempt to hold the city until nightfall when he would evacuate the garrison through the Rosario gate. The main body of the garrison was to make its exit while fourteen-hundred picked officers and men remained to hold the walls for as long as they could, only fleeing when the French broke through.

Ángel thought it was a mad plan, not least because Contreras had freely shared it with both officers and men, giving them detailed orders about their position on the walls or as part of the sortie. Morale was a delicate matter and Ángel thought that a man instructed to hold the wall but then given an approved bolthole was unlikely to fight to the death. Contreras had positioned some of his best regiments on the wall to the front but Ángel worried that they would have half their minds on the escape to the rear.

Ángel finished the wine because there was no point in saving it, then made his way out onto the front steps of the cathedral. The streets were busy with marching soldiers and a bustle of people making their way into churches and public buildings in the hope of finding refuge from the coming storm. Some of them were trying to get into the cathedral and the sentries were arguing with them, turning them away. Ángel wished them luck. There were several entrances to the old building and he had already seen two families making their way in through the cloister garden.

He sat on the steps and allowed the sunlight to warm his tired, aching body. The pain from the wound on his arm and the gash on his face was not as bad now, but his hand throbbed constantly. He had been grateful at night for the laudanum sent over from the *Blake*, but it made him sleepy so he preferred not to take it during the day, especially this day.

The guns continued to boom out throughout the long morning, but Ángel realised that the answering thunder from the Spanish guns was becoming less and less. More wounded were beginning to come in, many of them artillerymen, spilling out of the overcrowded cathedral into the cloister and then onto the street. A few infantrymen battered on doors of nearby houses, demanding that the householders give space to the wounded. Ángel could hear the crackle of musket fire punctuating any gap in the crashing of the artillery.

There was a pause in the French bombardment at around noon and curiosity sent Ángel up to the bell tower again. Two other officers occupied the space and made way for him. Ángel looked out over the lines and was appalled at the amount of damage already done, particularly to the wall by the San Juan Bastion.

"Why have they stopped?"

"They're repositioning the guns," one of the officers said grimly. He came to stand beside Ángel and pointed. "Look. They're having trouble hitting the San Pablo square on, and it's not coming down fast enough so they're going to concentrate all the guns onto the San Juan. They'll start up again soon. After that, I give it a couple of hours."

Ángel thought he was probably right. They stood together at the unpaved window watching the French activity until the guns were in position and the first cannonade thundered out towards the crumbling curtain wall. Ángel had spent so much time in battle that he was inured to the deafening sound of artillery, but this made him flinch and the man beside him, who had a chest wound and was heavily bandaged under his jacket, did the same.

"It doesn't feel right to be up here watching," he said, sounding almost apologetic. "I've never been this close to a battle but not fit to take part."

"I've never been seriously wounded before," Ángel said and he knew he sounded angry. "I'm as weak as a kitten, I can't use my left hand and my right arm aches if I hold a sword for more than two minutes. I'm useless."

His companion did not reply. There was nothing to say. The third officer disappeared back down the stairs. Ángel wondered if he was going back to his men. He did not look as though he was wounded. Ángel and his companion did not move but stood looking out over the rooftops of Tarragona which were becoming wreathed in black smoke, watching the French batter a breach in the San Juan curtain wall.

Chapter Seventeen

Bonnet had a surprisingly restful few days as the 30th was unexpectedly released from its position at the head of every action against the town. Instead, they had been given relatively easy sentry duty which gave them some time to recover. Bonnet had no idea if his comments to Suchet had contributed to this welcome change and did not care. It gave time for the men to rest and recuperate from minor injuries. His company was much depleted from the long weeks of the siege but those remaining were at least in better health and seemed eager for the fray.

On the evening before the storming began, he was surprised by the arrival of Bianca Ramos, who arrived in camp carrying a small bundle of possessions, escorted by a bewildered medical orderly. Bonnet greeted her warily, conscious of the astonished stares of his fellow officers and the men. Some of them would remember the Spanish woman from their time in the village but he had confided in nobody that he had met her again.

"I am sorry," Bianca said apologetically as Bonnet put her bundle in his small tent and seated her beside the camp fire. "They have been emptying out the hospital. The more seriously wounded have been sent with a convoy back to France and others have been sent back to their regiments."

"Have they closed it down?" Bonnet said in some surprise.

"They have left a surgeon and a few orderlies up there but they hope to use some of the buildings in the city for hospital provision if possible."

"If they're still standing," Bonnet said cynically and then remembered that he was speaking to a Spanish woman about a Spanish city. He winced internally and tried to think of a way to retrieve it but Bianca did not appear to notice.

"I could have remained, but the other women who worked there have gone back to their men. Dr Tellier will be working from a field hospital for the next few days until…anyway, he was concerned about leaving me there without him or Madame Savary."

"He was right. I was hoping we'd get this battle out of the way before turning to more personal matters, but I'm glad you'd the sense to come to me. Pierre was just about to cook my supper. Once we've eaten I'll introduce you around and make sure they know who you are and how they're to behave around you."

Bianca's thin face softened into a smile which made his pulse quicken. "I am sorry, Gabriel, I could give you no warning."

"That's all right. Where's Pierre? He was here two minutes ago." Bonnet glared around. His servant seemed to have vanished.

Bianca got up with a snort. "Just as well," she said. "I have tasted Pierre's attempt at cooking. It is surprising he does not poison you. Where is the food and your cooking pot? I will do it. That way I may be sure we will not die of his cooking."

Bonnet gave in and sat watching her as she bustled about. Within an hour she had made herself mistress of his fireside and his camp kit and he could not believe how much he was enjoying it. The meal was the usual tough beef and dry biscuit but he admitted that her way of slowly stewing it was a considerable improvement on Pierre's usual efforts.

His servant reappeared just as Bianca finished washing the pots, muttering an excuse about the pack mule needing attention. This particular pack mule was the most stolid animal in the army and required no tending apart from regular meals so Bonnet presumed that Pierre was simply trying to avoid either work or his Captain's new companion. Bianca seemed unimpressed with his excuses but she handed Pierre a mess tin with the remainder of the food and told him to wash it himself. Pierre's resentment was visible but Bonnet was utterly charmed.

When Pierre had taken himself off, Bonnet brought some of his precious supply of wine and handed her a cup. They sat opposite each other across the fire and he struggled for words, wondering dismally if he would ever feel comfortable enough with this or any woman, just to talk.

"This is a bit sudden," he said awkwardly. "But I'm glad you're here, Bianca. You've made yourself very much at home. I like that."

She sipped the wine. "I told you, Gabriel. I will take care of you. Though I do not think your servant likes me being here."

"He'll get used to it. He's a useless bastard, but he's not likely to give you any real trouble. If he's rude to you tell me and I'll deal with him."

"Thank you."

"I've spoken to Allard and Duclos and one or two of the others. Allard's servant is a good steady man, he'll keep an eye on you and if you need help while I'm not around, go to him and ask. I'd trust him ahead of Pierre."

"I am here to make your life better, Gabriel, not more difficult. You should not worry about me. Do you think they will take the town tomorrow?"

"Yes," Bonnet said briefly. "I'm sorry. They're your people, this must be hard for you."

"I do not like the thought of people dying, but Tarragona is not my city. I've only been there twice. I'm more worried about you. Is your wound…?"

"It's healed very well. You're a good nurse. If they get me again I'm going to tell them to bring me straight back here and avoid the army butchers."

"Try not to get hurt."

Bonnet took a deep breath, lost the ability to speak again and buried his face in the wine cup. He was desperately embarrassed. The woman opposite him studied him for a long moment, then seemed to come to a decision. She tossed back the rest of her wine, stood up and held out her hand for his cup. He finished his drink, his eyes on her face. Bianca held his gaze for a long moment then disappeared into the tent, dropping the flap. Bonnet's stomach knotted with nerves but he could hardly sit out here all night and he had an early start. He extinguished the dying fire, took a deep breath and ducked into the tent.

She was sitting upright on his bedroll under his blankets. The tent was small, with just enough space to sleep and store his kit. Bonaparte was known to dislike the use of tents for his army but many officers had acquired them unofficially, often looted from their enemies and Suchet did not seem to object. There were loose laces on the front flap and Bonnet took the time to tie them. When he turned back to her, her face was in shadow but he could see wide dark eyes studying him and he thought she was nervous too.

He shrugged out of his jacket and sat on a tiny folding stool to take off his boots and stockings.

"Bianca, we don't have to do this tonight. We can just sleep. I have to be awake early and you're probably tired."

"Do you not want me?"

There was a little tremor in her voice which told him how she was really feeling. He turned to look at her feeling ridiculous standing there in trousers and shirt, painfully aware of all his shortcomings.

"Of course I bloody want you, woman. I just don't want you to feel…"

"Then come to bed."

It was a clear instruction so he obeyed, stripping off his trousers and sliding quickly under the blankets. He was under no illusion that she had chosen to join him because she had been passionately attracted to him. He was a man approaching middle age with a slight paunch and an unpleasant scar and for much of his adult life, the sexual act had been a matter of commerce. He knew that Bianca had offered herself to him in return for his protection and because she had no wish to become a common prostitute in the army's tail. Such transactions were common and always gave the man the upper hand.

At the same time, he liked the girl and had a silly wish that she should like him too. He was afraid of making a fool of himself and it had not occurred to him until now that she might share his anxieties.

"Are you going to take off your clothes?"

Bonnet had got into bed with his shirt on and the thought froze him. "Are you?"

Wide brown eyes met his and Bonnet recognised embarrassment. "Do you wish me to? I am not…I do not think…"

Wisdom came to him from an unknown source. "Bianca, I think you're beautiful with a shift on or without. I think this is strange for both of us. Why don't we see how we both feel in a while?"

She smiled at him then, with real gratitude, and moved into his arms more easily. "Gabriel Bonnet, you are a very good man. I wish I was better at this."

"I wish I was too. Maybe we just need to practice."

It went far better than Bonnet had expected. She was shy but did not shrink from him. He decided to keep things very simple, but he could not resist kissing her. Most of his sexual experiences in recent years had been with prostitutes where his sole aim was to achieve satisfaction before the woman kicked him out to make way for another client. The thought that he could spend as much time as he wanted kissing and holding this woman made him slightly weak with longing. She seemed very happy for him to do so even after they had made love. She settled finally in the crook of his arm with her head on his shoulder and gave a little sigh which sounded surprisingly content.

"Are you warm enough? I can probably find another blanket."

"Gabriel, you are keeping me warm. Lie still, I am comfortable."

Bonnet twisted his head to look down at her. The dark hair was tousled and her face looked rosy and sleepy. "I can't remember the last time I went to sleep feeling this good."

"Nor can I," she said, surprising him. "When do you have to be up? Do you have everything you need? Is there something I should do to help you?"

He kissed her very gently on the tip of her nose. She had a very nice shaped nose.

"No, little bird. I'll be up before dawn. Stay here and keep warm. Pierre can do anything I need."

She rose anyway, emerging into the pale, early light as Pierre was lighting a fire, and took over the job of making coffee. Bonnet said little, aware of his servant's avid curiosity. When he was ready he kissed Bianca very gently and beckoned to Pierre to walk a little way with him on the pretext of giving him final instructions.

"You'll have noticed a change in my living arrangements, Pierre."

"Yes, Captain. Do you want me to get rid of her before you get back?"

"No, you scurvy bastard, I want you to be polite to her, she's staying. She'll help with my kit so you can show her around and explain what needs doing. But she's my girl not your maidservant so be civil and if I find you've so much as laid a finger on her, I'll fucking castrate you, are we clear?"

"Yes, sir." Pierre sounded sulky.

"Good, because I mean it." Gabriel turned and looked back to where Bianca stood watching them. He smiled and raised a hand and in response she blew him a kiss which made him blush. He turned away towards the trenches where his men were already beginning to assemble and thought how pleasant it was to have a woman to wave him off to battle, though he found himself wishing that he was not about to fight against Bianca's own countrymen.

By four o'clock in the afternoon there was a breach thirty feet wide in the curtain wall beside the San Juan and the Spanish guns along the front line had been silenced. A powder magazine had exploded during the artillery bombardment, completely wrecking the Cervantes Bastion at the far end of the Spanish line. Only the muskets still thundered defiance from the city walls. General Suchet made a brief assessment of the situation and, despite the narrowness of the breach, decided it was worth the risk. Gabriel Bonnet, waiting behind Colonel Lacasse at the head of the 30th légère, thought cynically that it was not of course Suchet who would have to lead the first storming parties over the rubble and into the city.

Three columns, each composed of four hundred men of the elite companies of the various regiments, waited in the closest trenches to the city walls; bayonets and swords slippery in sweating hands. Another thousand, led by General Habert waited in the foremost houses of the lower town while a force of five battalions under General Montmarie was positioned opposite the Rosario Gate out of range of the guns. If the assault succeeded, this column would advance to the gate to be admitted by the men already in the city.

The order was given at five o'clock and Lacasse led his storming party forward. The columns set off from different parts of the trenches, charging towards the breach at full speed. They could not avoid being within range of the Spanish muskets, but there were very few cannon left able to fire.

The intention had been for all three columns to arrive at the breach simultaneously but two of the columns, including the one led by Lacasse, found themselves briefly entangled with a spiky aloe hedge at the foot of the wall. It had been damaged in places but the section ahead of Bonnet was in excellent condition and surprisingly difficult to cut through.

The Spanish defenders greeted the first column with a solid wall of musketry fire, though only three cannon fired grape shot from the left of the bastion. As Bonnet's men approached they could see that a number of the first column were down but some seemed to be making their way into the breach already. Lacasse shouted an order and the 30th picked up their pace, scrambling over rubble and fallen masonry and into the narrow gap.

The muskets crashed again and Bonnet flinched as the man beside him gave a gurgle and fell. Bonnet glanced down then looked quickly away from the ruin of the soldier's head. He pushed forward, sword in hand, urging his men on. When attacking a defended position like this the worst possible tactic was to hang back, remaining within range of the muskets but separated from the enemy infantry. If his men could get into hand to hand combat with bayonets and swords it would be impossible for the Spanish to fire at them again.

Bonnet and his men were fiercely engaged within minutes. Two Spaniards scrambled over the stone towards him as he reached the top of the breach and Bonnet charged forward with a roar, swinging his sword. Beside him, Belmas drove his bayonet into one man's stomach while Bonnet cut the other across the upper body. Blood splashed onto his face and into one eye, partly blinding him. Bonnet swore and scrubbed at it with his sleeve. As soon as he could see again he charged on into the thick of the fight where men stood grappling like wrestlers, their bayonets locked together.

The air was filled with shouts and cries and the clash of steel on steel and over it all was the crash of gunfire although that was beginning to die out. Bonnet slashed his way through the press of men with single-minded savagery. His height and strength gave him an advantage in this kind of one on one combat. He had learned during his childhood on the streets of Paris, the art of bringing down an opponent by whatever means it took. He had always thought it useful not to be a gentleman in the middle of a bloody fight and when one of his opponents seemed inclined to stand and try conclusions with him he knocked the man's bayonet up with his sword and before the Spaniard could rally, floored him with a vicious kick to the knee which proved as effective as a sword thrust. Bonnet stabbed down once just to make sure and found himself at the head of his triumphant company at the summit of the breach.

Behind him he could hear the advance of General Habert's reserves, sweeping up and over the fallen men of both sides. This unexpected rush seemed to unnerve the Spanish troops. For the first time, with a moment to catch his breath, Bonnet realised that there were not as many manning the breach as he would have expected. Given that this was Suchet's only attack, he would have thought that Contreras would have packed the opening with his best troops but these men seemed unsure, looking behind them as much as ahead.

With a roar, Habert's troops came on and the Spanish defenders broke and began to run, leaping down the other side of the breach with no further attempt to stand. Bonnet lifted his sword, yelling encouragement to his men and the 30th followed him, ruthlessly cutting down the fleeing Spaniards. Some of the Spanish troops stumbled and fell in their haste to escape and the French bayonetted them on the ground then trampled over their bodies and swept down into the streets of Tarragona.

Once inside, Suchet's men separated into two sections. The first turned left, making for the Rosario gate to admit Montmarie's waiting troops. The other, headed by the 30th, turned right and began to clear the ramparts down to the ruins of the Cervantes Bastion. The Spanish melted away before them and those who tried to stand were slaughtered without mercy. Suchet's men had been waiting for this moment and Bonnet doubted that quarter would have been given even if the officers had tried to enforce it. They did not. Officers and men were caught up in the savagery of the fight, spurred on by the weeks of tedium and discomfort and the losses of friends and comrades in the various skirmishes for the outer works.

The rush into the town was brought up short at the second line of the defences. There was a broad street known as the Rambla which ran parallel to the walls and along it, the houses had been barricaded. Barrels filled with rocks and stones had been used to block every street and alleyway between the houses to form a solid inner fortification. It was surprisingly well constructed and manned along its length with Spanish troops. The men fleeing from the breach leaped over the barricades to join their comrades and most of them paused to reload their muskets before turning to join the defence.

As the muskets began to fire on the approaching French troops, Bonnet yelled at his men to halt and was faintly surprised when they obeyed him. He stood for a moment scanning the barricades and thought briefly how stupid it was that the Spanish had chosen to make their stand here rather than at the far more defensible walls they had just fled from. He hated this kind of prolonged, bloody street fighting but he knew from experience that it still paid to use his brain and after a minute he could see the vulnerable point; a wider alleyway where the barrels were stretched thinly and there were too few muskets positioned.

Bonnet bellowed to his men to follow, charging towards his target. His company followed him and seeing their concerted attack, some of the other men of the 30th broke away from the general mêlée and raced after them. Bonnet set a dozen men to firing their muskets at the upper windows of the two houses on either side of the alley, which may not have killed many Spaniards, but did keep them from shooting down at his impromptu storming party.

Leading from the front he dashed towards the barrels. The Spanish defenders stood ready with muskets. They appeared panicked by Bonnet's systematic attack and fired too soon but several of Bonnet's men were hit and one ball went so close to him that it grazed the sleeve of his jacket.

Arriving at the barricade, Bonnet and his men stabbed over it at the Spaniards who leaped back out of range. Belmas dropped his shoulder to one of the barrels and heaved, but it was enormously heavy and a Spanish infantryman saw his chance and dashed forward, stabbing down. Bonnet shouted a warning and struck the bayonet up with his sword, allowing Belmas to scramble backwards out of sight. The Spaniards were loading again and Bonnet swore and dived out of reach around the corner of the house, taking care not to get too close to the downstairs window where more defenders stood ready. Contreras' makeshift fortress was proving exasperatingly effective.

"Sir, get out of the way."

It was Lieutenant Allard and Bonnet turned to look, saw what was happening and sprang back, calling to his men. Allard and Duclos had set up a small column of men, five wide and four deep, with muskets at the ready. The Spanish had fired and were reloading again. Bonnet bellowed for his men to get out of the way and Allard called the order.

"Fire."

The first row fired at the Spaniards who dodged down behind the barrels. Allard called another order and the men peeled away and went to the back of the column to reload.

"Fire."

The second row fired. Bonnet was temporarily stunned at the simple brilliance of the ploy and then roused himself to play his part.

"Belmas, Dupont. Call up your men. Keep them low, below the muskets. Let's get these barrels over."

Allard's column kept up a steady rolling fire which made it impossible for the Spanish troops to stand up behind the barrels. Bonnet led a dozen men forward, bent low under musket fire from either side. On his command they put their shoulders to the weighty barricade and heaved. It was astonishing how heavy they were, but with the Spanish kept at bay by Allard's muskets, the men had time to put their entire weight behind it. Bonnet joined them, shoving as hard as he could.

There was something very satisfying about hearing his junior officer's calm voice calling the shots. The rolling fire was devastatingly effective and one of the Spaniards brave enough to make the attempt to reach over the top of the barrel with his bayonet fell back with a scream of pain. Bonnet heaved again and felt, unexpectedly, the barrel tilt.

"Keep going," he roared and as his men redoubled their efforts, Bonnet slid higher up the barrel, wedging his feet against a raised cobblestone and pushing with all his might. He was dangerously exposed to a musket ball from either side now and he heard Duclos yell at them to keep their fire high, well above his head. But the barrel was shifting, beyond the point of no return and then with a huge crash it fell.

The Spaniards jumped back in alarm as the structure toppled. As it hit the ground the wood split and burst, spilling huge chunks of broken stone out onto the pavement. Bonnet was caught off balance and fell backwards onto the ground, hitting his head painfully on one of the rocks. For a terrifying moment he was stretched out helpless and he waited for the stabbing agony of a Spanish bayonet but it did not come. The Spaniards had broken and fled down the alleyway without looking back.

A hand reached out and hauled Bonnet to his feet. Bonnet saw the face of young Duclos, grinning broadly.

"Are you all right, sir?"

"No, I've hurt my head and my arse, but who cares? That was fucking brilliant boys, you'll get my commendation for what it's worth. Come on, let's get after them."

The French troops poured into the alleyway and the barricade was overrun. Spanish troops manning the other barrels were shot down from behind or bayonetted as they tried to escape and the French poured into the houses, cutting down the defenders with ruthless efficiency.

The streets were rapidly filling up with French troops and Bonnet realised that the Rosario Gate must be open and that the reserves were in. The fight was over and Suchet's men were masters of the town. Bonnet paused, leaning against an iron balustrade outside one of the houses and took a few deep breaths, wondering if he had cracked a rib as he fell onto the broken masonry.

He had no idea where Lacasse had gone, which was a relief because if he could not find him, he could not receive any orders. Bonnet decided that he had earned a few minutes respite. He felt into his pocket for his flask and took a long satisfying swig of a very good brandy he had looted a month ago.

Around him the noise level rose to a cacophony as the French troops went through the town, chasing down Spanish soldiers. Bonnet wondered at what point the officers would intervene and insist on prisoners being taken. He hoped it would be soon so that he would not personally have to intervene to prevent wholesale slaughter but he decided sadly that he would not put money on it. Sometimes the officers were as excitable as the men and he supposed that in a moment he would have to put his flask away and go and round up the men of the 30th légère. It was exasperating.

He took one more long drink and was just stoppering his flask, ready to go in search of his men, when somewhere, in a house nearby, a woman screamed.

***

Ángel watched the fighting from the top of the bell tower until it became clear that the Spanish defence had crumbled. His companion had left some time earlier, though Ángel did not know if it was because he could not bear to watch any more of if he had some mad idea of rejoining his battalion. Ángel hoped it was the former. He had no idea what would happen to the wounded when the French broke into the Cathedral, but he thought their chances were probably better here than out on the streets where the French soldiers were slaughtering every Spaniard they found.

It was growing late. The French had overrun the city with terrifying speed. Eventually, reluctantly, Ángel moved away from his window. On the stairs he hesitated. He suspected that he was about to descend into chaos. Strangely nobody had climbed the stairs and he wondered suddenly what would happen if he remained up here. Would he be found days later, dying of hunger and thirst but still safe from the French troops who could not be bothered to climb the steep, winding staircase?

Ángel decided that a combination of pain and fear were affecting his brain and brought himself firmly under control. He descended carefully and was immediately assailed by the heat and the noise and the smell of the army hospital. There were other sounds too, shouted orders and the sound of running feet. Army boots echoed loudly on the stone flags of the nave and Ángel sped up, wondering what was happening. At the arched doorway at the bottom of the stairs he stopped, looking around him, appalled.

There were troops in the cathedral, clustering round the barred main doors and spread around the vast nave. Groups of men guarded each doorway. The medical staff, looking white and frightened, were moving those patients who could be moved into the shelter of some of the smaller chapels. Ángel thought furiously that it would make it much easier for the French to slaughter them when they broke in.

He strode down the aisle, forgetting his weakness in a rush of blind anger, and then stopped on the approach to the door when he realised that one of the men was Óscar García . He was filthy, his uniform black with smoke and his hair coming loose from the neat black ribbon he always wore. The young face was dirty and Ángel could see tracks of tears on his cheeks.

García saw him and ran towards him. "Where have you been? I've been looking for you everywhere."

"I went up to the tower to see what was happening. García, this is madness, what are these men doing here? The wounded might have been safe. Often they spare the hospitals. But if you turn this place into a fortress they will batter down the doors and slaughter them. Or burn it down. Can you not hear what is happening out there?"

"I have seen what is happening out there," García said fiercely and suddenly Ángel understood.

"The General," he said quickly. "Óscar, where is General Contreras?"

"He is either dead or wounded. In which case, he is a prisoner. I do not know which. We were overrun, Captain. The men…some of them fought bravely but too many did not stand. They fled and the French cut them down."

"I know. But the General?"

"He put himself at the head of the Savoia. It was our last undamaged regiment. He fought so bravely, but it was hopeless. He was cut down by the bayonets. He may be dead. I think he may be dead."

"Oh God." Ángel felt a wave of dizziness and fought it back furiously, angry with his own weakness. "What of the others?"

"General Courten tried to lead some of the men out by the Barcelona Gate but they had troops out there waiting. Some of them ran back into the city. Others scattered and ran up into the hills. I think General Velasco did that; I've no idea if he made it. Some of them ran to the beach. The British are sending boats in as far as they can and the men stripped off and tried to swim out. But there was French cavalry. They rode them down on the beach, slaughtered them. I don't know how many survived."

García was crying and Ángel could feel tears wet on his own cheeks. He could not believe that Contreras had gone. These past weeks he had found his General difficult and at times had been furious with him, but the thought of him bayonetted in the street trying to defend the city he had never wanted to command broke his heart.

"Lieutenant García."

Ángel turned. He recognised the commander of the troops now as Colonel José González, Governor of the city and the brother of the absent Marquis of Campoverde. Ángel had heard, over the past days, what the troops were saying about Campoverde. He wondered if González had heard them too and if it had affected his decision to make this desperate last stand. Ángel understood the sentiment but was appalled at what it might mean to the wounded and helpless men in the cathedral.

González approached and stopped at the sight of Ángel. Ángel drew himself painfully into a salute. It was meaningless, but it felt important that even in his weakened state, he behave as a soldier. González returned the salute.

"Captain Cortez, I had forgotten you were a patient. I am sorry about General Contreras."

"As am I, sir."

"García, my men and I will hold the door for as long as possible. When they break in we will try to force our way through to make our escape. I have designated fifty men to form a second line. They are under your command."

"Yes, sir."

"Fifty men?" Ángel said incredulously. "He's barely twenty-one and you're setting him up to be slaughtered…"

"There's nobody else," García snapped and Ángel looked at him in astonishment then looked around. There were no other officers present.

"There's no one else, Ángel," García said, more quietly. "It's all right. I'm ready to do my duty."

Ángel felt sick. He wanted to shout out in protest. He also wanted to elbow García to one side and take command but it would be a ridiculous thing to do. He was still in great pain and shaky on his feet and the men would quickly realise that he could not possibly fight a battle. After a long moment, he said quietly:

"I cannot lead men in my condition, García. But I ask that you allow me to stand beside you. I would rather that, than…"

"Of course," García said warmly. "Captain, I'd be honoured."

They waited inside the huge wooden doors, hearing the rising sounds of the city being sacked and the people dying in the streets. It did not take long for French troops to reach the cathedral door and realise that it was barred against them. Ángel could hear them battering at the door, yelling insults. He suspected that some of them had already begun looting the taverns and wine shops. It would be impossible, once they broke in, to stop them killing the wounded men.

The impasse seemed to go on forever. The huge doors of the cathedral were designed to withstand a siege and without artillery the French were never going to break them down. They were also never going to give up and Ángel thought that the long wait, while both sides screamed threats and defiance, was probably enraging the French more. He wondered if there was an officer out there or if they were going to be faced by an undisciplined mob of drunken soldiers.

There was a sound from within the cathedral and a soldier appeared from the steep steps to the bell tower, gabbling the words in his panic. It took Ángel a moment to understand him and then he wondered with sick misery why he had not thought of it himself. He looked at García and saw his own resignation in the younger man's dark eyes. García took a deep breath and turned to the General.

"If they set fire to the doors, every man here will burn to death. We cannot allow that, sir. We must open the doors and take the fight to them."

González nodded. "Of course. Call the men in from the rear doors, Lieutenant, we will make a stand in the square."

Ángel watched as González organised his men. Most of them had ammunition left and Ángel imagined the first line of drunken Frenchmen outside the Cathedral were in for an unpleasant shock. After that it would be over very quickly. He wondered if the Governor had considered surrendering but decided that it was too late for that. The first troops over the breaches, still sober and supervised by their officers would probably have taken prisoners. By now, these men were out of control.

González gave the order and two men ran forward to lift the heavy bar free. Ángel's heart was hammering in his breast, so loudly that he wondered if García could hear it. He glanced at the younger man's face and wished suddenly that he had made more effort to get to know him. He had dismissed García as a callow, inexperienced boy but he had displayed extraordinary courage over these past days. He was displaying it now, his face pale and set but very calm. Only the white knuckled grip on the hilt of his sword gave away his tension.

"Captain Cortez?"

"Yes?"

"I know you wish to fight and I know that you are willing to die in the service of Spain. But you are not fit for battle and it may be that you can speak for the wounded once we are…once they break in. It would be a service to me if you would consider returning to your place."

Ángel opened his mouth to utter a stinging reproof and managed to close it again. He wanted to say that it would make absolutely no difference whether he died here, with a sword in his hand or was stabbed to death on his pallet in the St Francis Chapel, but there was no time for an argument and he did not want the last words he said to García to be angry.

"If that is what you wish."

"It is." The men had removed the bar and were beginning to drag open the heavy wooden doors. They creaked ominously and the roar of the French troops became louder. García looked round and managed a gallant attempt at a smile. "Thank you. For this and for everything. If you survive, will you write to my father? Tell him…oh you will know what to say."

"I will tell him that his son died a hero of Spain," Ángel said. His voice was thick with tears and he knew he needed to move away before he began to cry openly. Sheathing his sword, since he was not strong enough to use it properly, he put his hand on García's shoulder for a moment then turned and made his way back up the aisle.

He had not reached the chapel when there was a thunderous crash of muskets, made louder by the echoing vastness of the cathedral. It was followed almost immediately by another volley from González' second line. After that, there was no more shooting, just the clash of steel on steel, the cries of wounded and dying men and the atavistic roar of the French soldiers.

Somewhere in the distance Ángel could hear muskets firing and the screams of the people of Tarragona as the French hunted them through the streets of their city. Ángel stood at the arched doorway of the little chapel and realised there were tears coursing down his cheeks. It must be over by now. In a moment the French would enter the building and begin the systematic slaughter of the wounded men. His choice now had nothing to do with García, who was already dead in the sunlit square of the Pla de la Seu.

Ángel looked down at his bandaged, splinted left hand and remembered that only yesterday he had still cared that he might never regain the use of it. He had no idea what he had done with his sling so he tucked his hand inside his coat for support then drew his sword again with his right hand. His arm ached badly and he was more tired than he had ever been in his life, but it did not matter. It would be over soon.

Ángel turned and walked back down the aisle towards the wide open doors. There were bodies strewn across the stone flagged floor and out onto the broad steps beyond and he could see pools of blood. They were dead, all three hundred men who had stood with González in a last desperate defence: blood pooled beneath the bodies, obscenely bright in the sunlight. There were French bodies among them, mown down by those two fearsome volleys, but after that the Spaniards had been massacred.

At the foot of the steps two Italian infantrymen were stabbing down with bayonets, finishing off a man on the ground. Ángel looked away quickly in case it was García. He walked to the top of the steps and waited. The French were milling about aimlessly. Some of them had already left in search of more drink, plunder and women. Others moved among the bodies, prodding them with their feet for signs of life. Several more looked up at the doors of the Cathedral, shading their eyes. At the sight of Ángel there was a murmur and then some of them began to move, stepping over the men they had killed in order to kill again. Ángel stood, his sword in his hand, ready to die.

As the first Frenchman reached the top of the steps, Ángel lifted his sword. It felt enormously heavy, dragging on his injured arm, but these men were visibly drunk and he thought he might kill one of them, possibly both, before the rest of the approaching mob overwhelmed him. He fell instinctively into a fencing stance. The first man was within two blades' length of his sword when an almighty roar from his left startled him. He glanced sideways and a sword struck his with brutal force, knocking it from his hand so that it hit the stone steps with a ringing sound. The sword was at Ángel's throat and Ángel closed his eyes, took a deep breath and waited for the blow.

"Stand still, don't move and for fuck's sake do not speak," a familiar voice said in Spanish. "It would fucking well be you again, wouldn't it? As if this day could get any worse."

Ángel opened his eyes, unable to believe what he had heard. The big Frenchman was beside him on the steps. He was dirty, unshaven and had blood in his hair. He gave Ángel a brief, unsympathetic glare, moved his sword and put the point at the chest of one of the approaching infantrymen. Without taking his eyes from the man he lifted his foot and booted the second man so hard in the gut that he fell backwards down the steps, knocking over several other men on his way.

"Halt, you miserable drunken bastards. The next one to make a move up these steps gets a sword in the gut or a pistol shot in the face, whichever one I feel like giving out first. Where's your officer? Who commands this fucking rabble?"

There was no reply. An uneasy silence had fallen over the men and they were looking around as if expecting an officer to materialise out of thin air. It did not happen, but instead, running footsteps sounded from the back of the Cathedral and two columns of men appeared, each led by a young officer. To Ángel's surprise and relief they appeared sober.

"Allard, Duclos. What's going on?"

"No other doors are breached, sir. We've set guards on all of them and six men in the cloister garden."

"Good. Duclos, get yourself in there, round up the Spanish doctors and tell them they'll be joined in fifteen minutes by some of their French counterparts and they're to treat all wounded coming in. You lot…" The Frenchman's voice dripped with disgust. "You're a bunch of drunken scum and you've done enough here. This is a hospital, there are wounded men in here and you're not slaughtering them. Get the fuck out of here and find another wine bottle before I get bored and start shooting. Move!"

The men were already backing up. Ángel suspected that it was not because of his rank but because he looked like a man willing to follow through on his threats without turning a hair and he had troops to back him up.

As the attackers melted away, the Frenchman turned to give orders for securing the hospital and protecting the wounded and Ángel, released from his temporary paralysis, realised that he needed to see what he could not bear to look at minutes before. Ignoring the French he bounded down the steps among the bodies of Gonzales' men. He could not see García. Bending, he hauled at men lying on their front, men lying on top of others, peering into the dead faces of men he did not know. He was sweating with pain and panting with effort: his legs trembling with the unaccustomed activity, but he had to know for sure.

He found Gonzales at the bottom of the steps and the sight broke what was left of his composure. The Governor had been bayonetted; stabbed over and over again so that his entire uniform was soaked in blood. Somebody had ripped away the medals he had worn on his jacket, the gold lace epaulettes and the gold buttons. His sword was missing. Worst of all, they had cut off several of his fingers to get at the rings he habitually wore.

Ángel felt his legs give way. He dropped to his knees on the pavement and vomited painfully, no longer able to keep his feet. In his mind he could imagine Contreras lying somewhere in a street in similar condition. It had been Ángel's duty to protect him and if necessary to die at his side and he was bitterly ashamed that had not been there.

A hand appeared before his face, holding out a tarnished silver flask. "Drink it," the French officer's voice said. "Take a swig and let's get you up before the next drunken mob comes past and decides to check the value of that ring you're wearing."

Ángel took the flask and drank. "You may take the ring, I do not care."

"I don't want the fucking ring, Spaniard. What I want is for this to be over, so I can get a wash, a shave, a meal and a peaceful hour with my new girlfriend. Unfortunately I can see that's not going to happen any time soon. Come on, up with you and back inside the hospital. My men will do sentry duty, your wounded will be safe enough."

Ángel allowed the man to haul him to his feet. He returned the flask. The Frenchman drank then slipped it back into his pocket. He nodded at González. "Who was he? Your commanding officer?"

"No. It is Governor González, the brother of the Marquis of Campoverde."

"Really? He gave a better account of himself than his bloody brother then. Brave man. I'll get a couple of my men to move him, they can lay him out in the cloister garden. We're a long way from burials yet, but General Suchet will want him buried properly."

The Frenchman turned away. Ángel caught his arm. "Wait. There is another. A young officer…he and I were aides de camp to General Contreras. He must be here somewhere. He should not lie here for flies to feed off, he should be buried alongside his General."

"That might be difficult, given that Contreras is still alive."

Ángel stared at him in astonishment. "I was told that he was dead."

"Well he's not. He was wounded though and he's a prisoner. Was this young officer a friend of yours?"

"Yes," Ángel said. He was not sure that it was true, but it ought to have been.

"All right, come on, we'll find him. After that, I want you back in that hospital and if I see you on the streets again I'm going to shoot you to spare myself the trouble of saving your fucking life every five minutes. I've got enough to do."

It was easier with the Frenchman to do the moving and lifting and they found García within minutes. He lay sprawled on the steps with his head pointing downwards and two other bodies on top of him. His fingers were still clutched reflexively around the hilt of his sword and he was bloody from a huge gash across his chest which had ripped open his uniform jacket. As with Gonzales, they had taken anything that might have been of value. García's rings had gone as had the saint's medallion he usually wore tucked inside his shirt. His rings must have been easy to remove because the fingers were intact.

Ángel knelt beside the body and lifted García's head into his lap awkwardly with one hand. He pushed the dark hair off his face and wiped away a smear of blood.

"I am sorry," he whispered. "But you see, I have survived to do as you asked. I will tell them how bravely you died, my friend, and that…"

The roar of the Frenchman's voice interrupted him. "Pascal, Delain. Get your lazy arses down here. We've got a live one."

Two men broke away from the group guarding the door and ran lightly down the steps. Ángel froze, staring down at García's lifeless body. He was still warm, but it had been less than twenty minutes since González had led his final, suicidal charge. It had not occurred to Ángel that anybody could survive it, but now that he looked properly he could see that the younger man's chest rose and fell very slightly. He was breathing.

"Oh my God. He lives."

"For now. Don't try to help lift him or you'll both end up at the bottom of the steps: look at the state of you. Pascal, get him in there and get a doctor to look at him. You – what's your name?"

"Cortez. Captain Don Ángel…"

"Cortez, he's your responsibility, I've other things to do. They won't have many nurses or orderlies, half of them will have run. Look after him."

"I give you my word." Ángel got up painfully and took a deep breath. "I owe you my life, Captain."

The Frenchman cut off his speech ruthlessly. "Twice, actually. Don't expect me to do it a third time."

He was gone before Ángel had a chance to think of a suitably caustic reply.

Chapter Eighteen

Hugh could not believe the speed with which the French overran the city of Tarragona. After weeks of delay and discussion and anxious speculation about how relief might be managed, and what part the Royal Navy might play, it was over in a few hours and the navy's only part was to watch helplessly and rescue those that they could.

The constant thunder of the French breaching batteries punctuated the entire day from when it began at dawn. Codrington gave orders that all boats were to be ready to launch and Hugh chose his crew for each boat with care and then summoned his servant and Bosun Geordie Armstrong to his cabin.

"I wanted to speak to you about tonight, Miles, because it's likely I'll be spending the night in one of the boats again. We think they'll storm the town today and if they do, we'll be trying to get as many of the garrison off as possible. I can't tell you where or how, it'll be a matter of making decisions as events unfold. Bosun, I'm leaving Lieutenant Paisley in command of the ship but I'll need you and the Master to be alert and aware of conditions if the weather suddenly changes."

"Aye, sir, we'll be ready."

Hugh turned his gaze to Miles. He could see by the boy's thoughtful expression that his servant was considering how best to put his case. Hugh was careful not to smile. Miles was very conscious of his dignity.

"Miles, you're to stay here. I know you want to come. I know you've the courage and I know last time you managed the oar very well for your age, but I need you to give me your word of honour that you won't try to sneak aboard one of the boats. We'll need every inch of space aboard every boat for one thing. For another, when it comes to hauling half-drowned men and possibly women and children out of the sea, we need grown men. If you take up a space and aren't yet strong enough or tall enough to do what needs to be done, you'll put lives at risk. Will you give me your word?"

Miles' expression had turned mutinous which Hugh knew meant that he had won. The boy gave his word in grudging tones and Hugh avoided Armstrong's gaze because he knew it would make them both laugh.

"I do have work for you, though. I've spoken to the purser and told him he's to open his stores to the refugees. They'll be cold and wet and possibly injured and they'll need space to rest and dry clothing. I'm putting you in charge of that. As they come aboard, you can find out their needs and see that they're supplied. Young Lewis will act as your second in command. Can you do that?"

Miles' expression had changed ludicrously and his eyes were shining. "Yes sir."

"Excellent. I suggest you station yourself on the poop deck. You might want to spend some time today touring the ship working out where the hell we can find space to put them. It will only be for a short time until we can drop them off further up the coast. And try to get some rest, I suspect we'll all be up all night. Off you go."

When Miles had gone, Hugh let his face relax into a grin and Armstrong returned it. "That's a stroke of genius, Captain, he'll love it. A bit young for the responsibility mind, but I think he'll rise to the challenge."

"He'll come to you if he's struggling, he's on good terms with you now," Hugh said. "I wondered if you'd think I'm mad, but I had to find him something to do or he'll be working out ways to get around my orders. I swear to God I've never had a ship's boy quite like him."

Armstrong laughed. "They're not common, though I remember a lad who served on the *Hera* for a couple of years with me. Most awkward young bastard I ever met in my life, but he was a good seaman and turned out well in the end."

"Officer material?"

"Oh definitely. He shouldn't have been there mind, he'd been illegally pressed. Captain Dalton was a bad old bugger but he got his comeuppance in the end."

"Kicked out, wasn't he?" Hugh said, a vague memory stirring.

"That's right, sir. Partly on the word of yon lad, though there was evidence of peculation and fraud as well. I heard he drank himself to death."

"Best thing he could do," Hugh said, getting up. "I might take my own advice and lie down for an hour. Not that I'll get much sleep with that racket going on. What happened to the boy?"

"He became a petty officer. Transferred to the *Triumphant* and fought at the Nile. The navy wasn't for him, but he joined the army later and did very well. We rather adopted him, me and Janet, and it broke our hearts when he left but he's kept in touch…"

"The *Triumphant*?" Hugh said in surprise. "I've a friend who spent some time in the navy in similar circumstances. He served on the *Triumphant*. Name of Van Daan."

Armstrong's weathered face cracked into a broad smile. "Well, well," he said. "I must tell Janet of it, she'll be that pleased. Aye, that's the lad."

Hugh was laughing. "I wish I had more time right now, but when this fiasco is over, Bosun, you and I will share a drink or two and swap stories about Paul van Daan."

"I'll look forward to it, Captain. And don't worry about Randall. After two years spent trying to stop that boy killing himself or somebody else, I can manage young Miles."

"I believe you," Hugh said with feeling, and went in search of an hour's sleep.

It was the *Invincible*, anchored out to the westward end of the squadron which raised the alarm, as the French began to gather in the trenches. Every boat was launched from every ship, carrying what weapons they could. The launches were joined by the Spanish gunboats, now temporarily commanded by a midshipman with an English crew. It was obvious to Hugh that every captain had been waiting on tenterhooks for the order and the boats were on their way towards the shore within the hour.

It should have been enough but it was not. From his gig, Hugh could only watch, appalled at the speed with which the French overwhelmed the Spanish defenders. At this distance it was impossible to see the detail of individual fighting but it seemed to him that the Spanish put up only a token resistance before being swept away.

It was still light, with the long summer evenings, and there was activity along the beaches. One or two of the gunboats made an attempt to annoy the French with longer range artillery but it was quickly clear that there was no way to mount an effective bombardment from the sea without hitting the Spanish troops or townspeople. Hugh ordered his six boats to move in as close as possible to the shore. Some Spanish troops were beginning to arrive on the beach and Codrington gave the order to his boats to row in and pick them up. Hugh signalled over to Durrell who was in command of the launch which was the largest of the *Iris'* boats, then gave the order to his coxswain to follow the *Blake's* boats in.

French cavalry were arriving on the low dunes above the beach long before the boats were close to the shore. At the same time the French appeared to notice the navy activity and began firing muskets down onto the boats. Codrington signalled for several of the gunboats to direct their fire back up to the city walls. Neither side could be said to have done much damage but it kept the French busy for a time.

On the beach, more and more Spanish troops were arriving, racing down to the edge of the surf and waving frantically to the approaching boats. Hugh kept his eyes on them as his gig cut through the surf, pulling ahead of the bigger, slower boats. It was not until movement above the beach caught his eye that Hugh realised they were rowing into danger.

"Hold her hard!" he yelled. "Muskets on the dunes. We need to stay out of range."

Alongside him other boats were coming to an abrupt stop. The Spanish troops were yelling, begging them to continue. Behind them, Hugh felt his stomach lurch as he watched the steady advance of the French cavalry.

He heard a yell and looked across to see Codrington on his feet, bellowing at the Spaniards. Having gained their attention he was waving his arms, pantomiming a swimming movement. In different circumstances, Hugh would have found his friend's performance hysterically funny and would have been waiting for Codrington to overreach himself and fall overboard but there was nothing remotely amusing about this situation.

Durrell had caught the idea and was up as well, shouting in Spanish at the men to swim. Already the Spaniards were catching on and beginning to strip off coats and kick off shoes and boots. Those most confident in the water were splashing through the shallows and beginning to pull out towards the boats with strong strokes when abruptly the muskets stopped firing and the cavalry charged.

The sound of hooves thundering towards them galvanised the troops on the beach into action. More and more of them hurled themselves into the sea. Some of them were clearly not swimmers and were quickly struggling. Others had not removed their heavy uniform and were being dragged down into the choppy waters. Hugh realised he was gripping the edge of the boat so tightly it hurt his hands. Some of his crew were shouting encouragement and advice to the swimmers in a variety of languages.

The first and fastest swimmers were beginning to reach the boats. Hugh concentrated on hauling them in and getting them seated in the most effective way to fill the boat to maximum capacity. The task kept his attention away from the beach where the cavalry rode through the troops slashing right and left with lethal effect. The sand was littered with the bodies of dead and dying men and their cries filled the air. It was brutal and heartrending and Hugh could not bear it.

There was nothing to be done for the men left behind except pray that eventually the over-excited cavalry would calm down enough to accept their surrender. Hugh saw several men with their hands raised in capitulation cut down savagely. When his gig could carry no more, he gave the order and the oarsmen rowed strongly, cutting through the water cleanly.

Ahead, the hull of the *Iris* loomed above them and men waited with ladders and ropes to get the Spanish troops aboard. Some of them were already wounded and had to be hauled up, but Armstrong was visible at the rail directing operations and the transfer was achieved smoothly and at remarkable speed. The moment the last fugitive left the boat, Hugh gave the order to return.

The cavalry was still milling about on the beach but with less purpose now, and the water was full of men swimming out towards the ships. Some of them were visibly struggling and Hugh gave a shout to aim for one man whose exhaustion had got the better of him. He went under twice and by the time Hugh's men dragged him up into the boat he was coughing and vomiting salt water, but he was alive.

They picked up men as they went and the boat was packed full long before they drew close to the shore. Looking around as the gig made its second return to the *Iris*, Hugh could see a lot of men treading water, waiting for the boats to return and he thanked God that they seemed to have calmed down enough to use their common sense. The sea was relatively flat in the mild evening air and there was no reason that they could not save all of these men.

On the third trip, he passed two men floating face down in the water. Hugh gave orders to leave them and concentrate on those who were obviously living. The cavalry had finally been called to order and in the distance Hugh could see a huddle of Spanish prisoners who had survived the slaughter, being led away. He wondered if any of the prone figures scattered on the beach were still alive. There were still a lot of men in the water. Hugh passed three packed boats heading back to the *Wren* and from another, Captain Charles Adam of the *Invincible* gave a weary grin and a nonchalant salute, which Hugh returned.

As the boats drew closer, Hugh concentrated once again on picking up men and helping them into the boat. They were shivering from cold and shock and some of them had bloody wounds from cavalry sabres, but these were the lucky ones. Full once again, they came about and were pulling strongly towards the *Iris* when a yell made Hugh turn. He called to his coxswain.

"Fletcher, wait. Turn about, and hold her steady."

As Hugh's boat turned back towards the shore he could see that a single cavalryman remained there. Hugh could not make out details from this distance but thought that he seemed to be an officer. He was standing with his horse up to its knees in the surf looking out at the boats. There was an air of concentration about him.

As Hugh watched, the officer drew his sabre and urged his horse further into the water. Hugh realised that the shout he had heard had come from his first officer. Durrell's launch was on its way back from unloading its latest complement of Spanish troops and facing the shore, he had realised before Hugh what the officer was about to do.

The horse waded through the surf towards the nearest men in the water and the officer held his sabre raised. Hugh could not quite believe it. The rest of the French cavalry had gone and this was an act of deliberate brutality which shocked him. He hesitated for a moment, but knew immediately that he could not go back to the shore with a boat full of men. Looking across at the launch, he saw Durrell at the stern. His First Lieutenant's eyes were fixed on the officer and Hugh decided that he could safely leave it in Durrell's hands.

He had almost reached the ship when he heard the first shot and, leaving it to his men to tie up and hand up the exhausted Spaniards into Armstrong's capable hands, Hugh twisted in the boat and looked back towards the beach. Durrell had taken his launch in close and his three marines were on their feet, muskets trained on the officer. Durrell called another order and one of the marines fired again. The shot hit the water close to the swimming horse and it squealed and thrashed about. The cavalry officer was no longer aiming his sabre at the Spaniards. All his attention was focused on managing the terrified horse as he urged it back towards the shore.

As the horse found its feet in the shallows, Durrell called another shot. It went nowhere near the horse but the noise panicked it into rearing up, throwing the officer into the water with an enormous splash. The horse, relieved of its irritating burden, took off at a gallop up the beach, disappearing over the dunes just as the officer struggled to his feet. He had lost his hat and the last rays of the fast sinking sun glinted off red hair. The man turned to glare out at the launch.

White's boats had come back for a final run and were picking up the last of the men in the sea. Durrell still stood, a tall figure in the bow of the launch, his face utterly without expression as he looked out at the man dripping in the water.

"Fire," he said and three muskets exploded at once. None of them hit their target; the muskets had little accuracy at that distance, but they came close enough to panic the officer. He took off at a clumsy run up the beach, spraying droplets as he went. Durrell watched him until he was out of sight then turned, surveying the sea around him to ensure nobody had been missed. As he resumed his seat, Hugh heard the crew of the launch erupt into cheers, whoops and laughter. Above Hugh, along the rail of the *Iris*, the applause was echoed back by the Bosun and the watching men.

"That'll teach that French bastard to piss off our first officer," one of the oarsmen said with deep satisfaction. Hugh grinned.

"Let's just hope the fella learns from it, Barnes. I wonder how long it'll take him to find his horse? Right, tie up and up you get. I want a quick change over to the relief crew and you can all eat and sleep. You might be needed again later, it could be a long night. Those are not going to be the only fugitives from Tarragona."

***

The night seemed endless to the wounded men who waited in the cathedral listening to the destruction of Tarragona. Those who remained unconscious were fortunate. Sleep was impossible for the rest. The air was filled with the anguished sounds of terror as the French soldiers ran riot through the city and the men, women and children of the town fled before them, tried to hide and too often died.

Ángel sat beside García. The younger man had awoken briefly when the surgeon came to treat his wounds but then fell into a restless doze. He had four bayonet wounds, any of which would have been fatal if they had been an inch or two either side but he was alive and in better condition than Ángel had expected. The surgeon dressed the wounds and bled him then hurried away to his other patients leaving García in Ángel's care. Ángel was glad. He did not trust the surgeon and could not forget the man's determined efforts to amputate his hand against his wishes. García had prevented that and Ángel spent several hours hovering over his companion like an irritable terrier ready to snap at any further attempt to disturb him.

News came in with each new admission to the hospital and the news was terrible. The Spanish garrison had either been slaughtered or had fled however they could. Some had tried to escape through the Barcelona Gate but had been intercepted and had scattered. Those who were chased back along the shore were ridden down by French cavalry though Ángel's spirits were a little lifted to hear that several hundred of them had escaped in the boats of the Royal Navy.

Through the city, small groups of Spanish troops made a desperate attempt to resist in houses and public buildings but they were too few and were either killed or rounded up and marched out as prisoners. Many surrendered with little resistance and after the initial bloodlust of battle, most French troops gave quarter to men in uniform and took prisoners.

No such quarter was given to the terrified civilians. Throughout the night, drunken troops battered down doors, set fire to houses and dragged people on to the streets. Men were murdered without excuse, woman were raped and often killed afterwards and children were hunted for sport. Everything portable was stolen and everything else was smashed and destroyed. Some of the French officers did their best to stem the tide of slaughter and put themselves at risk in the process. Others refused to become involved. Crucially, no order to stop the rioting came from General Suchet who seemed to have decided that the Spanish refusal to surrender was a reasonable excuse to allow the troops to sack the city and murder the inhabitants. When Ángel could listen no more, he retreated behind the chapel curtains and wept where nobody could see him.

By midnight, it was clear that the wounded would not be further molested and the conversation turned to prison camps in France. Ángel listened to the speculation and thought about it and realised he could not bear it. As an officer, he was entitled to fair treatment but the thought of spending years as a prisoner of the French was intolerable. He would rather die attempting to escape.

García was awake and had even managed some weak broth and a few sips of wine. They sat in silence listening to an infantryman from Valencia describing how he had tried to escape towards Milagro Point to reach the Royal Navy boats which had spent long hours trying to rescue both soldiers and civilians off the rocks. The climb was steep and difficult and some of the people fleeing in terror from the marauding soldiers had fallen to their deaths on the rocks below. Many had made it though, and crouched in soaked misery while the boats went back and forth through the darkness under constant fire from the French who were deliberately trying to target the helpless refugees, many of whom were women and children.

When the man became too exhausted to speak and fell asleep, Ángel sat quietly, fingering the hilt of his sword with his right hand. He thought García was asleep again until he heard him say very softly:

"If you go, I am coming with you."

Ángel turned his head to stare at him in surprise. "You will never make it, Lieutenant. You are too weak."

"And you have only one hand. Both of mine are working properly. Perhaps between us we can make one good man."

Ángel gave the witticism the perfunctory smile it deserved. "They will treat you well, García, you're the son of an eminent member of the Cortes of Cadiz. They may even agree to an exchange."

"And if they do, I will be sent back to Cadiz to wear gold lace and be a toy soldier guarding the palace, which is what my father wanted me to do all along." García jerked his head towards the big doors leading to the slaughter on the steps. "I did not do all this to rot away in a prison camp or be treated like a privileged child again. If you go, I will go. If I slow you down, you may leave me and I will try to make my way back here."

"We do not even know for sure if the Royal Navy boats are still operating," Ángel said.

"I have met Commodore Codrington. He is a man who does not know how to give up. If there is any possibility of taking off one more man, woman or child, he is still out there. We can make it out through the cloister gardens. The guards there have been drinking wine and there is a broken window in the abbot's store room."

"How do you know this?" Ángel asked in surprise.

"Because when men talk to me, Captain, I listen to them. You should try it yourself."

Ángel gave him a look, wondering what had happened to the quietly spoken respectful young officer who had joined Contreras' staff in Cadiz. He supposed the bloody bandages covering the deep bayonet wounds were his answer.

Their escape from the cathedral was childishly simple, because it clearly did not occur to the French guards that any Spaniard would be mad enough to go out onto the streets of Tarragona of his own accord. Their job was to keep the marauding French soldiers out, not to confine the wounded. Once on the streets, their progress was erratic because García was in considerable pain and Ángel was not in much better condition. They staggered through the shadows, ducking out of sight every time they saw enemy soldiers. It was easier than it might have been because the men were very drunk by now. Some were slumped asleep in the street and, outside a blazing building, two inebriated Italians were trying to drag their unconscious comrade away from a doorway where he appeared to have fallen asleep. Ángel hoped viciously that the building came down on all three of them before they made it.

The upper slopes of the southern part of the city were guarded by French musket men who were firing down at the rocks and the incoming boats. Ángel found a shadowy shelter behind a pile of rubble which had once been part of the city wall and watched for a while. García had been right, the boats were definitely still coming in. The blaze of some of the fires which lit up the city skyline outlined their dark shape on the water, some rowing in, others on their way out to the ships and transports with their complement of human misery.

Below him on the rocks Ángel could hear crying. It sounded like a young child and he closed his eyes and wished it would stop. It was a distraction, wondering where it was and who was taking care of it and if it was hurt or cold or hungry. He had no interest in children and had never bothered to feign it but this child's desperate misery pierced his heart.

"I think we can take that track there," García said softly. Ángel jumped. His companion was so close he actually tickled Ángel's ear. Ángel swore softly and rubbed it. García gave a breathy laugh. "Sorry. Look, to the right of those bushes."

Ángel looked. He could see the dark line, dotted here and there with scrubby patches of thorn bush. There did not seem to be any Frenchmen lining the track but that was because it was so steep that there was nowhere for them to crouch and no cover from returning fire from the gunboats and launches. It looked impossible and the thought of trying to make it down with a badly wounded man under threat from both French muskets and accidental fire from Codrington's rescue boats was horrifying.

For a long moment Ángel remained still, trying to gather his courage. He decided that he had faced death so many times during the past week that it was time he became accustomed to it. Eventually, reluctantly he got up and began to edge cautiously towards the track, hearing García move behind him. He had barely taken half a dozen steps when a dark form stepped out of the shadows and a voice said:

"If you go down there, they're going to blow your bloody head off, it's completely exposed to a line of muskets on that ridge. How did your mother ever let you out without a nursemaid?"

Ángel thought about drawing his pistol and shooting the big Frenchman in the chest but he was not sure it was loaded or if his powder would still be dry enough to fire. He stood still, searching for resignation, but was only aware of anger.

The French officer moved forward, his eyes on García. "As for you, look at the state of you. I know he's got no sense but I thought you might."

"What are you doing here?" Ángel asked because he no longer believed in this much coincidence.

"I was escorting this lady to the hospital as she's offered to help with the nursing." The Frenchman waved a hand and for the first time Ángel noticed a woman standing back in the shadows, her head covered by a dark shawl. "I went to ask about your young friend here and found you'd both disappeared. It wasn't hard to guess. You're an idiot, but you're not that stupid, you must have had some kind of escape plan."

"Then why did you not just let us go?" García asked in a strained voice.

"Because I know how well they've got these tracks covered and after all the efforts I've made to save your pointless lives it seemed a shame to let you get yourselves killed."

"I would rather die than be a prisoner of the French," Ángel said.

"Oh don't be so fucking dramatic. Though I should think most French prison guards would probably die rather than have to listen to you whining through the rest of this war. This way. And don't think I'm doing this for you. My girl has seen enough of her countrymen killed today and would like me to see you safe."

He turned away, indicating that they should follow. Ángel did not move, recognising a target for his anger and humiliation.

"I see that it has not taken long for the prostitutes of Tarragona to find their way into a Frenchman's bed," he said contemptuously.

García gave a furious exclamation. The Frenchman turned in one movement, surprisingly sure-footed on the slippery slope and there was the swish of a drawn sword. Ángel froze feeling the blade at his throat.

"I recently sent a dozen musket-wielding infantrymen away from this pathway to eat and rest. It's now unguarded and leads to several flat rocks which can't be seen from above. I've already directed a few Spanish refugees down there and fairly soon they'll be on a boat in the care of the Royal Navy. You can keep your mouth shut and go with them or you can say one more word about my girl and go over that fucking cliff the fast way. Choose wisely."

Ángel closed his mouth and forced himself to say nothing at all. The woman waited to bring up the rear of the small procession. As Ángel passed her, he shot her a surreptitious glance and found dark eyes staring directly back at him. She gave a disgusted snort and waved him on. Ángel felt oddly uncomfortable as he slithered down the slippery track, as though her eyes were boring into his back.

There were five people huddled on the rocks; a Spanish soldier bleeding steadily from a leg wound, two women, a baby and a girl of about five. The baby was feeding at the younger woman's breast, probably more for comfort than nourishment. The child sat huddled against her, huge eyes staring out of a white round face. She was shivering violently and every now and then gave a little sob as though she was too exhausted even to cry properly any more.

"Stay here," the big Frenchman told them in Spanish. His companion had crouched beside the child and was giving her what looked like a wizened apple. "The boats will pick you up very soon. You'll be safe from the muskets but take care as you get into the boats, they can hit you from there. You should be all right, these navy bastards look quick to me."

He turned away. García said quickly:

"Thank you, sir. I do not know why you have chosen to help us, but I am grateful. You will both be in my prayers always."

The Frenchman turned back and studied him for a moment then looked at Ángel. "You see, manners cost nothing," he said. "You keep it up, boy, it'll take you a lot further than your friend here. Good luck."

He disappeared up the narrow track and Ángel waited with the others in the shadow of the rock for the arrival of a boat.

***

The launch, having disgorged the latest collection of woebegone fugitives onto one of the transports, turned back to the shores of Tarragona and Durrell settled back in the stern, pulling his oilskin cape around him, and wondered how many more trips they could make. The rowers had swapped over several times but the officers commanding the various gigs and launches had been in the boats all night and Durrell was wet, cold and completely exhausted. Around him the boats from the other vessels passed in the darkness. He could still hear the rattle of musket fire and the occasional crash of artillery as the more determined of the French troops tried to shoot at the boats.

Cruelly, they had also been shooting at the rocks. It made Durrell sick to think of a man with a musket taking deliberate aim at women, children and wounded men. The refugees huddled together in the crevices between the rocks to try to protect themselves as best they could, waiting for rescue with resigned patience. Durrell's anger kept him going long after he knew he should probably have stopped. He had been told that while the fever which had almost killed him after the Walcheren campaign appeared to have receded, it might come back in times of stress or exhaustion. Durrell thought his London doctors would have thrown up their hands at the current state of their patient, but while there was any possibility that there were still people on the rocks he could not give up.

There had been some casualties through the long, miserable night. Codrington's barge had been hit and overturned, killing a woman and child, but the crew and the rest of the refugees escaped unharmed and the barge was salvaged for repair. More serious was a skirmish with French infantry on one of the beaches when the ship's launch of the *Centaur*, commanded by a young lieutenant, had to make a fighting retreat with its complement of Spanish soldiers leaving two crew members dead and three wounded, including Lieutenant Ashworth who looked likely to lose his leg. Durrell knew and liked Ashworth and the news had sobered him but did not alter his resolve. They had not managed to save Tarragona but Codrington was determined to save as many of its wretched inhabitants as he could.

Durrell's launch passed slowly along the coastline while he scanned the rocks and beaches for survivors. He could see none. It was becoming lighter with the first pink and gold tendrils of dawn streaking out across the dark sky, suggesting another fine day. Durrell thought that the weather at least had been kind to them. There had been a few short, sharp showers of rain during the night which had drenched the boats' crews but also doused the flames rising from burning buildings within the broken walls. The wind had remained light and easy and the surf, although choppy in the early hours, had never made it impossible for them to embark their fugitives.

As the light improved, Durrell could see a boat ahead of him which already had several passengers, one of whom was a fair haired woman who seemed to be wearing Hugh's blue coat. Some of the fugitives had arrived on board the ships and transports half naked where they had cast off their heavy clothing to keep them afloat while swimming desperately for the boats. In two cases women had made it to the rocks completely naked and bearing the marks of what had been done to them first by the French soldiers. Their stories were burned into Durrell's brain. He hoped passionately that the woman Hugh had picked up was merely cold.

Hugh's boat was pulling in towards the shore again and Durrell could see a small group waiting on a series of flat rocks. They stood well back against the cliff wall and Durrell thought that although they must have passed an uncomfortable night, they were fairly well sheltered from the firing above. He signalled to his coxswain to hold the launch steady, watching to see if Hugh needed any help, though he seemed to have enough space in his gig for the refugees. Hugh was on his feet, handing them into the boat while one of his crew held it steady against the edge of the rock.

The explosion of firing was so sudden that Durrell's heart flipped. His launch was well out of range of the mortars and muskets but Hugh's gig was an easy target. Shot and shells thundered out, shattering the relative peace of the dawn sky and Durrell swore as Hugh's crew member lurched forward, letting go of the boat before the last man was aboard. The seaman toppled into the creamy surf and Durrell knew he had been hit.

He could hear Hugh's voice, calm above a babble of frightened cries, bringing his crew to order. The gig steadied and came about and Hugh reached out a hand to the final Spanish soldier still stranded on the rock and hauled him aboard so hard that he fell into the boat. Hugh left it to his crew and the other passengers to help the man and turned his attention to his wounded crew member. The firing was intensifying and Durrell found himself praying, his eyes fixed on the drama.

The injured man was dragged aboard although Durrell could not tell if he was conscious or not and Hugh shouted to his coxswain to get them out of danger. Durrell watched, rigid with tension as the oars cut through the water and the gig swept towards him. It was somewhat overloaded and Durrell waited to make sure they did not need to transfer some of the refugees over to his launch.

There were more shots and a shell fell so close to the gig that Durrell flinched, thinking it had been hit. The gig rocked violently and Hugh, who was still kneeling up after his efforts at hauling Able Seaman Milton back aboard, overbalanced, ending up in a tangle in the bottom of the boat among the passengers' feet. Durrell felt an unworthy flash of relief. By the time his Captain untangled himself enough to get up again the boat would be out of range.

The gig came closer and now the shells were falling harmlessly into the deep slate blue of the water. The sun was coming up in a blaze of gold and orange, lending beauty to the broken walls and ruined houses of Tarragona, silhouetted against the glory of the morning sky. Durrell decided that it was enough. He would order the boat back with Hugh and they could eat breakfast and get some rest before going out to make another sweep of the coastline to see if there was anybody still alive that they had missed.

There was still a babble of excited voices from the gig as it pulled in beside Durrell. It took Durrell a moment, in his weariness, to realise that Hugh was still lying in the foot of the gig. He felt as though a cold hand clutched at his heart.

"Fletcher is the Captain…?"

"He's hit, Mr Durrell. I can't tell how bad it is, he's unconscious and he's bleeding real badly." There was panic in the coxswain's voice. "Musket ball, I think. Might even have been hit twice, in the back."

Durrell started to lean forward to look then pulled back. "Back to the *Iris*, now. We need to get him aboard and to the surgeon. Pull hard, Fletcher."

He waited until the gig was underway, surging through the water towards the distant ships of the squadron, then gave orders to his coxswain to follow.

***

Bonnet walked in silence through the darkness back up to the town. He was lost in his own thoughts, wondering what would become of the two young Spanish officers who had crossed his path so briefly. It had been a quixotic decision to give them their chance of escape but Bonnet did not regret it. There had been so much death and misery here in these past few days that he welcomed the chance of giving life.

A hand crept into his and gave a tentative squeeze. Bonnet looked down, startled, then smiled. He had almost forgotten she was there, but the sight of her lifted his spirits again.

"This is the wrong way to the cathedral, Gabriel."

"We're not going to the cathedral, I'm taking you back to camp. It was a generous idea, Bianca, but after seeing what's happened to some of the women and girls here today I'd rather you were tucked away in the French lines. I don't want some arsehole…"

Bonnet stopped as a man stepped out from the doorway of a house directly in front of him. He was a tall man, wearing the uniform of a cavalry officer though he was not as tall as Bonnet himself. He was very wet which made Bonnet wonder if he had fallen off his horse while riding down desperate men on a beach. He hoped so. Bonnet looked at the insignia, sighed and saluted.

"Captain. I've just walked up from the shore. I found a very good viewpoint. Perfect for watching a French officer betray his Emperor by allowing two Spanish prisoners to go free."

Bonnet studied the man without letting go of Bianca's hand and remembered why he had never been tempted to join the cavalry. "Have you, Colonel? That's interesting, you should report it."

"Oh, I intend to. What's your name?"

"Bonnet. 30th légère. Take it straight to General – soon to be Marshal, I imagine – Suchet. He knows me."

The other man's face quivered a little and Bonnet knew that his air of casual unconcern had rattled him. He had no idea what the cavalry Colonel wanted and did not care. He was tired, hungry and ached all over and he could not bring himself to worry about an unsubstantiated complaint from an officer he had never seen before in his life.

The Colonel moved his dark eyes to Bianca and he smirked. "I see why you don't have time for taking prisoners, Captain. I tell you what, I'm feeling generous today. I'll take her off your hands for an hour and we'll say nothing more about this."

Bonnet felt Bianca's hand quiver in his. He tightened his grasp firmly, hoping it would reassure her. "I've got no idea what you're talking about, Colonel, sorry," he said genially. "Why don't you talk to General Suchet, or else find my commanding officer, Colonel Lacasse. Make it official, that way we'll all know where we stand. Excuse me, I need to report…"

The cavalry officer made a contemptuous sound and stepped forward. He caught Bianca's dark hair in one hand and twisted painfully, dragging her towards him. "An hour. She's not worth more than that. If she behaves, you'll get her back then."

Bonnet felt a rush of sheer satisfaction. He realised he was sick of stupid orders from stupid men and he had been wanting to hit an officer in a French uniform for weeks. His fist swung and he struck the man squarely on the nose, just above a set of carefully trimmed ginger whiskers. The man went down like a stone, releasing Bianca's hair. He crashed to the ground and lay inert.

Bonnet gathered Bianca into his arms and kissed the top of her head. She was shaking. "I'm sorry, little bird. I told you there were arseholes about. Let's get you back to camp."

Bianca lifted worried eyes to his face. "He is a colonel," she said. "Gabriel, will you get into trouble?"

Bonnet looked down at the prone body. He prodded it with the toe of his boot and the man made no sound. "I might," he conceded. "But I think I might have broken his ugly nose, so it was worth it. And by the time he wakes up I hope my little bunch of escaped prisoners will be safely away. Who knows, he might not even remember me when he comes round. Come on."

Chapter Nineteen

By the time he and his companions were hoisted aboard the *Iris*, Ángel was in so much pain that he was not really aware of what was going on. García had been unconscious since the navy officer dragged him into the boat; his wounds had opened up and were bleeding badly again. Ángel found himself unceremoniously lowered to the deck and two sailors laid García down beside him then disappeared without a further word.

For a time, Ángel drifted in and out of consciousness. He discovered, during moments of wakefulness, that his right arm was bleeding again but he barely noticed the pain as it was swamped in the agony of his left hand. For a long time he could not move or speak. Even breathing seemed to hurt, so Ángel lay still on the unyielding wooden boards and listened to the chaos around him.

The *Iris* was packed with people. Men, women and children jostled for space, begged for help and sometimes cried out in agony, crammed into this small wooden world. Around them, the sailors went about their usual business as best they could. At one point, Ángel opened his eyes and found himself looking up at men scrambling up the rigging to set the sails. He had no idea which sails or why they were doing it but even the thought of it made him feel so sick that he closed his eyes again.

Gradually his stomach settled a little and the pain, although still intense, receded enough for Ángel to push himself up and look around him. The deck seemed to have been cleared of many of the refugees but there were a dozen wounded men lying around. Nobody was tending them and Ángel wondered if the officers had somehow forgotten they were there.

It was not cold although it must still be early, but Ángel's clothes were soaked through and he was shivering. He turned to look for García and the sight of his companion got him up onto his knees and then onto his feet. García's whole body was soaked in blood. Like Ángel, he was wet through and his body was shaking violently. The young face was completely white and the lips were unnaturally pale. He looked like a corpse and if he had not been shivering so much, Ángel would have thought him dead.

Ángel looked around him. There were a lot of seamen about but none seemed to be paying any attention to the wounded Spaniards. Ángel felt a flood of rage at their indifference. He turned about, his eyes scanning the decks for an officer. He did not immediately see one but eventually he spotted a young man in a blue coat standing at the rail. Ángel set off towards him although his furious march quickly turned into an undignified stagger at an unexpected motion of the ship. He arrived at the rail in a rush, clutching it with his right hand and trying to protect his left as best he could but the jolt forced a little cry out of him and the young officer turned in surprise and then quickly held out a hand to steady him.

"You should lie down," he said.

"I will not," Ángel ground out furiously. His brain was desperately scrambling to remember his hard-learned English. "We are dying. They are dying and you do not care."

The other man spoke again, gesturing but the flood of words passed over Ángel's head. He stood seething in frustration, trying to interrupt the officer but he realised that in his exhaustion and pain, his painfully acquired English had entirely deserted him and the other man clearly did not understand a word. Eventually Ángel stopped because he was feeling light headed and dizzy. Desperately he threw out an arm in the direction of the men on the deck. "Help," he said, and hated the plea in his voice. "Please help."

The officer stopped his lengthy explanation immediately. He studied Ángel for a moment and then seemed to relent. "Come with me."

Below decks it was hot and smelled strongly of tar and cooking and unwashed bodies. Ángel almost fell down the companionway and then stopped as his stomach revolted at the stench. He stood taking shallow breaths, trying not to be sick.

"Mr Barton, what are you doing?" a familiar voice barked, and Ángel saw the young officer spring to attention. He almost did the same. "I gave orders that the wounded were to remain on deck until the surgeon was ready for them. They're moving more cots into the sick bay to receive them."

Ángel gathered his wits. "They are dying," he said, knowing that this time he would be understood. "They cannot wait any longer, Lieutenant, or they will be dead. He will be dead."

Durrell turned blue-green eyes to study him. Ángel noticed that his eyes were red-rimmed and that his clothing, like Ángel's, was still soaked.

"Lieutenant García?"

"He was badly wounded during the fighting and his wounds have opened up again. He is bleeding badly. He shakes and he is so pale. I think he is dying."

Durrell said nothing for a moment then turned to Barton. "The surgeon and his assistant are still operating on the Captain," he said. "I had not thought…it should not be taking this long. But perhaps we can get these men to sick bay. At least they can be warmer. I didn't want to move them without the surgeon's advice, but…"

"Lieutenant Durrell."

Ángel turned to see another man standing in the wooden arch to the ladder. He was older, a grizzled seaman of fifty or more.

"Bosun?"

"Get them to sick bay and let my wife have a look at them. She's probably got as much experience as yon doctor, and at the least she can see them warmed and tended. She'll know too which are the most serious for the surgeon when he's done with the Captain."

Durrell hesitated. It was the first time since Ángel had met him that the Englishman had seemed anything other than utterly in control. He rubbed a hand over his bloodshot eyes.

"I'm not thinking straight, Bosun."

"Aye, and it's no surprise, lad. You're half-drowned, wholly exhausted and mad with worry. It's not your job to carry the whole ship on those shoulders. Let someone else share the load. Get back down there now, before young Miles breaks the door down. Send a message when he's out."

Unexpectedly, Durrell seemed to relax his taut body and Ángel belatedly understood. "Aye aye, Bosun," he said, with something like grim humour. "Thank you."

As the older man left, Durrell turned to Ángel. "This way."

"I should go back…"

"Don't worry, Bosun Armstrong will get them to sick bay. There's nothing you can do. I need a drink and I think you do as well."

Ángel followed him into the officers' ward room. It was empty apart from a skinny boy of around ten who was seated on a stool in the corner. He had obviously been crying but when Durrell entered he jumped to his feet, scrubbing his face on a dirty sleeve.

"Lieutenant Durrell, is there news?"

"Miles, when I know, you'll know. Do something useful and pour wine for me and Captain Cortez."

The boy obeyed quickly then returned to his corner with an air of defiance. Durrell surveyed him for a moment as if considering ordering him out then shook his head resignedly.

"You can stay there as long as you're quiet." Durrell turned to Ángel and spoke in Spanish. "I'm sorry, Captain, it was not my intention to abandon your men. Most of them are not seriously wounded and I thought they might be better up on deck until we had space to accommodate them. I had not realised that your Lieutenant was so bad."

"Nor did I," Ángel said bitterly. "He concealed it very well, though I think the wounds opened up in the boat. If I had realised I would not have allowed…"

He broke off. Durrell sipped his wine and gave a tired smile. "Could you have stopped him?"

"No."

"I thought not. It was a foolish thing to do but I might have done the same if I was faced with a lengthy term in a French prison."

"How is your Captain?"

"The surgeon is operating now. He was shot in the back. It looked…" Durrell stopped, gulped the wine again and took a deep breath. "It looked very bad to me but I am not a surgeon."

Ángel could think of nothing more to say. They sat silently, drinking their wine. Occasionally he could hear a sniffle from the boy in the corner. Ángel recognised him as Kelly's servant and found himself trying to imagine his servant crying over him. He could not do so. After a while, Durrell got up, collected a blanket from a nearby cabin and tucked it around the boy, then resumed his seat still without speaking.

It seemed a long time and Ángel was just considering asking if he could see García when there was a tap at the door. Both men and the boy rose as the door opened. The sight of the aproned figure made Ángel's stomach turn. The surgeon was splashed with so much blood that he looked like a butcher. Ángel glanced at Durrell's white, set face and felt unexpected, painful sympathy for the other man's anxiety.

Durrell went forward, holding up a hand firmly to the boy to stay back. He and the surgeon spoke quietly for several minutes and then the doctor departed. Durrell turned to the boy and Ángel felt a rush of relief at his expression.

"It's over and he's conscious, Miles. The doctor thinks he'll be all right, though he'll be laid up for a while. He's managed to remove the ball and it's touched nothing vital although there's some damage to the shoulder blade. They're bringing him down to his cabin. Get yourself cleaned up then go and see him. Dr Cavendish tells me that Mrs Armstrong is going to nurse him with your help. Are you up to that?"

The boy scrubbed away his tears again. His face was radiant. "Yes, sir. I can do anything I'm asked to do. I just don't like being shut out."

Durrell gave a faint smile. "Go," he said and the boy shot through the door without a backward glance. Durrell turned to Ángel and spoke in Spanish.

"You may have guessed that was good news, Captain. He…"

"I understood most of it," Ángel said pleased to find that some of his understanding of English had returned. "I am glad, Lieutenant. Captain Kelly has been a good friend to Tarragona and to Spain. He has my gratitude, as do you."

"Cavendish has been to the sick bay to look at Lieutenant García but he tells me that the Bosun's wife has cleaned and dressed the wounds and is feeding him some broth and one of her sleeping possets so he is leaving it to her for now. I have experienced Mrs Armstrong's nursing and I can tell you he's in the best hands possible. I'm going to see the Captain but I'll get Lewis to show you to sick bay. Once you've reassured yourself, Cavendish will have a look at you and find you a berth. Trust him, he's a very good surgeon."

Ángel could not speak for a moment. He felt oddly like bursting into tears. "Thank you," he said again, this time in careful English. "Please pass on my good wishes to Captain Kelly. I will never forget what he has done."

**

Hugh was feverish, drifting in and out of sleep for several days after the operation to remove the musket ball. He was vaguely conscious of the presence of the surgeon, of his young servant and often of Durrell sitting beside his bunk with one or both of the cats on his lap. Of the three of them, Hugh preferred Durrell who did not prod him and ask difficult medical questions or hover around him anxiously asking if he was all right.

When he woke properly it was dark in his cabin and there was a warm weight on his feet which told him that Molly was back in her rightful place. Hugh shifted slightly, winced at the pain and felt his chest which was covered in bandages. The room was quiet and Hugh needed to relieve himself so he gritted his teeth and tried to sit up.

"Can I get you anything, sir?"

Hugh swore loudly, collapsing back into his cot, his heart hammering. "Yes," he said. "You can bring me the chamber pot. And if that's beneath your dignity as my First Lieutenant, it serves you bloody well right for scaring me half to death."

Durrell appeared in the door in shirt sleeves. "Sorry," he said. "I didn't mean to make you jump. They've slung a hammock in your day cabin for me; I've given up my cabin to a Spanish officer. Besides, I wanted to keep an eye on you. You've not been well."

He brought the chamber pot then disappeared to empty it and Hugh lay back in his bed and admired his first officer's sang froid. Durrell reappeared with two cups of wine, arranged Hugh's pillows for him to sit up properly and sat beside him.

"How are you feeling, sir?"

"Better, I think. Bloody sore, though. Did they get the ball out properly? And have I already asked you that?"

"Yes, sir, but I doubt you remember, you've been feverish for almost a week. You were much better yesterday though, and you've slept well so I think you're on the mend. The surgeon removed the ball. There's some damage to the bone in your shoulder though, which will take some time to heal."

"Ouch. What about the others? In the boat."

"Milton was shot through the shoulder but he's doing well. No other casualties."

Hugh leaned back and sipped his wine, trying to make sense of his fragmented memories of those frantic moments in the boat. Something surfaced and he regarded Durrell doubtfully.

"Have I imagined it or was Cortez in the boat that night?"

"He was, sir. He and Lieutenant García were on the rocks, you brought them both off safely."

Hugh frowned. "He was injured. Struggling to get into the boat."

"They were both wounded, sir." Durrell hesitated. "Lieutenant García was in a bad way when we brought him aboard. He suffered several bayonet wounds while defending the cathedral and they opened up during his escape. He was bleeding very badly by the time we got him aboard. The surgeon was worried for a few days.

"Will he be all right?" Hugh asked quietly. Durrell's expression told him that he had not misjudged his first officer's regard for the young Spanish officer.

"He's still very weak, sir, but Mrs Armstrong took over the nursing and he seems much better."

Hugh studied him, noticing for the first time how exhausted Durrell looked. There were dark shadows under his eyes and his face was pale. Hugh felt a twinge of anxiety.

"What about you? Have you managed any sleep at all this week, between fussing over me and worrying about García? You know that the doctor told you…"

"I am perfectly well, sir. Better now that you're awake and treating me like a child again. I thought we agreed that you were going to stop doing this?"

Hugh opened his mouth to remonstrate and closed it again with an enormous effort. He agreed in principle that it was ridiculous to coddle a man of Durrell's age and experience as if he were a delicate boy, but the memory of those long hours when he had thought Durrell was going to die was too recent. He managed to keep any further strictures about his First Lieutenant's health to himself however.

After a moment, Durrell relented and grinned. "I'm tired. We had two more nights out in the boats, picking up stragglers off the rocks. Since then I've been helping Commodore Codrington with the refugees. It has been a challenge, since every Royal Navy vessel has been crammed full of them, but relief is at hand. Two of the Spanish frigates have just returned from transporting the first lot of refugees and they're going to take the rest of the wounded to the Naval Hospital in Menorca."

"Good," Hugh said fervently. "They must have been driving you mad."

"Not as much as they've been driving Commodore Codrington mad. The *Blake* has been overrun with Spanish women and children. We all have, sir. We've had to clear out the purser's stores and order more to feed and clothe them. The Commodore assures me he's written to get authorisation. I hope he gets it, but what else could we have done?"

"Nothing. Don't worry about it, Mr Durrell, Ned will get the money out of them. Sit back, drink your wine and tell me what's been going on."

Durrell complied. Most of his news concerned the arrangements being made for the Spanish refugees, the last of whom were ready to be be transferred to the transports and Spanish frigates for repatriation further up the coast or to the islands of Menorca and Mallorca. Hugh made a mental note to ask Codrington if his own refugees could go to the islands, along with the two wounded Spanish officers. With the current chaos of the Spanish forces after the comprehensive defeat at Tarragona, Hugh did not trust that other coastal towns would not start falling into French hands and he felt that the women and children who had made it out of Tarragona alive should not be put at risk of another French assault.

Over the next few days, Hugh kept to his bed and allowed Durrell to run the ship. Once he was sure Hugh was on the mend, he reclaimed his cabin and allowed Miles Randall to take over most of the nursing duties. As Hugh began to regain his energy he also regained his sense of humour which made Miles perfect for the job. After a week, Hugh decided to teach his servant mathematics. He was hoping that filling up that overactive brain with knowledge might leave less space for mischief.

Hugh was well enough to visit the two Spanish officers before their departure for Menorca. Ángel Cortez rose to greet him but García still reclined in his borrowed bunk, heavily swathed in bandages. Hugh was horrified at the younger man's frail appearance.

García did most of the talking, thanking Hugh for their rescue and for the help given by the Royal Navy to the city during the long weeks of the siege. He spoke largely in English. Hugh was impressed at how much he had improved and suspected that Durrell was responsible.

Cortez said little although he added his thanks to García's. He also spoke in English to Hugh's surprise and sounded reasonably gracious. Hugh thought he seemed subdued after his ordeal in Tarragona. He hoped it would be a permanent improvement although he was not entirely convinced.

The one thing which seemed to have definitely improved was his relationship with his young lieutenant. García retained his charming diffidence but had lost his painful deference to Cortez. He even went so far as to tease him when Hugh asked about the French officer who had allowed them to make their way to the boats.

"Oh we do not know his name, Captain Kelly. Me, I like to call him Captain Cortez' guardian angel. Was it three or four times that he saved your life, Captain?"

Cortez glared at him. "And possibly robbed me of the use of my left hand."

"My surgeon doesn't seem to think so, Captain," Hugh said mildly. "He tells me you've already recovered a little movement."

Cortez flushed and managed a small smile. "Yes. I was surprised. And grateful. This way he has of splinting the fingers is much better and he does not threaten to remove my hand every time he sees me."

"He doesn't have the time," Hugh said frankly. "Goodbye, gentlemen. I hope you'll both recover fully and be back in the field. I'd like to hear news of you some time."

"You will hear news of me, Captain, as it is agreed that I am to write to Lieutenant Durrell, to practice my English," García said.

Hugh was amused. "Mr Durrell is a good letter writer. He has correspondents in the most unlikely places."

"I look forward to reading them." Garcia grinned and the serious face was suddenly once again that of the boy Hugh remembered meeting just weeks earlier in Campoverde's briefing room. "Though I am unsure that he will enjoy reading mine quite as much."

Hugh returned his smile. "I think he'll be delighted you've survived to write them, Lieutenant. Good luck, both of you."

His next visitor was Commodore Codrington. By then, Hugh was able to sit up for most of the day and he greeted Codrington in his dining cabin with a glass of Portuguese red which brought a smile to the Commodore's tired face.

"Now this is an improvement. Where the devil did you get it from?"

"It's from the Douro region in Portugal. Durrell has a friend in the army who is now serving out there. Apparently he'd been complaining about the quality of the wine here and Fenwick sent it to him in sympathy. Durrell is currently trying to work out which local delicacy he can send to Fenwick in return."

Codrington laughed, sipping the wine again. "Tell him to make it something good, we need more of this. Hugh, I've received orders."

"Unless they involve shooting half the Junta of Catalonia, I'm not interested. Are you still playing go-between for the quarrelling Spanish generals, Ned? You look exhausted. In fact, I think you look worse than I do."

"I don't have a hole in me and a broken shoulder though. Sir Edward Pellew has arrived to replace Sir Charles Cotton in charge of the fleet and I'm sailing up to Toulon to meet with him. You, on the other hand, are going home."

Hugh froze for a moment then set down his glass. "Under what circumstances?"

"With a huge pile of tedious letters and reports for London and my warmest commendation, Hugh. This has been horrendous from start to finish, but you've had my back every inch of the way. I don't know what I'd have done without you. Thank you."

"You're welcome, Ned. Any time."

"I'm glad you said that, because I think they'll be keeping me out here and I want you back when you're fully recovered."

"I could stay and recuperate here. Or in Mahon."

"I know, but I'm using your injury as an excuse to get you back to England. I did my duty here, Hugh, and so far the Admiralty have been very supportive. Still, I'm nervous, particularly about the lavish amount of money I spent on clothing and feeding our refugees. I'm out of pocket personally and I know you are too."

"What do you need me to do?"

"Once they've read the volumes of nonsense I've sent them, they're going to call you in for a meeting. I'm hoping your Manx bluntness will get the point across."

Hugh smiled. "I think I can manage that. And it's excellent timing for me, because I had a letter this morning from my wife. I was beginning to think she'd forgotten about me, but it turns out she's been a little busy."

Codrington stared at him then broke into a smile. "Boy or girl?"

"Girl." Hugh paused for dramatic effect. "And girl."

"Twins? Oh good God, Hugh, you do like to show off. What are you calling them?"

"We'd agreed Aalish for a girl, but of course we've two of them. Roseen decided to call the other one Ruth, it was my mother's name."

"Aalish and Ruth. I like that. Jane will be wild to see them."

"Jane is going to; Roseen is making plans to go back to Chatham. She's missing her friends and she wants to be there in case I get a chance at some leave." Hugh pulled a face and indicated his bandages. "She doesn't know about this yet, but I can write to her now and tell her that I'm going to be fine. Don't worry about London, Ned, I'll deal with them."

"I know you will. You should know, by the way, that my letters have heaped praise upon you along with Adam, White and Winterton. I've also expressed my gratitude and admiration for the assistance of your very talented first officer."

"I appreciate that, Ned, thank you."

"I know there was talk after Walcheren of him being put on half-pay. I've done my best to put an end to that. He's an excellent man and you're bloody lucky, Hugh."

"I know I am."

Codrington drained his wine glass and reached for the bottle. "I am a very moderate drinker these days, but I intend to make an exception for this. If I can't walk, your men can lower me into my boat."

They talked for a time about the siege, about the deaths, the tragedy and the pointless politicking and in-fighting which had led to it. Hugh was growing tired but he was enjoying himself and did not want it to end since this would be the last such evening he would have with his friend for a while.

Eventually Codrington looked at the fading light through the windows and sighed. "I need to go. There are some gifts I've bought over the past months for Jane and the children. If I send them over with a letter or two, would you give them to her, Hugh?"

"Of course I will. And I'll write often to tell you what's going on."

"Thank you. I'm not too worried, but it will be good to know I have you there, arguing my side. Look, there's something else."

"Yes?"

"Earlier in the year, when you first arrived, I made a bit of an arse of myself."

"You didn't, Ned."

"Yes, I did. I was rude to you and snappy with Durrell."

"You apologised."

"Yes, but I didn't explain." Codrington hesitated. "I'm embarrassed," he said finally. "The whole thing...the legacy, the plantation...the slaves. I can't talk about it and I get angry when it's raised."

"It's all right."

"No, it's not, because you never raised it with me. You just got on with doing what you think is right. You always do, Hugh. It's what I admire most about you. But I've realised that I couldn't stand the thought that you might despise me for something that sometimes, I don't even like in myself."

Hugh did not speak for a moment. He was still trying to find the right words when Codrington said abruptly:

"My brother is an ardent anti-abolitionist. It was he who wrote to me, telling me about your involvement with the cause. My sister doesn't care that much. Jane...Jane speaks of it intelligently and with surprising compassion but she was raised on a plantation. She doesn't see it in the same way. And I..."

"What do you think, Ned?"

"I think the end of slavery is coming. I think it should come. I think those of us with a financial interest in it should be finding ways to make it happen before it is forced on us. But I find myself reluctant to go against the wishes and interests of my family and some of my friends to stand up for that. Which makes me feel like a coward."

Hugh took a deep breath. "You're not a coward, Ned. You're one of the bravest men I know. Family is the hardest fight in the world. You couldn't change this overnight even if you wanted to, the estate is held jointly. You couldn't just up and free the slaves without your brother and sister's consent."

"That's just an excuse," Codrington said. He looked as though the words hurt him to speak them. "There are other things I could do. I just...I don't want to be the one to throw our family into turmoil. Even if the cause matters."

Hugh studied him for a moment then he gave a little smile. "All right, then don't. Let me take up the cause for you. Let me be your speaker. You keep the family peace for a while longer. But if you want to do something, there are causes you could donate a little money to which would help things along. You can do it anonymously."

"That's cowardice, Hugh. It's not good enough."

"It might be all you can manage for now, Ned. And it's better than nothing. Think about it." Hugh paused, a sudden thought occurring to him. "Have you met Elijah Winterton?"

Codrington frowned, puzzled. "I don't think so. Is he related to Lieutenant Winterton?"

"Not exactly. He's master's mate aboard the *Wren*: he started off as Winterton's cabin boy and as he had no surname of his own, he took Luke's. He's a former slave who ran away to join the navy at the age of twelve. Mixed race. He has no idea which white man raped his mother and sired him."

"Oh fuck off, Hugh."

"Sorry. The thing is, Elijah is very ambitious, very bright and very personable. He could do with a patron."

Codrington sat watching him in silence for a long time, then his mouth curved into a smile.

"That's still not good enough."

"No, it's not, Ned. But it would be a very good start."

Codrington rose. "I need to go. I'll send those reports and letters over in the morning. Goodbye, Hugh. Send all my love to my wife...and yours. Before I leave for Toulon, I'll go over to the *Wren* and ask Winterton to introduce me to young Elijah."

Hugh watched him go and was content.

***

Bonnet was seated on the balcony outside his room, sunning himself with the contentment of a lizard, secure in the knowledge that for once, he had no responsibilities. If his company had been marching to battle, he would have ignored his battered body, hauled himself to his feet and pushed himself onwards. Unusually, there was a period of respite and Colonel Lacasse had given Bonnet leave to rest and heal, leaving the day to day management of his company to his lieutenants.

The brief period of respite was made all the more sweet by the presence of Bianca Ramos in his life. Bonnet was trying not to behave like a lovestruck boy, but he knew perfectly well that his fellow officers were laughing behind their hands at his obvious infatuation with the Spanish girl.

Bonnet had been right about Bianca. Army life was hard, but the bare existence she had eked out with her father on their bleak smallholding had been harder. After only a few weeks, regular food and some respite from the gruelling task of tending the land and caring for her elderly father, had brought colour to her cheeks and some much needed weight to the long, elegant bones. Before his eyes, she was turning from a skinny albeit attractive peasant girl into something of a beauty. She seemed very happy which astonished Bonnet.

Bonnet watched her about her tasks with the fascination of a man unaccustomed to female companionship. He had wondered if he might quickly regret his rash decision to offer her a place in his life, but instead he found himself revelling in her company. Free from the responsibilities thrust upon her from a young age, she quickly displayed a lively sense of humour. They talked all the time, exchanging memories of their younger days, stories of the war, and opinions about the world and the people around them. She was a generous and affectionate lover and devoted herself to his comfort and his interests in a way that he had never experienced. Life was good and Bonnet was stupidly happy.

"Your boots are ready, Captain. And this came for you."

Bonnet turned to take the letter, noting with grim amusement the tone of Pierre's voice. His servant loathed Bonnet's new living arrangements, and for the first few days had been openly scornful and extremely rude to Bianca Ramos. Bonnet had tried to ignore it, knowing that Pierre's moods usually burned themselves out after a while. He had lost his temper completely one morning when he had walked into the big kitchen to remind Pierre that his second horse needed to go to the farrier and heard him call Bianca a name that was disgusting even by army standards.

Bonnet was surprised at his own fury. He upended his slovenly servant into the stone cattle trough outside the monastery doors and dismissed him. Pierre returned the following day as he always did, outwardly contrite. Bonnet made him apologise to Bianca and gave him explicit instructions about his future conduct towards her. Since then, Pierre had been irritatingly obsequious towards Bonnet and done his best to pretend that Bianca did not exist. Bonnet was waiting to see if the situation improved before making a decision about Pierre's long-term employment.

"Is Bianca back yet?" Bonnet asked, breaking the seal on the letter.

"No, Captain. She went to the market. She said she wanted to buy shellfish."

Pierre's tone implied that he did not believe a word of Bianca's story. It was Bonnet's turn to entertain his fellow captains to dinner that evening, and he was surprised and pleased when Bianca immediately took over both the arrangements and the cooking. When the battalion found itself in a situation of relative comfort, the six captains took it in turns to entertain the others to dinner, but Pierre was an uninterested cook and Bonnet was always vaguely embarrassed by his offerings. He had not yet tasted anything other than plain cooking from his lover, but he had a feeling that his standing was about to improve dramatically.

"Well make yourself respectable, Pierre, because I'll expect you to wait on table as usual. And you can pick up the wine I ordered."

"I am surprised you have not asked your woman to join you at dinner," Pierre said with heavy sarcasm. "Maybe you do not trust her table manners."

"They're better than yours."

Bonnet scanned the letter and his heart sank. He had been waiting for the axe to fall over his behaviour towards the red-haired cavalry colonel, and he was surprised that Lacasse had not already spoken to him, but a summons to headquarters was ominous. Suchet had spent some time re-organising his troops and setting up a French administration in Tarragona, but he was ready to march out and Bonnet supposed that he was dealing with last minute administrative matters first.

He was glad that Bianca was out shopping because he knew she would feel responsible for his predicament. He dressed carefully for the interview with the Commander-in-Chief, enjoying the fact that his shirts were clean, his stockings were darned, his boots were polished and his jacket was brushed and mended. It was an entirely new experience.

General Suchet received him in a small panelled room in one of the public buildings of Tarragona. It still smelled of smoke after part of the building had been set on fire by the rampaging soldiers, but it was clean and neat. Suchet looked fresh and energetic and ready to conquer the rest of Spain. It made Bonnet tired just to look at him.

"Captain Bonnet. It is a long time since we last spoke."

Bonnet acknowledged it with a little bow. "You have been busy, General."

Suchet studied him in silence for a moment. "So have you," he said. There was a pile of paperwork on the table. Suchet touched it lightly then picked up a letter, glanced at it and put it down again. "I am a little disappointed, Captain."

Bonnet said nothing. Suchet looked up. "Have you no response?"

"I am waiting to find out what I am supposed to have done, sir."

Suchet gave a faint smile. "I have a complaint from Colonel Dupres, a cavalry officer, recently arrived from Portugal. He claims that on the night of our triumph in Tarragona you aided the escape of two Spanish officers and assaulted him when he confronted you. Have you a reply to this?"

Bonnet thought about a number of replies he might have made and discarded most of them. He kept it simple. "I discovered that two Spanish officers had left the hospital. Both were badly wounded. I went in search of them down at the shore but I didn't find them. I don't know if they fell, drowned or were taken off by the Royal Navy. I'm sorry, sir, I'm not omniscient."

"And the assault?"

"After I'd been looking for them I was on my way back up into the town when Colonel Dupres, if that's his name, accosted me. He made a variety of accusations which made no sense to me. I suggested he report the matter to Colonel Lacasse or even yourself. I'm sorry, sir, I had no idea what he was talking about and I wanted rid of him. At that point he became objectionable and assaulted my female companion. I punched him and knocked him out."

There was another long silence. Eventually, Suchet said:

"Is this the Spanish woman you spoke of?"

"Yes, sir."

"Is she still your companion?"

"Yes, sir."

"Did he harm her?"

"He took her by the hair and informed me of his intention to rape her. I prevented it. I've no idea if he meant it, I didn't take the time to ask. He hurt her. That was enough for me."

Suchet studied him and then sighed. "Sit down. Have some wine. I am disappointed, Captain. I had hopes for you after this campaign."

Bonnet, who was so used to his hopes in the army remaining unfulfilled that he had stopped hoping, appreciated the wine. When they were both seated, Suchet said:

"I am willing to share some information with you which is not for public knowledge. I am trusting you, Captain."

"You can, sir."

"Colonel Dupres is leaving us. He was already under something of a cloud when he arrived here. A number of incidents during this past week have convinced me that a post of a more administrative nature might be more suited to the Colonel's talents." Suchet waved a hand in the air in a vague arc. "Supplies or some such thing."

"I see," Bonnet said. There were a number of things that he did not see, one of which was why the Commander-in-Chief was telling him any of this.

"It appears that the Colonel was sent to us after several mistakes were made during the campaign under Marshal Massena in Portugal. The letter from Marshal Massena describes the Colonel as…let me see…a dangerously incompetent imbecile."

"I see, sir." Bonnet said again. He was no wiser at all but he was hoping that Suchet did not realise it.

"Given the difficulties of Colonel Dupres' behaviour, I do not intend to pursue his complaint any further. However, the man has contacts in Paris. Men close to the Emperor. He may write to complain of my conduct and your name will be mentioned. I had hoped to have you promoted, Captain, but your impetuous behaviour means that I cannot immediately do so."

Bonnet stared at him blankly. Having had no idea that promotion was even a possibility, he found it hard to summon up the requisite amount of disappointment but he made a heroic attempt. "I'm very sorry to hear that, General. I will try to do better in future."

Suchet sat looking at him and Bonnet found his expression completely unreadable. He continued to sip his wine, hoping for a clue. Eventually Suchet made an odd noise. Bonnet put his glass down, eyeing the General with some concern. He hoped he was not choking.

Suchet made the noise again and it resolved itself into a laugh. Bonnet picked up his glass and drank more because it seemed the best thing to do. Suchet sniggered again and then began to laugh loudly, big whoops of mirth. Eventually, Bonnet started to laugh too. He had no idea what he was laughing at but the General's mirth was contagious.

Finally Suchet got himself under control. He drank some wine, wiped his mouth on his sleeve which immediately endeared him to Bonnet and sighed.

"Thank you, Bonnet, that's the best laugh I've had in a long time. You allowed two Spanish prisoners to escape, knocked out a ranking colonel and lost your best chance of promotion for a while and you don't even care. While we're about it, are there any other misdemeanours I should take into account?"

"Are you going to send me for court martial, General?"

"Good God, no."

"I suppose I've been fraternising with an enemy woman," Bonnet said consideringly. "But I gave her a choice in the matter, so it's not a crime. And after all, she has been nursing our wounded."

"What's her name?"

"Bianca."

"Where is she now?"

"Shopping for shellfish. She's cooking dinner later for my fellow officers."

Suchet fixed him with an intent gaze. "Can she cook?"

"Very well, General."

"We march in three days. Do you have time to invite me to dinner?"

Bonnet was utterly shocked but made a heroic recovery. "Yes, General. Do you like fish?"

Bonnet walked back down to the monastery where the 30th was billeted. He checked on Bianca and found her singing happily in the kitchen. The smell was mouth watering. Bonnet left her to it and went in search of Pierre. He discovered him playing cards with Allard's groom in the stable yard. Bonnet beckoned and Pierre picked up his winnings and slouched into the house. He had probably cheated.

In the hallway, Bonnet turned to him. "Go into the kitchen," he said quietly. "I have arranged for a meal for you. After that, you will take your things and go. These are your wages. I am dismissing you."

Pierre stared down at the coins then up at Bonnet. His face was a snarl. "You are throwing me out because of that Spanish bitch."

"I am kicking you out because she has shown me what a useless lout you are. There is a young Spanish boy who is helping out in the stables. He's an orphan, thanks to this war. He's good with the horses and I'm taking him on as my groom. Eat your dinner, take the money and go. I can't believe I put up with you for this long. You'll find some other idiot to employ you in this army, Pierre, they're short of servants. But not in this regiment. I don't want to see you again."

Bianca's dinner party was a big success. The food was excellent and Bonnet persuaded her to join them at the table. She wore a blue muslin gown. Bonnet had bought it for her at an auction and tried not to wonder what had happened to its previous owner. His fellow officers were enthusiastic about the meal and when Bianca departed after clearing the table, they drank toasts to her and teased Bonnet unmercifully.

"What in God's name does she see in you, Bonnet. Is this witchcraft?"

Leaning back in his chair, Bonnet drank deeply from his wine glass and privately thought that it must be.

"She likes me, Garreau. Maybe my luck is changing," he said expansively and raised his glass. "After all, tomorrow I have invited General Suchet to dine with me and he has accepted."

Garreau stared at him for a long time then gave a guffaw of laughter and slapped his hand on the table. The other men joined in, hilariously suggesting ways in which the proposed dinner party might go wrong for Bonnet, if it had been anything other than an excellent joke. Bonnet laughed with them, impressed with how imaginative their suggestions were. He did not attempt to insist on the truth of his story. Sometimes, he decided, it was best to leave people to enjoy their prejudices in peace.

Chapter Twenty

The last few days before the march were a whirl of activity for Bianca. The dismissal of Pierre had removed the only part of being with Bonnet which had marred her happiness. She was surprised and touched when her lover approached her after his servant's departure and handed her a worn leather purse. Bianca, who was fairly sure that Bonnet was not wealthy, considered that he had already been remarkably generous. She looked down at the purse and then up into his face.

"What is this, Gabriel?"

"My worldly goods," Bonnet said seriously. Bianca, who was beginning to know him, recognised that he was nervous. She had also discovered that humour often helped during his awkward moments. She weighed the purse in her hand.

"It is too heavy. There must be something more in there."

Bonnet grinned. "There is something more in there," he admitted. "There is a gift from the new Marshal Suchet."

"Marshal Suchet? The Commander-in-Chief?"

"I'm sorry, Bianca, I know how hard you worked to cook for my fellow captains. Suchet called me in to give me a bollocking about that red-haired son of a whore, but he also invited himself to dinner. I don't think he's being fed very well. Do you mind?"

"As long as I do not have to sit down with him," Bianca said. She could feel her heart beating faster. "Gabriel are you in trouble because of me?"

"I don't think I am," Bonnet said. He sounded bewildered. "I've no idea why he wants to come to dine although I'm telling you his face lit up at the thought of well cooked seafood. He gave me some money. Ostensibly it's some kind of imperial award for courage in the face of the enemy but that's clearly bollocks because they never give you money for that, just a medal and some pointless commendation. I think it's a personal gift from Suchet and I've no idea why. But it will cover the cost of a very good dinner and a number of items for the march. Tomorrow we are going shopping. You need a cloak and a better shawl and finally some proper shoes or boots."

"You shall not spend this on me."

"I'll spend it on whatever I like. But I'm glad you're willing to take charge of the household budget. Because that's what I'd like you to do."

Bianca stared at him for a long time. When she could finally speak, she said:

"How do you know that I will not…"

"Because I know. If you leave me, you won't take my purse with you. I just know. That's why I want you to take care of it. As you take care of me."

Bianca's heart was full. She reached up and cupped the scarred part of his face in her hand, running her thumb over the long white mark. "You take care of me too."

"I'm trying. You know, don't you, how much…how I like having you with me? I mean, I'm not good with words. But Bianca, I've never been this happy. So if you need to go, know that for this short time…"

"Oh stop it, you big fool," Bianca said. She spoke in French, because she was beginning to feel very comfortable with the language and she knew it meant something to Bonnet. "Why do you think I am here?"

"I know why you came."

"No, you do not," Bianca said firmly. "I have wanted to tell you. I have tried to tell you."

"I understand," Bonnet said. Bianca had the impression that he had been working himself up to this speech so she forced herself not to interrupt him to tell him how stupid he was being. "But being on the march is different. It's hard for you to just walk away. I need you to make this choice of your own accord, Bianca, not because you're desperate. You could stay here, in Tarragona. If you stay here, you'll find a man one day, and you'll have a life. Not an easy one, but a life."

"And if I come with you?"

"Then you choose me. A real choice."

Bianca did not respond immediately, and Bonnet looked as though he had forgotten how to breathe. Eventually, when the silence became too much, he said:

"You don't need to tell me right away, we have a few days for you to think about it. If you…"

Bianca moved suddenly, forward into his arms. She wrapped her arms about his neck, pulling his head down to hers and kissing him fiercely. She could feel the immediate leap of response in his body but she could also see him talking himself out of it. Bianca gave him no time to do so. During the weeks of their friendly, affectionate lovemaking she had never found the courage to do this although she had wanted to. She had searched many times for the words to tell him how she felt but now, when it mattered, she discovered that words were not required at all.

Bianca did not speak other than to say his name, and Bonnet clearly had no idea what to say. She concentrated instead on her body, on the sudden rush of pleasure and on ensuring that he felt it too. Unexpectedly she was free. She felt no hesitation and no shyness and he seemed happy for her to take control. For the first time she let go of her wary caution and the result was something so shattering and so joyous, that as she lay wrapped in his arms in the aftermath, Bianca could feel tears on her cheeks. He lifted his hand to touch her face and she realised that he was crying too.

"Bianca. My beautiful little dove."

"More like a sparrow."

Bonnet pushed himself up and leaned over to kiss her for a long time. "That was no sparrow. More like a sparrow hawk. So fierce. And so beautiful."

"Does that answer your very stupid question, Captain Bonnet?"

She watched him think about it and understand.

"I didn't know," he said. "I didn't realise. I'm sorry, cherie. When did you…when did it…"

Bianca sat up and pushed back her long dark hair. "Did you seriously think I had to walk six miles to find a man who would take me on? There were Spanish partisans within three miles of the village. If I had sent a message that my father was dead, they would have come to collect me with a horse. That week with you, I was happier than I could ever remember being. I wanted to know if you might feel it too."

"Anything could have happened to you on the way here," Bonnet said. He sounded angry at the risk she had taken to be with him. "And why didn't you tell me?"

"Because I knew you did not feel the same way. I was hoping you might, with some time. I could not come here and beg you to take me with you, I have some pride. I knew you would understand starvation."

Bonnet kissed her again. "I'm so glad you came. Now up, little dove, and get yourself dressed. You are with the army now, there is no time to lie abed in the daytime. We will collect my new servant and go to the market. You will need a new cloak and a better shawl, that one will not be warm enough during the cold nights. And better shoes. Perhaps we can find some boots. And then we need supplies."

Bonnet watched her as they dressed and Bianca wished for a moment that she possessed a fluent tongue to tell him how she felt about him. When they were ready, she collected her market basket and gave him a warm smile. Bonnet smiled back and took her hand. It felt very natural and very right and Bianca reflected that perhaps with this man, practical signs of her affection would be enough.

***

Arriving back in England, Durrell was quickly absorbed into his Captain's family life as though he had never been away. Roseen looked remarkably well after the birth of her daughters and Durrell tried hard not to fuss too obviously over the babies and took charge of his Godson who seemed to have grown an alarming amount. Master Alfie seemed to have taken the arrival of two sisters very much in his stride, confiding to Durrell that it was going to be some time before the girls could actually do anything interesting but making it clear that when they were ready, he had a list.

Durrell thought that the content of the list was probably enough to send any normal parents into a panic, but given what he had seen so far of the Kellys' attitude to parenthood it might not be as bad as he thought.

There were the usual minor repairs to the *Iris* and the administrative matter of paying the crew and trying to make arrangements to retain as many of the men who were willing to sail again under Captain Kelly as possible. This short campaign had brought no prize money and Durrell was resigned to losing a number of the newer men but he knew that Hugh's long term crew members would remain loyal.

Hugh Kelly was recovering fast from his wound and divided his time between his family, his ship and meetings at the Admiralty in London. Durrell wondered if he should take the stage up to London to visit his mother and Abigail. He was still trying to balance his wish to see his sister with his reluctance to meet his brother and sister-in-law, when Hugh invited him into his study for a drink one evening after dinner.

"Mr Durrell, are you busy for the next week or so?"

Durrell regarded him wide-eyed. "Only with tasks you've given me, sir. I'm working with Bosun Armstrong on…"

"Excellent. I've a small errand for you. I'm negotiating for some replacements for two of our ship's boats. The captain's barge is antiquated and in poor condition and so is the second launch. I've been in correspondence with a company in Yarmouth who supply the navy at very reasonable rates and I've heard good things of them. I could wait and go through the usual channels but I want this done soon. The recent campaign highlighted our shortcomings and I want them improved before we sail again. Which might be soon. I've some drawings and estimates but I want you to go up there on my behalf to talk to them. Look over the quality of their work and I'll accept your recommendation."

Durrell was taken aback. "Yes, sir, of course. If you wish me to. Only…there are other men who could do this just as well. I don't mind. But…"

"I've another commission for you which is more social than professional and I'm hoping you can combine the two, if that is acceptable to you."

"Sir?"

Hugh reached out and picked up a letter from his untidy desk. "This is from my wife to Miss Faith Collingwood. You may not be aware that she has suffered a recent bereavement. After her father died, she removed with a companion to Wickham House. It's only about twelve miles from Yarmouth. You'll need to be there for a few days. No need to go overland, there's a cutter leaving for the dockyards the day after tomorrow. Would you be willing to deliver this to Miss Collingwood with our condolences?"

Durrell could not speak. He had never before been so obviously managed and Hugh was not even attempting to hide it. At the same time he realised that he had never wanted anything more in his life than an excuse to visit Faith Collingwood. He was embarrassed at how well his Captain and his wife understood his feelings and he was also passionately grateful.

Eventually he stood up and saluted, falling back on formality as he often did in moments of extreme emotion.

"Of course, sir. I would be honoured."

***

Arriving in Yarmouth, Durrell was able to conclude his business quickly. The previous correspondence with Hugh had given the boat builders most of the information they needed. Durrell found the proprietor, Mr Torkington both intelligent and efficient and the negotiations proceeded smoothly and to the satisfaction of both parties.

It was no more than eleven miles from Yarmouth to South Walsham. Durrell hired a horse at a local coaching house, a solid black mare with a surprisingly sweet temperament. Bramble was not a fast mount but her steady pace suited Durrell. He still had no real idea what he was going to say to Faith Collingwood, but he knew that his Captain had been right to push him into visiting her. Since their meeting in London, Durrell had thought of her every day.

The Norfolk countryside was flat and rather dull, but Durrell found that he was seeing it differently after his conversation with Faith about her painting. He watched out for birds and wildlife, remembering the sketches scattered around her studio and stopped for a while beside a stretch of marshland, busy with tall, elegant wading birds.

South Walsham was a pretty village with a church, a white painted inn and a collection of cottages and larger houses running higgledy-piggledy off a traditional village green. Durrell stopped at the *Ship Inn* for a drink and directions to Wickham House. The landlord looked him over with a critical eye as he paid for his ale.

"You'll be up to see Miss Collingwood, then?"

"Yes. I knew her father," Durrell said. "I was at sea when he died and had no opportunity to offer my condolences. I am over at Yarmouth on navy business, so thought I would call."

The landlord seemed to be waiting for more, but Durrell did not oblige. He was not given to sharing his personal business with strangers and under normal circumstances he would not have said as much, but he knew that in a rural area such as this, gossip spread quickly and Faith Collingwood was vulnerable.

"I can give you directions all right," Mr Rallison said finally. "It's nobbut two miles west of here and the road's good."

"Big changes up at the house," his potman said, emerging from the kitchen quarters with a barrel on one shoulder. He had clearly been eavesdropping. "Everyone said house'd be sold, once old Collingwood could find a buyer, but that girl of his has had 'em turning it inside out and making it fine. Painters and plasterers and some fancy draper from London come up to measure for curtains and suchlike. There's been no woman out of work these past two months with the cleaning she's ordered."

Durrell was surprised enough to forget his determination not to gossip. "That sounds as though she intends to keep the house."

"Aye. Though what her husband'll say to it when she marries, I can't think. Not natural for a girl so young to be setting up house like she means it. And not even a proper lady living with her."

"Now you know that's not true, Billy Goodrum, so keep your tongue between your teeth and get that barrel set up," Rallison said sternly. "She's got Miss Abi living there with her and a nicer young person you couldn't meet."

"I still say it's not right," Goodrum said direly. "She should have a proper English lady looking after her."

Durrell drained his tankard and set it down. He was full of curiosity. "My thanks for the directions, landlord. Good day to you both."

Wickham House was set back from the road behind a high red-brick wall with freshly painted iron gates which were set wide open. A long, gravelled driveway swept around a formal lawned area up to the house, whilst to the rear, more lawns were bordered by mature trees and shrubs. The house itself was an elegant building with a symmetrical façade which had clearly been newly painted, a gleaming white. There was still scaffolding at one end and workmen were busy with what seemed to be repairs to a chimney.

Durrell dismounted and looked around. There was a building which looked like a stable block and possibly an old coach house over to the right. Durrell led his mare towards it, but before he drew close, a groom appeared at a run.

"Take your horse, sir?"

Durrell handed over the reins and turned back to the house. The front door was open and a housemaid stood waiting. Durrell trod up the steps.

"Is Miss Collingwood at home?"

"Miss Collingwood is not receiving visitors, sir, due to her recent bereavement."

"I understand," Durrell said. "I am in the area for only a short time, however and I would like to see her briefly, to offer my condolences. I also have a letter from my Captain and his wife, who knew Mr Collingwood. I wonder if it would be possible to take in my card. I understand that she may not wish to see me, but I've come a long way and I would like to wait. Outside, if you prefer."

The girl hesitated, looking down at the card. Durrell could see her trying to make up her mind, when a decided voice called:

"Leave the card for Miss Collingwood, Nell, she's not in the house at present. But I think she'll want to see Lieutenant Durrell."

Durrell recognised her accent immediately. She came forward and Durrell bowed.

"Miss Danjuma, it is good to see you again. How are you?"

The dark eyes sparkled with amusement. "You have a very good memory for names, Mr Durrell, mine is not an easy one to remember. I am very well, as you see."

Durrell did see. She was dressed with great propriety in floating white muslin which was definitely a cut above the servants dress she had been wearing in Ackerman's. He was amused to see that she also wore a cap on her braided hair, a small wisp of lace which was clearly intended to indicate her status as a respectable chaperone. Durrell understood now, the doubts expressed by the potman at the *Ship Inn*. Abisola Danjuma looked nothing like the kind of woman who might generally have been employed as a live-in companion for an unmarried girl. Durrell could also see that she was enjoying his surprise immensely. He smiled back at her.

"I am glad to see you here, Miss Danjuma. I have been wondering who is taking care of Miss Collingwood."

"She does not really need anybody to take care of her, sir, she is very well. I am glad you are here, though. She is painting down at the river and I promised to take some food down to her as it is such a beautiful day. Miss Faith never eats much at breakfast, she'll be as hungry as a horse by now. You could carry the basket?"

Durrell felt a little lift of happiness. He had been hoping for at least a few minutes in the drawing room with Faith, but this was much better. "If you think she will not object."

"I think she will be delighted, you're an old friend not a caller. I'll get it. It isn't a long walk."

She returned with a sturdy picnic basket and Durrell took it from her, then followed her around the back of the house. They strolled across the lawn towards the shrubbery at the back of the garden. Between the trees and bushes there was a small wicket gate and Abisola pushed it open and took a path through a cool wooded area which opened up unexpectedly onto a sunny river bank with a wide view over the river and wetlands towards the coast.

Faith was standing at her easel wearing a loose painting jacket over her black mourning gown. The picture showed the flat, smooth water of the river, with the broad vista of marshland beyond it, dotted with several birds and a clump of weeping willow. The subject was deceptively simple, but she had caught the light superbly.

"Miss Faith, you have a visitor."

Faith turned and her eyes widened in surprise. "Lieutenant Durrell. Oh. Oh my goodness, what a surprise. Look at me, I'm not at all dressed for a visitor."

Durrell bowed. "My apologies, Miss Collingwood. I would have left my card…in fact I did leave my card…but Miss Danjuma thought…"

"Miss Danjuma thought it was a lot of nonsense when a gentleman has come a long way to pay a call. We shouldn't have the same rules out here as in Town and I knew you'd want to see him. Here, let me help you off with that painting smock or we'll have green vermilion in the strawberries. Lieutenant Durrell, why don't you set out the picnic?"

Durrell looked uncertainly at Faith, but she was looking at Abisola, laughing. "You are a terrible chaperone," she said.

"I know it, Miss Faith, you should never have hired me," Abisola said cheerfully. She dropped the loose smock over Faith's folding stool and straightened her gown with a proprietorial air. Durrell decided to obey orders and set down the basket. He took out a large tablecloth and unfolded it onto the grass.

"Let me do that, you're here to see Miss Faith, not to act as butler," Abisola said. Durrell straightened obediently and went to join Faith.

"I am sorry just to arrive like this. I wondered if I should have written first, but I am only in Yarmouth for a short time, and I did not want to miss the opportunity to see you."

"Oh please don't, I'm so glad you came. I'm not at all lonely here and I have had so much to do, but it is very good to see a friend."

"Yes it is." Durrell glanced over at Abisola who was setting out the picnic. "I didn't mean to intrude though."

"You are not intruding. When I am painting, I have a tendency to forget about mealtimes. It does me no harm at all, but Abisola insists on bringing me a nuncheon; she is of the opinion that I will starve myself otherwise. She behaves as if she were my mother."

Faith raised her voice a little on the last sentence. Abisola was uncovering a bowl of strawberries. She did not look round. "If I were your mother, Miss Faith, I'd have taught you to have breakfast before you go out. It's surprising you don't faint with hunger by noon. Sit down and eat something. You too, Lieutenant Durrell. I brought a bottle of the champagne, ma'am, as you have a guest."

Faith surveyed the basket. "That is a very good idea, Abisola, but there are only two glasses."

Abisola looked astonished. "Well now, I know I told Cook to put in three. Don't you worry about it though, Miss Faith, I will be right back."

She was gone before Durrell could speak, walking briskly up towards the house. Durrell glanced uncertainly at Faith. She was laughing.

"Would you mind opening the wine, Mr Durrell? She is going to take her time over finding that glass, and I am not waiting for her, it will serve her right if we have eaten everything before she gets back. She's outrageous."

Durrell could not help smiling at her complacent tone. "If you will excuse me saying so, Miss Collingwood, you seem very happy in your choice of companion."

"I am. Abisola is like the sister I never had. Mr Glinde was very annoyed at me for making such an unsuitable choice, but I have no regrets at all. Would you like some bread and butter?"

"Yes," Durrell said, uncorking the wine. "But I don't want to steal your nuncheon, Miss Collingwood."

"There is always too much food. Please, sit down. The grass is quite dry."

Durrell obeyed. He accepted a plate, thinking that he had not been expecting, when he set out this morning, to be picnicking by the river with Faith Collingwood.

"This reminds me of that day on the beach in Walcheren," he said.

Faith laughed. "Me too. I was so shy that day, I had no idea what to say to you. But I enjoyed it so much."

"I was so tongue-tied I was an embarrassment," Durrell said, pouring champagne. He handed her a glass. "Here. I'll stand the bottle over in the shade."

"What brings you here, Lieutenant?"

"I am in Yarmouth for a week or so, on navy business. Captain Kelly had heard about your father's death and that you had come back to Norfolk. I must say that I was surprised."

"That I should come back to the place of my exile?" Faith smiled. "You should not be. This is a fine house, although it had been very neglected. I used to look around and wish I had the means to restore it. Now I have. There is still work to do, but I am very happy with how it is going. I would like to show you the work I have done, and what I still intend to do."

"I would like to see it. Do you not intend to return to London once your mourning period is over?"

"I have not decided yet," Faith said, sipping the wine. "Mr Glinde is adamant that I should do so. He has all kinds of plans for bringing me out formally next year and finding a good husband for me. It worries him terribly that I am my father's sole heiress with no restrictions."

Durrell raised his eyebrows. "That's certainly unusual."

"I am twenty-one. It would not be at all unusual if I were a boy."

"I suppose not. Do you not wish for a debut?"

"I don't know. This is all so new to me. I thought that once my father died, I should have time to think about it, but from the moment his death was announced in the *Times*, the door knocker sounded, and it did not stop. I was plagued by every family in London with an eligible man in need of a fortune. They offered me condolences and comfort and in one case, even a temporary home while I recovered from my grief. Really, if they had any idea how little grief I actually feel, they would be shocked." Faith lifted her eyes from the contemplation of her food and met his gaze steadily. "Do I shock you, Lieutenant?"

"Not at all, ma'am. I know what he was like with you. Is that why you came back to Norfolk?"

"Yes. I wanted to go somewhere I could be myself for a while. And I have been so happy here, Lieutenant. I have enjoyed redecorating this house and beginning to bring it back to beauty again. Abisola and I have indulged ourselves beyond permission. She is much bolder than I am in choosing colours and she bullies me shamelessly. I'm learning so much."

Durrell realised that he could not stop smiling. "I remember when I first met you. It brings me joy to see you so happy, Miss Collingwood."

"Thank you. I'm so glad you came. I've thought of you a lot these past weeks, and I realise now that I wanted you to see what I have been up to. I also wanted to know what you have been doing. Will you tell me about the campaign? I read something of it in the newspapers, of course."

"If you wish."

"All of it, mind. I do not want you to edit what you tell me because I am a lady. I have had enough of that all my life."

Durrell sipped the champagne. He watched Faith as he talked and thought how strange it was that he should feel so comfortable with this young woman. They had only met a dozen times, but he had liked her from the start. He thought that their promising friendship might have been destroyed by his brother's appalling behaviour when he had terminated his betrothal to Faith, but their shared misfortune seemed to have drawn them closer. It was very easy to talk to her. She asked intelligent questions and did not flinch when he told her of the horrors of the end of the siege although she went very quiet.

When he had finished his telling, Durrell inspected the picnic, reached for her plate, and added several items. "My reward for telling you all the horrors is that you prove to me you are not too upset to eat."

Faith gave a splutter of laughter. "You sound like Abisola. It was upsetting, but I imagine more so for you in the telling of it."

Durrell suddenly realised there was no sign of Faith's companion. "Where is Miss Danjuma? Surely she…"

"She will be here in plenty of time to be able to claim, if asked, that we were properly chaperoned. She must like you. She was the fiercest duenna at times in London. My very unwanted suitors had no idea what to make of her, it was very satisfying. I'm sorry to hear about Captain Kelly's injury. How is he now?"

"He seems almost fully recovered, although Mrs Kelly is keeping a close eye on him."

"You must have been very worried."

"I was frantic," Durrell said honestly. "I didn't immediately realise he'd been hit and then I was so busy getting him back to the ship along with the refugees that I'd no time to think. It was afterwards, knowing the surgeon was operating on him and not knowing how serious it was."

"You're very attached to him, aren't you?"

"He's my closest friend. More than that, really. He's like my family."

Durrell stopped, uncomfortably aware that their conversation, once again, was becoming more personal than was proper. He eyed Faith warily and decided that she did not seem to care.

"What of your sister? Has she enjoyed her first forays into society?"

They talked, picking at the food and drinking champagne, and Durrell forgot his concerns for propriety until he realised that Abisola had returned and was sitting quietly beside the river, tactfully out of earshot. He got up with a brief apology to Faith, filled a plate and a glass and took them to the African girl who was reading a book.

"Thank you."

She gave him her broad, friendly smile. "You're very welcome, Lieutenant Durrell. It is worth it to see her so happy."

The words made him thoughtful. As the afternoon became cooler, Faith suggested they go up to the house. Durrell helped the two girls pack up the picnic and took charge of carrying the basket and some of Faith's painting equipment. In the house, he followed Faith around as she showed him, with considerable pride, some of the work she had done in restoring the house.

Several rooms had still to be decorated and it made Durrell realise the conditions she had lived in during her exile. He wished very badly to be able to speak to the recently deceased Mr Collingwood to give him a piece of his mind.

It was early evening when they walked finally out onto the carriage drive, waiting for the groom to bring Durrell's horse. Faith had become quieter, and Durrell struggled to find the words to express how much the afternoon had meant to him.

"Do you remember the end of our afternoon in Walcheren," Faith said suddenly.

"Yes. I attended a very tedious meeting at army headquarters and worried about what would happen if your father found out."

"I didn't care," Faith said. "It was so lovely, and I enjoyed it so much. I have had another lovely afternoon, Mr Durrell. Thank you."

"At least I don't have to worry about you this time," Durrell said, glancing at the house. "You'll probably have to find an older chaperone if you do decide to make your debut, but in all else, she suits you perfectly."

"I am glad you approve," Faith said. "Although I must tell you I would not have cared one whit if you did not. Goodbye, Mr Durrell. I do hope this will not be the last time we meet."

Durrell hesitated. He desperately wanted to ask her permission to write to her, but the request was wholly against his sense of propriety. Her father would never have allowed it, and any respectable chaperone would have quickly pointed out the unsuitability of a correspondence with a young navy officer of limited means who was not related to her.

"Abisola tells me I am a great coward," Faith said abruptly. "I have been brave enough to set the town talking by coming here, taking on all kinds of responsibilities considered most unsuitable for a young lady and choosing a paid companion who would not be allowed in half the drawing rooms of London, but I am too afraid to ask a gentleman whom I consider to be a friend, if I may write to him from time to time. I expect it must be because I was brought up to believe that would be a shocking thing to do."

She spoke very quickly, the words tumbling out, and then took a deep breath. Durrell could see that she was forcing herself to stop speaking and he knew so well how that felt, that it was painful.

"Abisola would think that I am even more of a coward," he said. "I have faced a French broadside aboard a warship, but I am not sure I would have managed to ask that if you hadn't been brave enough to do it first. The mail takes a long time to reach me sometimes, but I would very much like to hear all your news and I would like to tell you mine. I feel as though I'm doing something wrong, because there is no guardian or chaperone I can ask permission of."

"I have already asked my chaperone and she considers it ridiculous," Faith said with a rather tremulous smile. "How do I address my letters?"

***

Faith took a long time to settle to sleep that night and woke early. She lay for a while, enjoying a sense of well-being. Her bedroom had been one of the first rooms she had decorated, and it was by far the most attractive bedroom she had ever slept in. She had kept the heavy oak furniture, which she liked, but the wallpaper was a pretty design of blue flowers, with bedcovers, curtains, and upholstery to match. Remembering the damp mattress and mouldering walls of her previous stay, just looking around this room gave Faith an immense feeling of satisfaction.

This morning she was too restless to remain in bed. Abisola was a naturally late sleeper and Faith saw no reason to disturb her, so when she was dressed she went out into the garden and went to inspect the new planting by the south wall.

It was another fine day, still cool enough to need her pelisse but promising to be warm later. The grass sparkled with morning dew and the newly-planted shrubs were a delight of spiders' webs, glistening with moisture like some exotic beaded lacework. Faith admired the view then walked back up to the house through the rose garden and past the main gates.

A horseman was approaching at a steady trot along the deserted road from the village. Faith paused by the gate, curious about who might be abroad this early on a road which led only to this house and then on down to the river and the ford. She recognised the horse first, having seen it only yesterday, and then the man. He had seen her and reined in, looking at her for a long moment. Then he walked his horse forward, dismounted and bowed.

"Miss Collingwood. You're abroad very early."

"Mr Durrell. Not as early as you. What time did you have to rise to get here at this time?"

"I set off in darkness," Durrell admitted. "I must not miss the tide so I cannot stay for long. I was not expecting to see you."

Faith was completely bewildered. "Then why did you come?"

"I wanted to deliver…there is something I wished you to have. As a matter of fact, I have wished you to have them for a long time, and it was one of the reasons I came to call on you, to give them to you. Then I could not do it, and I rode all the way back to Yarmouth last night cursing myself for a coward and a fool. I'm sorry, I'm not making any sense, am I?"

"Not a great deal." Faith realised she was smiling broadly and could not stop. "Now that you are here, you must come up to the house and have some refreshment…"

He was shaking his head, but he was smiling as well. "No. A picnic by the riverside is bad enough but arriving for breakfast is going to have some of your servants wondering if I ever really left."

Faith felt colour scorch her cheeks and Durrell looked stricken. "Oh, I'm sorry, I shouldn't have said that. You know what I'm like when I'm nervous, my tongue runs away with me. I only meant that even out here, I need to have a care for your reputation; it is surprising how gossip reaches Town."

"It is perfectly all right, Mr Durrell. But I still don't know why you came when you should be aboard your ship."

"Not my ship, she is at Portsmouth. I came in a cutter…I'm sorry, I'm doing it again. I came to give you these."

Durrell reached into the saddlebag and withdrew a fat package wrapped in brown paper and tied up with string. Faith took it in surprise. "What is it?"

"Letters. Just letters. Please don't open it until I have gone. I hope you will not be offended by this. I have wished for so long that you should have these, although I never thought I would have the opportunity to give them to you. But then yesterday, when I received your permission to write to you, I suddenly realised on my way back that your permission is the only thing that I require. And although it is very shocking, that feels right, somehow." Durrell stopped speaking with a visible effort.

"It is right," Faith said gently. "When did you write these, Mr Durrell?"

"I wrote the first one as soon as I heard that my brother had broken your engagement in such a cruel way," Durrell said. "I knew I couldn't send it, but I felt so terrible. And also, I had so much to tell you. It was very foolish, but at times it has given me great comfort."

Faith looked down at the packet then back up at him. "A year. You have been writing to me for almost a year."

"You must think me a madman."

"No. Oh no. I am…I'm delighted. You are very much ahead of me, Mr Durrell, but then your life has been so much more interesting than mine during that time. I look forward to reading them, thank you so much for bringing them to me."

"I must go," Durrell said. He reached for Faith's free hand and raised it to his lips. "Goodbye, Miss Collingwood."

"Goodbye, Mr Durrell. I know you will always do your duty, and that will take you into danger. But please take care as far as you are able. Your welfare is important to me."

Faith felt his hand tighten around hers for a moment and she knew a sudden, shocking wish that he would kiss her. He did not do so, but he did kiss her hand a second time, then stood holding it as though he could not bear to let go.

Eventually he released her and swung himself back into the saddle. Faith lifted her hand in farewell and Durrell saluted gravely.

"Oh – there is just one thing I should mention. I fear the letters are improperly addressed. I am sorry. I didn't expect you'd ever read them, you see. Goodbye, ma'am. Please give my regards to Miss Danjuma."

Faith watched him ride away, then walked quickly back up to the house and into her big, bright studio. She rang for tea and gave instructions about breakfast when Abisola awoke, then unwrapped the package. There were ten letters, neatly folded but unsealed. Durrell's hand was a rather spiky but very legible copperplate and he had dated each letter.

Faith sat staring at the pile. She realised that her heart was beating unevenly. She could visualise him so clearly, writing by lamplight in his small cabin, possibly in shirt sleeves, bending his tall form over his writing desk. She had thought of him often, remembering their meetings and wondering if he ever thought of her as anything other than the girl his brother had rejected. She had thought of him for more than a year and before her was the evidence that he had been thinking of her too.

After a long time, Faith reached for the top letter and unfolded it. The ink had faded a little, but still stood out in bold, black letters across the page.

"My dearest Faith."

***

Hugh was in his study writing to Isaac Moore when the door knocker sounded. He raised his head and listened, waiting for the noise. It came as he had expected, a shout of excitement followed by the thundering sound of feet on the stairs. A crash suggested that Alfie had overdone it and arrived at the bottom in a heap. Hugh debated about whether to get up, but there was no howl of pain, so he returned to his letter with a grin.

"Master Alfred, you need to come back up here right now," Beth called from the top of the stairs. "If your Ma sees you taking those stairs at that speed, she'll skelp your bottom for you. Come along, it's time for your milk, leave Susan to do her job in peace."

"I'm helping," Alfie said with great dignity.

The rest of the exchange at the front door was lost to Hugh. He did not know where Alfie's sudden enthusiasm for behaving like a butler had come from, but every time the knocker sounded, the housemaid was accompanied by a solemn small boy who stood beside her with the dignity of an upper servant of many years standing. Hugh wondered what callers made of it. Susan had spoken to Roseen about it, and his wife had laughed.

"I am sorry, Susan. I've no idea what started this, but I suppose if he decides against the navy, he'll have excellent training to go into service. Don't worry about it, he'll get bored with it far more quickly if we ignore it. And actually, he's very good at bringing calling cards and messages."

The truth of this was borne out several minutes later when there was a firm knock at Hugh's door. Hugh put down his pen.

"Come in."

Alfred marched in with great dignity, executed a little bow and handed Hugh a letter. Hugh took it gravely.

"Thank you, Alfie."

"Is it important, Papa?"

Hugh looked at the seal. "Yes," he said. "From the Admiralty, son. I wonder if it's my orders."

Alfie abandoned his dignity and came forward, scrambling up onto Hugh's lap. "Read it," he commanded.

"I don't need orders from the Admiralty when I've got you around. Is that you hovering outside, Beth? You can leave him here for a bit, I'll send him up when he's finished enquiring into my private correspondence. Wait – will you find my wife and ask her to come down if she's free, please?"

"Yes, Captain."

Hugh broke the seal, unfolded the letter and began to read. Alfie peered at it intelligently, although he could not read a word of it.

"What does it say, Papa? Where are you posted next?"

Hugh noted, with a little pang, his son's calm acceptance of the inevitability of parting. He was grateful to Roseen, who had always made a point of treating Hugh's sudden departures as a usual part of life, thus ensuring that Alfie did the same.

"Spain," he said, skimming the letter. "A squadron along the north coast. Under…"

Hugh stopped himself just in time from uttering an oath wholly unsuitable for his son's ears. Alfie seemed to pick up his tone and twisted round to look at him.

"Under who, Papa? Is it a bad man? Is it someone you don't like?"

Hugh controlled his expression with an effort. "Not at all. I was just surprised. It's a fella I've worked with several times in the past, Alfie. Captain Sir Home Popham is commanding the squadron."

"I think you should be in command," Alfie said. "Popham. That's a funny name. Popham."

Hugh did not speak as his son wriggled to the floor and in the way of a four-year-old, began to run around the room at high speed, chanting at the top of his voice.

"Popham, Popham, Popham, Popham, POPHAM! Popham goes POP! Popping Popham on the poop deck. Poopy Popham."

Despite his sudden sense of gloom, Hugh could not help laughing. He stood up and caught Alfie on his next circuit, swinging him up into his arms before he endangered either the furnishings or himself.

"Enough, before you deafen me, you noisy whelp."

"Do I understand you have orders?" Roseen said from the doorway.

"Popham," Alfie roared. "Papa is serving under Popham the Poopy."

Roseen met Hugh's eyes in rueful understanding. "That is more than enough, Alfred Kelly. Sir Home Popham is a very well-respected officer and can't help his name. Stop shouting right now, or you won't get bread and butter with your milk."

Alfie stopped wriggling. "I'm hungry," he announced, as though he had just made the discovery.

"Well best get yourself off to Beth before she eats it all," Roseen said.

Hugh watched as his son took the stairs at a terrifying pace then went back into his study with Roseen, closing the door. Roseen went into his arms and hugged him for a long, silent moment of understanding.

"I'm sorry, Hugh."

"So am I. I can't decide if this is pure bad luck or if I've upset somebody. I was hoping to go back to the eastern coast under Ned."

"It's possibly neither, Hugh. You told me that Popham has been pushing for this assignment. It may be that they've given it to him, but they want a man of sense to prevent him sailing off to invade South America when he gets bored."

Hugh could not help laughing. "Bless you for your common sense, Roseen. You're probably right. Not that I could stop him, but I'd make sure London was informed of it very quickly."

"What's worrying you, love?"

"I'm probably over-reacting. Popham has that effect on me. But I'm concerned that Popham has asked for the *Iris* specifically. He's a man who holds a grudge."

"Why would he ask for you if he dislikes you?"

"Because if you're in a tight corner and you're a man like Popham, it never hurts to have a ship you don't care about to take the worst of any action. And it's even better to have a ready-made scapegoat if things go wrong."

"Oh, surely he's not that spiteful, Hugh?"

"I don't know. I hope not. But I have my orders, I've no choice but to obey them. At least by now I know how Popham operates, so I'll be on my guard. He wants to meet with me before we sail. He's offered to come here, but I'll write to him now and tell him I'll meet him at the Admiralty."

"Is that for convenience or because you want this meeting to be very public?"

"Both," Hugh said. "We know Popham's tendency to forget inconvenient meetings or invent those that never happened. I want this well-documented, and I want to know exactly what our orders are so that I know if Popham is exceeding them. Will you come up to London with me, Roseen?"

"Of course. I think we'll leave the children at home though. Beth can manage them perfectly well and as much as I love the sound of my son shrieking 'Popham the Poopy' in the confines of my own home, I am not ready for the rest of the world to hear it. I'll write to Maria." Roseen hesitated. "Should I tell her that Mr Durrell will be accompanying you?"

Hugh thought about it. "Yes. I'm not sure about taking him to meet Popham. But if we're likely to be at sea for a while, he might want to spend some time with his mother and sister, I should give him the chance."

Roseen smiled. "Possibly. I suspect Alfred has made the most important call for him."

Hugh grinned. "Matchmaker," he said.

"As though you had not thought of it," Roseen retorted. Reaching up, she kissed Hugh very tenderly. "I am sorry about this, love. I can see how worried you are. But I honestly don't think Popham is in a position to do you any damage now, you're in very good standing at the Admiralty. More so than he is."

"Durrell isn't, though."

"He has you to watch out for his interests, Hugh. And didn't you say that Ned was going to put in a good word for him?"

"Yes, and he did so. I should stop being so over-protective of Durrell, shouldn't I? He complains that I coddle him. That damned Walcheren fever." Hugh sighed. "I'd better write that letter first and then I'll tell my First Lieutenant the good news."

When Roseen had gone, Hugh sat at his desk for a long time, the ink drying on his pen, thinking about the months ahead. After a while, he stirred and mentally shook himself. The posting was decided, and Hugh was not a believer in agonising over what could not be changed. Reaching for a new sheet of paper, he dipped his pen in the ink again and began to write, his mind already ranging over what needed to be done to have the *Iris* ready to sail.

Author's Thanks

Many thanks for reading this book and I hope you enjoyed it. If you did, I would be very grateful if you would consider leaving a short review on Amazon or Goodreads or both. One or two lines is all that's needed. Good reviews help get books in front of new readers, which in turn, encourages authors to carry on writing the books. They also make me very, very happy.

Thank you.

Lynn

Author's Notes

This book is out a year later than I intended. When I finished writing *An Unmerciful Incursion,* book six of the *Peninsular War Saga*, I intended to go back to the *Manxman* series and write book three. I made a good attempt. I did loads of research and reading, planned the book out and wrote about eight chapters, but it just wasn't working for me. For the first time ever I was halfway through a book and I just couldn't finish it.

I've no idea why. I was in the middle of lockdown-induced-madness and possibly it had something to do with that. Perhaps it was because I'd become so involved with Paul and the 110th in book six that I wasn't able to make the switch. I honestly don't know, but writing it was like wading through treacle. Eventually I gave up and moved on to book seven of the *Peninsular War Saga.*

When that book was published in April, I came back to *This Bloody Shore* with some trepidation but there was no need. Amazingly, when I read what I'd written, I understood immediately what was wrong with it and how to put it right. The rest of the book went very smoothly and I'm delighted to feel that I've got my writing mojo back.

The 1811 Siege of Tarragona was fascinating to research and I was able to find out a surprising amount of detail. Marshal Suchet wrote the French account of the siege, while General Contreras wrote from the Spanish perspective after the war. From the English point of view I had the memoirs of Edward Codrington which gave an excellent account of the Royal Navy's evacuation of the Spanish refugees.

I've taken the usual liberties of an author of fiction, while keeping to the known facts as far as possible. The ships of Ned Codrington's squadron during this campaign are all real, as are their commanders, with the exception of Hugh Kelly's *Iris* and Luke Winterton's *Wren*, both of which are my own invention. I've apologised in previous books for inadvertently using the name of a real ship and I hope the spirits of the original crew of the *Iris* will forgive me.

Having introduced Captain Gabriel Bonnet in *An Indomitable Brigade*, I've thoroughly enjoyed going back to an earlier part of his life. Writing part of this book from the French perspective has given me the opportunity to explore aspects of the campaign that my navy characters couldn't possibly have known. The 30th légère (light infantry) is a fictional battalion as are all its officers. There was in fact a real 30th but they were disbanded in 1802. I've chosen to reinstate them for the purposes of my stories and I'm hoping you'll see more of Bonnet and his comrades in future books.

I decided that if I wrote from the French perspective, I should do the same for the Spanish, and out of that came Captain Don Ángel Bruno Cortez who is one of the most difficult characters I've written for a long time. Generally speaking I try to write about a broad spectrum of characters, but those given their own point of view in the books tend to be people I like. I'm not sure I like Ángel yet, but he's interesting to write. Ángel's attitudes towards rank, honour and the position of women in society aren't always comfortable but they are firmly rooted in the period.

Captain Edward Codrington is not a fictional character. He's a bit like Lord Wellington, Sir Home Popham and Colonel Andrew Barnard; I couldn't make Codrington up. His memoirs are absolutely hilarious and I thoroughly enjoy reading and writing about him. Having discovered him during the writing of *This Blighted Expedition*, I unhesitatingly set him up as a good friend of Hugh Kelly. He's exactly the man who would have been.

When further research revealed that Codrington was also an absentee slave owner I was seriously cross. It's not that surprising as so many people had connections to the trade during this era, but I'd already made Hugh Kelly's abolitionist opinions clear in book one. I decided that I couldn't ignore this aspect of Codrington's story but at the same time I didn't want it to dominate this book. For anybody who wants to know more, I wrote a blog post on my website, www.lynnbryant.co.uk. In the end I decided to leave the debate between Ned and Hugh open. We'll see more of Codrington in the future and I'm sure we've not heard the last of it.

Book four of the Manxman should be out some time next year and Hugh already knows where he's going next and who he'll be serving under. In the meantime, it's back to the Peninsula where the Light Division is marching on towards France in *An Unattainable Stronghold,* book eight of the Peninsular War Saga. I can't wait.

I now include one of my free short stories at the end of each book as a bonus. They're all free on my website so if you enjoy this one, why not go and have a look at the others. *The Pressed Man* fits perfectly with this book as it tells the story of an earlier episode in Bosun Geordie Armstrong's career involving the most difficult ship's boy he ever encountered…

The Pressed Man

April, 1797

The wind began to pick up ten days after leaving Antigua, after a week of depressing calm. The crew were restless and the captain morose and the Boatswain, who had been wishing for months that Captain Dalton had not been appointed to command *HMS Hera*, awoke to an unaccustomed noise from the men's quarters. The bell had not sounded, so something was clearly wrong. Geordie Armstrong groaned and swung his legs over the edge of the narrow bunk he shared with his wife.

"What is it, my dear?"

"No bloody idea, Janet. Stay there, bonny lass, it's freezing."

His wife ignored him and got up, reaching for her gown. "It can't be far off the bell, lad and you'll want your tea. I'll get to the galley while you find out."

Geordie stepped to one side to let her reach her shawl. A private cabin was one of the many perks of being Bosun, but it was small, especially for two people. He and Janet had shared such cabins for so many years they were expert in moving around it without getting in each other's way, as if in the carefully learned steps of a well-known dance. Outside on the wooden companionway they parted, Janet on her way to the galley for hot water, while Geordie made his way down to the lower deck where the crew slung their hammocks.

It was not yet light, but someone had lit a few lanterns. Most of the men were up, in various states of undress, huddling together talking in small uneasy groups. Nobody had given an order yet, probably because it was too early for the bell. Geordie took out his pocket watch and saw that it was thirty minutes to first bell. He debated with himself. He could pipe for the removal of hammocks then send them about their usual business early, which would get them out of the way, but he knew Captain Dalton loathed even the slightest deviation from routine and he was reluctant to have the argument without knowing what had happened first.

"Bosun. Pipe up hammocks and send a message to the galley. I know it's early, but we need to get them moving."

Geordie obeyed, dying of curiosity. He had a lot of respect for First Lieutenant Daniel Eaton, and he knew he would find out in time. It was clear that something unusual had disturbed the crew, but Geordie could not imagine what.

He was too busy during the next hour and a half for speculation. Returning to his cabin, he found that Janet had tea ready for him and he gulped it down gratefully, then set off on his inspection of the rigging, while Rashford, the ship's carpenter inspected the gunports, hatches and boats and Sharpe, the gunner, checked the guns. The three men met at seven-thirty in Captain Dalton's day cabin to make their reports. They found Lieutenant Torbin, the officer of the watch, already there making his report. Dalton listened in stony silence to the end. When Torbin saluted to indicate he had finished, Dalton said:

"Haven't you missed something, Mr Torbin? What was that Godawful racket that brought me from my bed early?"

Torbin, who was red-haired and had a very fair complexion, went scarlet and saluted again. "Yes, sir. Sorry, sir, it's just that Lieutenant Eaton said he would report to you about that, he'll be here any minute."

"Well unless he's invisible, he's not here now. What happened?"

Torbin gulped nervously. "There was a death, sir. Among the crew."

"Death? Death? What kind of death? Fever? Cholera? By God, if that bunch of scurvy louts we picked up on Antigua have brought sickness aboard my ship, I'll throw them overboard."

"Not fever, sir," Torbin said, in agonised tones. His awkwardness was painful, and Geordie was desperately trying to think of a way of rescuing him without drawing Dalton's fire himself, when there was a knock on the door and First Lieutenant Eaton entered, saluting.

"Ha, there you are. What's going on? Torbin is blathering about a death in the night. Is that good enough reason to disturb my sleep at that hour?"

"My apologies, Captain," Eaton said politely. Geordie hid a smile. Eaton's unruffled manner made him the best first officer Geordie had ever sailed under, but he knew it infuriated Dalton who was rude, bad-tempered, and incompetent and seemed to find Eaton's placidity a personal insult. "Perhaps I should wait until these gentlemen have given their reports."

"No, they can bloody wait. What happened? Who died?"

"It was Mackay, sir."

"Mackay?" Dalton sounded surprised, probably because he knew the man. Dalton did not bother to learn the names of most of the crew, but Mackay had sailed with him for many years. He was in his forties, a big man from Inverness who was an excellent seaman and an inveterate drunk. "What happened, did he fall out of his hammock onto his head?"

"He was murdered, sir."

"Murdered?" Dalton froze and sat for a while, his mouth hanging open in surprise. Geordie shared his astonishment. He had been at sea since he was ten years old, almost thirty years, and he had never heard of a murder on board. There had been one or two deaths after a fight which had been tried as murder, but nothing worse.

After a long time, Dalton jerked his head. "Out. You can make your reports later."

Geordie left and went in search of breakfast with Janet. After the meal he went up to the quarterdeck and smoked a pipe while watching the ship's marines on their morning parade. He was not disappointed. Just after nine o'clock, as they were beginning drill practice, Lieutenant Eaton appeared and came to join him at the rail. He lit his own pipe and stood smoking in silence.

"The surgeon is inspecting the body at the moment," he said finally. "He'll write up a report for the captain and we'll bury him later today."

"Aye, sir. Do we know what happened? I mean is there any doubt?"

Eaton shot him a sideways look. "Able Seaman Mackay was found in a dark corner of the hold with his throat slit from ear to ear. Not much doubt."

"Holy Mary. Anyone suspected?"

"Yes. We've arrested one of the new men we picked up in Antigua. He was out of his berth without leave or reason."

"Any other signs? There must have been blood."

"Oh there would have been, and that's what's suspicious. It seems this man fell overboard with all his clothes on."

Geordie was startled. "In the dark? How the devil did they find him? And why didn't I hear the call?"

"There was no call. Nobody saw or heard him go over. His story is that he felt sick and went up for air, came over dizzy and went over the side. He was lucky enough to be near the ladder and the shock of the water woke him up fast. He grabbed hold and pulled himself up."

"I'm surprised the watch didn't shoot him."

"He'd the presence of mind to call up as he was climbing, to identify himself. They pulled him in and hauled him before the watch officer, who was just ordering him put in irons for roaming the ship without permission when they found Mackay's body."

"It looks suspicious, sir, no question. But why the hell would anyone kill Mackay?"

Eaton did not speak for a long time. Eventually he said:

"Don't be bloody naïve, Bosun."

Geordie felt an odd little lurch in his gut. "Christ," he said softly. "Do you think that perverted bastard finally went after someone big enough to give him what he deserved?"

"I didn't tell you the whole," Eaton said flatly. "They found him dead in a corner. The slash was huge, he'd have bled out in minutes. But whoever killed him cut off his balls and stuffed them in his mouth. I don't think there's any doubt why he died."

Geordie felt sick. "Who could do that? And why?"

"I don't know, Bosun, but I'm guessing it's to make a point that any other man who tries buggering the boys is going to get the same. I don't know if there's anyone else on this ship who shares Mackay's nasty habits with the young ones, but if there is, I think he'll keep it in his trousers from now on."

"Bloody hell." Geordie considered himself unshockable, but admitted to himself that he had been wrong. "I wonder what made this man set himself up to defend the ship's boys? It's a reet shame he's like to hang for it, that bastard Mackay has had it coming for years. I've only served with him on this one voyage, and I've been haunting him ever since young Price went overboard and drowned. It was down as an accident, but the whole crew knew Mackay had been at him for months. I couldn't get him to testify."

"You can't blame him, Bosun. Sodomy is a capital crime, and if Mackay were brought to trial he could easily claim the boy consented."

"It's impossible to prove anyway as there have to be witnesses to every detail. I didn't blame Price, he couldn't hide from Mackay forever, and he'd have got a good hiding on top of everything else. I tried talking to the captain about it."

"Several of us tried, Bosun, but Captain Dalton simply said that Mackay was an excellent and very experienced seaman and that's all he cared about. I'm not sorry the man is gone, it infuriated me knowing he was getting away with it. But it will be a shame if this boy gets hanged for defending himself."

"Boy?" Geordie said, startled. "It's one of the boys?"

"Fourteen or fifteen at a guess. I've had nothing to do with him. He was picked up with the rest of the crew of that shipwrecked merchantman. All the others did the sensible thing and signed up as volunteers, but this boy refused to do so. He's a pressed man, and Marshall, who's the petty officer in charge of his mess, says he's been difficult from the start. At best, he'll get a flogging for being where he shouldn't be. At worst, they'll hang him."

"But no blood on his clothing," Geordie said softly.

"A few stains that might be, but we can't be sure. If he went in before it dried, chances are there wouldn't be."

"Clever little bastard."

***

Prisoners awaiting trial were kept in irons in the half-deck, an area beneath the quarterdeck which was covered but not fully enclosed. It was used partly for storage, but there were often one or two prisoners chained up to heavy metal rings set into the bulkhead. Discipline aboard ship was largely Geordie's responsibility, with the help of his bosun's mates, so when he had given his delayed report to the captain, he gave instructions to his juniors, made a tour of the ship, checking that all was well, then went to inspect the accused. The boy was the only prisoner chained there, a leggy form huddled against the wooden wall in an attempt to keep him out of the brisk wind. His clothing was still very damp, the regulation loose trousers, rough shirt and blue jacket clinging to his body. His tousled fair head was bowed, and his arms wrapped around his knees. He was visibly shivering, and Geordie swore under his breath.

"On your feet, boy."

The boy looked up, giving Geordie a glimpse of startling blue eyes, then unwrapped himself and got to his feet in one smooth movement. He stood straight, tall for a boy of his age but still heartbreakingly young. Geordie looked him over curiously. He looked well-nourished when compared to the skinny children who often came into the navy from poor households and although he kept his eyes lowered to the deck, he bore himself with a certain arrogance which aroused Geordie's curiosity even more. Listening to Mr Eaton's bloodthirsty tale, Geordie had doubted that any boy of this age could undertake the murder of Jemmy Mackay then endure the freezing waters of the Atlantic. Looking at this boy, Geordie was suddenly not so sure.

"What's your name?"

The boy looked up. "Van Daan. Paul van Daan."

Geordie did not respond for a minute. The voice was surprising and raised immediate alarm bells. He had served, during his time, alongside men of all nationalities and all social classes. It was not at all unusual for a young gentleman of this age to join the navy, initially as an officer's servant, and then as a midshipman, with a view to taking the lieutenant's examination and becoming an officer. Geordie recognised this boy's accent, and it did not come from any fisherman's cottage or dockyard slum. He was beginning to wonder why this boy was below decks as a pressed man.

"Van Daan? That's not an English name."

"My father is Dutch; I was raised in England."

The alarm bells were growing louder. Geordie often supervised the signing on of new crew, but the dozen pressed men picked up during their stop at English Harbour had been from the crew of a shipwrecked merchantman. They were obvious targets for the press gang; all were experienced seamen and Geordie had seen no need to get involved. He had a feeling he should have.

Geordie reached for his whistle and summoned one of his bosun's mates. "Smith, let the watch officer know I'm taking Van Daan below to Janet for a spell. He's injured and he's still soaked, and he needs feeding. I'll return him when he's fit, and I'll speak to the captain later to see what charges he's bringing, if any. Unchain him."

Smith moved forward readily, but shot Geordie a wary look. "You sure, Bosun? You want to watch this one, he's like a wild thing. Pushed Marine Bennet right off the dock when they was bringing him aboard and punched the lights out of Snyder when he used his cane on him. Snyder had to give him half a dozen of the best before he went down."

Geordie studied the boy. He still had the over-long limbs of boyhood, but he had the grace of an athlete and Geordie wondered if he boxed. Geordie had been a very good boxer in his youth and still entered the odd bout during shore leave, just to keep in practice. He was glad of Smith's warning. Pointedly, he drew the baton he wore at his waist.

"You try that with me, laddie, and you'll be back in irons with a couple of buckets of cold water over you and a thumping headache to go with it," he said.

The irons clanked as they were removed, and Van Daan flexed his wrists in relief and rubbed them. "What would be the point out here?" he asked. "There's nowhere to run."

There was something about the bald truth of that statement which tugged at Geordie's heart unexpectedly. He motioned for Van Daan to follow him and led the way to the galley. At this hour the huge stove was roaring, and the ship's cook and his assistants were busy over the main meal. A savoury smell reminded Geordie of how hungry he was. It was almost dinner time and the captain and the master would be on the quarterdeck taking the noon sight.

There was a wooden bench and table outside Geordie's cabin which was located in the bow of the ship. Geordie indicated that Van Daan should sit. He opened his mouth to warn the boy again about the consequences of moving, then caught his eye and stopped himself. He did not know why, but he was absolutely certain Van Daan would simply remind him again that he had nowhere to go.

"Janet, are you there, bonny lass?"

"Aye, where else would I be at this hour?" Janet opened the door, a shirt she was mending in her hand and surveyed the prisoner thoughtfully. The boy stared back.

"And who's this half-drowned rat you've brought for dinner, husband?"

Geordie opened his mouth to explain, but the boy was on his feet, and the bow he executed chilled Geordie to the bone. "My apologies, ma'am, I had something of an accident in the small hours. I was feeling sick and leaned over too far. It's lucky I'm a strong swimmer. Paul van Daan. Pressed man."

Geordie saw his wife give the youth a long sweeping glance, then she smiled. Janet was a very comely woman with a lovely smile. To Geordie's complete astonishment, the boy smiled back. "And a bit of a drowned-rat," he said apologetically.

Geordie put his hand on Van Daan's shoulder and shoved him back onto the bench. "Will you have a look at that gash on his hand, bonny lass, while I get some dry clothes from the slops for him? He might be about to hang for murder and he's definitely due a flogging, but we can't have him freezing to death, it's not in the regulations. You can eat your dinner here with us and warm up a bit and then you'll need to go back where you should be."

"Thank you, it's very good of you, sir."

"Not sir, laddie. I'm not a commissioned officer, you should call me Bosun."

"Sorry, Bosun."

"And try and pretend to do it respectfully, you arrogant little shit. Do you know how much trouble you're in?"

"Yes, Bosun."

Geordie studied him, grunted, and disappeared to find clothing. He allowed the boy to change in the cabin, while Janet set the table and went to collect the food. As Van Daan emerged, Geordie ran his eyes over him, and the boy held out his arms at his sides.

"I've not stolen anything, I swear, you can search me. I'm not that stupid. Like you said, I'm in enough trouble."

Geordie could not help smiling. "Oh sit you down and drink your grog. Here's my lass with the food. Eat."

Geordie watched the boy covertly as he ate, while telling Janet about the events of the morning. He did not give the full details of Mackay's murder, but he could see she was still shocked. Van Daan did not look up from his meal, eating stew with the concentration of a boy who had not eaten for a while.

"I just stopped for a chat with Petty Officer Marshall about you, Van Daan," Geordie said, when the bowl was empty. "He says you've not made a good start aboard the *Hera*. You've barely gone a day without a punishment in the log. Insolence, abusing your seniors, fighting in the mess."

"If I didn't fight, I wouldn't eat, Bosun."

Geordie eyed him with reluctant respect. "Aye, there's probably something in that, lad, they'll steal your rations if you let them. But to put another boy in the sickbay for two days…"

"He had a knife. But I did hit him too hard. I was…I got angry."

Geordie wondered if he had been about to say that he was scared. He glanced at Janet, who got up. "I'll get you some more," she said, sounding alarmingly maternal. "If you've been fighting over every meal, it'll make a nice change to sit and eat like a decent human being."

Van Daan looked up quickly and smiled. "Oh it does, ma'am. But please, I don't want to put you out."

"It's no trouble for a lad with manners like yours," Janet said, and bustled away. Van Daan's smile faded, and Geordie thought that without it he looked very young and very lost. He wondered again what the hell this boy was doing below decks as a pressed man.

"All right, laddie," he said gruffly. "You've been fed, and you've had your grog. At least…you've barely touched it. Don't you want it?"

The boy gave a somewhat embarrassed smile. "I can't stand it," he said frankly. "I'd rather have water, actually."

Geordie studied him, then sighed. He got up, went into his cabin, and returned with a bottle and two glasses. Setting them on the table he poured.

"Sip it," he said shortly. "This is not rum grog."

Van Daan picked up the glass and sniffed suspiciously at the amber coloured liquid. "What is it?"

"Scotch whisky, laddie. Comes from a little distillery just over the border from where I grew up. My sister sends it to me from time to time. Try it."

Van Daan took a sip. Geordie watched his expression. He swallowed and coughed a little as the peaty spirit caught in his throat then looked up. "That's excellent."

"Spoken like a connoisseur," Geordie said ironically. Janet was back, setting another plate in front of the boy, along with a chunk of dark bread.

"I need to turn the laundry, husband, so I'll leave you to it," she said, with her accustomed tact. Van Daan got to his feet with instinctive courtesy. Janet studied him for a moment.

"Eat," she said. "You'll need your strength for whatever comes next. And then talk to my husband, tell him the truth, and listen to his advice. He's a good man."

The boy offered his charming smile again and Geordie decided that he was glad Van Daan was not ten years older. "Thank you for your kindness, ma'am. Whatever happens, I won't forget it."

When Janet had gone, Van Daan returned to his meal. Geordie finished his grog, since it should not go to waste, then sipped his whisky and waited for the boy to finish. He was looking better, with more colour in his cheeks, and the fair hair had dried to a dark gold, shoulder length and tied back with a grubby strip of linen. Eventually, Van Daan set his spoon down.

"That's the most I've eaten since I came on board. Worth getting hanged for. Thank you, sir…I mean, Bosun."

"Tell me what happened?"

"I already told the lieutenant. There's not much to tell. I felt sick. I'm over it mostly during the day, but sometimes at night…I went up on deck because it's not civil to cast up accounts where men are sleeping."

"You're not allowed to wander around the ship at night, boy, they must have told you that."

"I'd forgotten, I was feeling so ill. Anyway, I must have had a dizzy spell and gone over. Thank God I didn't hit my head on the way down or I'd have drowned."

The blue eyes were limpid and innocent. Geordie studied him. Despite his height and surprising air of self-assurance, this was still very much a boy. Geordie thought again about what had happened to Mackay. He could imagine this lad striking out in self-defence, but the cold-blooded killing and mutilation of a man seemed beyond him. At the same time, his story sounded carefully rehearsed rather than natural. Geordie had sent his bosun's mates to make enquiries among the crew and there was no evidence of anybody else being away from his proper place at that time.

"You must be a very strong swimmer," Geordie said.

"I am. I learned in the lake as a boy."

"Which lake?"

"At Southwinds, where I grew up. It's in Leicestershire."

"How did you cut your hand?"

"It must have been when I was trying to grab the ladder from the water."

"A thin cut for a splinter. Almost looked like a knife."

"No, I'd have remembered if I'd cut it on a knife."

"You bloody liar," Geordie said softly. "You killed him, didn't you?"

"No, Bosun."

"Well somebody killed him and cut his balls off. Now why?"

"I don't know, Bosun."

"Don't you? I bloody do. Able Seaman Mackay had some very nasty habits with the younger boys aboard ship. I've been trying to get somebody to speak up about it for months. One young lad, a boy called Harry Price, drowned himself a few months back, and I've always wondered if it was because he couldn't stand it any longer. What do you think, Van Daan?"

Paul van Daan looked back at him. He had flushed a little, but to Geordie's surprise he neither turned away or dropped his gaze, although Geordie could see that his fists had clenched together until the knuckles were white.

"I don't know what to think, Bosun, I wasn't there when Price drowned himself. But do you know what? I wish I fucking had been."

The obscenity sounded odd in Van Daan's well-spoken accent, but his tone told Geordie everything he needed to know. Reaching for the bottle, he poured another shot into each glass.

"What did he do to you, Van Daan?"

"Nothing, Bosun."

"What did he try to do?"

"Nothing, Bosun. I never met Able Seaman Mackay."

Van Daan reached for the glass. Geordie watched as he inhaled the rich aroma of the whisky and swirled it around the glass a little before sipping it appreciatively. Somebody had taught this boy how to enjoy good wine or good brandy.

"You're a bad liar, Van Daan."

"I've been told that before, Bosun."

"Don't you know they could hang you for this?"

"Don't they have to prove it?"

Geordie met his eyes for a long time. He was fascinated by Van Daan's odd blend of boyish vulnerability and adult intelligence. During his years at sea Geordie had come across a lot of boys of this age, but he had never encountered one quite like this.

Finally he reached for his own glass. "Let's try a different question. What the bloody hell are you doing here, boy? For one thing are you even old enough to be pressed? And secondly, from your voice and your manner, you're not a common seaman."

"No. I'll probably need to work on that if I'm going to survive the next few months."

"Who are you?"

"I told you. Paul van Daan."

"Your family?"

"My father owns a shipping company."

Geordie stared at him very hard for a while. The boy's gaze did not waver. Eventually, Geordie said:

"You're a gentleman's son?"

"Yes. And I'm almost fifteen. Not quite old enough to be pressed, but close."

"Did you tell them that?"

"Do I look stupid? Of course I did. Repeatedly. Then I hit people and tried to escape. That didn't work either."

Geordie closed his eyes. "Oh shit. Somebody is going to be very sorry for this."

"Yes, they are."

Geordie opened his eyes at the tone. Abruptly he was absolutely sure Van Daan had killed Mackay. Geordie suspected he also knew what had been done to him to drive him to commit such an appalling crime. He understood why Van Daan refused to talk about it. Geordie could only imagine the terror of a gently-bred boy thrown into a situation so far removed from the life he was used to. Mackay's assault, coming before Van Daan had time to even begin to adjust, would have been enough to break most boys. Geordie wondered what it would take to break this particular youth and hoped passionately he was not about to find out.

"Bosun. Captain wants to see you."

Geordie sighed. "I'd be willing to bet it's about you, you troublesome wee bastard. Finish that drink and get up."

Van Daan obeyed, getting to his feet. "If I can stand. It's stronger than I'm used to."

"You'll need to get yourself a stronger head and stomach if you're going to survive the navy, laddie."

"You might not have to worry about that for much longer," Van Daan said. It was a creditable effort, but Geordie could hear the tremor in his voice. He silently applauded the boy. Only a fool would claim not to be afraid when faced with a hanging, but this slender youth was controlling it very well, and Geordie knew that in the noise of battle or the screaming height of a storm at sea, that was what mattered. He regarded Van Daan and decided to be honest.

"You're going to get hanged or flogged, Van Daan. I'm going to the captain and I'm going to tell him the truth about you. I'm also going to try to convince him that a young sprig of the gentry couldn't possibly slit a man's throat and mutilate the body. That won't be difficult because until today, I wouldn't have thought it myself. But Captain Dalton's an awkward man and I can't tell what he'll do."

"It's all right, sir. I mean Bosun. Just...thank you for this. Thank Mrs Armstrong as well, will you? Whatever happens, I'm grateful."

Geordie studied him, troubled. "No point in asking you why in God's name you did it that way, I suppose. Given that you didn't do it."

"Is it bothering you?" Van Daan said unexpectedly. "I'm sorry. Look...your wife said I should trust you, but I don't know you yet, it would be stupid. So I didn't do it. But if you want me to guess, I'd say the man who did that was pretty sure Mackay hadn't done that for the last time. Maybe he could have found another way to protect himself. I don't know what's possible, I've not been here long."

"I know. You poor little bastard, you don't know your head from your heels, do you? And then this. But Christ, to mutilate him like that…"

"Once again, Bosun, I can only guess," Van Daan said gravely. "I don't know how common it is in this navy for a man to do what he did and get away with it for years. How many boys, I wonder? He needed stopping. Not just for one attack but for all the others he was going to do in the future. And if there's any other perverted bastard aboard this ship thinking about doing the same thing, I don't think he'll be in any doubt about what's going to happen to him if he does. Maybe you don't think that's worth risking a hanging. Maybe I don't. But I can tell you for sure, that whoever killed him did."

Geordie suspected that was the closest he was ever going to get to an admission from this boy. Van Daan's reasoning made terrifying sense given what had happened to him although Geordie was still astonished that a lad of not quite fifteen had not only come up with the plan but carried it through. He felt oddly flattered that Van Daan had admitted even this much. Geordie reached for his whistle to summon one of his mates. Derbyshire was in his twenties and of medium height and watching them walk away back to the half-deck, Geordie realised Van Daan was already as tall and probably still had a few years of growing to do. He hoped the boy survived long enough.

***

Geordie found Lieutenant Eaton with Captain Dalton. The captain was in a foul temper, which was very common. He barked out questions and Geordie responded, keeping his answers short and factual. When he had finished, Dalton sat back in his chair.

"Did he do it?"

"I don't think so, sir," Geordie said without hesitation. "He's a tall lad, but he's very young and Mackay was a big man. Besides, I don't think a boy from his background could do what was done. I don't think it would occur to him."

"He was the only man away from his hammock."

"The only one who was caught, sir, but a murderer would be canny enough to sneak back to his place without being seen."

"What about the blood?" Eaton asked. "He'd have been covered in it."

"He could have changed. It's not impossible that he'd purloined spare clouts from somewhere. Dumped the bloody clothing over the side in the dark, sluiced himself down with a bucket of water and got back to bed. Nobody searched, sir, because everybody thought we'd got our man."

"Damn it, I still think he's guilty," Dalton snarled. "He should be hanged."

"I think he'd get off at a trial, Captain," Eaton said quietly. "No witnesses and no evidence. They searched his hammock and the few possessions he has. No knife, no bloody clothing. Nobody saw or heard anything apart from Van Daan scrambling back up onto deck half-drowned. He's a landsman and a pressed man, it's not impossible to believe he was seasick and fell overboard."

"Well who the hell killed Mackay?" Dalton roared. "What if he does it again? What if he kills an officer? What if he kills me?"

Geordie met Eaton's eyes and looked away quickly, suppressing a snort of unsuitable laughter. "I don't think that's likely sir," Eaton said gravely. "It seems pretty obvious that whoever did this was either a victim of Mackay's unsavoury practices or a friend of a victim. He's gone. No reason to kill again."

Dalton did not reply. He was looking down at a log book. Eventually he looked up. "Well that little bastard isn't getting away with this. I'm ordering a flogging."

"What's the charge, Captain?"

"Being bloody annoying," Dalton said.

"That's not actually a crime, Captain," Eaton said patiently.

"Although with this lad, it probably should be," Geordie said, mostly under his breath.

"Well he's been in the punishment book every day since he got here, and he was bloody well out of his hammock when he shouldn't have been. Maybe fifty of the best will teach him a lesson. See to it, Bosun, tomorrow."

Geordie froze and looked at Eaton. The first lieutenant stared back. Neither spoke. A captain could only order twelve lashes without a formal trial. It was not unheard of for a captain to order more, and within reason, it would be quietly ignored, but fifty was too many.

"Sir, we'd need a trial for that. And besides, you can only use the cane on him, he's fourteen."

"He commits a man's crime, he gets a man's punishment, Mr Eaton. Anyway, I don't believe he's fourteen, any more than I believe the rest of that nonsensical story he told you."

Geordie looked again at Eaton. "Look, sir, I really believe this boy has been pressed illegally. I talked with him for a long time and it's obvious he's well-spoken and educated. I don't think he should be here."

"He's taken you for a fool, Bosun. He's a practiced liar and probably a thief."

Geordie could feel his temper rising. He opened his mouth to speak then closed it again at a very tiny shake of the head from Eaton.

"Whatever the boy has or hasn't done, Captain, I think it would be a mistake to administer as many as fifty without a formal trial," Eaton said. "It is up to you of course, but even if the boy is over fourteen, he is still young, and we do not know his state of health. If anything should go wrong, I am afraid you could lay yourself open to serious criticism."

"I am the captain of this ship, and I will not be held to ransom against the word of a dirty little ragamuffin with a fluent tongue!" Dalton exploded. "Flog him. Thirty lashes, and with the cat, not the cane, during the punishment hour tomorrow. As for this pack of lies about being a gentleman, I want to hear nothing more of it. Get out of here."

Outside, Eaton beckoned for Geordie to follow him to the starboard rail. "You need to stop pushing him about an illegal impressment, Bosun."

"Talk to that boy for ten minutes, sir, and you'll agree."

"I believe you. But for the boy's sake, you need to shut up about it. It's recorded in the log that the boy protested his impressment. Dalton failed to listen, he failed to investigate, and he took that boy to sea in the full knowledge that his impressment might well be illegal because he was drunk, and he didn't care."

"That's no surprise to me, sir."

"Or me. But if it turns out that young Van Daan really is the son of a man of influence, and he makes it out of here in one piece, it could mean the end of Dalton's career. I would rather Dalton didn't work that out."

Geordie felt suddenly very cold. He turned his head. "You don't think he would…?"

"I don't know what he'd do. I've served under him for five months and the minute I get the chance, I am leaving this ship. I don't care if I have to go onto half-pay, or take a post as a second lieutenant again, I'm not working under that man."

"I don't blame you, sir. I've been with the *Hera* a long time, but if he doesn't go, I might."

"A bosun of your experience won't have any trouble finding another ship, Armstrong. It might take me longer, but I don't care."

"Can't we get a letter out to his father?"

"Not without Dalton knowing. He should write one, though, and I'll take charge of it. If we're in port, I predict that boy stands no chance of leaving this ship even if he signs up as a volunteer. But I might be able to send it off."

"If you're right about the captain, that won't help, sir," Geordie said. "Because if the boy's father goes to the Admiralty about getting him back, they're going to write to Captain Dalton directly, asking him about it. All he has to do is make sure Van Daan has an accident and is buried at sea and then he can throw up his hands and claim he knew nothing about it. Without the boy to speak up, who will care?"

"Dear God, you're right."

"The only thing we can do is pretend we all believe the captain, let him flog the boy and say nothing more about it. After a few weeks of quiet, the captain will have convinced himself the boy was nothing but a liar and a troublemaker and as long as Van Daan stays out of trouble, he'll forget about him. When we reach a port with an English consulate, we can get him ashore and out of Dalton's reach."

Eaton looked troubled. "How the hell are you going to manage to persuade that lad to keep quiet and keep his head down, Bosun?"

Geordie had already made the decision. "I'm going to tell him the truth," he said.

***

Geordie brought the boy into the small cabin and closed the door to have the conversation, stationing his wife on the bench outside in case of eavesdroppers. It felt ridiculous to be taking such precautions aboard ship, but Eaton's words had convinced Geordie.

Van Daan sat at the opposite end of the bunk and listened without saying a word as Geordie related what had happened and repeated his conversation with Lieutenant Eaton. At the end of it, he sat in silence for so long that Geordie wondered if it had, after all, been wrong to speak to such a young boy as though he was an adult.

Eventually Van Daan stirred and looked up. "What do I need to do?" he asked.

Geordie caught his breath and realised that he had not, after all, got it wrong. "Take the flogging," he said bluntly. "I can't get you out of it, and it's bloody painful, lad. I'm sorry. You don't deserve this."

Van Daan sat silently for a moment, staring at his linked fingers in his lap. Then he looked up. "To some degree, I do, Bosun."

Geordie could not help smiling. "Is that a confession, lad?"

"Oh no."

"I didn't think so. I'll take care of you, you'll be all right, and Mr Eaton will make sure it doesn't go too far. After that, I'm going to get you signed up as a volunteer. I want you to behave. Keep your head down, do as you're told and stop demanding to be taken to the nearest English port."

"Will that work?"

"The captain's not that bright, laddie. If you stay out of trouble he'll forget about you. I don't know how long it will take, but eventually me and Mr Eaton will find a way to get you off this ship. I wish I could do better, but for now Dalton is in charge and you're a long way from home."

"I'm sorry, I'm causing you a lot of trouble and you've been very good about it. I understand, and I'll do the best I can."

Geordie studied him. "What does that mean?"

"Only that I'm not that good at keeping my head down. I'm not sure I can manage it for that long. But I think I know what to do to fit in better. So don't worry."

***

Geordie had both attended and arranged many floggings but had never before felt such distaste for the process. Van Daan was the only miscreant up for punishment the following day. At eleven-thirty, Geordie gave the order for the ship's company to muster by watches on either side of the main deck. Van Daan was brought on deck. Tradition allowed him to plead his case to the captain. On this occasion, Geordie could not imagine what the captain would ask or what the boy would say. He found himself rigid with tension as Van Daan stepped forward. He looked very young, the fair hair lifted in the breeze away from the smooth lines of his face.

"You are accused of absenting yourself from your berth, boy, along with numerous other offences since your arrival aboard ship," Dalton said, his voice harsh. "Have you anything to say?"

"No, sir."

"Nothing? No excuse for your behaviour?"

"Only that the life is new to me, sir, and I'll try to improve."

It was perfect and Geordie thanked God he had not tried to coach Van Daan since he could not have done better. If he had been in Dalton's place he would not have believed a word of it, but Geordie could see the captain relax. He appreciated humility and seemed completely unable to see that the boy's stance radiated contempt.

"Thirty lashes Bosun."

Geordie gave the order, and Smith stepped forward with the cat. The handle was covered with red cloth and the whip consisted of nine thin pieces of line with each section knotted several times along its length. A new cat was made for each flogging by one of the bosun's mates. It was their duty to administer the flogging, swapping over after each dozen to ensure that a tired arm did not lessen the punishment.

Geordie had selected the three mates with care and had spoken to them in advance very specifically. He could not prevent the boy's suffering, but he could ensure that over-zealous administration did not make it worse.

Van Daan was stripped to the waist and bound by the wrists to the wooden grating situated at the gangway. Lieutenant Gordon stepped forward to read the Article of War pertaining to the boy's crimes aloud and then stepped back. There was complete silence across the deck. Geordie wondered if it was his imagination that the atmosphere was more tense than at a normal flogging, possibly because of the victim's youth and possibly because of the spectre of Mackay's unsolved murder hovering in the background.

The cat fell across Van Daan's back, leaving long red weals. The boy's body jumped but he made no sound. The cat fell again and again. Geordie felt himself flinch internally with each blow. He had never felt like this before at a flogging and he could not decide if it was the injustice of it or if it was because of his enormous liking and respect for the boy being beaten.

At the first changeover, the ship's surgeon went forward to inspect Van Daan's back. Geordie thought he looked uncomfortable. Eaton had told him that Dr Baird had insisted on registering a formal objection to the cat being used on a boy this young, and Geordie respected him for it.

At twenty lashes the skin broke. Van Daan had still not made a sound, though his body convulsed at each blow. Geordie realised he was clenching his fists so hard that his nails were digging into his palms, leaving marks. He imagined himself punching Captain Dalton over and over until he did not get up and it helped a little.

At twenty-six lashes, Van Daan's back was bloody and for the first time he uttered a little cry, quickly bitten back. Geordie thought about the other injuries, the bruising and the muscle damage and the battering to the internal organs, and he wondered if the crew would support him if he drew his pistol and shot Dalton through the head. He thought they might.

At thirty lashes, the third bosun's mate, Petty Officer Ferris, lowered the cat with an air of relief. The surgeon moved forward.

"One moment, Doctor."

Captain Dalton walked across the deck towards Van Daan. Geordie moved forward as well, ignoring the frantic signals from Lieutenant Eaton. He wanted to hear what was said. Dalton reached up and caught the long fair hair, wet with sweat. He twisted his hand in it and yanked the boy's head back.

"Do you hear me, Van Daan?"

"Yes, sir."

"Did you kill Mackay?"

"No, sir."

"Louder, Van Daan."

"No, sir."

"What if I told you I could whip you until you confess?"

Geordie realised he was poised, ready to attack. He had never felt such an urge to kill in his life.

"Well I can't stop you, sir." Van Daan's voice was faint but his tone was loaded with so much contempt that even Dalton could not miss it. Geordie groaned inwardly.

Dalton stepped back. "Another dozen, Ferris," he said loudly.

Ferris looked over at Geordie, appalled. Geordie took a deep breath. He decided that he was about to commit mutiny and he prayed that whatever happened, Janet would be all right.

"Belay that order, Petty Officer Ferris," Lieutenant Eaton called out.

Ferris lowered his arm, looking relieved. Dalton swung around. "What did you say, Mr Eaton?" he demanded.

"Sorry, sir, it's just that you've miscounted. The sentence was thirty, and I remember you didn't want more than that on a boy this young, especially with the cat. It's recorded in the log, sir."

There was a long moment of agonised silence across the deck and Geordie silently thanked God that Daniel Eaton had all the intelligence and integrity that his captain lacked. He hoped somebody at the Admiralty realised it soon and gave the man a command of his own. The ship's log was inviolate and if Dalton continued with the punishment it would be recorded and could be used against him.

Dalton glared at his first lieutenant with sheer hatred then turned to the surgeon and nodded. Geordie felt as though the entire crew let out a collective sigh of relief. He called the order and two of his mates went forward to untie the prisoner.

Abruptly, Dalton stopped and stooped. He picked up a wooden pail of salt water, turned back to the boy on the grating and threw the entire contents over the boy's back. Van Daan screamed. Dalton turned away and stomped back to his cabin, leaving Geordie and the first officer to stand the crew down.

Geordie ran to the boy as the mates lowered him face down onto the deck. After that one agonised yell, he had made no further sound and Geordie felt a sense of panic. The damage done to a man by a flogging could be completely unpredictable, depending on the physical condition of the victim. Paul van Daan was young, much too young to have been beaten by the cat which was usually reserved for adults. He was also, Geordie discovered, a mass of bruises all over his fair skin, presumably due to the over-enthusiastic use of the cane on the recalcitrant new recruit during his first week aboard ship. Geordie had known a man die from damage to his kidneys after a flogging and he knelt beside the boy, running his eyes over the bloody mess of his back, seeing new bruising coming up beneath the existing marks.

"Van Daan. Can you hear me?"

"He's fainted, Bosun."

"Carry him to the sick bay," Geordie said, getting up. "Dr Baird will see to him there."

"I will. And please understand, Armstrong, that I will be keeping detailed notes of this boy's condition. If he dies because of what has been done to him aboard this ship, it will be fully recorded, and I intend to complain to the Admiralty."

"Good," Geordie said. "Lift him carefully, Ferris."

"Get your fucking hands off me," a voice said distinctly. "Or I will break your fucking fingers."

The men froze. Geordie motioned them back. "It's good to see your punishment has settled you down proper, Van Daan. They're trying to help you, you mannerless young twat."

"If this is their idea of help, I'll live without it." The boy turned his head to look at Geordie. "I wouldn't mind a hand up though, Bosun."

"Let them carry you."

"I'll walk."

Geordie said nothing. He watched as, slowly and painfully, Van Daan heaved himself onto all fours. He stopped, wincing at a sudden pain, and put his hand to his side. "Christ, that hurts."

"You may have a broken rib, it's not uncommon," Dr Baird said, coming to his side. "Will you not let them carry you, boy?"

Van Daan turned his head to look at him, and surprisingly managed a shadow of his charming smile. "Thank you, Doctor. I probably sound mad, but I really need to walk away from this. Would you?"

Baird offered his hand without speaking and between him and Geordie, they got Van Daan onto his feet. The tall form swayed for a moment and Geordie stood ready to catch him, but Van Daan steadied himself. He shook his head at the doctor's proffered arm but did it with a faint smile. He walked carefully, but seemed reasonably steady. Geordie trod behind him trying not to fuss like a hen with one chick. He wished the obstinate whelp had remained unconscious.

Once he had reached the sick bay, Van Daan became more cooperative, and Geordie left him with Baird and went to find Janet. He was not surprised to discover that his wife had expressed her sympathy by laundering and mending Van Daan's few items of clothing. She had also added to them, and Geordie recognised an old shirt and trousers of his own, spotlessly clean, and neatly darned. He hid a smile, wondering if Van Daan knew that he had been adopted by the fiercest creature on the ship.

Geordie went through the rest of his day as normal, forcing himself to leave the boy alone. Van Daan needed rest in order to heal, and at least in the sick bay he would get solitude and relative quiet. He looked in at five o'clock, after the men had been issued with their second grog ration, and the mess cooks were beginning to collect provisions for supper.

There were eighteen berths in the sick bay which was on the starboard side of the ship. Half a dozen of them were occupied by sick or injured sailors, but Baird had put his newest patient in one of the two curtained alcoves which he reserved for more serious cases, where privacy might be required. Van Daan was asleep, lying on his front, the rough blankets pushed down to his hips to avoid touching his wounds.

Geordie stood looking down at him. In sleep, the boy looked more like the child he really was. What Geordie could see of his body was a mass of red bleeding stripes and black bruising, overlaying the yellowing remains of older injuries. Geordie thought he must have been in pain ever since he arrived on board and was thankful that at least now he would have no choice but to rest and heal. All the same, as he left he paused by the surgeon's table, where Baird's assistant was writing up the daily returns in a ledger.

"Keep an eye on Van Daan, will you, Harris? If he makes any attempt to get up and go back to his duties, tell him I'll give him a kicking that'll make that flogging look like a picnic."

Harris grinned, showing yellowed teeth. "Already told him once, Bosun. Don't worry, we'll keep him quiet. Poor little bastard. Got balls though, I've seen grown men break down sooner than he did. He still a pressed man?"

"I'll be down to get him properly signed up as a volunteer tomorrow. When he's fit for duty, I'm getting him assigned to the rigging."

"He's a landsman, Bosun. He'll kill himself."

Geordie glanced back at the cubicle where the sleeping boy lay. "You need to trust me with this one, Harris. If we don't keep him busy, he'll stir up the entire crew of this ship until somebody really does kill him."

Harris looked amused. "You adopting him, Bosun?"

"I'm going to train him. And I'll speak to the schoolmaster about moving him up to take lessons with the older boys. He can already read and write, so he can study seamanship. At least it'll keep him out of mischief. For now, just let him rest. He bloody needs it after what he's been through."

***

May, 1798

Geordie was writing up the Boatswain's accounts in his store cabin, a job he loathed, when First Lieutenant Eaton appeared in the doorway.

"Do you have a minute, Bosun?"

"I've got an hour, sir, if it'll get me away from this."

"Come down to your dinner bench. I've got some news and we're celebrating."

Eaton lifted a wine bottle and Geordie grinned and got up. He locked the door carefully behind him. He could guess Eaton's news and he was pleased for the man although he would miss him. Seated at the wooden table, Eaton poured two cups.

"To the third rate, *HMS Triumphant* and her new post-captain, Bosun."

"Congratulations, sir, it's well deserved. Came with the mail boat, did it?"

"Yes. I'm to sail back with her almost immediately, the *Triumphant* is with the fleet off Toulon. An old ship and in need of an update, but my first post command."

"You'll be missed."

"I wish I could take you with me, Armstrong."

"You'll have a good bosun of your own, sir, who knows the ship. Mediterranean Fleet then?"

"Yes, and in a hurry. They're sending a fleet under Nelson, hoping to engage the French."

Geordie hid a smile at Eaton's attempt to sound nonchalant. At his age, Geordie had also longed for battle and glory and the chance to shine. These days he preferred the long, easy days of blockade duty and would be happy to never hear a gun fired in anger again. He raised his cup.

"Good luck, sir."

"Captain Dalton is going to get Powlett to act up as first lieutenant."

"Is he sorry to see you go, sir?"

"I can't tell, Bosun, he's such a miserable bastard all the time, I'm not sure how I'd know the difference. But I wanted to speak to you about Van Daan."

"No reply to your letter, then?"

"No, and there should have been. I think it got lost or went down with a ship. I was hoping I might be able to get the boy ashore, but they're ferrying me straight to the ship, there's no time. And I've no wish to dump him somewhere he might get picked up by another press gang. We need to get him to the British authorities and do this properly. A long way from Captain Dalton."

"Once you're away, you'll be able to write again, sir. Dalton has taken no notice of Van Daan for a long time."

"He might, if he receives a stiff letter from the Admiralty asking why he has an illegally pressed gentleman's son aboard and hasn't returned him to his proper place. Dalton got himself into this because he was too lazy and too much of a drunkard to do his job properly, but if he finds out Van Daan really is everything he claimed to be, I wouldn't trust him not to quietly find a way to shut him up before he can give evidence about what was done to him. Look, Bosun, I know Van Daan is a bit of a favourite of yours and Janet's. But I was thinking of taking him with me as an officer's servant. Once aboard, I'll promote him to petty officer. I'll write again immediately to his father, and I'll write to the Admiralty as well."

"You're taking him into battle, though, sir." Geordie felt slightly sick.

"Probably. I can't turn the ship round to get him to safety. But the first chance I can, I'll drop him off at an English consulate. If he wants to go."

Geordie laughed. "I see right through you, you duplicitous bastard, sir. You're going to promote him to midshipman as fast as you can and hope he'll decide to stay on and try for an officer's commission, aren't you?"

"Oh come on, Bosun, what would you do in my place? When did you last see a boy with his talent for leadership? I'd be mad not to try."

Geordie got up. "Just so long as you give him a choice."

"You'll miss him."

"Like a piece of my heart," Geordie said simply. "We never had children, Janet and me. Told ourselves it was just as well, since it's meant we've been together all these years. But the Van Daan boy reminded both of us what we've missed. Still, I'm proud of the man he's going to become. If he can get there without getting himself killed, the reckless young bastard. Come and find him and tell him the good news."

Up on deck, there was a flurry of activity up in the rigging as the officer of the watch had ordered the main topsail to be set. The topmen were clambering up the shrouds towards the main top. Geordie and Eaton stopped to watch them, shading their eyes against the sun. They were fast and nimble, scrambling barefooted over masts and sail.

First to the top was a tall slim figure. He had removed his blue jacket and hat, and the sun sparked an occasional golden light off his fair hair. Arriving at his destination, he looked back at his fellows and pantomimed waiting impatiently for the others to be in place, the young face alight with laughter.

The sail had been tightly reefed in and Geordie watched as the men loosed the sail then kicked it out and down, where other crew members eased on the lines. It was a process Geordie had watched a thousand times during his time at sea, and probably performed as many. He watched now as the topmen completed their task then swarmed back down the rigging. It was not supposed to be a race, but the younger men often made it so. When Van Daan was firmly back on the deck, Geordie raised his voice.

"Van Daan. I catch you using the rigging as a race track again, you'll get a clip round the ear. Get yourself over here, the officer wants a word with you."

The boy approached at a run, scooping up jacket and hat from a grating along the way and managing to arrive looking vaguely presentable.

Geordie reached out to give him an affectionate cuff, knocking his hat off again, partly to prove that he was still just tall enough to make it possible and partly because he knew how much he was going to miss that simple act after tomorrow.

"First Lieutenant Eaton wants to speak to you. When he's done with you, come down to the stores, I want a word."

"Yes, sir. Yes, Bosun." Van Daan eyed him warily. "Am I in trouble? What have I done?"

"Oh, wipe that innocent look off your face or I'll do it for you, it doesn't sit well there. And pick up your hat or I'll charge you for it."

Van Daan picked up the battered straw hat with a grin. "You couldn't legitimately charge me a halfpence for this, Bosun, look at the state of it."

"Well you're not getting a new one, you'd wreck it in a week. Get along with you."

It was thirty minutes before Van Daan joined him in the store, and the laughter had been replaced by an unusually serious expression. Geordie pointed to a stool and went for beer.

"So you'll be leaving us. Officer's servant, no less."

"Only until we reach the *Triumphant*. Then it's to be petty officer."

"I'll be saluting you one day, laddie, I've known that for a long time."

"I don't think so, Bosun. I've been honest with Mr Eaton because it's only fair. I'll go with him this voyage. I think I owe him that. But afterwards, since it looks as though it will be possible, I think I'll go home."

"To see your father?"

"I'd be happy never to set eyes on him again," the boy said flatly. "He doesn't want me there, he sent me to sea in the first place, to teach me discipline, since he couldn't be bothered to do it himself. Well I think I've learned it."

"Then why leave? You're good at this, Van Daan. You'll be a midshipman in a year or so, and you'll pass the lieutenants' examination without any effort at all."

Van Daan gave a little smile. "And post-captain a year later? It's a nice story, Bosun. Don't think I've not considered it. There are things about the navy I like. But too much has happened here. And besides…a ship is too small."

Geordie considered it and knew he was right. "Aye, that's the way of it with you. Some of us feel secure within these wooden walls. Some feel trapped by them. Go home then, laddie, and make your peace with your Da however you can. But if you take my advice, you'll not let him push you behind a desk in a shipping office, or into the silk suit of a gentleman. You're not cut out for that. Think about the army. Mr Eaton is right, you've the makings of a bloody good officer if you can learn some respect for your seniors and keep your mouth shut occasionally."

"The thing I will miss about this ship, is you. And Mrs Armstrong. Does she know?"

"Aye, I've told her. She's in the cabin, mending everything you own twice over. You should go and see her and be prepared for her to cry over you, for she will."

"I might cry over her too," Van Daan said, getting up. "The packet ship leaves early. I was wondering…"

"Eat your dinner down with us today, laddie. It'll be the last time, and I'll miss sampling the whisky with you."

The boy smiled. "I'll write," he said. "And I'll send you a bottle myself when I can. To remember me by."

"I'll not be forgetting you, Paul van Daan. The ship'll be a lonelier place without you."

"You'll be all right, Bosun, while your wife is here to look after you. You've been like my family. Some day…I wonder if I'll ever marry? If I did, I'd like it to be the way you are with her. You're so close."

Geordie could feel tears tightening his throat. "Go and see her. And don't worry about it. When you've done sleeping with every pretty girl that's willing, now you've found what to do with them, there'll be a bonny lass waiting for you somewhere. Write and tell me about her if I'm still alive."

"I promise I will."

Van Daan was outside the door when Geordie had another thought. "Van Daan – what are you going to do about the captain? Will you report him, d'you think?"

Van Daan raised his eyebrows. "I don't see that I can do anything else, Bosun. My father might not like me, but he's a proud man and he'll be furious about this. He's going to want Captain Dalton's head on a plate with an apple stuffed in his mouth when he sees the scars on my back, and I'm not covering up for the drunken, spiteful bastard. Why, will it bother you?"

"Not at all. I was thinking, it would be good to serve under a different captain. It's a fine ship, the *Hera*. Could do great things under a better man."

The boy studied him for a long moment then gave one of his broad smiles. "I'll see what I can do for you, Bosun."

***

The boat left as dawn was just beginning to stain the sky with a pink wash. Geordie stood beside his wife at the rail, his arm about her, watching the oarsmen pull smoothly through the water. Eventually they could no longer see the boy's face clearly, but Geordie remained there as the rising sun spilled amber and gold across the water. Several sea birds swooped low past the hull, diving for fish then soaring up again. The packet ship waited at anchor, its rigging outlined against the glory of the morning sky. Geordie could see the figures clambering out of the boat and climbing up the side of the fast little ship, and he felt a sudden fierce envy of the boy, setting out on a new adventure with no idea where it might take him.

"I hope he'll be all right, Geordie. Do you think he'll write, as he promised? A young gentleman, back with his own kind, he might well forget."

"Well we'll have to wait and see, bonny lass. But I do wonder you know, if yonder lad is going back to his own kind or if he's just left them."

"I wish he was going directly home," Janet said. "Packet ships are often ambushed and sunk, and even if he makes it to the *Triumphant*, he's likely to be in a battle before he's safe with his family."

"He's fought with us in two skirmishes, Janet, and he's a man grown now, or very near."

"He's just sixteen and I want to know he's safe."

"I think he'll write. I'm sure he'll write. Now dry those tears and let's get some tea before the bell."

They had finished their tea and Geordie had just called the pipe for hammocks to be stowed for the day when he heard a noise from the quarterdeck above. There was a commotion of shouting and then Geordie heard the Welsh accent of First-Lieutenant Powlett calling down the companionway.

"Bosun, get yourself up here. There's something wrong with the captain."

Geordie arrived at the door to the captain's bedroom, which was on the starboard side of the ship beside the master's sea cabin, where the charts and navigation equipment was stored. The captain's servant, a skinny thirteen year old by the name of Fletcher, was holding a jug of steaming water. Beside him was Kingsley, the ship's master and Lieutenant Marshall who commanded the marines.

"I know he's in there, sir, he's been making funny noises. I think he must be ill. Maybe he's had a seizure."

"The door?" Geordie asked.

"Locked from within," Powlett said briefly. "I've sent for the carpenter."

The ship's carpenter arrived looking exasperated rather than worried, his curly dark hair untidy as if he had just emerged from his bed. The last rays of the glorious dawn gave a slightly garish light to the deck as they waited for Rashford to open the door. Geordie gently removed the heavy water jug from Fletcher and set it down out of the way.

Eventually the door was open. Rashford stood back with the air of a man who did not much care what was found within. Geordie looked over at him.

"I'd get to your inspection, Rash. Will you call Dr Baird first in case he's needed?"

"I will, but we all know he's probably dead drunk," Rashford said contemptuously. "Let me know when I can put the lock back."

Powlett was stepping cautiously into the cabin. It was spacious, with a curtained bunk, a wash stand and clothing chests, a red velvet armchair and small side table. The furniture was arranged incongruously around the two nine pounder guns and on the opposite wall was a closed door which led into the captain's day cabin, in which he dined, entertained, and took his ease. The bed curtains were closed.

As Geordie followed Powlett into the room, motioning for the others to stay back, the first thing he noticed was a muffled squawking sound from the bed. The second was the smell, which was appalling. At first, Geordie wondered if somehow a chamber pot had been kicked over, but this was far worse. The livestock pens were situated in the waist of the ship and it was often possible to smell them throughout the vessel if they were not regularly cleaned, but never this strongly.

Powlett seemed frozen in surprise, so Geordie walked forward and drew back the bed curtain. For a long moment, he stood very still, unable to believe his eyes. Captain Dalton lay on the bed. He was naked and had been neatly trussed at both wrists and ankles, which were then tied together at the back leaving him in a painfully unnatural position. The bedclothes were in a heap on the floor and Dalton's teeth were chattering with cold around the gag which had been stuffed into his mouth.

The only garment which the captain was wearing was his wig. It had been placed very firmly upon his head, glued in place with a dark sticky substance which Geordie was easily able to identify as animal manure. He had a strong suspicion that the animal pens would not need mucking out this morning as they had been very thoroughly cleaned out during the night. The rest of the manure had been plastered over the captain's body in huge reeking dollops. Beside the bed, left very neatly, was the bucket and shovel that the assailant must have used. The captain's chamber pot was beside them, pointedly empty. Geordie could not be sure and had no intention of checking, but he suspected that the captain was also wearing the contents of that.

"Oh my God," Powlett whispered. "Who in God's name…and how? Fletcher! Get yourself in here and help the captain. Bring the hot water. In fact, we'd better send for more hot water. A lot of it. This is going to take some cleaning up."

Geordie retreated to give the orders. Then, as he was fairly sure he would not be observed in the mayhem of the captain's deliverance, he slipped through the opposite door into the day cabin and stood looking around. It was an elegant room, with long windows which let in the light and could be opened to let in fresh air. It was clear that somebody had decided the room needed a good airing because one of the windows was wide open.

Geordie went to the window and stuck his head out, looking upwards towards the poop deck. It would be a scramble, but Geordie decided that should the mad idea ever take him, there were enough handholds for a man to pull himself upwards. It would be even easier for a slender, agile boy.

Geordie went back through the cabin and joined the master on the quarterdeck. "Any ideas?" he asked.

"God knows. The captain isn't the only victim. The boy who guards the livestock was found tied up, and so was the marine on duty by the captain's cabin."

"I'd keep looking," Geordie said cheerfully. "Check on anybody you think might be suspected of being involved in this, and I think you'll find them safely tied up and remarkably unharmed. Just free of suspicion. Was the captain hurt at all, do you know? Apart from his pride."

"Only one injury. He didn't see the face of his attacker, he wore some sort of black mask over his head with the eyes and mouth cut out. And he never spoke. But before he left he gave the captain a huge whack across the nether regions with what looks like a cat o' nine tails. Some nasty weals."

Geordie took his pipe from his pocket and began to fill it. "Aye, that can hurt. All the same, I reckon he got off lightly, when all's said and done. He can rest easy now. At least until the next packet ship reaches him with letters from England. If you'll excuse me, I should be starting my inspection."

By the Same Author

The Peninsular War Saga

An Unconventional Officer (Book 1)
An Irregular Regiment (Book 2)
An Uncommon Campaign (Book 3)
A Redoubtable Citadel (Book 4)
An Untrustworthy Army (Book 5)
An Unmerciful Incursion (Book 6)
An Indomitable Brigade (Book 7)

The Manxman

An Unwilling Alliance (Book 1)
This Blighted Expedition (Book 2)
This Bloody Shore (Book 3)

Regency Romances

A Regrettable Reputation (Book 1)
The Reluctant Debutante (Book 2)

Other Books

A Respectable Woman (A story of Victorian London)

A Marcher Lord (A story of the Anglo-Scottish borders)